The

Newcomer

Also by Mary Kay Andrews

Hello, Summer

Sunset Beach

The High Tide Club

The Beach House Cookbook

The Weekenders

Beach Town

Save the Date

Christmas Bliss

Ladies' Night

Spring Fever

Summer Rental

The Fixer Upper

Deep Dish

Savannah Breeze

Blue Christmas

Hissy Fit

Little Bitty Lies

Savannah Blues

The
Newcomer

Mary Kay Andrews

ST. MARTIN'S PRESS   New York

First published in the United States by St. Martin's Press, an imprint of St. Martin's Publishing Group

THE NEWCOMER. Copyright © 2021 by Mary Kay Andrews. All rights reserved. Printed in the United States of America. For information, address St. Martin's Publishing Group, 120 Broadway, New York, NY 10271.

www.stmartins.com

Design by Donna Sinisgalli Noetzel

Library of Congress Cataloging-in-Publication Data

Names: Andrews, Mary Kay, 1954– author.
Title: The newcomer / Mary Kay Andrews.
Description: First U.S. Edition. | New York : St. Martin's Press, 2021. |
Identifiers: LCCN 2020053277 | ISBN 9781250256966 (hardcover) |
ISBN 9781250277855 (international, sold outside the U.S., subject to rights availability) | ISBN 9781250279385 (signed) | ISBN 9781250256935 (ebook)
Classification: LCC PS3570.R587 N49 2021 | DDC 813/.54—dc23
LC record available at https://lccn.loc.gov/2020053277

Our books may be purchased in bulk for promotional, educational, or business use. Please contact your local bookseller or the Macmillan Corporate and Premium Sales Department at 1-800-221-7945, extension 5442, or by email at MacmillanSpecialMarkets@macmillan.com.

First U.S. Edition: 2021
First International Edition: 2021

10 9 8 7 6 5 4 3 2 1

*For my pandemic writing partners, otherwise known
as the co-founders of Friends & Fiction. Adversity brought us
together, but love and luck kept us going. With thanks and love to
Kristin Harmel, Kristy Woodson Harvey, Patti Callahan Henry,
Mary Alice Monroe, and managing producer, Meg Walker.*

1

~~~~~~~~~~

I T WAS STILL DARK WHEN Letty pulled into the parking lot. The car bumped slowly over the rutted oyster-shell pavement and she turned around to check on Maya, grateful that the child was finally sleeping. Her head slumped against the side of the car seat, her curls dampened with sweat, her rosebud lips pursed as she softly snored, and Ellie, her ever-present toy stuffed elephant, was clutched tightly to her chest.

A large hand-painted sign was posted at the entrance to the motel lot: GUEST PARKING ONLY IN ASSIGNED SPACES. TRESPASSERS' CARS WILL BE TOWED. THIS MEANS YOU.

Letty yawned. Her eyes burned and her shoulders and arms were cramped. She ignored the sign and backed the silver Kia into a space at the far end of the lot, which was near capacity, with two dozen or so cars parked in spaces marked off with numbered wooden signs, so that she'd be able to spot anyone approaching her car. The yellowing fronds of a huge palm tree draped over the spot, which was next to a dumpster. Surely nobody would mind a crappy little Kia tucked away in a parking slot nobody else wanted. Right?

She turned off the engine, locked the car doors, and slid her seat back as far as it would go. She sighed wearily and her eyelids fluttered as the motel sign's neon-blue waves, waving green palms, and pink lettering flashed on and off, on and off. THE MURMURING SURF. FREE WI-FI. POOL. COLOR TV. She'd paused, before pulling into the lot, after spotting the yellow NO VACANCY notice, but maybe, she thought, there really was a room. Maybe someone would be checking out this morning, after the sun rose.

Letty picked up the carefully folded article she'd placed on the passenger seat. It was a faded page torn from a back issue of *Southern Living* magazine. "Florida's Hidden Gems: Four Family Motels You'll Want to Discover." There was a photo of the Murmuring Surf at the bottom of the page, which had been circled with a black Sharpie pen, but from the looks of the place now, the photo had been taken some time ago.

Sunrise was probably half an hour away, with just the faintest promise of pink streaks in the midnight-blue sky, but she could make out a series of little concrete-block units arranged in an asymmetrical horseshoe shape. In the center of the horseshoe was a glowing aqua kidney-shaped swimming pool, shaded with tall palm trees and ringed with lounge chairs and tables. No lights shone in any of the windows, but at the curve of the horseshoe, a two-story unit, double the size of the others, had a small neon OFFICE sign posted in a window, and there was a lit-up Coke machine near the door.

She slid her window down a few inches and sniffed, inhaling the cool, salt-scented breeze and listening to the gentle wash of waves from somewhere very nearby. God, what she wouldn't give for a moonlit walk on the beach, just a moment to sink her toes into the sand and feel the warm tickle of water lapping at her ankles, washing away the terror and trauma of the past thirty-six hours.

Maya stirred, mumbling something in her sleep, bringing an abrupt end to Letty's daydream.

Her face softened as she regarded the little girl, her face so calm and untroubled in sleep. What had she seen? What would she remember? "Poor little chickadee," she whispered, unconsciously using the endearment her grandmother always used when referring to her and her younger sister.

During the long drive from New York, Maya had cried for hours, at first racking sobs, which finally subsided into whimpers and sniffles. She'd refused to eat anything, sweeping away her favorite (and usually forbidden) chicken nuggets during a raging tantrum in a roadside fast-food restaurant in West Virginia, screaming "I want my MOMMY!" so loudly that a panicky Letty had hustled her out of the place so fast that she'd left behind her own dinner. Hours later she'd pulled into the drive-through line of another fast-food joint, bribing Maya with a chocolate milkshake, which she'd greedily sucked down—and then barfed up half an hour later, which meant yet another gas station pit stop.

She picked up her cell phone. Six text messages, all of which she deleted. The last two texts were from Zoey.

WHERE R U?

OMG! CALL ME! R U OK?

She hesitated. Zoey had been her first real friend in the city. She had to trust somebody, didn't she? No, she decided, shaking her head. Nobody could be trusted. Not after everything that had happened. The less Zoey knew, the better off they'd all be.

Her eyelids fluttered again, and she descended into a black, dreamless sleep.

She was awakened by a sharp metallic rapping on her car window. "Ma'am? Hey, ma'am? Wake up!"

"Huh?" The sun was shining in through the windshield.

Maya began whimpering. "Letty? I'm hungry."

"You can't sleep here, ma'am." It was a man's voice. He was peering at her through the driver's-side window. He was wearing aviator sunglasses, and some kind of dark blue shirt with a badge pinned to the breast pocket.

Despite the heat inside the car, a cold shiver ran down her back. A cop!

She shook her head, trying to dispel the cobwebs. "Huh? I wasn't sleeping."

"So what, you were passed out drunk? With a kid in the car?" The sunglasses obscured his eyes, but he was youngish. Late thirties, very tan, very judgey.

"Letty?" Maya again, her voice pleading. "I need to go pee-pee."

She ignored the cop and turned to her niece. "Okay, baby. We're gonna go inside the motel now, and find you a bathroom. Can you wait just a minute?"

She turned to the cop, trying to tamp down her fear and annoyance. "Look. I'm totally sober, just really tired. I've been driving all night, and I pulled in here about an hour ago. I was waiting for the motel to open, so I could get us a room. Now, can you please go away, so I can take my little girl to the bathroom?"

"You didn't see the no-vacancy sign?" He pointed at it.

"I figured somebody would probably check out this morning."

She opened the car door and swung her legs out, but he was blocking her way. "There aren't any vacancies," he said. "They're full."

"If you don't mind, I'll just go inside and speak to the manager myself," Letty said. "Besides, I really need to find my child a bathroom. Okay?"

"There's a Citgo down the street," he said, pointing.

"Would you let your kid use the bathroom there? The parking lot is filthy."

Maya was wriggling, trying to unfasten her seat belt. "I gotta goooo," she wailed.

Letty opened her door all the way and got out, sliding past the cop. She opened the back door, extricated Maya from the car seat, balanced her on one hip, and grabbed her purse and phone.

"Excuse me," she said, not bothering to turn around, race-walking toward the motel office. It wasn't just Maya who needed a bathroom now.

She glanced backward just as she reached the door. The cop was standing by the Kia, hands on his hips, watching.

Letty yanked the plate-glass door open and an unseen electronic bell dinged. There was a front counter, with a blond fiftyish-looking woman standing behind it, talking into the phone. She looked up and frowned.

"Are you the owner of that Kia out there?" the woman asked. "I'm just getting ready to call for a tow truck."

"Bathroom," Letty said tersely. "Please? My little girl . . ."

"Pee-pee," Maya wailed, right on cue. The kid's timing was flawless. Like her mother's, Letty thought ruefully.

The woman paused, then shrugged and pointed to a narrow hallway. "Right there. But it's for motel guests only."

"Fine," Letty said, hurrying toward the bathroom door.

She took her time in the bathroom, first washing Maya's tearstained face and hands, finger-combing the damp curls, then doing her best to try to make herself look, as Mimi would have said, "respectable."

Letty sat Maya on the closed toilet seat. She washed her own hands, then splashed water on her face and neck before gathering her straight brown hair into a ponytail. She fished lipstick from her purse, which was bulging with all the last-minute items she'd tossed in before fleeing the city.

She closed her eyes and tried to choke back the suffocating sense of panic she'd been seized with at the sight of that cop in the parking lot. Common sense told her she should back the Kia out of here and ride on down the road.

But.

That magazine article. There was something about this place that meant something to Tanya. Her sister was not particularly sentimental. She was not a saver of magazine articles. And yet, she had saved that article about this particular place. Why?

Breathe, Letty, she told herself. *Inhale. Exhale.*

When she opened her eyes again, the face that stared back from the bathroom mirror was pale and gaunt. Her hazel eyes were bloodshot, ringed with dark circles. She glanced down at the blue-and-white-striped T-shirt she'd grabbed from Tanya's closet, after she'd realized her own white blouse bore a blood smear on the cuff.

"You look like you were rode hard and put up wet," she muttered, unconsciously slipping into Mimi's West Virginia twang. For the first time she noticed the price tag fluttering from beneath the sleeve of the shirt. She plucked it from the fabric. The designer brand was one she didn't recognize, but the price took her breath away. Tanya had paid 325 dollars for this simple boat-necked blue-and-white-striped knit shirt, which she'd never even worn, and probably didn't remember having bought. The walk-in closet in her sister's town house was crammed with expensive clothes like this, many never worn.

Tears stung her eyes as she ripped the tag in half and stuffed it in her pocket.

"Letty?" Maya's bright blue eyes studied her. "You crying?"

"No, baby," Letty said, leaning down and kissing the child's forehead. "I'm fine. We're both gonna be fine. Let's go talk to the nice lady about a room, okay?"

The nice lady was standing right outside the bathroom door, arms folded across her chest. The cop from the parking lot was standing next to her.

"Hi," Letty said, forcing a weary smile. "Thanks so much for letting us use the bathroom. It was kind of an emergency."

"You're welcome," the woman said. She wore a pink polo shirt tucked into high-waisted mom jeans. A name badge pinned to her collar said MURMURING SURF. MANAGER, AVA DECURTIS. Her ash-blond hair was worn in a short, bad perm. She nodded at the cop. "Joe tells me you said you're looking for a room."

"Yes, ma'am," Letty said, deliberately laying on the Southern accent she'd worked so hard for so long to erase. "We don't need anything fancy, just a clean place to sleep."

"I'm sorry, but like the sign outside says, we're full up."

"I told her that," Joe said. He'd removed his sunglasses, and if he weren't busy being such a prick, Letty thought, he could actually be considered semi-hot.

"Yes," Letty agreed. "He did tell me that. But I was hoping maybe somebody would be checking out this morning. We drove all night, and I haven't slept in hours and hours. Are you sure you don't have anything? I mean, at all?"

"I'm really sorry, hon, but if you'd called ahead, I could have told you we're booked solid. It's still high season, you know."

"Oh." Letty's shoulders sagged and she felt like she'd been kicked in the gut.

"There's probably rooms back up the road by the interstate," Ava offered. "I could call Mark over at the Econo Lodge."

Letty shook her head. "I really had my heart set on this place. I've heard so much about it, and I promised Maya we'd be at the beach."

"It's that doggone *Southern Living* article," Ava said. "Forgotten motel, my ass. It's been five years, and I'm still turning folks away."

Joe the cop stared at her. "You're not gonna find anything on the beach this time of year," he said. "It's March, and it's Florida."

"I realize that," Letty said, fighting against the urge to kick him in the nuts. She sighed heavily. "I just . . . well, this place has some very special memories for my family."

Once again, she'd slid into another persona. Was this the failed actress speaking now?

"Is that right?" Ava asked. "I've owned the Surf since the eighties. Maybe I know your family?"

"My mimi and granddaddy honeymooned here, but I guess maybe that would've been back in the sixties." The lie was seamless. "Mimi used to tell us stories about swimming in the ocean . . . and eating shrimp at the seafood place down the street . . ."

"It's the Gulf of Mexico," Joe cut in. "And we still don't have any rooms available."

"Joe!" Ava said sternly. "Don't be rude." She knelt down and looked at Maya. "This sweet baby needs to be on the beach, don't you, sweetheart?"

Maya batted her extraordinarily long, spiky dark lashes. She really had gotten all the very best DNA from the gene pool, Letty thought. "I wanna go swimmin'."

"What's your name, sweetheart?"

"Maya Abigail. And I am four years old, and I go to big-girl school."

The manager was instantly besotted, Letty saw. Maya had that effect on people. Like her mother.

"They have a pool at the Econo Lodge," Joe pointed out.

Ava stood up and looked around the motel lobby with a sigh. "Maybe the old storage unit?"

"Mom!"

Letty looked from Ava to Joe. "She's your mom?"

"Guilty," Ava said, giving her son a warning glance. "Look, we haven't rented it out in years, because it's the only efficiency unit in the place, and it's tiny, but there's nothing magical in there. Just a bunch of old broken lounge chairs and faded bedspreads and random junk I've been meaning to get rid of. . . ."

"As long as there's a bed and a bathroom, I'm fine with small. I'm used to small," Letty said, thinking of all the roach motel rooms she'd rented back in New York. She sounded desperate, but that was because she really *was* desperate.

"And who's gonna haul away all that crap in there?" Joe demanded.

"I will," Letty said.

"In that piece-of-shit Kia?"

Letty really, really wanted to kick him in the nuts. "I saw a dumpster in your parking lot."

"That's true," Ava said. She glanced at her son, and then down at Maya, with her bedraggled stuffed toy elephant.

"Tell you what. If you want to clear it out, and drag all that stuff to the dumpster, you got a deal. I know there's a bed in there, but I can't vouch for what kind of shape the mattress is in. The bathroom is nasty, but the last I knew it worked. And there's a sort of kitchenette. You probably don't need more than that."

"I don't," Letty said. "That's enough for us."

"I can't spare a housekeeper to help you," Ava warned.

Letty nodded and thought about the wad of cash she'd stuffed under the front seat of the Kia. She could already feel it shrinking. "If I empty it out and clean it up, what would the weekly rate be?"

"No housekeeping?" Ava asked.

"No, ma'am," Letty said, laying it on thick. "My little girl and I just need a place to stay, at the beach. I'm used to working hard, and cleaning up after myself."

"For how long?" Joe asked.

"Not sure," Letty said. "Can we figure it out as we go along?"

Ava looked at her son, who just shrugged and looked away.

"Fine with me," Ava decided. "How's three hundred a week?"

"If I paid in cash instead of a credit card, could you do a little better?"

Ava shrugged. "I guess I could knock off ten bucks. One thing, though. You can't tell any of my regulars what you're paying. I don't need a riot up in here."

"You got a deal," Letty said, sticking out her hand. "I'm Letty, by the way. And I promise, you won't regret this."

Ava grasped Letty's hand in both of hers and shook. "I'll get the key. You can use the wheelbarrow that's back behind the pool pump house."

"I want to go on the record here and say I'm against this," Joe said, shaking his head in disgust.

"Okay, noted," Ava said. She held out her arms to Maya, who normally didn't take to strangers, but immediately allowed herself to be picked up. "Precious baby," Ava cooed, running her fingers through Maya's curls. "I can't remember when was the last time we had a little one around here."

"Wait until the Feldmans find out you've got a kid staying here," Joe said. "They'll shit a brick."

Ava stared at her son. "Doesn't your shift start soon?"

2

~~~~~~~~~~~~~

THE EFFICIENCY UNIT WAS LOCATED at the north end of the row of pastel-painted concrete-block cottages. It was tiny and painted bubble-gum pink, to her niece's delight. "It's the Barbie house," Maya giggled.

The glass of the unit's jalousie windows was thick with salt spray and grime, and the paint on the door was a peeling, unattractive shade of pea green.

"Here we are," Ava announced, unlocking the door and shoving it open. "Like I said, it's not much."

"Oh my," Letty said, surveying her new home. It smelled of mildew and old socks.

As advertised, the unit was small. And it was packed, within an inch or two of the ceiling, with decades of motel discards. Letty spotted a stack of aluminum-frame lounge chairs with rotted plastic webbing, seven televisions of various vintages, plastic bins stuffed with faded bedspreads and yellowing towels, and stacks of hideous framed mass-produced paintings. Three rusted window air-conditioning units teetered totem-pole style in one corner of the room. Sagging mattresses covered the windows, and shoved in among everything else were a washing machine and three toilets.

Ava sighed and kicked at the edge of a laminate-topped dresser that had seen better days. "Guess I kind of forgot how much stuff was in here." She scowled. "That's what I get for carrying on with the damned handyman. By the time I figured out the only thing he was really handy at was drinking beer and losing money at the

Seminole Indian bingo over in Tampa, he'd already wrecked my car and managed to fill up this room with stuff he was supposed to be fixing."

Letty offered a sympathetic smile.

"Take my advice, Letty. Don't ever get your honey where you get your money."

"My mimi used to tell me that all the time," Letty said.

"You ever been married?"

"No."

"So, you didn't ever marry Maya's daddy?" Ava asked. "I mean, I'm not judging you if you didn't. Come to think of it, I've got two kids and I thank God for 'em every day, but I wish now that I hadn't married either of their daddies."

Letty glanced over at Maya, who was busily digging through a bin of bed linens.

"Actually, Maya is my niece," Letty said quietly, letting her guard down just a little.

"Look, Letty," Maya said, holding up a flowered purple and yellow polyester bedspread. "For Ellie's bed."

"Ellie? So you've got two kids?" Ava asked, looking confused.

"No. Ellie is Maya's best friend. The stuffed elephant."

"Oh." Ava smiled at Maya, then turned back to Letty, her voice just above a whisper. "Where are her parents?"

"Deceased," Letty said sadly. This was not exactly a lie. After all, Tanya was dead and Evan was dead as far as she was concerned.

"Sorry," Ava said. She was about to say something else when her hip buzzed. She grabbed her phone from the back pocket of her jeans.

"Oh Lord. Sorry. That's my electrician saying he's on his way. I'm gonna leave you to it then. Just put stuff in the dumpster right by where you're parked. When you're ready for cleaning supplies come on back to the office and I'll give you one of the housekeeping carts. Okay?"

"Thanks," Letty said.

When Ava was gone she looked around the room and sighed. "Where do I even start?"

She heard Mimi's voice in her ear. "The only way to begin is to just dig in."

Letty and Tanya had spent two summers during their trouble-some teen years with her mother's parents, Mimi and BopBop, on their farm in Indiana, this while Terri was in the honeymoon phase of life with her third husband, Bobby Ray Braithwaite.

Eventually, and to absolutely nobody's surprise, the marriage im-ploded, and after BopBop's stroke and subsequent death, their sum-mer sojourns ended and they'd moved back down to a seedy mobile home park in Tennessee, where Terri had taken possession of Bobby Ray's double-wide. Mimi had driven them down to Knoxville in Bop-Bop's Chevy Impala, helped move them into the trailer, filled the re-frigerator and cupboard with groceries, then, reluctantly, two days later, returned to the farm.

"You girls look after each other, y'hear?" Mimi had said, wrapping an arm around each of the sisters. "Your mama, bless her heart, it's all she can do to take care of herself, so it's gonna be up to you, Letty, to look after Tanya. And Tanya, you listen to what Letty tells you. Promise me that, okay?"

The girls had nodded dutifully, and waved, as Mimi drove away, honking the Impala's horn until she was out of the girls' sight. It would be the last time they ever saw their only grandparent.

Now Letty loaded a pile of linens into the wheelbarrow, plopped Maya on top, and trundled it out to the dumpster. After heaving the contents into the dumpster she unlocked her car and retrieved an armload of Maya's things: her battered copy of *If You Give a Mouse a Cookie*, a small pink plastic lunch box containing Maya's crayons and coloring book, and the girl's suitcase, which featured her favorite Disney character, Elsa, from *Frozen*. She glanced around to make sure she wasn't being watched, then grabbed the canvas tote she'd taken from Tanya's closet. She was already uneasy about letting that tote bag out of her sight, even inside her locked car.

"Let's go for ride, Letty," Maya said, climbing back into the wheelbarrow.

"Okay, but when we get back to the room, Letty has to work, and you get to play, okay? I've got your book and your crayons. Can you do that and be a good girl while I get our room cleaned up?"

Maya nodded vigorously, sending her curls shaking. "I'm a good, big girl."

Letty dropped a kiss on the top of her head. "You are the biggest, bestest girl in the world."

By noon, she'd managed to clear debris from half the room, making dozens of trips back and forth to the dumpster, while Maya constructed a pillow fort from the least objectionable sheets and pillows Letty salvaged from the piles of rejected bed linens.

Tanya would have a fit, Letty thought, if she could see her daughter now. She'd become a major priss-ass after Maya's birth, requiring that all visitors leave their shoes at the door, installing bottles of antibacterial soap in every room, refusing to let her daughter eat, touch, or play with anything that wasn't certified organic.

But Tanya wasn't here, Letty thought grimly. And germs were the least of their problems. She was hot and grimy, her legs and arms were aching, and her stomach was rumbling.

"Come on, ladybug," Letty said, peeking down between the makeshift tent flaps at her niece. "Let's get lunch."

"Yay," Maya said, scrambling to her feet. "Chicken nuggets!"

"Not," Letty said firmly. "Salads. And fruit. And milk."

"And cookies?"

"We'll see."

She was unlocking the Kia when Ava stepped out of the office and waved them down. "Y'all want some lunch?"

"Yes!" Maya answered.

"We were just going to go grab some groceries," Letty said,

walking over to the motel manager. "I meant to ask—where's the nearest store?"

"There's a Publix a couple of miles away, but in the meantime, why don't you just let me give you lunch? Nothing fancy. Just some ham salad sandwiches, carrot sticks, and a few grapes."

"And cookies?" Maya said, always hopeful.

Ava took the child's hand in hers. "Why yes, I think I can probably rustle up a couple of cookies."

Letty followed Ava into the office, through a door, and up a narrow flight of stairs.

"Here it is. Home sweet home," Ava said, pushing through the door at the top of the stairs.

They were standing in a large, sunny room with polished pine floors, pale blue walls, and a bank of windows looking out over the sparkling waters of the ocean. The room looked comfortable and lived-in, with a squashy denim-slipcovered sofa facing a flat-screen television in the living area, and a pine farmhouse table surrounded by painted rattan chairs in the dining area.

"This is so nice," Letty said, trying not to sound envious. Her old apartment back in New York would have fit in the space occupied by that dining table. She found herself blinking back tears at the thought of that apartment. In her haste to flee the city she'd only taken time to throw a few belongings into the car, her laptop, toiletries, whatever clothes would fit into her smallest carry-on suitcase. Everything else had been left behind. By now she was sure Evan would be pawing through all of her things; her clothes, her books, the few family pictures she'd kept over the years, seeking some clue to her whereabouts. The thought of his hands—the same hands that were responsible for Tanya's death—on her things made her skin crawl.

"Does your son live here with you?" Letty asked, looking around at the room that was decorated with a decidedly feminine look.

"Joe? Not a chance. He's got his own place down the beach a

ways. No, it's just me and my youngest, Isabelle. It's nothing fancy, but it's mine, and it's mostly paid for. Come on in the kitchen. I bet you two are starving."

The kitchen was smaller and more dated than the front rooms, with a bank of metal cabinets, a four-burner stove, a refrigerator, and a chrome-and-Formica dinette set pushed up against a picture window that looked out through the tops of towering palm trees onto the motel's sandy parking lot.

Ava set three plates on the table and placed a child's booster seat on one of the four yellow vinyl-covered chairs.

"I knew there was a good reason I didn't take this to the Goodwill," she said.

She slid a platter of sandwiches in the center of the table, then added a plate of carrot sticks and apple slices. "What can I give the baby to drink?"

"Juice box!" Maya said, pounding a fist on the tabletop.

"Milk would be fine," Letty said. She'd barely placed a sandwich half on Maya's plate before the little girl snatched it up and began gobbling it down. Letty had to force herself to chew slowly, savoring every bite.

"Mmm," Maya said, chomping away at a carrot stick.

Ava beamed her approval as she added a second sandwich half to Maya's plate. "That young'un was hungry. She fell on that food like a rat on a Cheeto."

Letty choked back her laughter. "Sorry. We had a long drive down last night, and we did stop for dinner, but then she had an upset tummy, so I was afraid to let her eat too much after that. I've got to get us both back on a regular schedule, just as soon as we get settled into our room."

"Where did y'all come from? I noticed the South Carolina tags on your car."

"New Jersey," Letty said, being deliberately vague. "But I bought the car secondhand, and I haven't had time to get a new license plate."

"I had an ex-sister-in-law from New Jersey, from around Newark," Ava said, sipping from a glass of iced tea. "But she got run over by a garbage truck. I always thought that was poetic justice. Whereabouts are you from?"

"Hoboken," Letty said. This was semi-true. She had lived in Hoboken, briefly, when she first moved to New York.

"How long have you been here at the Murmuring Surf?" she asked, eager to change the subject.

"Let's see. Joe was just a baby. He was so little, and we were so poor, he slept in a dresser drawer until I could afford to buy a secondhand crib. He's thirty-eight in July, so I guess it's been that long."

Letty stared out the window at the parking lot. A silver sedan pulled alongside her Kia and she felt herself tense. But then an older woman got out and began unloading a wheelchair from the trunk and she allowed herself to relax a little.

"Does Joe work here too? I mean, when he's not being a police officer?" she asked.

"He's actually a police detective, and he'd tell you he works here full-time, cop or no cop," Ava said, rolling her eyes. "Both my kids work in the business. Joe does maintenance for me, and security, when we got problems, and Isabelle, she's still in high school, when she's not at school, she answers the phone and helps out some. I raised 'em like I was raised, to take responsibility early in life. What about you, Letty? What line of work are you in?"

Letty remembered the advice she'd gotten from Siobhan, the acting coach she'd briefly studied under during her first few months in New York. "Dig deep. Find your truth in every story, even the ones that are total bullshit. If you're good enough, the audience will buy your truth, even when it's a lie."

She offered her audience of one a rueful smile. "I thought I was going to be a famous actress. And I did some of that, but mostly I've done whatever needed doing so that I could pay the rent. Sometimes it was waitressing. I did some office temp work, worked at a bagel shop and in a rental agency. Like that."

"I thought I was going to be a badass rock 'n' roll singer like Linda Ronstadt," Ava confessed. "There was a time I could really belt out 'You're No Good.'" She shrugged. "Now that I think about it, that could have been the story of both my marriages. Anyway, the only singing I've done since high school has been for my supper."

Letty glanced at the kitchen clock. "This has been such a nice treat for us, Ava, but I guess I'd better get moving again if I'm gonna get our room cleaned out enough to sleep in tonight." She pushed away from the table and lifted Maya down from the chair.

"Okay, sweetie. Lunch break is over. Time to get back to work. Can you thank Miss Ava?"

"She said we could have cookies." Maya's face began to crumple and redden. Letty sensed a meltdown on the horizon.

Ava jumped up and went to a kitchen cupboard. She brought out a box of vanilla wafers. "Bless her heart. I did promise cookies. Put out your hand, sweetheart."

Maya held out two grubby hands and Ava shook the box until her hands were full.

"They might be stale," she whispered to Letty, as the child shoved a cookie into her mouth. "Isabelle fusses at me if I bring sweets home."

Letty smiled and began herding Maya toward the door. "She's not really supposed to have too much sugar either, but I guess I'm just getting the hang of this parenting thing."

Ava followed her through the living room and down the stairs. "Let me know if you ever do figure it out."

TANYA CAME TO HER IN her dream. After hauling junk back and forth to the dumpster for three straight hours, so tired and dirty she couldn't take another step, Letty finally dumped a mattress onto the floor of the hotel room, spread a blanket atop it, and pulled Maya down beside her.

"Nap time," Letty said firmly, and for once, Maya didn't resist, spooning up beside Letty with the stuffed elephant tucked in the crook of her arm. In a moment, she heard her niece's breaths slow, felt her warm body relax against her own. She touched her niece's plump, pink cheek and closed her own eyes, falling into an almost trancelike sleep.

Tanya appeared almost immediately. Her lovely face was pale and agitated, her pupils dilated. "Promise me," she said, poking Letty in the chest. "If something happens to me, promise me you'll take Maya and run."

They'd had this conversation numerous times in real life and now Letty was hearing it again in her dream. Tanya swore she'd gotten sober, was going to her meetings, had thrown away the pills. Letty wanted desperately to believe her.

"Nothing is going to happen to you," Letty would always reply. Tanya was overreacting, nearly hysterical. Forever the drama queen.

"You don't know that. You don't know Evan. I mean the real Evan. He'll do anything to get Maya away from me. He won't stop until he gets his way."

"Okay, whatever," Letty had said, not wanting to get her sister more agitated.

"I mean it, Letty. If something bad happens to me, it will be because of him. He's got detectives following me. I think he's got my phone tapped. I'm being super careful, but he's rich as shit, you know? And he knows important people. He always gets his way. Always."

"But not this time," Letty had said, trying to calm Tanya. "You're doing all the right things. You've been in counseling, going to your meetings. That arbitrator lady told you herself. You're a good mom. Evan can't prove otherwise."

That was when Tanya did it. She leaned in and whispered, "I know you think I'm being paranoid, but I'm not. If something bad happens to me, you've got to take Maya and get the hell away from here. Don't tell anybody where you're going or why. Just go. Promise me you'll keep my baby away from him."

"All right," Letty said, spooked by her sister's intensity. "I promise, Tanya. It won't happen, but if it does, I'll keep Maya safe."

That day, what? Six, seven weeks ago?

"I want to show you something," Tanya had said, taking Letty by the hand and leading her into her master bedroom.

Letty had never liked this room. Evan's interior designer—a former girlfriend, Tanya claimed—had pulled out all the stops, covering the walls in an antiqued silver mirrored wallpaper that Tanya claimed cost four thousand dollars a roll. The ceiling was mirrored, too, and the floor was covered in a thick, furry white carpet that reminded Letty of a shaggy dog, but not in a good way. There was a crystal chandelier over the heavily draped canopy bed, and the bedspread and piles of pillows were all shades of gray and silver and white. Letty thought it was too new, too shiny, too everything, but of course Tanya proclaimed it chic and elegant.

"In here." She followed Tanya into the walk-in closet, which was as big as Letty's studio apartment. The closet had its own chandelier, and an antique silver-gilded trifold mirror, and a little silk-covered sofa that the designer called a canapé. A cabinet in the middle of the room held a treasure trove of Tanya's jewelry. Three walls held racks and racks of designer clothes and accessories. Tanya had organized them by size, from what she called her "pre-Maya" days as a size two, to her "disgusting-pig post-baby body" size, which was, after all, still only a size eight.

One whole wall of the closet held shelves and shelves of hand-bags and shoes. Her boots, dozens of pairs of them, were lined up in rows on the floor of the shoe rack. Tanya reached around and pulled out a tall black suede boot with a wicked three-inch-high spike heel.

"These boots are made for walking," she said, her tone con-spiratorial. She shoved her hand down in the boot and pulled out a canvas tote, the kind fancy grocery stores gave to customers who thought they could save the planet by buying thirty-dollar-a-pound wild-caught salmon.

"What's that?"

"My go-bag," Tanya whispered. "Like Mama always had."

Terri had drummed into her daughters' heads that they should always be ready to leave any situation when, in her words, "the house burns down."

"Girls," she'd say to them. "A man will tell you he loves you. He might believe it too. But one day, he's gonna wake up and decide you're too old, too fat, too loud, or just too you. You gotta be pre-pared. Like they told you in Girl Scouts.

"Start by putting a little money away, every payday, no matter what. I mean cash money, where you can put your hands on it, day or night. Hide it good. And make a plan, so you can grab that bag and get out fast when the time comes."

That day in the closet, Tanya gave Letty a peek into the bag. She got a glimpse of a velvet-covered jeweler's box that she knew con-tained Tanya's diamond ring push present, and fat wads of bills, fas-tened with rubber bands, before her sister snatched the bag away and returned it to its hiding place.

"Promise me," dream Tanya said now, tugging at her arm. "Promise you'll take Maya and get the hell away from him."

"I will," Letty murmured. "I promise I will."

"Letty, Letty." The tugging continued. She opened her eyes slowly and Maya, her very real niece, was pulling at her hand. "Letty, I need to potty."

"Oh, honey." Letty stood up and went to door of the bathroom, which had a pink tile floor and pink fixtures. The pink sink was stacked with more piles of discarded linens, and the pink-tiled shower stall was full of dust-covered collapsed cardboard cartons. The room smelled sour, but it held the only thing Letty really needed at the moment.

She pulled Maya's shorts down and dangled the child inches above the pink plastic toilet seat. "Go ahead and go, baby," she urged. Maya giggled and did as she was told.

"Gotta get that cleaning cart, stat," Letty said. She pushed the linens aside, found a shriveled-up sliver of soap, and washed her own hands as well as her niece's.

By six o'clock, she was standing in the mostly cleared-out motel room, her hands on her hips, staring at the stuff that had proven too heavy to move by herself. "How the hell am I gonna get this junk out of here?"

Seconds later there was a rap at the door, followed by an impatient male voice. "Hey! You in there?"

Spooked, Letty ran to the window and peered out through the fly-specked glass. She shrugged, then opened the door. Joe's badge and gun were gone; he was dressed in jeans, a T-shirt, and flip-flops. So maybe he didn't intend to arrest or shoot her just yet.

"Yes?" her voice was deliberately cool and she stared directly at him. Another trick from her short-lived acting class.

Without asking, he stepped inside the room and looked around. The only remaining discards were the commodes and the washing machine and one of the mattresses. After her uneasy nap session,

she'd unearthed a bed frame and set it up with the least objectionable mattress, and from beneath a pile of faded floral draperies she'd
uncovered a sturdy but ugly double dresser that could hold what
little of their belongings she'd brought along. She'd found a worn-
down broom in the bathroom and managed to sweep away the top
layers of cobwebs and unspeakable crud.

"Not bad," he said. "You did all this by yourself?"

"Me and the wheelbarrow," Letty said.

He pointed at the washing machine. "Were you planning on leaving that here?"

Letty rolled her eyes. "Sure. I'm gonna plant a palm tree in it."

"Okay, well, then you don't need me."

"Actually, I was just trying to figure out what to do with it," she
admitted.

"That asshole Chuck," Joe said. He went outside and came back
with a heavy-duty furniture dolly. "I told her he was a bum, but she's
always had a soft heart for a stray."

"Your mom?"

"Who else?" He wheeled the dolly over to the washing machine.
"Okay. I'm gonna stick the lip of this under the washer, and you're
gonna push it forward—carefully, until it tilts backward. Like a lever.
Got that?"

"I think I can manage."

Maya was watching the grown-ups with interest, her thumb in
her mouth. Letty reached over and gently pushed the thumb aside.
"You sit on the bed now and try to stay out of the way. Can you do
that, ladybug?"

Maya nodded and returned the thumb to her mouth.

Joe wrapped a webbed belt around the washer and fastened it to
the dolly's handles.

"Go," he said.

Letty placed both hands on the machine, closed her eyes, and
leaned hard into it. Seconds later, she heard a loud thud.

"Owwww," Joe howled.

She opened her eyes. The belt had snapped in two and the washing machine seemed to have landed on his foot.

He somehow managed to shove it aside, and dropped onto the floor, cradling his bare right foot in both hands, rocking back and forth, his face contorted—either with pain or anger, she wasn't sure which.

"Goddamn," he cried, glaring at Letty. "I think my toe is broken."

"I'm sorry," she said. "Let me see it."

He scooted backward, away from her. "No way."

"I'm not gonna hurt you," she protested. "Just let me look. Which toe is it?"

"None of your business," he snapped. He picked up a gnarly-looking rubber flip-flop, slid it gingerly onto his injured foot, stood up, and leaned against the offending washer. "Christ, it hurts."

"Well, I said I'm sorry. But shouldn't you have been wearing real shoes? I mean, who tries to do heavy lifting wearing flip-flops?"

"A guy who just got off work after an eight-hour shift," he said. "A guy who was minding his own business and drinking a cold beer until his mom guilt-tripped him into helping out her newest guest."

Letty felt her cheeks burn with a mixture of anger and her own guilt. "I said I was sorry. If you'll let me look at it, I'll go get some ice and try to help you wrap it up."

"Forget it," he muttered, "I'll live." He turned back to the washing machine, examining the mover's dolly. "That asshole Chuck. Shoulda known he'd let this thing get dry rot. Even the tires are shot."

"What now?" Letty asked.

"Now I take this piece of crap to the dumpster, go back to my place and get a decent furniture dolly. And a pair of boots." He grabbed the dolly and walked out of the room, slamming the door as he went.

Letty sighed and sat down on the bed beside Maya, who'd witnessed the debacle. "He got a bad boo-boo," the child whispered.

"Not that bad," Letty said. "He's just being a big crybaby, that's all."

When he returned twenty minutes later Joe was wearing dusty work boots. He wheeled the dolly into the room. "Let's try this again. Go slow, okay?"

The second time went much smoother than the first. He wrapped the strap securely around the washer. She pushed the washing machine onto the dolly, its weight shifted, and he was able to roll it out of the room with comparative ease. He followed suit with the toilets and the remaining mattress, and when he came back from the dumpster he carried a crumpled brown paper sack, which he thrust at her.

"What's this?"

"Peace offering," he said, his voice gruff. "You were right. It was an accident, and I shouldn't have blamed you. Definitely shouldn't have cussed in front of a little kid."

"Nothing she hasn't heard before," Letty said guiltily. She opened the bag and pulled out a bottle of chilled white wine and two plastic cups.

"It's screw-top, because I figured you might not have a bottle opener, but it's not cheap screw-top." He shoved his hands in the back pocket of his jeans and looked at her uneasily. "You drink, right?"

She smiled despite herself. "I've been known to."

He held out another bag. "This is for your little girl."

It was a pint bottle of chocolate milk. "Her name is Maya."

"I knew that," he said, bristling.

"That's nice of you," Letty said. She held up the bottle and showed it to her niece. "Maya?"

"Chocolate milk!" Maya snatched the bottle from Letty's hand.

"What do you say?" she prompted.

Maya was busy trying to remove the plastic seal from the bottle's neck. "Thanks."

"Yes, thank you," Letty said, remembering her own manners. "How's the toe?"

"Hurts like a mother."

"Well," she said, feeling uneasy. "Guess I better get back to work now."

"What about food?" he asked.

"Ava gave us a late lunch," Letty said. "I'll hit the grocery store in a few minutes."

"Mom wanted me to check the fridge, to see if it works," he said, pointing to the kitchenette area just outside the bathroom door. There was a single-bowl stainless-steel sink, which was piled with a jumble of sixties-era electric percolators, and as advertised, an apartment-size refrigerator sitting beneath a chipped Formica counter that held two electric burners.

"I've been so busy clearing the place out, I haven't even gotten to the kitchen," Letty admitted.

Joe knelt on the floor and opened the fridge door. He put his hand inside and shrugged.

"Needs a good cleaning, but it's cold." He stood up and dusted his hands on his backside.

"Looks like you're good to go," he announced.

Letty followed him outside. A pair of elderly women sat on rusting metal chairs in front of the unit two over from hers. They were dressed alike, in flowered pastel blouses, white knit pants, and pastel sun visors. One was tall and skinny, with long bony arms and short gray hair, and the other was shorter, softer, and rounder, with shoulder-length hair worn in a stiff pale blond pageboy.

"Hello there, Joseph," the tall skinny one said, peering up at Letty from behind thick tinted glasses.

"Hey, Miss Ruth," Joe said, nodding. "Miss Billie."

"Who's your friend?" the round one asked. She wore cat-eye

glasses on a chain around her neck and she put them on now and stared, unsmiling, at Letty.

"Oh, uh, this is Letty."

"Hello," Letty said.

"Are you moving in?" The skinny one pursed her lips and shook her head. "To the storage unit?"

"Yes, ma'am," Letty said, lapsing into the Southern manners Mimi had drummed into both her granddaughters. "I've spent the day cleaning it out. Joe just hauled the last load out to the dumpster."

"We noticed," Ruth said. "We were wondering what was going on over there." She nodded in the direction of Letty's room. "Ava didn't notify us that she would be renting out the storage unit."

"It was a last-minute decision," Joe said cheerfully. "Okay, ladies. If you have any questions, I'm sure my mom can answer 'em."

Ruth, the tall one, pointed an accusatory finger at Maya, who clung to Letty's hand. "Whose child is that?"

Maya retreated behind Letty, hiding her head.

"Mine," Letty said, instantly on the defensive.

"Joseph?" Ruth said, raising her voice. "Is Ava aware that this person has a child?"

"Yup," Joe said. "Like I said, any questions, concerns, bring 'em up with Mom." He scuttled away toward the parking lot without even a backward glance.

"Well . . ." Letty said. Her hand was on the doorknob. "Nice to meet you ladies."

"Dear?" Billie said. "Since you're new, I think I should let you know that most of us here at the Murmuring Surf have been staying here for years."

"Years and years and years," Ruth added.

"We're used to things a certain way," Billie said.

"Ava never used to rent to people with young children during the season," Ruth said sternly. "We thought we had an understanding."

"You have something against children?" Letty heard her own voice harden.

"Only when they're living in the room in proximity to ours," Ruth said. She peered over her glasses at Maya, examining her as she might a dead roach. "This is a quiet place. That's how we like it. No stinky diapers in the trash cans, no screaming kids splashing in the pool, leaving toys all over the place for folks to trip over."

"I'll keep that in mind," Letty said, turning to leave.

These two! Terri would have called them nosy old biddies, or worse. She knew the type from her own childhood. She had a vivid memory of pursy-lipped church ladies, peering at her and Tanya as Terri dropped them off at whatever Sunday school was closest to wherever they were living at the time.

"Isn't your mother coming to church? Where do you girls live? Will your daddy be picking you up after services?"

Letty, mortified, would shrug and look away, but Tanya, her feisty little sister, wasn't having it. "None of your business!" she'd shout.

"Where's the child's father?" Ruth asked, one eyebrow raised expectantly.

Maya wound her arms tightly around Letty's knees, sniffled, and ducked her head.

"I really couldn't say," Letty said. She gave the two a curt nod, picked up the child, and retreated to her room.

4

M AYA SPOTTED THE MOTEL'S SWIMMING pool as
soon as Letty pulled into the Murmuring Surf parking lot after their
grocery-shopping excursion. The rippling turquoise water beckoned
in the gathering darkness.

"Swim! Letty, I wanna go swimming," Maya called, kicking her
sandal-clad feet against the back of the driver's seat.

Letty was worn out from the long day of cleaning and hauling,
followed by an exhausting shopping trip to the nearest big-box store,
where the four-year-old had clamored to buy every bright-colored
item that caught her eye.

"Oh, ladybug," she said, turning around to face her niece. "Aren't
you tired? Maybe we could go for a nice swim in the morning. . . ."

"No!" Maya cried, her face starting to crumple, a sure sign that
tears were about to start. "I wanna swim. I wanna swim now."

"All right," Letty said hastily. "Let's put our food away and then
we swim. But just for a little while. I think we both need an early
bedtime."

She knew it probably wasn't good to give in so easily to Maya's
demands. She already felt guilty about feeding the kid yet another
fast-food dinner, but she just didn't have it in her tonight for one
more battle.

It took three trips to unload the car. Fortunately, along with the
juice boxes, milk, cereal, fruit, coffee, and other groceries, Letty had
tossed new bathing suits for both of them into the shopping cart, as
well as an inflatable swim ring.

As soon as they were inside their room, Maya happily began to shed her clothes. She stood in the doorway of the bathroom, dressed only in her tiny white sandals, chanting, "Swim, swim, swim, swim."

"Okay," Letty said, laughing. She reached into a bag, ripped the price tags off the pink-and-white-striped two-piece she'd bought for her niece, and held it out.

"Swimmy, swimmy, swimmy," Maya hummed under her breath, stepping into the bottoms.

"Swimmy, swimmy, swimmy," Letty agreed, pulling the top over the child's head.

"Now you," Maya said, handing Letty the modest navy-blue one-piece she'd chosen for herself.

When they were dressed, with the inflated swim ring and newly purchased beach towels in hand, they stepped outside their room. Maya trotted determinedly toward the pool, which was enclosed behind a fence lined with neatly trimmed hibiscus bushes.

A large sign was posted on the gate. NO LIFEGUARD ON DUTY. NO GLASS IN POOL AREA. POOL CLOSES 10 P.M.

As they pushed through the gate, they saw two women swimming laps down the center of the pool.

"I can swim too!" Maya said, pointing. Which was true. As soon as her daughter could walk, Tanya had enrolled her in an impressive array of "Mommy and me" classes. Music appreciation, pottery, ballet, and even swim classes, which her father had arranged for her to take at a private club in the Hamptons the summer she turned three.

Evan, she reported, would happily pay for anything that smacked of self-improvement. Maya, as it turned out, was tone deaf, uninterested in pottery and ballet, but a natural in the water.

"Evan says it's her genes," Tanya said. "He was on his prep school water polo team."

The pool at the Murmuring Surf was a far cry from the tony Hamptons. It was ringed with aluminum-framed tables and chairs, each grouping shaded by large faded yellow-and-white-striped beach umbrellas. Letty sat down and pulled a squirming Maya onto her lap. She unbuckled her sandals and pulled the swim ring over her head and around her torso.

"Now we swim," she announced, standing up and reaching for the child's hand.

Before Letty could stop her, Maya ran to the edge of the pool and jumped in, landing directly on top of one of the lap swimmers, who'd just reached the shallow end of the pool.

The woman stood up, pushed her swim goggles on top of her bathing cap, and batted her arms at the child bobbing contentedly in her orange swim ring.

"You!" she hollered. She glared up at Letty, standing helplessly at the edge of the pool.

She recognized the swimmer as Ruth, one of the motel guests they'd met earlier in the day.

"I'm so sorry," Letty said, plunging into the pool. Maya reached up and wrapped her arms around Letty's shoulders, hiding her head in the crook of her aunt's neck. Letty patted the child's back, but could already hear her sniffling and feel warm tears trickling down her neck.

The other swimmer reached the shallow end and stood up. It was Billie, their other neighbor.

"What happened?" Billie asked, looking from Ruth to Letty.

"Some people have no manners," Ruth said indignantly. "She just let this kid jump on top of me."

"It's adult swim!" Billie said. "No kids in the pool during adult swim."

"I'm sorry," Letty repeated. "I had no idea. There wasn't a sign or anything."

"It's common courtesy," Ruth said. "Everybody here knows we swim laps from eight to nine every night. You didn't see us? You just let your kid run loose, like a wild animal or something? I bet she's not even wearing a swim diaper."

"She's not a wild animal. She's a four-year-old child!" Letty exclaimed, feeling the rage building in her chest. "She's been cooped up in a car or a motel room for three days and she just wanted to get in the pool and swim. Is that a crime? I've said I'm sorry she jumped on you. She won't do it again, but there's no need to get nasty."

"I'm going to speak to Ava about this," Ruth said. She turned to the other woman. "Come on, Billie. Let's go."

Billie nodded. "Newcomers!" she muttered, as she dog-paddled past Letty and the now-wailing Maya.

The two women climbed slowly up the concrete steps, water streaming from the baggy seats of their floral skirted swimsuits.

Maya lifted her head. "I'm sowwy, Letty," she whispered.

5

~~~~~~~~~

S HE'D FINALLY MANAGED TO FALL asleep when she heard her phone ding softly from beneath her pillow. Letty looked anxiously down at Maya, who was burrowed into her side like a small, determined hedgehog. Or maybe a barnacle was a more apt description. *Don't wake up,* she thought, reaching for the phone. *Please don't wake up.*

It was another text from Zoey.

OMG. Evan showed up at my work today, yelling and carrying on about how I better tell him where you are. He almost got me fired. And then a cop came and asked a bunch of questions too. I told them I don't know anything, because I don't. They think you killed your sister. It's crazy. Be careful, please.

Letty stared at the text, then deleted it without a response. She'd already disabled the GPS on her phone. She'd been debating getting rid of it, buying one of those cheap burner phones they sold in convenience stores, but she wasn't ready to give up the lifeline her phone represented. Yet. She switched it off and willed herself back to sleep.

We're safe, she thought. Nobody would look for them in this out-of-the-way town. She had been careful not to leave any tracks that could lead Evan to a place like the Murmuring Surf. The door was locked, the dead bolt engaged. Tanya's go-bag, with the money and the ring, was hidden away. They were hidden, too. Maya was safe. She stroked the little girl's curls, and listened to the reassuring sound of the child contentedly sucking on her thumb.

True, there was a cop sniffing around, asking prying questions. But Letty had questions of her own, so she intended to stay put and stay vigilant.

Letty still didn't know how much her niece understood about what had happened to her mother, or how much she'd witnessed. Her prayer was that Maya had slept through Tanya's violent murder, because she couldn't bear to think about the alternative. At some point, she thought, she would need to get Maya counseling.

Tomorrow, Letty vowed, she would make a plan. Start thinking about finding a job and a better place to live. A ratty motel room was no place to raise a child. Was that what she was going to be doing now? Raising a child? It was a deeply unsettling idea. Letty had always harbored some vague notion that someday she would have the normal things that normal people had: a career, a stable marriage, a mortgage, a dog, and yes, even a child of her own. Preferably in that precise order.

But there was nothing normal about her life on the run.

She was waiting tables at a diner in Tribeca, sharing a crappy apartment in Queens with three other girls she'd met through a Craigslist ad. Evan was a regular customer. He had the kind of looks that, if you passed him on the street, you'd turn around and take another look. He was on the short side, yeah, maybe five foot ten, but he had these arresting amber-colored eyes, a square jaw, hair with the beginnings of a silver streak.

He was a regular customer at the diner, always sat alone at table 2, in the window, dressed casually in fashionable designer jeans, and a heavily starched dress shirt, Gucci loafers, no socks; the only jewelry a wristwatch and heavy gold signet ring on his right hand.

Although he frequently had business meetings, with clients filtering in and out over the space of a couple hours, it hadn't gone unnoticed that Table Two, as the girls all called him, was rarely joined by a woman.

Later, she learned from one of the other waitresses that he owned half a dozen apartments in the neighborhood, and was using the diner as a de facto office. Zoey said he had an understanding with Arthur, their manager, so they left him alone, kept him supplied with coffee and his standing order: a poached egg on unbuttered rye toast, bacon crisped but not burned, and a small glass of unsweetened grapefruit juice. He was a great tipper, polite, but somewhat aloof.

She'd been late to work that wiltingly hot morning in August, had survived a tirade from Arthur where he'd threatened to fire her, and was confiding to Zoey about the fact that her roommates were kicking her out, and she had no idea how she'd find an affordable place to live before the end of the month.

"Excuse me," the customer at table 2 said, when she stopped to refill his coffee. "I uh, overheard you telling your friend that you need a place to stay."

Letty regarded him warily. She was used to being hit on by customers, but Table Two had never shown any particular interest in her.

"Yeah," she said, shrugging. "Sucks. I mean, the apartment was a dump, but it's all I can afford. I was splitting a room with one of the girls, but now her boyfriend is moving in, so they voted me off the island."

"I might know of a place," he said slowly. "If you're interested. It's in the neighborhood."

"This neighborhood?" she laughed. "No way I can afford anything around here."

"You might be surprised," Table Two said. He pulled a business card from a slender leather portfolio, jotted something on the back, and handed it to her. The address was a building two blocks from the diner.

"The tenant just moved out, and I don't like my places to stay vacant. It's bad for business. Let me know if you want to take a look."

She shook her head. "I appreciate it, but honestly, whatever you're charging, I can't afford it."

"Where are you living now, and what are you paying?"

"Don't laugh. My share is nine hundred dollars, and it's a stretch. My credit card is already maxed out."

"You'd be living alone? No boyfriend in the picture?"

"No," she said, already regretting the weird turn this conversation was taking.

"Okay, well, I think we could work something out," Table Two said. "What time do you get off today?"

"After lunch."

"Just think about it. You've got my number. If you want to take a look, I can meet you over there, probably between two and three."

By then, Letty had been living in New York for nearly two years. During her first subway ride she'd seen a man in a clerical collar expose and fondle himself while staring directly into her eyes. She'd had her wallet stolen in an H&M, been casually groped by more customers than she could count, and actually fended off an overly aggressive grill cook with a five-pound block of frozen ground chuck.

"I'm interested in an apartment," she said coolly, "but that's it. I'm not gonna sleep with you, and I'm not into kinky shit, so if you are, forget about it."

He tilted his head and seemed to be considering her in a new light. "What's your name?"

She hesitated for a moment. "Letty."

Table Two pointed at the name badge pinned to her uniform. "According to that, your name is Chynthia."

"Oh, yeah. Long story. It's actually the name of a character I played in a *Law & Order* episode. I played the hooker who finds the politician's body in the bathtub in a motel room at the start of the episode. You know, like, the part before the music goes, 'BAH-BUM!' I liked the sound of the name, so I borrowed it."

"You're an actress?"

"Sometimes. Not enough that I can afford to quit working here."

The cell phone he'd left sitting beside his plate buzzed. He looked down at the phone, then back up at her. "Okay, Letty, I gotta take this. I look forward to hearing from you."

"Maybe."

He picked up the phone. "Not that you asked, but I'm Evan."

6

~~~~~~~~~~

FRIDAY MORNING, JOE LEANED AGAINST the front counter, sipping his coffee and watching the motel's newest guest making her way across the courtyard, a plastic laundry basket under one arm, with the little girl in tow.

Letty was dressed in shorts and a tank top, and the little girl was dressed in the same pink-and-white bathing suit she'd been wearing all week.

"There's something off about that woman," he told his mother.

Ava looked up from the computer screen, lowered her reading glasses, and followed his gaze. "Why do you say that? I think she's perfectly nice. Look how hard she worked, getting that unit cleaned out so she'd have a place to stay. She's quiet, minds her own business. And that Maya is adorable. I wish we had half a dozen guests like Letty."

"Tell that to the Feldmans."

"Those two! They're not happy unless they have something to complain about," Ava said. "They came in here Wednesday, in a snit, wanting me to post a sign at the pool saying that it was reserved for lap swimmers from eight to nine P.M. I told 'em to blow it out their bungholes!"

Joe laughed softly. "I bet that went over great with Ruth."

"They think they own the place just because they've been coming here all these years."

He finished his coffee and tossed the paper cup in the trash. "I gotta get to work."

"You still haven't told me why you think there's something off about Letty."

"Didn't you tell me she paid you cash?"

"Yeah. So what? Several of our guests do that. As far as I'm concerned, it's the perfect arrangement. That money goes right in my pocket, and what Uncle Sam don't know, won't hurt."

"Don't tell me that!" he said sharply. "I'm a cop, remember? And income-tax evasion is a federal crime. Besides, it's not just the cash. It's the whole situation. She's not some retired schoolteacher from Buffalo. She's half the age of our guests. She admits the kid isn't hers. No job. She just shows up, out of the blue. What's she doing? And why here?"

"Why does anybody come to Florida?" Ava gestured toward the plate-glass picture window. Outside, the fuchsia blossoms of a bougainvillea vine clambered across the office's concrete-block façade, and palm fronds rustled gently in the breeze. "The cost of living isn't too bad. No state income tax. The weather's great, the water's warm. I read online that they had snow squalls in Chicago yesterday. It's why your father and I came down here, all those years ago. And why we stayed."

"But why this motel? Why the Murmuring Surf? Remember how upset she got when I suggested she find another motel? It was like she was desperate to stay here. I don't like it."

"Go on to work," Ava said, making a shooing gesture. "Lock up some tax evaders or something. I've got a business to run."

He pulled his phone from the breast pocket of his jacket. "I'm gonna run the tag on that car of hers. Just to make sure she's legit."

"The trouble with you is that that you don't trust anybody. Just because you're a cop, you think everybody's a criminal. Look at you, Joseph! You're thirty-eight and still single."

"Take a look at yourself, old lady. The trouble with you is that you trust everybody. You're fifty-seven and you've had two husbands. And don't get me started about that loser Chuck. And yet you're still trolling Match.com, looking for love in all the wrong places."

"It's Silver Singles, smart-ass. And yes, I'm still hopeful that I'll meet somebody. I know he's out there, somewhere."

"Yeah, probably at a halfway house on work release," Joe said. "See you later."

Letty loaded the sheets and towels into the washing machine, dumped in a detergent pod and a cup of bleach, inserted two dollars' worth of quarters, and punched the start button.

The laundry room was tiny, with two commercial washing machines and two dryers, and sweltering.

"Let's sit out here," she told Maya, guiding her to a row of metal chairs stationed right outside the laundry room door. She would have liked to go back to their room, but the day before, when she'd left the laundry unattended, someone had dumped her wet clothes on the floor instead of placing them in the dryer, or even in the plastic basket she'd left on top of the machine, and now she had to wash them all over again.

She suspected that the "someone" was one of the Feldman ladies, but she had no proof, and she had no idea why they'd taken such an instant dislike to her. She'd even asked Ava about the pair, the morning after the swimming-pool debacle.

"Don't mind those two," Ava said. "They've been coming here for twenty years, so they think they run the joint."

"Are they sisters?" Letty asked. "They sure don't look anything alike."

"Sisters?" Ava hooted. "No, honey, bless your heart." She lowered her voice. "They're lesbians! Got married right here on the beach, as soon as it was legal. Of course, Ruth insisted that Billie had to take her name."

"Juice box," Maya said, tugging at Letty's arm.

"Juice box, please," her aunt corrected.

"Pees?" Maya batted her eyes. She was Tanya's daughter, all right.

Only four, and she'd already figured out that the best way to get her way was to look cute and turn on the charm.

Letty's chest contracted in a sudden spasm of grief. She couldn't get the image of her sister out of her head, her blond hair splayed out on that black and white floor. The puddle of blood. The single shoe, the glass of vodka.

Today was Friday.

Less than a week ago, Tanya was alive, making plans to move to LA and reinvent herself. She'd found a bungalow to rent in Holmby Hills—"Ellen DeGeneres has a house there!" she'd said, showing Letty the photos from the online real estate listing. "It's way small, actually, I think it's the guesthouse behind some gigantic mansion, but you'd have your own bedroom and bathroom. And there's a pool for Maya. She could go swimming every day."

Tanya refused to accept that Letty didn't want to move to Los Angeles. "Think of all the career opportunities," she'd said. "Show business is *the* business there."

"I'm not in the business anymore," Letty reminded her. "And that's fine with me." She didn't remind her sister that Evan intended to fight tooth and nail to keep Tanya from taking Maya across the country with her. And she didn't point out that she was pretty sure Tanya mainly wanted Letty to accompany her to California as in-house childcare.

While Maya sucked contentedly on her juice box, Letty tapped her phone and forced herself to read the headlines of the tabloids back in New York.

BLOND BEAUTY SLAIN, TOT ABDUCTED, COPS SEEK SISTER was the headline in the *Post*. A huge color photo of Tanya and Maya, dressed in matching outfits for a children's charity fundraiser, was plastered across the front page, and below it was a smaller photo of Letty, handcuffed and dressed in orange jail scrubs. It was a screenshot from the other walk-on she'd done three years earlier for a *Law & Order* episode, but it made Letty look like a hardened criminal.

The *Daily News* was even worse. WHERE IS MAYA? the headline screamed. Beneath it was a blown-up shot of Maya, hands clasped beneath her chin, her cupid's-bow lips curved into a dreamy smile. Letty recognized it as the school photo from the exclusive preschool Maya attended. The subhead and accompanying story made her want to gag.

HEARTBROKEN DAD OFFERS REWARD
FOR KID'S RETURN

Real estate entrepreneur / philanthropist Evan Wingfield is still reeling after last week's brutal murder of his estranged partner, Tanya Carnahan, and the apparent abduction of his four-year-old daughter, Maya.

Through a family spokesman, Wingfield announced a $10,000 reward for information leading to the recovery of his daughter.

"Although they were no longer in a romantic relationship, Evan admired and respected Tanya, and he is devastated by her tragic death. For now, though, all his energies and resources are concentrated on finding his daughter," said the spokesman, Charles "Skipper" Hallowell. "He has fully cooperated with the police, and he will not rest until Maya is brought back to safety."

Tanya Carnahan, an aspiring model and actress, was found sprawled on the floor of her lavish Upper West Side brownstone last Sunday morning, after an anonymous tipster, believed to have been her older sister, 33-year-old Scarlett Carnahan, called 911 to report Tanya's death. A source close to the police investigation told the Daily News that Tanya Carnahan suffered a blow to the head. Although the actress had reportedly been in rehab for unspecified substance abuse issues, the source said preliminary lab results revealed substantial amounts of Xanax and alcohol in her system.

When authorities arrived at the town house, which is one

of several in the neighborhood owned by Wingfield, they discovered Tanya Carnahan's body. The child, however, was missing.

Evan Wingfield admitted to police that he'd seen his former girlfriend that morning, and that the two had a loud argument after he accused her of drinking, in violation of their custody agreement. He insisted, however, that Tanya Carnahan was alive when he left the home shortly after noon on Sunday.

Wingfield and Tanya Carnahan were in the midst of a very public and very bitter court battle over their daughter. Carnahan claimed that her former fiancé was a serial cheater who was indifferent to their daughter's needs, while Wingfield claimed that Tanya Carnahan, who'd had only modest success with her acting and modeling career, was an unfit mother.

Friends of the couple say the two were introduced by Scarlett Carnahan, who at the time was employed by and in a relationship with Evan Wingfield. The relationship ended when Wingfield turned his attention to Carnahan's troubled younger sister, a recent arrival from Atlanta.

"Troubled?" Letty exclaimed out loud. "She wasn't troubled until she hooked up with that scumbag."

Maya, startled, looked up at her aunt, her mouth puckered.

"It's okay, ladybug," Letty assured her. "Everything's okay."

The child smiled, uncertainly, before turning her attention to a handful of seashells they'd gathered during yesterday's morning walk on the beach.

According to one friend, the 42-year-old real estate entrepreneur struck up a relationship with Scarlett Carnahan when she was working as a waitress at the Lazy Daizy diner in Tribeca.

At the time, Carnahan was struggling to find acting work, and needed a new place to live after roommates evicted her from her apartment in Queens.

"Evan befriended her, let her stay in an apartment he owned nearby, even gave her a job managing some of his real estate," the friend said. "He helped her find a new agent, who got her some acting gigs. Eventually they started dating, in a casual kind of way. Letty then invited her younger sister, who'd been living and working in Atlanta, to visit her in New York."

But as soon as Tanya Carnahan arrived in the city, the friend said, everything changed.

"Evan fell hard for that girl. Letty, obviously, was furious. It caused a serious rift between the two sisters. They didn't speak for years."

Maya patted her knee and held up her juice box. "All done."

"Okay," Letty said, taking the empty box. "Would you like some Goldfish?"

"Pees," Maya said, holding out a rather grubby hand. Letty took the bag of cheddar crackers from her backpack and poured some into the child's hand.

"What do you say?" Letty prompted.

Maya shoved all the crackers into her mouth and chewed happily. "Fank you," she said, sending showers of orange crumbs down the front of her swimsuit.

Letty resumed reading the *Daily News* story, fuming. She knew exactly which of Evan's bitchy pals the reporter had quoted.

Sascha Hallowell was married to Evan's Princeton classmate Skipper. She'd pretended to like Letty, but as Tanya later confided, "She thinks we're both a couple of hillbilly hayseeds. What Sascha doesn't know is that good ol' Skippy tried to put his hand up my skirt the last time we had dinner at their place."

Letty could picture the sneer on Sascha's face when she referred to Tanya as "that girl."

She was scanning the rest of the story when she spotted Ava's son Joe sauntering out of the motel office toward the parking lot.

She watched as he walked slowly through the parked vehicles, stopping behind her Kia. He took out his phone and clicked off a few frames of the license plate, did a slow circle around the car, then got in his own truck and drove away.

Letty froze. She thought she'd been so smart buying that car. After renting a car at Newark Airport the previous Sunday night, she'd driven as far south as Raleigh, North Carolina, before checking into a fleabag motel.

Maya had finally stopped crying, and the two of them had fallen asleep almost as soon as they hit the bed, not waking until glaring sunlight blasted through the thin draperies. She'd been horrified to see that they'd slept past noon. She'd hustled Maya out of bed, put her in the shower with her, and headed back toward the interstate.

Of course, the child screeched with joy when she spotted the golden arches at the strip of shopping centers and fast-food joints near the interstate on-ramp. They were devouring their chicken nuggets and French fries when Letty noticed the car parked several yards away, facing traffic. It was a silver Kia with a FOR SALE sign posted prominently on the dashboard, and it offered the solution to something she'd been worried about since leaving the Hertz lot at Newark.

She'd rented an Acura with Tanya's credit card. Although Letty was three inches shorter with hair several shades darker than Tanya's, on a driver's license photo she could easily pass for her younger sister.

The police would probably be looking for her by now. Maybe they had found Tanya's Mercedes in Newark already, or maybe not. Maybe they had traced the credit card and seen that it had been used at the Hertz counter. Maybe she was already the subject of a multi-state manhunt. She needed to ditch the rental car, and fast.

From the plastic booth in McDonald's, Letty called the number on the Kia's dashboard sign and, after a short discussion about price and the car's mileage, arranged to meet the seller in the Hertz lot at the Raleigh-Durham airport. He pulled up alongside her at the appointed time, got out of the Kia, and seemed surprised to find someone who looked like Letty standing there, clutching the hand of a little girl, surrounded by two small suitcases and a child's car seat.

"Here's the keys," he said. "And the title. You gotta sign it right there."

She wrote her name on the registration in a deliberately illegible scrawl, then handed him the money. He counted the bills and nodded. "I gassed it up like you asked."

"Thanks," Letty said.

Now she didn't know what to do about the Kia, or Joe the cop. Should she move on? Where would she go? The Murmuring Surf seemed like as good a place as any to lie low and figure out her next move. Tanya must have had a reason for saving that magazine article about the motel. But sooner or later she'd need a job. She didn't want to touch any more of the money in Tanya's stash than was absolutely necessary. That was Maya's money, as far as Letty was concerned.

Right now, though, her most urgent concern was to keep as far away from Maya's father as possible.

"Letty," Maya said, tugging at the hem of her shirt. "Let's go to the beach now, okay?" She kicked her sandal-clad feet. "Swimmy, swimmy, swimmy."

"Okay," Letty promised. "As soon as the laundry's done."

~~~~~~~~~~~~~~

7

J OE PAINSTAKINGLY TYPED THE LICENSE tag number into the South Carolina Division of Motor Vehicles database. After a few moments, he had the answer to one of the questions in the list he'd compiled about their newest guest at the Murmuring Surf.

The Kia was registered to a Myles Nordan, in Pickens, South Carolina, a town he'd never heard of. He wrote down the name, then entered Nordan's name into the South Carolina DMV database.

Nordan, it seemed, owned lots of cars. Eight, to be exact. So maybe he was a small-scale used-car dealer?

He rested his stubby fingertips lightly on the computer keyboard. He would have liked to type Letty's name into the National Crime Information Center Database, but he didn't actually know her last name. As he'd pointed out to his too-trusting mother earlier that morning, there was very little they did know about this newcomer.

His sergeant poked his head into Joe's cubicle. "Hey, ace. Got a situation at Sharky's. Some drunk parked in their lot and wandered off to the beach. Their security guard called for the tow truck, which arrived at the same time as the drunk, who decided to take a swing at the guard."

The Treasure Island Police Department was small, with eight uniformed officers and two detectives, including Joe DeCurtis, but with a department that small, the distinction between patrol and detective was frequently blurred. Like today.

"On it," Joe said.

He didn't get back to the computer until two hours later. By then, he had a last name to go with Letty's first name. It was Carnahan. When he typed her whole name into the search engine, his screen lit up.

He shook his head as the pieces to the puzzle began to fall in place. Shit. Letty Carnahan was a fugitive, wanted for murder, who, if you believed the tabloid news accounts, abducted that little girl who'd already claimed Ava's heart. She was living at the Murmuring Surf. It would only take one phone call. Just one.

If he went by the rule book, he'd make that call. But his cop's intuition, which had never failed him, told him that there was much more to this story. He would hold off on that phone call until he had all the pieces of the Letty Carnahan puzzle.

Maya sat in waist-deep water, the gentle waves washing against her chest. She leaned back against Letty. "Fishes," she said, pointing at the small shadowy green shapes darting beneath the surface of the water.

"Minnows," Letty said, giving the child a hug. "Little baby fishes, just like you."

"I'm not a baby. I'm Mommy's big girl." Maya turned to her aunt. "Where's Mommy?"

Here it comes, Letty thought. Time to tell truth. For five days now, she'd dodged the child's questions about her mother's where-abouts.

She lifted Maya onto her lap and smiled sadly. "Mommy's gone to heaven, ladybug."

Maya frowned. "You take me to see Mommy in heaven, Letty."

"I can't," Letty said, kissing her niece's forehead, already sun-browned despite the layers of sunblock Letty slathered all over both of them. Unlike Letty, whose fair skin freckled and burned after only fifteen minutes at the beach, Maya tanned easily and beautifully, like her mother.

"I want you to," Maya said, her upper lip quivering. "I want to see Mommy in heaven."

"Someday," Letty said. She and Tanya had attended church and Sunday school strictly as a matter of convenience to Terri. Her own grasp of theology was sketchy at best, so she felt totally inadequate to the task of explaining death and mortality and the hereafter. How was she supposed to explain the hereafter to a four-year-old when she wasn't sure she understood it herself?

Instead, she fell back on the only coping mechanism she'd ever learned from her mother. Denial, with a strong helping of distraction.

"Come on," Letty said, standing up. "I'm hungry. Let's go get some lunch."

Letty had taken to opening the windows in the mornings in an effort to air out the room.

After lunch she sat in a chair by the door, watching, as Maya drifted off to sleep. She wished she had a television, or a book, or something to keep her mind off the avalanche of anxiety that seemed to be her constant companion.

Instead, she picked up her phone and scrolled through the Craigslist ads for help wanted, which was yet another depressing, anxiety-inducing time suck.

It wasn't that the pickings were lean. This was Florida and tourist season seemed to be a year-round state of mind. Restaurants needed servers and experienced cooks. Hotels needed housekeepers. Stores needed cashiers. She'd found a few listings for real estate management, but these all seemed to be full-time jobs. And right now, her full-time job was softly snoring from inside a pillow fort.

A wisp of acrid smoke drifted into the room. She jerked the door open and stepped outside.

An elderly man lounged in a folding lawn chair directly in front of her window. His bald head gleamed in the sunlight. He was bare-chested, exposing a narrow expanse of wrinkled, sun-bronzed skin and a hairy, beach ball–size belly. Spindly legs poked out from baggy shorts that reached to his knees. His eyes were half closed and a cigarette hung limply between pale lips.

"Mr. Jensen!" she said sharply.

"What?" He didn't even open his eyes or bother to look at her.

She flapped her hands, trying to dispel the cloud of smoke. "I've asked you more than once. Could you please not do that? Your smoke is pouring into my room. I don't want my niece or myself exposed to that."

He inhaled and exhaled a thin stream of smoke through his nose. "So? Close your windows. That's why God invented air-conditioning."

"There's a no-smoking sign right there," Letty said, pointing at the sign affixed to the concrete column.

He shrugged. "I'm not smoking there. I'm smoking here. It's a free country, you know."

"Couldn't you go over there?" Letty pointed to the plastic chairs grouped in a semicircle beneath a palm tree. The smokers' lounge, the regulars called it.

Every night, around six o'clock, after the early-bird dinner hour, a few of the Murmuring Surf guests wandered out to the palm tree and took up positions in what seemed to be a rigorously enforced seating chart. The two men, one a Hispanic man who puffed on cigars, the other a short, pudgy man she'd never seen dressed in anything except a short terry-cloth bathrobe, always sat together. There were three elderly, birdlike women, who shared a single bottle of wine and a large clamshell they used as an ashtray. Letty surmised, from the overheard tone of their conversation, that they, too, were retirees and longtime regulars at the motel. Once, Letty had seen Billie, the shorter, nicer of the Feldmans, slink out to the palm tree. She'd borrowed a cigarette from one of the bird ladies, leaned against the tree, and smoked exactly the one cigarette, keeping her eyes trained on the door of their unit, probably worried that Ruth might catch her sneaking a smoke.

"Too hot out there," Mr. Jensen said lazily. "I like it right here in the shade."

"Oscar!"

They both looked up to see Ava bearing down on them, trundling a plastic cart loaded down with cleaning supplies.

"How many times do I have to tell you? Put that thing out and get the hell out of my breezeway."

Ava's usually placid face was pink and perspiring.

"Okay, already," Jensen said. He pinched the end of the cigarette between his fingers and dropped it to the concrete floor.

"Oh no you don't," Ava said, pointing at him with a dustpan. "I'm not your mother, and I'm not cleaning up after you. Pick that up and put it in the trash. The next time I find one of your disgusting cigarette butts laying around out here, you'll forfeit your security deposit."

"I'm not the only one here who smokes," he protested.

"You're the only one who smokes outside this room, and you're the only one who never heard of an ashtray," Ava said.

"Okay, okay," Jensen muttered. The chair creaked beneath him as he stood up, and he walked slowly back to his room.

Ava shook her head and sighed. She looked over at Letty. "Sorry about Oscar. Since his wife died, he's gotten lazier and more ornery every year. Sue kept him on a pretty short leash, didn't let him smoke or drink at all. You see what he's like now. He pays in cash, right before he goes back home to Rochester every year. Arrives in January, leaves in May. I could probably ask a lot more money for that unit of his, but I just don't have the heart to kick him out."

"He doesn't bother me that much," Letty said. "I guess I could just keep my windows closed."

"You doing okay otherwise?" Ava asked.

"We're good, thanks. How come you're doing the housekeeping?"

"Had another girl quit on me yesterday. No call, no show, nothing. That's what it's like this time of year. People can have their pick of jobs. Somebody offers fifty cents an hour more, they take it, and they don't look back."

Ava hesitated for a moment. "I don't suppose you'd be looking for work, would you?"

"I need to," Letty admitted. "But what would I do about Maya?"

"You have any family living around here?"

"No."

"There's day care," Ava pointed out. "The Methodist church up the street has a program. Some of our housekeepers have had their kids there."

"I don't think so," Letty said. "Maya's been through a lot. I can't see myself leaving her with a bunch of strangers."

"Here's a thought," Ava said slowly. "My Isabelle is in a baccalaureate program at the high school, and she's a senior, so she only has classes for half a day. She's back here every day by lunchtime."

Letty had seen Ava's pretty teenage daughter coming and going in the jaunty red Jeep that was parked near the motel office. The girl always waved and smiled when she caught sight of Maya.

"What would you want me to do?" Letty asked cautiously.

"Anything and everything," Ava asked. "I reckon you're probably more interested in an office job. Are you good with computers? Joe's been after me to do more online marketing, and to put our reservations system online too. He even bought me the software, but I never have had the time to learn to use it—or maybe I'm just too old a dog to learn new tricks. Maybe you could start with that?"

"I wouldn't say I'm a whiz or anything, but I used to work in real estate management up north," Letty said.

"Hate to ask, but do you think you might also pitch in with the housekeeping? Just 'til I hire somebody else? I've still got Anita, thank God, but fourteen units is too much for her to manage by herself. She leaves by three every day, because her dad just moved in with her, and he's pretty high-maintenance."

It was Letty's turn to ask questions. "Has Isabelle ever done any babysitting?"

"She used to watch my niece's two hellions every summer," Ava said. "To be fair, that was more like zookeeping than babysitting."

"Won't she mind you volunteering her to babysit Maya?"

"I promise you, she'd rather babysit than change beds and scrub toilets," Ava said. "What do you think? You'd work for me however many hours a week you can manage, and I'll cut you a break on the room."

Letty's mind was already doing the math. "What would I do with Maya in the mornings, while Isabelle's at school?"

"Same thing I used to do when mine were that age," Ava said, smiling broadly. "I'd sit them down in the office with a picture book, or a puzzle or some crayons. And yeah, some days they watched more television than they should have, but I don't think it did 'em any permanent harm. Joe, he was class valedictorian, and Isabelle's already been accepted to Emory, with a full ride."

Letty felt her spine stiffen at the mention of Joe, the nosy cop.

"I don't think your son likes me very much," she said. "What's he gonna think about me working for you?"

"Probably think it's a terrible idea," Ava said cheerfully. "At first. But he'll get used to the idea, and he'll get used to you. Anyway, I'm the boss around here, not him. What do you say? Do we have a deal?"

"Letty?"

Maya stood in the doorway of the room, naked from the waist down, clutching the stuffed elephant under her arm. "I think Ellie did pee-pee in the bed."

Ava chuckled and handed Letty an armload of freshly laundered sheets. "Looks like you're gonna need these. How about you start in the morning? Is eight too early?"

"I'll see you then," Letty said. "Thanks, Ava."

8

~~~~~~~~~~~~~~

ZOEY SPOTTED TABLE TWO THE moment he stepped into the diner. The balls of this guy! He sat right down at his old spot, unfolded the newspaper, and tapped his fingertips on the table-top while he read.

When Hailey headed that way with the coffeepot, Zoey grabbed it from her. "Hold up. That's the guy I told you about. The one who used to come in here all the time. Messed with my girl Letty."

Hailey's eyes widened. "That girl who killed her sister and kid-napped the baby?"

"Hush! That's some bullshit right there," Zoey said. "Letty would never. You take my table and I'll take yours. And I'll split the tip with you. Okay?"

"I guess." Hailey was new, but she wasn't dumb.

Zoey eased over to the table. Evan held out his coffee mug and she filled it. He looked up and she could tell he recognized her. Vaguely. Men didn't look at Zoey the way they did girls who looked like Letty.

"Long time, no see," Zoey said.

"Uh, yeah."

"The usual today?"

"That's right. Rye toast, dry. Poached egg. Crisp bacon. Small grapefruit juice. Oh, and, I've got somebody joining me."

"Should I go ahead and put in your order?"

He glanced at his watch and frowned. "Yeah. She's late."

Ironic, Evan thought. Vikki Hill had never been late when it came time for an under-the-table payoff. She'd turned up, unannounced, at his building in Tribeca two months earlier, and demanded to see the apartment on the third floor, his most recent purchase.

Naturally, he'd been alarmed. Where, he'd asked, was Norman, the city housing inspector he'd been dealing with for the past few years?

The new inspector had shrugged. "Gone. That's all I know."

Which was obviously a lie. Vikki Hill seemed to know quite a lot. She let him know, subtly, that she could be "influenced" to overlook his illegal short-term rentals. And she seemed to know exactly how much she could expect as reward for turning a blind eye.

Just then the door opened and the new inspector walked in. She spotted him at his table and hurried over to join him.

Interesting, Zoey thought. The woman was definitely not the guy's usual type. She was skinny, no boobs to speak of, probably around Table Two's age. Dressed in jeans and Chuck Taylors with a black turtleneck sweater under a boxy no-name navy blazer. A light-skinned black woman with flat-ironed hair. Or maybe she was biracial.

Zoey grabbed a menu and the coffeepot.

"Morning," she said, sliding the menu onto the tabletop. "Can I get you started with coffee?"

"No thanks. Just some ice water." The woman glanced at the menu. "I'll have a bagel egg sandwich, and you can bring me two packets of mustard."

When the waitress was gone, Evan thumbed through photos on his phone, found the one he wanted, and handed it across the table to his guest.

She studied the photo, enlarged it with her fingertips. "She's a lot prettier than that photo they ran in the *Daily News*. Is this the most recent one you've got?"

"Yeah."

"Okay, text that to me. And any other photos you've got of her. And the kid, of course."

"Maya."

"Right."

Zoey was back with the coffeepot, but Evan waved her away.

Vikki Hill sipped her ice water. "I talked to the detective running the investigation. I worked on a housing-inspection thing with him a couple years ago that ended up also being a child-endangerment case. He's pretty straight."

"Did he tell you anything useful?"

"Just that they recovered the Mercedes in Philly yesterday. Stripped and abandoned."

"Figures."

"She used your wife's . . ."

"Girlfriend," Evan corrected. "Ex-girlfriend."

Vikki plowed ahead. "A woman who fits the description of Scarlett Carnahan used your ex-girlfriend's credit card to rent a car at the Hertz counter at Newark Airport, then turned it in at RDU."

"That's the airport in Raleigh?"

"Yeah. Do you know if the girl has any connections down that way?"

"Not that I know of. She and Tanya moved around with their mother a lot when they were growing up. They lived in West Virginia for a while, and then I think there was a relative who lived in Indiana. To tell you the truth, I didn't pay much attention to any of that. But neither one of them ever mentioned Raleigh."

"Have you talked to the mother?"

"No," he said succinctly. "They weren't close. I know her name was Terri, but Tanya and Letty didn't talk much about her."

"Okay. You say the sister worked here, when she first moved to the city?"

"Yes."

"All right, I'll check with the manager. Maybe she used her mother's contact info as next of kin on her job application."

"Doubtful," Evan said. "But I guess you could ask."

"Tell me more about Letty," Vikki Hill prompted. "What was she like? Who were her friends? Places she hung out, like that."

He gave it some thought. "She was sharp, you know. No college that I knew of, but she read a lot and she was street smart. You couldn't hustle Letty, that's for sure. She'd been doing acting, but not getting very far with that. She was pretty enough, but nothing like her sister. Tanya had presence, you know? Like, drop-dead gorgeous."

His lips twisted. "Of course, as it turns out, Tanya, unlike Letty, was a major head case."

"Friends?"

He jerked his head in the direction of the counter, where Zoey was busily trying to look like she hadn't been staring at them.

"That waitress? She was a friend of Letty's. There's another girl, who quit around the same time as Letty. Corinne Tapley. She's working at a boutique in the East Village. I went to see her, but she claimed she hasn't heard from Letty and doesn't know where she might have gone."

"Did you believe her?"

"Not really."

"Text me the girl's name and the name of that shop. I'll talk to her. Let me ask you something. What motive would Letty have for killing her sister?"

He raised an eyebrow. "Who knows? Jealousy? Letty was living the good life up here. And then little sister shows up and poof! Everything changes."

Every morning when she woke up in what she still thought of as Monica's apartment in *Friends,* Letty felt like she was living in a dream. She arose early, sipped coffee on the balcony, and planned her day.

Managing the Airbnb guests was more involved than her new

employer had led her to expect. One of the tenants on the second floor had begun to complain about all the people coming and going from Evan's unit there, so she'd taken to meeting guests in the lobby, wheeling their suitcases as though they were hers, and ferrying them into the unit.

"The doorman keeps giving me these weird looks," she reported to her boss. "Do you think he thinks I'm a hooker or something?"

"Sidney gets paid very well not to ask questions or give you weird looks," Evan said, sounding annoyed. "I'll speak to him."

Every guest who checked into one of Evan's Tribeca units—which were located within a six-block radius—was given Letty's cell phone number. They called or texted at all hours, day and night, to complain about the air-conditioning or the furnace. Or the Wi-Fi speed. Or the lack of a corkscrew, toilet plunger, or ice cream scoop.

Guests lost their keys. They wanted early check-ins and late checkouts. And, as Evan had warned, none of them could figure out how to work the television remotes.

Her new responsibilities quickly escalated. She gave notice at the diner. Working alone from the apartment, she was surprised how much she missed the camaraderie and friendship of the Lazy Daizy crew.

"You need a better agent," Evan told her bluntly one evening, when they met at a nearby bistro to discuss the upcoming week's bookings.

"No." She shook her head. "Leslie's been great to me."

"How long since she got you an actual job?"

"I got two callbacks for that paper-towel commercial."

"I'm not talking about callbacks. I'm talking about paid gigs."

Letty shrugged.

"Dammit, Letty, if you want to be an actress, you need to be acting. I've seen what you've done, you're terrific. You really stood out as the juror in that Denzel Washington flick, and I realize you only had a couple lines, but the *Law & Order* episode you did was great."

"You've seen my work? How?"

He smiled. "IMDb." He slid a card across the table to her. "Give this guy a call. Ronnie's the best. Knows everybody, reps all the up-and-coming actresses. More importantly, he owes me a favor."

In retrospect, it was shocking how easily she agreed to do whatever Evan suggested. She cried the morning she let Leslie know she was seeking new representation, but within a week, Ronnie Silver managed to get her a walk-on in a CBS pilot and an actual speaking part in a low-budget indie horror flick. She got cast as the jealous ex-girlfriend in a Hallmark Christmas movie. The pay was crap, but she got to spend a week in Canada, in August.

The boost in her income allowed her to sign up for classes with a prestigious acting coach.

When Evan tactfully mentioned that her slight underbite could be keeping her from getting bigger roles—and when he referred her to an orthodontist he knew—she dutifully got invisible braces, which cut her lower lip and made her jaws ache. And when he pointed out that she might get bigger roles if she let her hair grow longer and went lighter, that's exactly what she did.

Evan Wingfield was a patient man. He waited a month before he casually asked Letty to dinner. She was frankly shocked when he didn't make any overt moves, just giving her a chaste kiss on the cheek when he dropped her back at the apartment.

There were more dates: to a charity fundraiser, the soft opening of a new French restaurant owned by one of Evan's friends. The kisses became less chaste and more urgent. She enjoyed the attention and began to have second thoughts about her pledge that she would not sleep with him.

Letty hadn't heard from Tanya in a while. The last she'd heard, her little sister was living down south somewhere, doing some modeling and living with an on-again, off-again boyfriend. Tanya was not big on phone calls or emails, so Letty was shocked to get a call from Tanya early one Saturday morning.

"Lettttttyyyy," Tanya sobbed.

"What is it?"

"Rooney's gone."

Letty wasn't sure whether Rooney was Tanya's boyfriend or her cat.

"Gone? Oh my God, is he dead?"

"I wish. No, the fucker moved out. I came home last night and there was a for-sale sign in the window of the condo. There's a multi-lock on the door, so I can't get in, but I looked inside and it's completely empty. All my stuff is gone. My clothes, my shoes, everything. Thank God I was carrying my Louis Vuitton, or it would be gone too."

"Did you try calling him?"

"Only like a gabillion times. Nothing. He's gone and my shit's gone. And P.S. He owes me like a couple thousand dollars. I'm officially broke."

"This happened last night? Where are you staying?"

"I slept in my car last night, because it was too late to do anything else."

"Oh, Tanya," Letty said with a long sigh.

Her sister had a long history of short, disastrous relationships with men, but even for Tanya, this was the Tanya-est thing ever.

"What are you going to do?" Letty asked.

"I'm not sure. I'm supposed to do a catalog shoot down in Florida next week, but I don't have any place to stay until then. I don't even have a change of clothes. Literally, all I have is what's on my back. And my car, which I have to keep moving because the bank wants to repo it."

"And the Louis Vuitton," Letty pointed out. "How much is that thing worth?"

"Don't even go there. I'm not hocking Louis."

Letty waited for the other shoe to drop.

"I was thinking," Tanya said slowly. "What would you say about my moving up there?"

"Here? You'd move to New York?"

"Why not? I could probably get a lot more magazine work. Definitely more runway. Maybe take some acting classes. Like you. Hey,

I meant to say I loved you in *Christmas in Charleston*. You were the only one with an authentic Southern accent. Maybe you could hook me up with your new agent?"

For a moment, Letty was seized with an irrational—and selfish— urge to scream "No!" But she would never do that. Tanya was her baby sister. Okay, technically half sister. The two of them had been on their own since they were sixteen and seventeen. Scarlett and Tanya against the world.

"Maybe," she said. "Where would you stay?"

"I was thinking maybe I could camp out on your sofa or something? Just until I get my feet on the ground, start getting some work?"

The waitress arrived back at the table with their order. She lingered, arranging the plates just so, pouring more coffee and water. "Anything else?"

"That's all," Evan said.

"Hold up," Vikki said. "I understand you're friends with Scarlett Carnahan?"

Zoey shrugged. "She used to work here, so yeah, I knew her. But she quit, so I haven't seen her in, like, forever."

"But you know your friend is in trouble, right?"

"I read about it in the *Post*, but you know how newspapers are. They make up most of that crap they print. Anyway, I know Letty wouldn't hurt anybody. Especially that sister of hers."

"Okay," Vikki said. She tore the mustard packets apart, squeezed mustard on top of the egg, then picked up her bagel and bit into it.

"She's lying," Evan said, when Zoey was gone.

"I know. I'll get back with her later, when you're not around."

She took another bite of sandwich and chewed slowly. "Let's talk about you for a minute. I see from the tabloids that things were pretty bad between you and your ex. You'd already moved on, right?

New girlfriend and all? You don't exactly look like a grieving widower to me."

Evan's jaw tightened. "Tanya was the mother of my child. And now that child is missing. Who knows what kind of situation Letty has gotten her into? Maya is only four. She's very sensitive and highstrung. She was seeing a therapist even before all of this."

"Why not just let the police find Letty and Maya?" Vikki asked. "Don't get me wrong. I'm happy to take your money, but be straight with me here. This isn't just about finding the person who killed Tanya, and it's not just about the kid. Am I right?"

He sipped his coffee and then carefully composed his answer.

"As I mentioned on the phone, Letty worked for me, until I met Tanya. She was privy to some, uh, confidential business arrangements, and then, while Tanya and I were living together, she obviously was around all the time, while I was doing business, talking to associates, that kind of thing. She asked a lot of questions. Tanya was a head case, but she was no dummy."

"Ohhhhh," Vikki said, nodding. "Letty and Tanya knew the dirty details about the Airbnbs, and you were afraid they'd spill the beans to the city. Am I right?"

"Not in so many words," Evan said. "Tanya was determined to move out to LA. She thought she'd get more acting jobs there. I was happy to let her go. . . ."

"And get her out of your hair, and off your payroll," Vikki interrupted. "But she wanted to take the kid. And you weren't having it."

"Tanya was just out of rehab. Booze and pills. She was . . . unbalanced. And Maya's own therapist—the one Tanya insisted she see, by the way—thought the move to LA was a bad idea. A kid that age needs structure and routine."

"Which you would have provided?"

Evan glared at her. "What's this got to do with finding Letty and Maya?"

"I like to know all the underlying issues," she said.

"These are the issues. Tanya is dead. My daughter is missing and I want her returned to me."

"Let's say I find them. What happens next?"

"You tell me where they are. I'll handle the rest."

Vikki took another bite of bagel. She chewed, swallowed, dabbed at her lips with a napkin, and then frowned. "What's that mean? Handle? I don't like the sound of that."

"It means I want to talk to Letty before the police do. I just need to make her understand that anything she thinks she might know about my business is confidential, and it needs to stay that way."

"Not sure I like the sound of that either. But back to Letty. Where was she living after she stopped working for you?"

"Brooklyn. But I've been to her place, there's nothing to see."

"You went to her apartment and searched it?"

"That's right."

"Do I want to know how you got in?"

He sipped his coffee but said nothing.

"I'll still need to see the place. You said Letty quit working for you?"

"Yes."

"She broke up with you? And quit? Because you hooked up with her little sister?"

He nodded.

"Must have been pretty awkward between the two of them, right?"

"Yeah. You could say that. Letty was so pissed, she wouldn't even come to the hospital when Maya was born. She totally ghosted her own sister. It was unbelievable."

"How long did that go on?" Vikki asked. "The feud, I mean."

"Let's see. I remember, Letty came to Maya's third-birthday party. Begrudgingly. By then, things were pretty bad between Tanya and me. I hadn't moved out yet, but the handwriting was on the wall. She'd supposedly quit drinking, but I went into the kitchen in the middle of the party, and caught her spiking her Fresca with vodka.

I blew up at her. I mean, getting wasted at your own kid's birthday party? Letty heard us fighting, and of course, she took Tanya's side. That was it for me. I walked."

Evan had placed his phone on the tabletop. The screen lit up, and he tapped it to dismiss the call. "Okay, I need to get going. You've got all you need, right?"

"For now," she said.

He reached for his billfold.

Zoey and Hailey were standing behind the counter when she saw Table Two getting ready to leave. She nudged Hailey.

"Time to take your smoke break."

"Now? I just took one a little while ago."

Zoey gave her a look. "Just go stand outside the window where they're sitting. Take your phone. When the woman gets up to leave, get a picture of her. And try to be subtle, okay?"

"What's this for?" Hailey asked, sliding her phone into the pocket of her apron.

"It's for our girl Letty," Zoey said. "Hurry up. Go, go, go."

9

~~~~~~~~~~

MAYA WAS USING THE BACK of her spoon to mash the banana rounds into her Cheerios, before happily stuffing the cereal into her mouth with her hands.

"Okay, doodlebug, finish that up now," Letty said, using a paper towel to mop up the spilled milk on the tabletop. "We've got to get moving."

"Where we going, Letty?"

Letty lifted her down from the booster chair. "This morning, you're going to the office with me, and we're going to help Miss Ava."

Maya went to the dresser and picked up her pocketbook and slung it over her shoulder. "Okay. Let's go."

"Not quite yet," Letty said, laughing. "Let me finish getting dressed."

She examined her reflection in the cloudy dresser mirror and sighed. It had been a tough twenty-four hours, and her face showed the stress.

They'd spent most of the previous day at the beach. It was Sunday, and crowds lined the expanse of wide, white sand. Maya had been in her element, swimming and gathering seashells. Ava had given them a plastic bucket and a small kitchen strainer, and the child spent hours trying to net the minnows that darted safely out of her way. They'd built an elaborate sandcastle, which Maya declared was for Elsa, even though Letty was fairly certain ice princesses would never survive the Florida sunshine. Late in the day they'd eaten somewhat sandy peanut butter and jelly sandwiches and potato chips and fed the leftovers to the seagulls, which dipped and swooped in for their meal and generally terrorized and annoyed the tourists sitting nearby.

It had been a carefree, golden afternoon. They'd packed up the beach umbrella and toys when suddenly, in the distance, Maya spotted a long-legged blond woman in a red bikini, walking along the shoreline.

"Mommy!" Maya screamed, dropping her sand bucket. "That's my mommy!" She streaked toward the woman, with Letty close behind. "No, Maya. Come back!"

The startled woman turned, just in time to see the child hurtling at her, and then desperately clinging to her knees, crying, "Mommy, Mommy."

"I'm sorry," Letty said breathlessly, as she tried to peel Maya away from the stranger.

"Noooo!" Maya screeched, clawing and kicking as Letty carried her away. "Noooo!"

It was quite the scene. People were staring, their expressions a mixture of amusement and sympathy.

"She's just overtired," Letty murmured, as a young mother stopped to ask if she needed help.

Maya screamed all the way past the Murmuring Surf pool, where the regulars were arrayed in their self-assigned lounge chairs. Letty was vaguely aware of the silver-haired women and balding men turning to stare in their direction.

When she finally reached the room, she had to lock the door, because Maya repeatedly threw herself at it, crying out for her mother.

That morning, Joe had arrived at the door to their unit with a small "extra" flat-screen television that he claimed Ava had discovered in the office supply room. Now, Letty turned the television on and tried to distract Maya with *PAW Patrol,* but to no avail.

Finally, in desperation, Letty ran a warm bath, stripped off first her own and then Maya's sandy swimsuit, and climbed naked into the tub. She held the sobbing four-year-old close to her chest, patting her back, rocking back and forth until the tears slowly began to subside. She hummed and sang "Let It Go" over and over until her voice was hoarse and the water was cold.

When Maya's breathing grew slower, signaling sleep, Letty finally climbed out of the tub. She dressed them both quickly and tucked Maya into the bed. The child stirred once, but fell back to sleep immediately. Letty congratulated herself on how expertly she'd handled what could have been a dangerous situation. What if someone had stopped and questioned her on the beach? What if someone demanded to know who Letty was? And where Maya's mother was?

Fortunately, that day, the beachgoers were busy minding their own business.

Letty tortured herself for hours, considering all the dire consequences of Maya's meltdown, finally falling into an uneasy sleep shortly after 2:00 A.M.

When her phone dinged softly, signaling an incoming text, her whole body tensed.

The message was from Corinne.

Hey. Heads up. Zoey called today. E showed up at the Daizy yesterday, with a lady detective. This woman had lots of ? about u and Tanya and Maya, but Zoey played dumb. She hung around long enough to hear the woman say they found the Mercedes in Philly. They know you rented a car and left it in Raleigh. And the woman has a picture of you. Be careful, okay?

Letty's fingers flew over the phone's keyboard. *Thanks. Will be in contact. You be careful too.*

Three little bubbles indicated Corinne was still typing. A photo popped up on her phone screen, of a woman, standing at what Letty recognized as Evan's favorite table at the Lazy Daizy. She was dressed casually, sneakers, jeans, blazer.

Zoey managed to get us a photo of the detective.

Tell her I owe her one. Xoxo L.

She shouldn't have been shocked that Evan had hired a detective.

Tanya had warned her, as recently as the week before her death, that her dealings with her ex had taken an ominous turn.

"He thinks he's so smart," Tanya said, while they were sharing take-out sushi. "I know all his dirty little secrets. And if he keeps messing with me, trying to take Maya from me, I told him, I'll go public. And he'll go to jail."

Letty had begged Tanya not to threaten Evan, but Tanya was beyond reason.

"Did I tell you about his new arm candy? Her name is—get this—Juliette. After Maya got back from the weekend with them it was all JuJu this and JuJu that."

"So? You know he's always got a new chick on the string. You're over him, so why do you care?" Letty asked.

"Because this chick is different. He let her move in. It's the first time he's done that since I left." Tanya scowled. "Of course, Maya's in looooove with her JuJu. She's totally buying my daughter off with fancy toys and clothes. Who gives a four-year-old her own goddamn iPad?"

"Tanya, listen to what the mediator is telling you," Letty said. "Stop picking fights with Evan. If you stop threatening him, he'll settle. If you do that, you can move on and put all this crap behind you."

"I'm moving on all right, all the way to California," Tanya retorted. "I'm taking Maya with me, and there's not a damned thing Evan Wingfield can do to stop me. Not if he wants to stay out of prison."

Letty could feel her anxiety spiraling. Tanya's prediction had been devastatingly accurate. Evan Wingfield had killed her sister, she was sure. And now he was after her. Her first instinct was to run—to pack up this child, asleep in the bed beside her, and flee into the darkness.

Maya sighed softly and burrowed into Letty's side, flinging an arm across her chest. Letty inhaled the sweet smell of baby shampoo and brushed a damp curl off the child's forehead.

Now was not the time to run, she decided. Maya needed to feel safe. She needed time to forget the trauma of whatever she had witnessed. And Letty needed time. To think, and plan. To figure out what their future would look like and yes, to find out what Tanya's attachment was to the Murmuring Surf.

This morning, Maya was bright-eyed and cheerful, as though nothing had happened at the beach on Sunday, but Letty was what Mimi would have called "a hot mess."

She donned the pink polo shirt with the Murmuring Surf embroidered logo, dabbed some concealer onto the dark circles under her eyes, and pulled her hair into a ponytail. "Okay, let's go to work," she told her niece.

"You're early," Ava exclaimed, as Letty and Maya entered the Murmuring Surf office.

"Gotta make a good impression on my first day," Letty said.

"How are you this morning, Miss Maya?" Ava asked, kneeling down so that she was at eye level with the little girl.

"I got all my stuff in here," Maya said proudly, holding out her *Frozen* pocketbook for inspection.

Ava dutifully looked inside the purse, holding up each item for examination. "Mmm-hmm. Lipstick, comb, granola bar, jewelry box . . ."

"What?" Letty grabbed the black velvet box, her heart pounding. "Maya, you're not supposed to have this."

The little girl's upper lip began to quiver. "Mommy said it was for me. I want it."

Letty didn't dare open the box in front of Ava, but as she tucked it in her pocket she could feel something rattling inside the box. Maya had always loved playing with the contents of Tanya's jewelry box, draping her neck and wrists with ropes of fake pearls, gaudy colored beads and gold chains. Before Tanya split with Evan, when she still wore the push present diamond ring, she'd sometimes allow Maya to slip the ring onto her thumb to admire it.

"It is for you, sweetie, but not until you're more grown-up," Letty said gently, hoping to forestall another temper tantrum. She had no idea how or when Maya had managed to find Tanya's tote bag when she'd gone to such pains to hide it in their room, but the first chance she got she would check to make sure Maya hadn't appropriated anything else—like cash. And she would find a new hiding place for the go-bag.

"Here," Ava said impulsively, removing the jeweled pink flamingo brooch she wore pinned to her blouse. "Why don't you wear this today, since it's your first day on staff."

"Oh no," Letty protested. "That's not necessary."

"I want her to have it," Ava said. "It's just junk jewelry. I went through a flamingo phase a few years ago and I've got more flamingo coffee mugs and napkin holders and pins and earrings than I know what to do with. I probably have three or four more of those pins the kids gave me for Mother's Day or my birthday."

Maya looked down at the flamingo's glittering pink stones and grinned. "Mine."

"Now that we've got that settled, you two, come around back here," Ava said, beckoning to the reception desk.

A red plastic child-size table and chair stood behind the counter, with a small box of crayons and a pad of paper. "That was my Isabelle's when she was your age," Ava told Maya, who promptly seated herself at the table and began sorting the crayons. "Good thing I decided to hang on to it for those grandchildren Joe still hasn't given me."

"He doesn't have kids?" Letty asked.

"No wife, no kids. I think that last girlfriend of his did a number on him. Too bad, because I really thought maybe she was the one."

Ava shook her head. "Oh well. Let me show you my command center."

She powered up the computer monitor and clicked on an icon, and the screen lit up. "This shows all our bookings by the day, week, and month. If you arrow over to the right, you can see next month's bookings. We're full up right now, which we almost always are this time of year, with all our regulars."

Letty nodded.

"The Polaceks went back home to Pittsburgh yesterday," Ava said, pointing to a square on the screen. "Earlier than usual, because their daughter is having a baby, and Dorothy wants to be there. So this afternoon, if you're up to it, you can help Anita turn unit twelve. That's the aqua one with the hot-pink door."

"I'm up for whatever you need me to do," Letty said.

"Good. Because Bill and Alice Sheehan are supposed to get in tonight from Boston. They usually stay in unit nine, but when I let them know the Polaceks were going home early, Alice jumped at the chance to get their unit, because it's got that nice screened porch on the back."

"All the units aren't the same?" Letty asked.

"Oh no. The Surf only had ten units when it was built right after the war," Ava said. "The Doughertys, the couple we bought it from, added onto it over the years. The original units in the north wing are pretty simple, a bedroom, kitchenette, sitting area, and bathroom." She gestured to the office. "If you can believe it, this was where the Doughertys lived. This front room was the office, and the back, which I use for storage and supplies, was their living area. They raised two daughters in that little bitty space! But when the oldest was a teenager, Elsie finally got Dick to add the second story where we now live."

"And the additional units?" Letty asked.

"Dick and his brother built those back in the sixties," Ava said. "My understanding is, there was an old wood-frame house on the south side of the property. It got hit pretty bad in a hurricane, and the owners sold it for eight thousand dollars to the Doughertys, who then tore it down and built those other six units."

"Eight thousand for a Gulf-front lot?" Letty asked.

Ava shrugged. "That was a lot of money back then. Anyway, all those units on the south side of the property have either a small screened porch or a little patio on the back. They have a proper dining area and the living room is big enough for a pull-out sleeper sofa, which our regulars love, because it means they can have their kids or grandkids come down for a few days, without paying for a motel."

"I'll bet those units are pretty popular," Letty said.

"Well, the Gulf-view units on the west are the ones everybody wants. You better believe it. If I had ten more of the bigger units, I could keep 'em full year-round. As it is, I have a waiting list."

"So, no check-ins until tonight?" Letty asked.

"That's right. No checkouts, either. It should be a pretty boring morning for you. Just answer the phone, take messages, deal with the guests. I've got a dentist's appointment at nine, and then I'm meeting an old friend for coffee after that. I should be back before lunchtime."

"Got it," Letty said.

Ava pointed to a stack of glossy colored flyers. "Our new brochures and rate cards. Just picked them up from the printer. The mailing labels are there too. If you would, insert the rate cards in the flyers, staple 'em closed, and stick the mailing labels on the front."

She held out her hand. "Give me your phone. I'll put my number in it, and if you have any questions or run into trouble you can give me a call."

"Okay," Letty said, and took a deep breath. "I guess Maya and I are on the job."

"MOD," Ava said.

"Huh?"

"Managers on duty. Good luck."

10

~~~~~~~

THE CHIMES ON THE OFFICE door sounded. Her guest was an elderly man with a fringe of silver hair and an aggrieved expression on his suntanned face. He was dressed in one of those violently patterned terry-cloth beach jackets and matching trunks.

"You're not Ava," he said, looking over her shoulder.

"No," Letty agreed. "Ava's out running errands. Is there something I can help with?"

"Who are you?" He spied Maya, who was busy stapling together the pages she'd finished coloring.

"I'm Letty," she said.

"Oh yeah. The newcomer. With the kid. I heard about you."

"Well, I hope you didn't hear anything bad," Letty said, flashing him what she hoped was a disarming smile. "And you are?"

"Merwin Maples. Unit four."

The door opened again and a woman pushed through, leaning on an aluminum walker.

"What'd she say?" the woman asked. "Can we get the Sheehans' unit, or no?"

He went to the door and opened it wider. "Ava's not here." He jerked his thumb in Letty's direction. "This is the woman Ruth told us about."

Merwin turned back to Letty. "This is my wife, Trudi."

"Nice to meet you. I'm Letty."

Trudi Maples had creamy, almost unlined skin and pale blue eyes. She wore a broad-brimmed straw hat, a knee-length snap-front housecoat, and sensible thick-soled lace-up walking shoes. But the oddest thing about her was the white cotton gloves she wore on both hands.

"Don't I know you?" she asked, studying Letty's face.

"I don't think so. We just moved into the pink unit this week. I'm going to be helping out here in the office."

"Where are you from?" Trudi asked, inching closer to the reception desk. "I could swear I've seen you someplace before."

Letty felt a tickle of fear. "I've pretty much lived all over. Most recently in New Jersey."

"We're from Jefferson City. Ever spent any time in Missouri?"

"Not really," Letty said. She needed to change the subject. "You were saying something about moving into the Sheehans' unit?"

Merwin spoke up. "Yes. Word on the street is that Bill and Alice are moving into the Polaceks' unit. So we'd like to move into the Sheehans' unit."

"Is there something wrong with the unit you're in?" Letty asked.

"No view," Merwin said. "You can see the water from the Sheehans' place."

"All you see out our window is the ice machine," Trudi griped.

"Oh," Letty said. "Ava should be back around lunch, so I'll tell her you came in and made that request."

"Write it down," Trudi instructed. "I know for a fact that the Weidenauers have been angling to move. But we've been coming down here way longer than they have, so by rights, we should get first shot at it."

"Okay," Letty said, dutifully scribbling a note to that effect. "I'll let Ava know."

Trudi looked past Letty at Maya, who was peeling the paper off a purple crayon.

"Pretty little girl," she said. "Whose is she?"

"Mine," Letty said, not bothering to explain. "Was there anything else I can help you with?"

"I never forget a face," Trudi Maples said. "And I know I've seen you someplace before."

"People tell me that all the time," Letty said. "I'm always hearing that I look like somebody's high school classmate or second cousin."

"No. It's nothing like that," Mrs. Maples insisted.

Merwin rolled his eyes. "It's her superpower. Sooner or later, she'll figure out how she knows you. And it'll probably come to her at four in the morning, so she'll wake me up to tell me all about it." He touched his wife's shoulder. "Come on, Trude. I want to start packing our stuff so we can move into the Sheehans' unit as soon as Ava gives us the go-ahead."

Letty recognized the next visitor as one of the women she thought of as "the bird ladies"—the three skinny women she saw gathered together most nights at the Murmuring Surf's smokers' lounge, laughing easily and sharing a bottle of wine.

Today's visitor was easily the most youthful-looking of the women—with hair dyed blue-black and a still-shapely figure she accented with snug-fitting capris and T-shirts. She pushed through the door and looked right past Letty.

"Where's Ava," she asked breathlessly.

"She's out. Is there something I can help with?"

"God, I hope so. My bathtub is stopped up and I've got a small river flowing straight into my bedroom. Is Joe around? He usually fixes stuff."

"I haven't seen him this morning," Letty said. "Is there a plumber I could call?"

"How do I know? Call Ava. Get her back here now."

Letty picked up her phone to call the motel owner, but her call went immediately to voice mail.

"Ava's probably still in the dentist's chair," Letty said. "Hang on." She walked into the supply room and returned with the plunger and a plumber's snake she'd spotted earlier while looking for a roll of Scotch tape.

"Good Lord," the woman said, pointing to the long hand-cranked drain-cleaning tool. "Do you know how to use that thing?"

"Hope so," Letty said. She held out her hand to Maya. "Come on, doodle, let's go."

"What's your name, by the way?" the woman asked, as they walked toward one of the larger units on the south side of the property.

"I'm Letty."

"And I'm Arlene Finocchia. Sorry to be so panicky, but the carpet in my unit is new, and I don't want to lose the security deposit if it gets ruined. What's your little girl's name?"

"Maya."

"Such a sweet face," Arlene said. "This is me. Unit thirteen."

She was pointing to a mint-green concrete-block unit with a deep blue front door. A thin stream of water trickled out onto the concrete doorstep.

"Oh shit," Arlene said. "Sorry," she said, glancing down at Maya. "Excuse my potty mouth."

"Unfortunately, she's heard it before," Letty said. Arlene opened the door and they followed the water into the bathroom, which had a powder-blue ceramic tile floor and matching powder-blue fixtures.

"Stupid me. I left the water running while I ran to the laundry room to switch out the machines . . . and when I got back, I saw this mess."

Damp towels were piled up on the floor, which held more than an inch of water.

"Uh-oh," Maya said, pointing to water splashing over the top of the tub.

Letty sat down on the edge of the tub, ignoring the resulting gusher.

"I'll just take Maya into the other room while you work," Arlene said, holding out her hand to the little girl. "Okay if I give her a snack? I've got some tangerines from the produce stand."

"She'd love a tangerine," Letty said.

Ten minutes later, Letty emerged from the bathroom with a triumphant smile. She was soaked from the knees down and held out a paper cup with what she estimated was a good four-inch-thick blob of matted jet-black hair caked with what looked like cream rinse.

"All done," she said, holding out the paper cup for inspection. "Here's the culprit."

Arlene Finocchia's face turned pink with embarrassment. "Oh my God." She clutched her head. "I knew my hair was thinning out, but not that much. That's disgusting."

"These old pipes are probably kind of corroded inside," Letty said. "I used to live in a building where this happened all the time. You ought to buy a gallon of white vinegar and pour some down the drain every day or so to clear out the gunk."

"I will," Arlene said.

"Have you got a mop and bucket handy?" Letty asked. "We should get that water up before it has a chance to sit."

"You're amazing," Arlene said, as Letty prepared to leave. "An honest-to-God lifesaver. Wait, I have something for you." She disappeared for a moment, and when she came back, she pressed some bills into Letty's hand.

It was two ten-dollar bills. "Oh no," Letty said. It was her turn to be embarrassed. "That's not necessary, not at all."

"Sure it is," Arlene said, waving away Letty's objections. "My security deposit is five hundred bucks. And I'm pretty sure Ava didn't hire you to do plumbing work."

"I'm here to do whatever needs doing," Letty said, trying to hand the money back. "Please, I can't take this."

"Maya," Arlene addressed the little girl. "Hold out your hand."

"Okay." The girl grinned as Arlene closed her chubby fingers over the cash. "You two run along now. And thanks a million."

Letty had devised a system for completing the flyer mailing. She folded each flyer in three, inserted the rate card, affixed a preprinted mailing label to the front, then handed it off to Maya, whose sole responsibility was stapling the flyers together. The little girl chortled gleefully each time she mashed the glossy paper beneath the stapler.

Letty was so absorbed in her task she lost track of time until the door chimed again and Joe walked in, carrying a large cardboard carton. He glanced around the room. "Where's my mom?"

"She had a dentist's appointment and a coffee date. She said she'll be back before lunch," Letty said.

He walked around and joined them behind the counter, setting the box on a console table and ripping it open with a box cutter. He lifted out a bulky package wrapped in a plastic foam cube.

"I picked up her new printer," he said, cutting away the foam. "I'm just gonna go ahead and set it up now, because otherwise I'll have to come back and do it after I get off work tonight."

"You're on duty?" Letty asked. "Isn't that against the rules or something?"

"We're a small department. My sergeant knows where I am and he knows how to find me," Joe said. He cleared a stack of file folders from the console top, set the printer up, and began plugging cables into the back of the printer, and then into the wall socket.

He tapped some buttons on the printer's control panel and nodded in satisfaction when it lit up. "There's paper on the shelf in the supply room," he told Letty. "Grab a stack and let's see how it works."

She found the paper and inserted it into the printing tray. Joe sat at the computer monitor and typed, and a moment later the printer whirred to life.

"Good," he said, nodding. He looked down at Maya, who was trying out the stapler on the discarded blocks of foam. "Hey, I recognize that table and chair."

"Ava said they used to be your sister's."

"But they were mine first," Joe said. "She used to sit me there while she worked. I watched a lot of television sitting at that table. Ate a lot of baloney sandwiches there too."

"How nice," Letty said. She picked up a stack of flyers and began folding them, hoping he'd get the signal that she was very, very busy.

"Where'd you grow up?" he asked. "I swear, just now when you said 'How nice' I detected a Southern accent."

"We moved around a lot when I was a kid. Tennessee and West Virginia, places like that," Letty said, being deliberately vague. "Could you hand me those rate cards over there?"

She wished he'd go.

"Were your parents from the South?"

"She was, but he wasn't. They split up when I was little."

"My old man took off when I was seven," Joe volunteered.

Despite herself, Letty found herself curious about this cop's background. Maybe if she asked the questions he'd be so distracted he'd forget to interview her.

"Your mom told me your folks bought this place when you were a baby. What was that like? Growing up, living in a motel?"

"Until I went to high school, I thought everybody lived like this," Joe said, gesturing around the small office. "Especially after my old man left, there was always a lot to do around here. I started off emptying garbage cans, cleaning the pool, sweeping the breezeways. When I got a little taller, Ava had me mowing the grass, painting, washing windows."

"Had your family always been in the motel business?"

"No. My dad sold cars for a living. The folks came down here from Michigan on vacation one January, Mom said they thought they'd found paradise. The water was blue and the sun was shining. My dad told her he never wanted to see another snow shovel for as long as he lived. According to her, he was always full of big ideas. They were staying at a little tourist court up the road from here, and one day he spotted the for-sale sign out front of the Murmuring Surf. Without consulting her he borrowed money from his folks and hers, did some fast talking to the previous owners, the Doughertys, and next thing Mom knew, they were in the motel business."

"And she stayed on, running the place, after he split?" Letty asked.

"She didn't have much of a choice. My old man met a cocktail waitress over at Derby Lane, that was the local greyhound track, and the next thing Mom knew, even though she'd always been a housewife until they moved down here to Florida, she was running a motel and raising a kid."

"Must have been tough," Letty said.

"She's a tough lady," Joe said. "But she's a soft touch for a sob story. Which is why I try to run interference when I can. Because people take advantage." He gave her a hard stare.

Letty stared right back. "I don't have a sob story. I'm just trying to live my life and take care of my niece. Is that some kind of a crime?"

"You tell me," he said.

The door chimed. Ava breezed in with an armload of grocery bags. "I'm back."

She looked from Letty to her son. "Everything okay here?"

"I met Mr. and Mrs. Maples," Letty said. "They came in to tell you they want first dibs on the Sheehans' unit."

"Here we go," Joe said. "Musical motel units."

"I also met Arlene, the lady in the mint-green unit? Her tub was stopped up, but I took care of it."

Joe looked skeptical. "What'd you do?"

"I got a plunger and the plumber's snake and I extracted a huge hairball from the drain," Letty said.

"Good work," Ava said, beaming at her new employee.

"Speaking of work, I gotta get back to mine," Joe said. "I hooked up your new printer."

"Did you show Letty that new software, so she can teach me how to use it?" Ava asked.

"No time today," Joe said.

~~~~~~~~~~~~~~~~~~

11

"HI MOM!" ISABELLE DECURTIS DROPPED her backpack on the reception desk. She pretended to be surprised when she spotted the small person busily coloring at the miniature red table.

"Who's this?"

Maya looked up, giving a shy smile. "I'm Maya. I'm four."

"Hey!" the teenager said, kneeling down beside her. "I'm Isabelle and I'm almost eighteen." She pointed to the "cover" of the booklet Maya had stapled together.

The picture showed a small stick figure with a headful of vivid yellow circles, holding hands with a taller figure with flowing golden tresses, spiky black eyelashes, and cartoonish high heels.

"Did you draw this?" Isabelle asked, her eyes widening in admiration.

Maya nodded.

"No way!" Isabelle exclaimed. She tapped the smaller figure. "Is this you?"

"Me and Mommy," Maya said. "We're going to a birthday party."

Isabelle looked up at Letty, and then at her own mother.

"Will they have cake at the birthday party?" Isabelle asked.

"Uh-huh. Pink cake. And pink candles. And pink balloons," Maya said.

"Whose birthday is it?"

Maya pointed at Letty with her purple crayon. "It's Letty Spaghetti's birthday!"

"Is it really?" Isabelle asked, looking at Letty.

"Not until November," Letty said, blinking back tears. "She, uh, really loves birthday parties."

"Okay," Isabelle said. She stuck out her hand. "So Maya. Would you like to hang out and have some fun with me today?"

Maya smiled, showing her dimples. "Yes."

Isabelle wore ripped and faded jeans and a navy T-shirt with EMORY in block letters across the front. She was slender with her dark hair worn in a single braid.

Now she swept Maya off the chair and propped her on her hip. "Do you know how to swim, Maya?"

"I'm a big girl," Maya declared. "I put my face in the water and kick my feet."

"Me too!" Isabelle said. She consulted Letty. "Okay if I take her to the beach for a while?"

Letty hesitated.

"Isabelle worked as a lifeguard at the Treasure Island pool for the past two summers," Ava said.

"We'll be super careful," Isabelle said. She tickled Maya's belly. "Won't we, Maya Papaya?"

"I guess that would be okay," Letty said. "But she hasn't had lunch yet."

"That's cool. I haven't either. We could walk down the beach to Lazy Larry's and grab a bite. They've got a kids' menu," Isabelle said.

"You'll need money." Letty hesitated.

"I got moneys," Maya said excitedly. She reached into the pockets of her shorts and pulled out the ten-dollar bills Arlene had given her earlier, waving them in the air.

"Whoa, dude," Isabelle said, laughing. "We're rich!"

"Mrs. Finocchia insisted on tipping me for unclogging her bathtub," Letty told Ava. "When I wouldn't take the money, she gave it to Maya."

"That's perfectly fine," Ava said, patting her employee's hand.

"Arlene is always very generous. But she's probably the only one of our regulars you'll ever see do something like that."

"Yeah," Isabelle agreed. "The last time I got a tip, it was fifty cents, from Mr. Maples, after I helped him carry in, like, a thousand bags of groceries from Publix, in, like, two-hundred-degree heat."

Ava rolled her eyes. "That's Merwin, all right. The last of the big spenders. He used to own a company that printed those color advertising inserts you get in the mail. Sold it and made a ton of money. But I promise you, he hasn't spent a nickel of that money since he retired. It's like a game with him. They drive that beat-up fifteen-year-old Honda Odyssey minivan all the way down here from Poughkeepsie every winter, and after they get here, he loves to bore everybody here with what great mileage he got. He even makes poor Trudi eat dinner at four thirty when they go out, so they can get the early-bird special."

"I was wondering about his wife," Letty admitted. "What's with the gloves?"

"Trudi's got some kind of problem with her circulation. Her hands and feet don't get blood like they ought to, so she's always cold, which is part of why they spend winters down here."

"It's called Raynaud's disease, Mom," Isabelle said, and spelled it out. "Trudi told me all about it. She's really nice, Letty. She doesn't get out a lot, with the walker and all, so she watches a ton of television. Like, she's seen every episode of *Buffy*, ever. We usually order Chinese takeout and watch *The Bachelor* together on Monday nights."

"Because Merwin has a coupon, of course," Ava put in.

Letty felt the now-familiar tickle of fear. Could Trudi have spotted her in one of her rare television appearances over the years? She'd adopted a stage name early in her nascent acting career, because she didn't want to be confused with the megastar Scarlett Johansson, but it wouldn't take much digging for a shut-in with an uncanny memory for faces to discover that Chynthia Chase was actually Scarlett

Carnahan, who was wanted for questioning in New York in connection with the murder of her sister and abduction of a small, adorable little girl named Maya.

"Isabelle, let's go to the beach!" Maya said, tugging at her babysitter's braid. "Swimmy, swimmy, swimmy."

Ava watched the two girls walking hand in hand toward Letty's room so that Maya could change into her bathing suit.

"That little one about broke my heart with that picture she drew of her mama. Do you think she really understands what happened to your sister?"

Letty busied herself stacking the assembled flyers. She wanted desperately to confide in someone, and Ava seemed like a person with a genuinely good heart, but she knew she couldn't divulge what was troubling her, especially to a woman whose son was an overly inquisitive cop.

"No," she said finally. "I've told Maya the truth, or as much of it as I think she can handle. I've told her that her mother has gone to heaven and isn't coming back, but she doesn't really believe it. She keeps thinking she sees her mama, on the beach, on the television. I keep thinking it too."

"Can I ask?" Ava said gently. "How long since your sister died? How did it happen?"

Letty shook her head. "I can't . . . I'm sorry. I can't talk about it. It's too soon. I haven't really processed it myself."

"I understand," Ava said, patting her hand.

"I wish I could say the same," Letty whispered.

Evan arranged to meet Vikki Hill in an apartment he'd just purchased in SoHo. "Nice place," she said, running her hand over the marble countertops in the kitchen. They were seated on chrome-and-acrylic barstools in the kitchen. "How much does a place like this rent for?"

"I haven't decided yet," he said, feeling rising irritation. He gazed out the floor-to-ceiling window.

"It's been nine friggin' days now."

"Yep."

"And yet you still can't find her?" He turned and fixed her with a cold stare, but she was not a woman to be intimidated.

"I warned you from the beginning, these things take time," she said.

"The police have been all over me, asking questions," Evan snapped. "It's total harassment and it's affecting my business. I need this thing settled."

"What's the hurry?" she asked. "They haven't said you're a suspect, right?"

"They haven't really told me anything. The big problem is, several of my most valuable properties were in Tanya's name. For tax purposes, of course."

"Ahhh," she said. She let that hang there in the air.

Evan tugged at his ear. He did that, she noticed, when he was agitated.

"Tanya left a will," he continued. "Her attorney drew it up, and I wasn't even aware of it, until recently. Everything she had goes to Maya, our daughter, of course. But Letty is listed as her guardian."

"Not you? Her domestic partner? She chose a sister who wouldn't even speak to her for a couple years?"

"Yes."

She bit back the sarcastic comment that came immediately to mind. "Just how much property are we talking about?"

"A lot. Several million dollars' worth. The most valuable portion of my investment portfolio."

"But in the eyes of the law, it's not actually yours, right? It's her kid's now. And the aunt's, by default, because the kid is a minor. Although, if this aunt is charged with murder, by law she wouldn't be allowed to profit from her crime."

"True," Evan said.

"Do you think the sister is aware of this will? Of what she and the kid stand to inherit?"

He tugged at his ear again. "I don't know."

12

~~~~~~~~~~~~~~~~~

Letty had only herself to blame. Moving to New York had been Tanya's idea, but Letty hadn't exactly discouraged her. She offered the pull-out sofa in the Tribeca apartment, loaned her money and clothes, showed her how to buy a MetroCard.

And the first night Tanya was in town, she introduced Evan to her little sister.

"Wow!" Tanya said, later that night, as she was making up the sofa bed. "You didn't tell me your boyfriend was, like, smoking hot. Seriously, Letty, he's amazing. And this apartment is so cool! I feel like I'm living in a *Friends* episode. Tell me again, what is it you exactly do to earn this place?"

Letty was hard put to explain her job.

"I'm the on-site manager. We had six units in this building when I started, but Evan just closed on two more. And he owns ten more units in the neighborhood."

"Do you happen to have any white wine?" Tanya asked, poking her head in the fridge. "That Italian food we had tonight was soooo salty. I'm parched."

"There's a bottle of Sancerre on the door," Letty said.

Tanya found the bottle and filled a wineglass nearly to the rim with the sixty-dollar-a-bottle wine Letty had splurged on the previous week. She held up the bottle. "There's like half a glass left. Want some?"

Letty shook her head.

Tanya sat back down on the sofa, her lovely nose wrinkled

in disapproval. "So, you're like Evan's receptionist? I don't get it. I thought you moved to New York to act."

"So did I. But breaking in isn't easy. In the meantime, like most actors when they get here, I started waiting tables. And then I met Evan. You might say I work in guest relations. All his units are rented out as Airbnb. No long-term tenants. But we're strictly on the down low, because the co-op board in this building, actually in all our buildings, prohibits short-term rentals. I make things run smoothly. It's not exactly what I planned to be doing with my life right now, but it's a living. And I get to live here."

"Okay, so this dude? He owns all these apartments? And he's rich?"

"I assume so," Letty said.

"Super rich? Like, Mr. Big rich?"

"I don't know," Letty said. "That's his business. Not mine."

"As soon as I start making some serious money, I'm going to get me a place exactly like this!" Tanya said, running her hand over the sofa's cool leather surface. "How much does an apartment like this cost, in this neighborhood?"

When Letty told her, Tanya flopped backward, pretending to faint. "That much? Seriously? You could put a down payment on a house for that back home."

"You could *buy* a house for that, back home," Letty said. "Or at least a double-wide. Which reminds me. Have you talked to Mama lately? Does she even know you've moved up here?"

"No." Tanya unzipped her jeans and let them drop to the floor. She wriggled out of her bra and added it to the pile of discarded clothes. She gathered her long blond hair into a careless knot on top of her head and fastened it with an elastic band and walked toward the bathroom, dressed only in her T-shirt and a pair of panties. Her legs were long and slim and tanned, and Letty noticed her sister had a new tattoo high on her right hip. A tiny shamrock.

A moment later she popped her head around the doorframe. "Hey, Letty Spaghetti? Do you have any decent skin cream? My face is like sandpaper. I swear, I can feel the zits popping up right this minute."

"Top shelf in the linen closet," Letty said. "But you didn't answer my question. When was the last time you talked to Mama?"

"It's been a while," Tanya admitted. "How about you?"

"I've lost track. Last I heard, she'd moved out to Lake Tahoe for a 'new job.'" Letty's fingers flashed air quotes.

"Yeah. New job is mom code for new boyfriend," Tanya said. She sighed heavily and started to close the door. "Okay if I take a bath?"

A month later, Letty was asleep when she heard the apartment door click open and softly close. She rolled over and picked up her phone. It was ten 'til three.

"Tanya?" she called.

Her bedroom door opened and Tanya appeared. "Sorry," she whispered. "Didn't mean to wake you up. Go back to sleep."

"Where've you been?" Letty asked, sitting up.

Evan had taken the sisters to a new restaurant on the Upper East Side. They'd just started on the calamari when Letty's phone pinged with a text. She looked up at Evan and shrugged. "It's the guest at Houston Street. Three-F says the doorman won't let him in."

"That's not possible." Evan frowned. "Wait. Didn't you tell me Dontae was going on vacation this week? Did you talk to the new guy?"

"No," Letty said. "I thought you were going to take care of him. You know I don't keep that kind of cash."

"Dammit!" His lips tightened and he took his own phone from the inner breast pocket of his linen blazer. "I'll text Dontae and tell him to talk to the guy. Let him know the deal. In the meantime, you better get over there. I don't want that busybody on the third floor making any more trouble for us.

"Here." He pulled a bundle of bills from his pocket and peeled off five hundreds. "Tell him it's a retainer."

By the time Letty arrived at the building, smoothed things over with Enrique, the substitute doorman, and spirited their guest inside and up to the apartment, it was past nine o'clock. She texted Evan that she was going home, picked up take-out ramen at the corner bodega, and was in bed by eleven.

"The service at that place was super slow," Tanya said, sitting on the edge of Letty's bed. She rubbed her fingers back and forth over the comforter's satin binding. "We were just about to leave, and an old friend of his stopped by the table. When Evan told him I was new in town, and a model, the guy invited us to this new club he's invested in. Like, insisted. Because he said I'd meet a lot of important people there. Evan says it's all about networking."

"And did you? Meet anybody important?"

Tanya giggled. "Who knows? I drank a lot of champagne. Like, a lot! I don't really remember anybody's name. But I had the most incredible time. And it's all because of you, because you invited me to come to New York." Tanya bent down and brushed her lips across her sister's cheek. Letty caught the scent of a familiar men's cologne. "Love you, Letty Spaghetti."

Letty felt funny going back to the Lazy Daizy after she'd quit working there. The other girls refused to meet her eyes. Zoey told Letty they thought she was stuck-up, now that she no longer waited tables. Instead, she'd begun meeting Evan for Friday breakfast at the Tip Top, a diner across the street from Letty's new apartment.

He was sipping coffee and finishing his toast when she seated herself at their usual booth.

"Am I late, or are you early?" she asked, nodding at the waitress who appeared with her iced tea.

"Neither." He propped his elbows on the table. "Did Tanya speak to you?"

She cocked her head. "I haven't seen her. She got in way after midnight and had an early call for some pilot that's shooting over in

Jersey. Seems like Ronnie's been able to get her plenty of work since she hit town."

"She's got a certain look that's in demand, right now, that's all," Evan said. "But you're keeping busy, right? I mean, with those two new units, I don't know when you'd have any more time to go on auditions anyway."

Letty sat up straight in the booth. "What's this about, Evan? What is it Tanya was supposed to speak to me about?"

He shook his head. "Dammit, this is awkward."

She thought back to the past few weeks. Ever since Tanya had arrived, she'd had a nagging sense that something was amiss. And now, looking at Evan, as he picked at a morsel of bacon on his plate, she knew exactly what was amiss.

"Oh," she said slowly. "So what? You've been sneaking around, sleeping with my little sister? You want my permission or something?"

"No. It's not like that."

She toyed with the packet of artificial sweetener the waitress had tucked under her glass. The girl should have known the packet would get soaked and the sweetener would be ruined. It was true what people said. You really couldn't get good help these days.

"Not like what? You're not sneaking around? Or you're not sleeping with her? Or maybe you don't actually want my permission. Which is it?"

Evan let out a long sigh. "Admit it, Letty. You like me, but there was never any real chemistry between us. Which is probably why you'd never sleep with me, which, looking back now, was a good thing. Ours is a working relationship, and unfortunately, I let things get . . . personal. But, as I told Tanya, I want to be honest with you. She and I? We just clicked. Like, right away."

Letty felt her face redden. "Clicked? Is that a polite euphemism for fucked?"

He wadded up his napkin and threw it onto his plate. "See? This is why Tanya didn't want to tell you herself. She knew you'd overreact."

"Overreact?" She leaned across the table. "I paid for her plane ticket up here. Loaned her money to get new headshots and set her up with my agent. Right now, she's wearing my favorite bra and living in my apartment. So you'll excuse me if I 'overreact' to the news that she's now sleeping with the guy I've been dating."

"I don't need this headache," Evan muttered. He tucked a twenty-dollar bill under his plate. "It is what it is, okay? You and I have a business arrangement. If I'm not mistaken, it's worked out pretty well. For both of us. You don't want to throw that away, Letty. Think about it, okay? In the meantime, Tanya's moving in with me. I'll send somebody over to pick up her stuff."

He slid out of his side of the booth, brushing toast crumbs from the front of his immaculately pressed white dress shirt, then glanced at his wristwatch.

"Don't forget, you've got a walk-through at the new unit in SoHo at three today. And you need to meet the guys delivering the furniture at noon."

"I'll be there," she said, her tone as detached and businesslike as his. "Please tell my sister I expect her to have the clothes she borrowed dry-cleaned and returned to me by this weekend."

Letty found a tiny, windowless studio apartment in Brooklyn. Ronnie Silver never formally fired her as a client, but the acting jobs dried up as she began to distance herself from Evan and Tanya.

She told herself it was a blessing in disguise and threw herself into her new job, working for a rental agent at a big midtown real estate company.

Tanya showed up at the door of the Tribeca apartment the day Letty was moving out, a bag of dry cleaning in one hand and an expensive bottle of champagne in the other.

"How'd you get up here?" Letty said coldly, not bothering to invite her sister inside.

"Sidney let me up," Tanya said.

"Oh that's right. I forgot. My doorman has a crush on you too."

Her little sister had the grace to blush. "Come on, Letty, please don't be mad at me. I didn't deliberately set out to hook up with Evan. It just happened. Neither of us understands why you insist on quitting and moving out. I wish you wouldn't be so damned stubborn."

"I made a mistake," Letty said. "Well, lots of mistakes, but the biggest one was getting mixed up with Evan Wingfield. I know you probably won't listen, but believe me, Tanya, you don't know what you're getting into. This guy is bad news."

"No," Tanya said, shaking her head. "You don't know the real Evan. He puts on this tough-guy act, but that's all just a show. If you got to know him like I have, you'd see, he's this incredibly tender, vulnerable man." She thrust the champagne bottle at Letty. "Aren't you even going to invite me inside?"

Letty opened the door wider and gestured at the stacks of boxes in the living room. "I really don't have time for this today. The movers will be here in another hour."

Tanya's beautiful blue eyes filled with tears. "Please? Please, Letty Spaghetti. Don't be mad at me." She lowered her voice to a whisper. "Letty? I'm pregnant!"

"*That* was certainly fast work," Letty said, handing Tanya a bottle of water. "When are you due?"

"Maybe November?"

They'd pushed aside enough boxes to seat themselves on the white leather sofa.

"I didn't plan this," Tanya said. "Like I told you, when Rooney ripped me off, I lost everything including my birth control pills. I tried calling to get the prescription refilled, but my doctor in Atlanta was being a butthead. His nurse said I'd have to come in for an exam, but how was I gonna do that, since I was already living up here?"

"How's Evan taking the news that he's going to be a daddy?"

Tanya's face lit up. "I was dreading telling him, but he's thrilled. Letty, it's the sweetest, cutest thing. He's already started ordering furniture for the nursery! I told him it's bad luck to do that stuff during the first trimester, but you know Evan. Once he gets an idea in his head . . ."

Her voice trailed off and she reached for her sister's hand.

"And how do you feel about being a mom?" Letty asked. "I thought you were gung-ho on having a serious acting career."

"I still am," Tanya said. She patted her perfectly flat abdomen. "My obstetrician says I'm healthy as a horse, and there's no reason I shouldn't keep working as long as I feel good. And I do. I feel amazing! Evan says I've never looked sexier. He can't keep his hands off me."

"TMI," Letty said.

"Oh, sorry."

They'd left the apartment door ajar, and now they heard the elevator doors slide open, and the sound of men's voices coming from the hallway.

"That's the movers," Letty said, standing up abruptly. "Look, Tanya. These guys get paid by the hour."

"Okay. Sure." Tanya stood up and flung her arms around her sister's neck. "Oh, Letty. You're all the family I have. Mimi's dead and Mom's out in Nevada somewhere, and you know how she is. Please be happy for me. Please?"

A man's voice called out from the hall. "Ma'am? Are you all set for us?"

"Coming," Letty called. She patted Tanya's shoulder. "I'm happy for you. We'll talk soon."

"Call me as soon as you get settled," Tanya said. "Promise?"

Letty walked slowly around the apartment, checking that the closets and cupboards had been emptied of her belongings.

"Okay," she said, to the lanky man standing in the doorway with a half-full mover's dolly. "That's everything. You can take this last load down. I'll meet you at the new place. You've got the address, right?"

He read it back to her from his clipboard, and she started for the door, key in hand.

"Wait, ma'am?"

She stopped. He pointed at the kitchen counter. "You forgot your champagne."

"Leave it," Letty said.

13

~~~~~~~~~~

As she dressed for work on Friday morning, Letty reflected that it felt good to have a routine again. Or as close to a routine as a person could get, while on the run from the law and a murderous ex—with a frightened four-year-old in tow.

Maya woke up at seven, so that's when Letty got up, too. She ate a breakfast of cereal topped with local strawberries and watched *Curious George* on PBS, while Letty had yogurt with strawberries and checked her email.

Earlier in the week, she'd reluctantly bought herself a new iPhone with a new phone number and acquired a new Gmail account, both of which she'd texted to Zoey.

HOW ARE U? HOW'S M? her friend texted back now.

Letty glanced at Maya, who was seated on the bed, dressed in her favorite outfit du jour—a bathing suit top and pink tulle princess skirt—happily sorting through the contents of her plastic pocketbook while softly humming the *Peppa Pig* theme song.

I'm adjusting. Working. M is okay. Not as many nightmares. Dry bed last night.

She paused typing, wanting to know, but dreading the answer.

Any more E sightings?

No, but that detective lady came back & asked Art for your job application.

Letty's mind raced, trying to remember the kinds of questions that had been on that long-ago perfunctory job application. Name, age, phone number, address, previous experience. All routine. And then she remembered. Social Security number. Her Social Security number would have been on that job application.

Just as she was considering all those implications, and starting to panic, Zoey texted back.

Don't worry. Art laughed, told her it'd been nearly 6 years & he didn't keep files that old.

"Thank God," Letty breathed. Ava had given her a job application, which she'd promised to fill out and return. She hadn't yet, and wouldn't, she decided, unless her new employer made an issue of it.

So far, her arrangement with Ava was extremely casual. She suspected that was because her boss had a casual attitude toward things like unemployment insurance and Social Security deductions. For Letty, this was the ideal situation.

Not having to make decisions about what to wear was a relief, too. She had three pink Murmuring Surf polo shirts in her wardrobe rotation, a pair of jeans, and two pairs of shorts she'd picked up at the big-box store in the nearest shopping center, along with a new pair of white Keds. Today was a shorts day.

She packed two sack lunches with turkey sandwiches, grapes, and carrot sticks, then quickly straightened the room. Their unit was so tiny and otherwise grim-looking that the only way Letty could stand to return to it in the evening was knowing it was neat and tidy.

Ava was waiting for them when they got to the office. A shopping list in one hand, her purse slung over her shoulder.

"Good morning, ladies," she sang out. "Letty, the coffee's made. I'm headed out to run errands. We've got the Carlisles checking into unit two this afternoon, but those weirdos from Orlando are still taking their own sweet time about packing up and getting out. I knew it was a mistake renting to those people."

Ava disliked what she called "short-termers"—guests who only checked in for a few days, as opposed to her long-term seasonal renters who booked rooms for weeks and months at a time. But since her motto was "heads in beds," when she had a rare midweek unit become available she reluctantly lit up the vacancy sign out front.

"Anything I can do to hurry them along?" Letty asked, settling Maya at her table and unpacking her art supplies and Ellie.

"I told 'em checkout's at ten sharp," Ava said. She turned and gazed out the plate-glass front window in the direction of unit 2, one of the original, smaller postwar cottages. It was painted soft coral, with a turquoise door and window shutters. "Don't see any signs of life over there."

"Not surprised," Letty said. "I heard them partying 'til late last night."

"Don't I know it," Ava said. "Ruth Feldman called and woke me up at midnight to report that those people were still playing loud music and splashing around in the pool. I had to get up, get dressed, go over there, and tell 'em to shut it down. You won't believe this, Letty."

She looked down at Maya, who was preoccupied with drawing flowers, and lowered her voice.

"The two of them were butt naked and goin' at it like a pair of rabbits. Right there in the shallow end of my pool. In public!" Ava's face was pink with a mixture of outrage and embarrassment.

Letty started to giggle.

"Frolicking around like it was nothing," Ava went on. "I'm just glad Isabelle didn't see them."

"What did you do?" Letty asked.

"I yelled at them to get dressed and get the hell out of my pool," Ava said. "And then that man—I bet they aren't even married—got out of the pool and had the balls to stand there—stark naked with his wangdoodle hanging out—and try to tell me I should calm down and mind my own business!"

Maya looked up, suddenly interested. "Miss Ava, what's a wangdoodle?"

Letty clamped her hands over her mouth to keep from laughing out loud.

"It's uh, a uh . . ."

"It's a grown-up kind of toy," Letty said. "Sort of like a float.

Sweetie, why don't you go into the supply room and get the stapler and some more Scotch tape so you can make another book?"

"Sorry," Ava said, as Maya went in search of more supplies. "I forgot about little pitchers having big ears."

"It's okay," Letty said. "What did you say then?"

Ava wrinkled her nose. "I could tell they were both high as kites, so I threatened to call the cops, and report them for public indecency. And then I told them they better clear out of my motel first thing in the morning."

"Oh my," Letty said.

"I hate to put his on you, hon, but with the Carlisles coming in, we're going to need to turn that room fast today. If they're not out of there on the dot of ten, I want you to call Joe on his cell."

"Is that really necessary?" Letty asked. "I don't mind knocking on their door and politely telling them it's checkout time."

"Absolutely not," Ava said, her voice firm. "There's no telling how those two dope fiends would react to you. Just call Joe. I'll let him know what the situation is. But in the meantime, I better scoot."

The next hour dragged by. She fielded phone calls from prospective guests asking for room availability and telemarketers, delivered additional towels to the Mitchells, and accepted what looked like a mountain of packages from UPS for Arlene Finocchia. Every fifteen minutes she got up from the reception desk to peer across the courtyard at unit 2, but there was no change in status.

At ten after ten, Oscar Jensen and Merwin Maples marched into the office. "Ava!" Oscar hollered, looking right past Letty. "Where are you?"

"Not here," Letty said, leaning forward on the counter. "What do you need, Oscar?"

"Need to talk to Ava," he growled. "When will she be back?"

"I'm not sure, but I can tell her you'd like to speak to her when she returns."

"Not good enough," Merwin said. "We've got a crisis brewing. The sooner we get this thing settled, the better off we'll all be."

"Crisis?"

"At the shuffleboard court," Oscar said, pointing out the window. His finger shook with barely suppressed rage. "Those women!"

Letty walked around the desk and joined him at the window. The shuffleboard court was on the south side of the pool enclosure. From where she stood she was barely able to spot two figures, one in a pink sun visor, the other in a floppy white sun hat, standing at opposite ends of the court.

"Is that a problem? Are they Murmuring Surf guests?"

"Of course they're guests. It's those Feldman girls," Merwin snapped. "Everyone here knows that Oscar and me play shuffleboard at ten o'clock. *Everyone* knows that. But for the past two days, when we get out there, those two are on our court. We've tried asking politely, but they refuse to acknowledge our long-standing court time."

"Oh." Letty's gaze strayed to the door of unit 2. The dusty maroon Impala with the Orlando license parked in front of it hadn't moved. The curtains were still drawn. It was well past ten o'clock.

Oscar snapped his fingers in front of her face. "Hey, hey! Pay attention here."

Letty took a step away backward and swatted his hand away. "Please don't do that, Oscar. I am paying attention. Is there a sign-up sheet or something like that, where guests reserve court time?"

"No," Merwin said. "It's just understood. It's always been understood. Up until this week."

"So, in other words, the shuffleboard courts are used on a first-come, first-serve basis. Maybe you two gentlemen could simply arrive at the courts a little earlier in the day? To make sure you're there first?"

"You're missing the whole point," Oscar said, shaking his head. "We play at ten, before it gets too hot. Merwin and I have other obligations until then. Those two girls, they're not even serious players."

"Don't even know the rules," Merwin said. "It's outrageous, is what it is. We need Ava to go out there and lay down the law to them. Or you. You could tell them."

Letty gave the men a sympathetic smile. "Sorry, I don't dare leave the office unmanned while Ava's gone. Plus, I don't have that kind of authority. Why don't you try working out a schedule with them? Like, maybe playing at ten on alternate days?"

"Never mind," Oscar said. "Should have known you'd side with those Feldmans. It's a women's-lib thing, right? Feminazis and all that?"

Her smile disappeared. "You should probably go now, Oscar. Before I decide to let Ava know you were smoking outside my room again last night." She pulled out her new phone and showed him the photo she'd snapped through her window, of a man matching Oscar Jensen's exact profile, leaning against the veranda column, letting out a long plume of smoke.

He looked at the photo. "You can't prove that's me."

She stood her ground. "Who else?" She went back to staring at the door to unit 2. It was ten thirty and nothing had changed.

Ava had programmed Joe DeCurtis's number into her phone. She sighed and scrolled through the short list of contacts.

"What are you doing?" Merwin demanded. "Who are you calling?"

"I'm calling Ava's son, Joe," she replied.

"The cop? No need to go overboard," Oscar said, scuttling toward the door. "We'll discuss this with Ava later."

When the shuffleboard players were gone, Letty picked up the house phone and dialed the number for unit 2. The phone rang five times with no answer. She hung up, waited five more minutes, and called again. Five more rings.

She *really* did not want an encounter with the police today, especially Detective Joe DeCurtis.

On her third call, someone in unit 2 picked up. "Who is this?" The man's voice sounded groggy.

"This is Letty, in the office. Checkout time was thirty minutes ago. I'm going to have to ask you to . . ."

"Fuck off," the man drawled. He hung up.

"I tried," Letty said with a shrug. She called Joe DeCurtis.

"Hi," she said. "It's Letty, at the motel? Your mom said I should call. . . ."

"On my way."

Five minutes later, the white pickup rolled up beside the maroon Impala and the manager's son got out. He wore a navy polo shirt with POLICE stenciled on the back. He looked over his shoulder at the office, saw her standing at the window, and gave her a thumbs-up.

She watched while he walked around the Impala, peered in the windows, then moved around to the rear of the car, knelt down, brought out his phone, and photographed the license plate.

Then he strode to the door of unit 2 and knocked loudly.

When there was no response, he waited another minute, then extracted the heavy flashlight from his belt loop and banged it against the door. Letty could hear his voice from across the courtyard.

"Sir? This is Detective DeCurtis with the Treasure Island Police. The hotel management needs you to vacate this room, immediately."

She saw the door open a crack, and could see the chain lock. A hairy arm poked out, flipped a bird, and then the door slammed shut again.

"Uh-oh," she muttered. She looked over at her niece, who was pretending to feed some broken crayons to the stuffed elephant.

"Maya, why don't you take Ellie into the supply room," she said, guiding the child by the shoulders. "I saw some empty boxes that would make her a nice bed."

She pulled out some empty cardboard shipping cartons, and when Maya saw that they were filled with foam peanuts, she gleefully climbed inside with her toy.

Letty went back to the front office to watch the unfolding drama with a mixture of dread and excitement.

The cop banged on the door of unit 2 again, and she saw the curtains part. A bearded, bare-chested man stared out briefly, and then the curtains closed again.

Joe went back and leaned against the truck. He pulled the two-way radio from his shoulder rig and spoke into it, then walked briskly toward the office, pushing through the glass door.

"What's going on?" Letty asked nervously.

"Just another low-life scumdog," Joe said. He walked past her into the back room. "Hi, Maya," she heard him call. "Playing hide-and-seek?"

"I'm playing house with Ellie," Maya said.

"Great idea. You guys stay in there, okay?"

He emerged from the office with a pair of lethal-looking bolt cutters, and stopped at the desk again to pick up what Letty knew was the master key to every unit in the motel.

"What now?"

"Just checking to see the name of the dude I'm fixing to arrest," Joe said. He flipped through the pages of the reservations book, ran a finger down a column of handwritten names, and rolled his eyes. "Mr. Benjamin Dover," he muttered. "Real cute. Dammit, Ava. I bet they paid with cash, so she didn't even ask for ID."

"Should I be worried?" Letty asked.

"No," Joe said. "Mr. Dover is the one who should be worried. That Impala was stolen a week ago from a truck stop in Ocala. I just called for a tow truck and a backup unit. Looks like Mr. and Mrs. Dover will be checking out of the Murmuring Surf and into the Graybar Hotel."

14

JOE USED HIS FLASHLIGHT TO knock on the door of unit 2 again. He waited a moment and announced himself again.

"Sir? This is the Treasure Island police. This is your second warning. I need you to vacate this room immediately or face arrest for trespassing."

Letty stood just outside the office, irresistibly drawn toward the unfolding drama.

The door opened a crack with the chain lock engaged. "Fuck off," the man yelled. "I paid for this room."

Joe shoved his booted foot against the door, picked up the bolt cutters, snapped the chain, then tossed the tool aside and pushed the door all the way open.

"Oh God," Letty breathed. She glanced back into the office, toward the door to the supply room, reassured that Maya was still safely ensconced in her cardboard playhouse.

Joe disappeared into the room, leaving the door ajar. She heard sounds of a struggle, shouted curses, the splintering of wood, then a woman's shrill scream. "Leave him alone!"

Letty clutched the phone in her hand. Should she call 911? Where were the backup unit and the tow truck he'd called for?

A moment later, the door opened, and Joe pushed the occupant of unit 2 out into the blazing midday sunlight. He was tall, with greasy dark hair that fell to pale, bony shoulders, barefoot, and naked except for a pair of tight-fitting red satin briefs. The man struggled, but ineffectively, because the cop had his hands clamped tightly behind his back.

Joe shoved the squirming suspect facedown onto the hood of the Impala. He drew his handcuffs from his belt and was in the process of fastening them when the woman appeared in the doorway of unit 2.

She was pudgy, with a blond bird's nest of hair and angry close-set eyes, and was dressed only in a grungy oversize white T-shirt that fell far short of covering fleshy pink butt cheeks.

Letty watched in horror as the woman darted from the room, wielding a baseball bat, advancing on the two men struggling against the car.

The woman planted her feet apart and swung the bat up, poised inches above the back of the cop's skull.

"Joe!" Letty screamed. "Watch out!"

He turned, startled. The bat came smashing down, missing his head by millimeters, landing with a vicious thud onto the hood of the Impala.

The woman, enraged, raised the bat to strike again, but this time, Joe grabbed her arms and knocked the bat to the ground. "Motherfucker!" she screeched, kicking and clawing at him. Letty hesitated, then ran toward the scuffle, launching herself onto the woman's back. The woman tried to shake her off, slapped back at her, landing a dizzying blow to her assailant's ear, but Letty hung on for dear life, her fear dissipating as the adrenaline rush took over. She yanked out a handful of hair and the woman yowled in pain, striking out, grabbing at Letty's face and arms, raking her flesh with razor-sharp nails.

In response, Letty opened her mouth and sank her teeth into the woman's fleshy arm, clamping down with her jaws. Her victim screeched and flailed with her left hand at Letty's legs, which she'd wound around the woman's thick waist.

Suddenly, without warning, the woman went limp and slumped forward. Letty slid to the ground, gasping for air.

Joe DeCurtis wrapped a plastic zip tie onto the woman's wrists, fastened it tightly, then knelt on the crushed-shell pavement beside Letty.

"You okay?" he asked.

"I . . . I'm not sure," she said. The side of her face throbbed where the woman had landed a blow, and she felt warm blood trickling from her arms and legs. He helped her to her feet. Her legs were shaking so badly she had to lean into his arm for support.

The blonde was on the ground, too, still moaning and writhing. "What happened?" Letty asked.

"I tased her," he said, his expression grim. He looked around. "Where'd the boyfriend go?"

"I don't know," Letty admitted. "I was concentrating on her."

Just then they heard an approaching siren. A police cruiser, blue lights flashing, sped into the parking lot. The uniformed officer, a powerfully built black woman, jumped out and approached, her hand resting lightly on the butt of her holstered service weapon.

"DeCurtis?" she said, her gaze taking in the blonde on the ground. "Everything okay here?"

"I'm good, but you're late," he said ruefully. "This one," he said, pointing at the woman, "is under arrest for trespassing, resisting arrest, assault and battery, and assaulting a peace officer. And that's just for starters."

"I thought the dispatcher said two suspects, including a white male. Where's the other one?"

"He must have booked it while we were tussling with his girlfriend," Joe said, looking chagrined. "But I don't think he'll get too far, considering the dude is barefoot, mostly naked, and handcuffed." He pointed at the Impala. "That's their vehicle."

The cop pointed at Letty. "Who's this?"

"Officer Shauna Arthur, meet Letty, the newest employee of the Murmuring Surf, who just saved me from suffering a life-threatening blow with a baseball bat upside my cranium."

Shauna Arthur shook Letty's hand. "Good work, although with

a head as hard as DeCurtis's, it probably wouldn't have done that much damage."

"Nice to meet you," Letty said, trying to steady the tremor in her voice.

"Hey Joe. Joe. Over here!" A man's voice called in a loud stage whisper.

Oscar Jensen stood, wide-eyed, in the shady breezeway outside his unit, an unlit cigarette dangling from his lower lip. He gestured wildly with his head, then jabbed his forefinger in the direction of the pair of five-foot-high ornamental concrete jardinieres that flanked the parking lot entrance. *In there,* he mimed. *He's in there.*

DeCurtis nodded his understanding. He and the other cop approached the jardiniere. Officer Arthur jumped without hesitation onto the pedestal and peered down into the urn. "Come out, come out, wherever you are," she called. She waited a moment, then took out her nightstick, banging it loudly against the side of the concrete urn. "Dude," she said, her tone conversational. "You're trapped. Call it a day, man."

Slowly, the man's head, then shoulders, then torso rose out of the urn. His face and chest were scraped and bloody, his expression meek. "Don't shoot, okay?"

"Okay," Shauna Arthur said. "You're under arrest. Now haul your ass on out of there." She looked over at Joe DeCurtis. "What'd you say his name is again?"

"Ben," Joe said. "Mr. Ben Dover."

Letty ran-walked back to the office. The phone was ringing but she ignored it. "Maya?" she called, poking her head into the storeroom. She tiptoed over to the large cardboard shipping carton and peeked inside. The child was asleep, head back, lightly snoring.

She went back to the front desk and collapsed into her chair. Her heart was still pounding in her chest. What had she been thinking getting mixed up in that crazy altercation? The blonde outweighed her by at least fifty pounds. She could easily have gotten injured or killed. And then, what would become of Maya?

Letty clutched her throbbing head between both hands. She had to be more careful.

She heard the chimes on the office door. Joe walked past her and into the storeroom. She heard him close the bathroom door, heard water running. When he emerged, he was toweling off his damp face and hands.

"Hey," he said, standing beside her. "Seriously, thanks for what you did out there. I mean, you shouldn't have, but I guess, if you hadn't, things could have gone south in a hurry."

He gently touched the side of her face. "You're gonna have a hell of a bruise here. You're pretty scratched up too. There's some antiseptic spray in the medicine cabinet in the bathroom. Better get yourself cleaned up before you get cat scratch fever or something."

Letty found herself suddenly tongue-tied. "I can't believe I jumped that chick," she said, laughing nervously. "I've never done anything like that in my life."

"We found Bonnie and Clyde's ID when we searched the room," Joe said. "They're both bad news. Multiple arrests for possession and manufacture of meth, burglary, auto theft, you name it. She was released last week, from a women's prison in Georgia, and there're warrants out for his arrest in Alabama and South Carolina."

"Wonder what they were doing here?" Letty said.

"His story is that they were headed to her mom's house, in Clearwater, to visit her kids. The court took 'em away from her after her last arrest. And here's the kicker—she's his ex-stepmother."

"Wait. The dude she was having sex with in the pool out there last night was her stepson? *Eeeeewww.*"

"Ex-stepson. Wait. What? Sex in the pool? Who told you that?"

"Oh. Well, your mom did. They were out there partying pretty loud, disturbing the other guests. I even heard them. Ava told me this morning she went out to tell them to shut it down—and they were,

naked and uh, in the act. That's when she told them they needed to
clear out first thing this morning."

"Jesus!" he exclaimed. "She didn't tell me any of that when she
called. All she said was that they were supposed to be out by ten and
if there was any trouble, you were supposed to reach out to me."

"Maybe she didn't want to worry you," Letty said.

"And maybe she needs to stop renting rooms to lowlifes and fu-
gitives from the law," he said. He pointed out the window, where a
tow truck was in the act of hitching up the Impala. "Shauna found
a loaded thirty-eight under the driver's seat of their car. I don't want
to think about what might have happened if . . ."

The chimes tinkled and Ava bustled in. "Hey, what's going on
out there? I've been calling and calling, but nobody answered. . . ."
Her face paled when she saw the scrapes and scratches on the faces
of Letty and Joe.

"Dear God!" she exclaimed, clutching at Letty's arm. "Are you all
right? Where's Maya?"

"Letty!" A thin wail drifted from the storeroom.

"Maya's fine," Letty said. "She was asleep the whole time, back
here."

The little girl was standing up, rubbing her eyes, with foam peanuts clinging to her knit top. "I'm hungry, Letty." She held up the
stuffed elephant. "Ellie's hungry too."

As Letty lifted her niece out of the carton, Maya touched her
cheek. "You got a boo-boo," she said. "I kiss it."

Back in the outer office, Ava and Joe were deep in what looked
like an unpleasant conversation. "You've got to be more careful,
dammit," she heard Joe say. "Those two were honest-to-God des-
peradoes. They used to cook meth for a living, Mom. They had a
loaded gun in their car. You're lucky they didn't decide to set up a lab
in that room you rented them."

"I know, I know," Ava said, running her hands through her hair in
agitation. "It was stupid of me. I won't do it again. No more walk-
ins. Never again. I swear, Joe."

"Okay," he said, his shoulders slumped. "I believe you. I gotta go get those two booked in at the jail." He pointed a finger at Letty. "We'll need a witness statement from you for the arrest report. I'll be back later. In the meantime, put some antiseptic cream on those scratches."

When he was gone, Ava wrapped her arms around her desk clerk and hugged her tightly. "Oh, Letty, I'm so sorry to have put you in danger. Joe's right. I should have known better. If anything had happened to you or Maya, I'd never forgive myself."

Letty hesitated, then awkwardly patted the older woman's back. "It's not your fault. You couldn't have known what would happen. I probably shouldn't have waited so long to call Joe, so it's partly my fault too."

"No," Ava insisted. "This is on me." She held out her hand to Maya. "Come here, little one. You run ahead upstairs and then I'm gonna order us some pizza for lunch. How does that sound?"

Maya clapped her hands together. "Pizza. Yay!" She scampered off in the direction of the stairs.

"Now, Letty," Ava said, her expression suddenly serious. "I need to show you something important."

She walked behind the reception desk and Letty followed. Ava took a key from the ring she wore on a lanyard around her neck and unlocked and opened the cash drawer. The black plastic tray inside held neat stacks of bills, and a slot to one side held coins.

"You showed me that the first day I came to work," Letty said, puzzled.

Ava took a step to the side. "Reach your hand all the way in the drawer there," Ava instructed. "All the way to the back."

Letty slid her hand over the cash tray, extending her fingertips until they touched cold steel. She gave Ava a quizzical look.

"Go on," the older woman said.

The gun fit in the palm of her hand, snub-nosed and black. Letty stared down at it with distaste.

"You ever fired a gun before?" Ava asked.

"Yes, ma'am," Letty whispered.

"That's good," Ava said, nodding. "Most girls like you are afraid of guns. I'm afraid of 'em myself. But I'm more afraid of what could happen if there's trouble. You know what I mean?"

"I do," Letty agreed. "But Ava, I don't think . . ."

"You don't have to think. You just need to know it's there, and know how to use it."

"Letty, I'm hungry!" Maya's plaintive voice drifted down from the top of the stairs. She shoved the gun back into the drawer. Ava locked it.

"Coming, ladybug," Letty called.

15

~~~~~~~~~~~~~~~

SHE WAS WATCHING MAYA PLAYING at the water's edge with another little girl when a shadow fell over her. Letty looked up. It was Joe. But not no-nonsense spit-and-polish Detective Joe DeCurtis. This was Joe Sixpack, bare-chested, barefoot, dressed in gaudy floral board shorts, holding a small Yeti cooler.

"Hey," he said, looking down at her. "Ava told me you guys were down here. Mind if I join you?"

She shrugged. "It's a public beach."

"Wow. Okay. Never mind." He turned and began to trudge back toward the motel.

Letty regretted the words as soon as she spoke them. She glanced toward the beach, where Maya and the other little girl were busily drizzling wet sand on each other's legs, and shrieking with delight.

"Joe!" she called.

He kept walking.

She jumped to her feet and ran after him. "Hey. Slow down!"

But he didn't stop or slow down, so she sped up, caught him by the arm.

"What?"

"I'm sorry," she said. "That was a bitchy thing to say. Come on back, please?"

"I'm good," he said, his expression flat. "Wouldn't want to impose."

"It's not an imposition." She bit her lip. "Look, I'm kinda rusty at making new friends. Give me another chance, okay?"

"You sure?"

"Yeah." She pointed toward the beach blanket, actually one of the motel's old floral bedspreads, where she'd set up camp. "Plenty of room."

Joe followed her back to her spot and looked around. "Where's Maya?"

"Down there by the water. She's having a ball. Living her best life."

He sat down and opened the cooler. "Beer or hard cider?"

"Don't judge me, but I do enjoy a hard cider," she said, and he handed her a can flecked with bits of crushed ice. She examined the label. "Three Daughters. Never heard of it."

"It's a local craft brewery. One of my high school buddies started a brewery. They've got a tasting room in downtown St. Pete. I work security there sometimes if they're having a big event. It's pretty good stuff."

Letty popped the top and took a sip. "Nice and light. Very refreshing. Thanks."

He leaned back on his elbows and looked out at the horizon. The beach was packed with sun worshippers, polka-dotted with bright-colored umbrellas and beach chairs. Music drifted from radios, and seagulls pecked at something in the sand. A cluster of older women, dressed in modest swimsuits, had set up nearby beneath a pop-up tent, and were playing cards.

"Not bad for March, huh?" he said, glancing over at her. "Looks like you're turning into a real Floridian. Am I allowed to tell you that I like that bathing suit, or does that make me sound like a perv?"

She'd splurged and bought herself an inexpensive bikini from a surf shop a few blocks away. It was black with hot-pink piping, and showed off her deepening tan. But she felt suddenly self-conscious under the warmth of his gaze.

"Not too pervy," she said finally. "Thanks."

Joe nodded at Maya, who was dumping buckets of water into the moat of the castle Letty helped her build earlier in the afternoon. "Who's Maya's new friend?"

"Just a little girl who's here with her parents, visiting her grandma," Letty said, pointing at the women gathered under the tent. "I think her name's Esme. I'm so glad that they're playing together outside in the fresh air. It's hard, you know? Maya's either at work with me or Isabelle all week, or cooped up in our room. I feel guilty that I let her spend so much time watching television, or playing the little games I have on my phone."

"Doesn't seem to have hurt her," Joe said. "You, on the other hand, look like someone who could use a night off. I've seen you running around the Surf. You're like the Energizer Bunny. You never stop."

"I'm grateful to have a job, grateful to your mom for letting me bring Maya to work with me," Letty said. "Most nights, after dinner, I put Maya to bed and I'm so tired I fall asleep after maybe thirty minutes of trying to watch television."

"But you're taking a beach day today," he pointed out.

"Seems almost criminal to be *at* the beach, yet not *on* the beach," Letty said. "This weather is so amazing, I still can't believe it's winter in the rest of the country."

"You mean, like, in New York?" He said it casually, but Letty heard the intent behind the question. She decided it was best not to evade the question.

"Yeah."

"How long did you live there?" he asked.

"Five or six years." She needed to shut down this line of questioning. "Hey, what's going to happen with Ben Dover and his stepmom? Are they still in jail?"

"They're still there, and I don't see either one of 'em getting out anytime soon," Joe said. "That story about going to visit her kids was bullshit. When we popped the lock on the trunk of that Impala we found an electronic credit card skimmer and boxes of credit card blanks. Those two are bad news."

"Did you tell Ava about what you found?"

"Oh yeah," he said, taking a swig of beer. "She says she's learned her lesson now, but she always says that. The problem is, in her mind she's a hard-nosed, take-no-prisoners businesswoman. She can't stand the idea of having an empty room for even one night."

Letty thought about the gun Ava had hidden in the front-office cash drawer and wondered if Joe was aware that he had a pistol-packing mama. And just how much did he know about her own complicated situation?

"But the reality is my mom is a pushover. Which is why all these sad-sack hard-luck losers are attracted to her like flies to honey."

"You mean people like me?" she asked.

His face flushed. "That's not what I meant. You didn't show up here looking for a handout, or to rip her off. I was thinking about her shitbird ex-boyfriend."

"The unhandy handyman," Letty said.

"The one who set up a scam business out of one of the rooms right here at the Murmuring Surf, right under my nose." He scowled. "Chuck and Rooney, the dynamic duo of rip-off artists."

Letty almost choked on her hard cider. "Rooney? Did you say the other guy's name was Rooney?"

Rooney. Tanya's ex-boyfriend. That Rooney?

"Yeah. Chuck was just a boozer and a loser, up until he met up with Rooney, who, it turned out, was a hard-core criminal."

"What kind of 'business' were they into?"

"Precious metals. It's a classic Florida scam, because they preyed on retirees or people desperate to make a buck. They'd set up in motels around here, including the Murmuring Surf, and run ads about paying top dollar for estate jewelry and gold coins. Some old lady would bring in her mother's wedding ring, or a bunch of old coins or the sterling silver tea set they never used. They'd make a big show of weighing it—of course the scales were rigged. And maybe they'd tell somebody her diamond was worthless—flawed, but they'd buy it for the weight of the gold in the ring. Pennies on the dollar."

"How did Chuck hook up with this Rooney guy?"

"Where else? A bar. I only figured out what they were up to after one of our guests came to me and said she was afraid she'd been ripped off. She'd decided to sell a watch she'd inherited. Begged me not to tell her husband because she was embarrassed. After I looked into it, we set up a sting. We got a female undercover agent to sell them a ring we'd had a certified gemologist appraise at fourteen thousand dollars. They offered her two hundred and eighty dollars. We had the Florida Department of Law Enforcement, the sheriff's office, St. Pete Police, several different agencies involved, because these other two had been working this scam all over the state."

"There were three of them? I thought you said it was just Chuck and Rooney," Letty said.

"They had a woman working with them. A redhead, and she was a knockout. They used her as window dressing, to gain the trust of these old ladies. Because how could a sweet-faced girl like her possibly rip them off?"

"Rooney and the woman were staying right up there in unit six," Joe went on. "Our undercover agent said she saw thousands and thousands of dollars in cash, boxes and boxes of gold and silver coins when she went to the room to sell the ring. But when the raid went down, the room had been cleaned out. Rooney and Chuck were long gone. Along with all the money and jewelry and coins. The only person arrested was their female accomplice."

Letty felt sick. "The female accomplice was arrested? Do you remember her name?"

Joe screwed up his face as he thought about it. "Something with a T. Teresa? Or maybe Tammy?"

"What was she charged with?"

"Fraud. Her lawyer worked out some kind of deal with the district attorney's office. I don't even know if she did time."

"What about the two men?"

He shrugged. "Gone. Mom had pretty much figured out that Chuck was a loser, although she didn't know he was a criminal loser. She'd kicked him out of her apartment, but was letting him stay in that room where you're living now, if you can believe it. I've got no idea what happened to Rooney."

"Kind of a funny name, Rooney."

"I think his first name was Declan, but everybody just called him Rooney. Even his wife."

"Wife?" Letty said. "He was married to the female accomplice?"

"So she claimed," Joe said.

Letty took another sip of the hard cider, but it had grown warm and now, she thought, had turned her stomach sour. She emptied the rest into the sand.

"How long ago did all this happen?" she asked.

"Let me think." He opened the cooler and offered her another drink, but she shook her head. "No thanks."

"Maybe five years ago?" he said finally. "None of the money or coins or jewelry was ever recovered."

Maya rushed toward them, her face alight with joy. Her little pink sun hat was askew, her arms and legs and tummy were coated in the sugar-fine white sand, and she was toting the plastic bucket Ava had given her, water sloshing over the sides as she ran.

"Letty, Letty," she said, when she reached the blanket. She held the bucket out triumphantly. "We catched a fishy!"

"That's a beautiful minnow," Joe said, admiring Maya's catch. "It's a greenback. See how its back is green, but when it swims, you catch a flash of the silver on its underbelly?"

Maya peered into the bucket and nodded. "Her name is Minnie. I'm gonna keep her. Okay, Letty?"

"Oh, I don't know," Letty said. "I don't think Miss Ava allows pets, does she, Joe?"

"Afraid not," Joe said. "But even if she did, a minnow is a fish, and a fish can't live in a little bucket like this. They have to be able to swim in the ocean with fresh water moving through their gills, because that's where they get oxygen to breathe."

"Really?" Letty glanced over at him. "I didn't know that. Must be a Florida thing."

Joe laughed. "Not a Florida thing. More like a high school biology thing."

"Oh yeah. High school. Mine was in a hick town in West Virginia, and probably only five percent of my graduating class went on to college," Letty said. "And our biology teacher really was a perv." She scowled at the memory of Mr. Parker, trying to corner her after class, using the ruse of "helping" her pass her midterm exam.

"I think we need to put Minnie back in the water, Maya," Joe said, his tone gentle.

"Noooo," Maya wailed. "It's mine minnow. I catched her."

Letty reached out and touched her niece's hand. "Joe's right, sweetie. Let's put her back in the water. It'll be fun to see her swim away with all her friends!"

Maya's lower lip began to quiver. "I don't *want* to." She pressed the bucket tightly to her chest.

Joe stood up. "Maya," he said impatiently. "If we don't put the minnow back in the water, it can't breathe. It'll die. You don't want Minnie to die, do you?"

Letty winced at the harshness of his response. He couldn't know about Tanya. Couldn't know what Letty herself didn't know—whether or not Maya had witnessed her mother's murder.

The child's reaction was instant. Her face crumpled as she dissolved into tears. "My mommy died," she whispered. "She's in heaven and she can't come back anymore."

"I'm so sorry," Joe said, looking over at Letty. He knelt down beside the sobbing child. "Come on, Maya. I'll help you put the minnow back in the water. And then we'll build a fort. Okay? Like, a cowboys and Indians fort."

"I'll help too," Letty said, scrambling to her feet. She used a towel to dab the snot and sand from the little girl's face.

"Okay," Maya said reluctantly. She put her face to the edge of the bucket. "Bye, Minnie."

"You coming to the cookout tonight?" Joe asked hours later, as they walked up toward the motel from the beach. He had the cooler and beach blanket tucked under one arm, with Maya asleep on his shoulder.

"There's a cookout?" Letty asked, struggling to keep up with his pace.

"Oh yeah. It's a Murmuring Surf tradition. The Doughertys always did a Sunday-night cookout for their guests during the season, so Mom just kept it going. We provide the main course. Tonight we're doing barbecued chicken. All the guests bring a side dish. And their own beverage. Afterward, everybody meets in the rec room for bingo. I'm telling you, it's a *big* night."

"Wish I could," Letty said. "But I need to get Maya hosed off and into bed. You saw how she wore herself out this afternoon."

"Pretty sure you could get Isabelle to stay with her. These days she thinks she's too cool to hang out with all the oldsters for an entire night," Joe said.

"I appreciate the offer, but I don't think so. I'm not really a guest, am I?"

"You'd be my guest," Joe said. "But okay, I won't press it."

They'd reached a rusty iron gate that separated the public beach from the Murmuring Surf property. Joe turned on a spigot and they rinsed the sand from their feet; then he walked Letty to her unit.

"Here," she said, reaching out her arms for the drowsy little girl. "I can take her now. Thanks for helping out today."

"Not a problem," he said, lowering his voice. "And I'm sorry again about the dead-minnow thing. I mean, I know you told me about her mom, but it didn't occur to me . . ."

"It's okay," Letty reassured him, retrieving the room key from her beach bag. "She's four. You saw how she was, five minutes later, splashing in the waves. She was completely over it."

"And what about you? Her mother was your sister, right?"

"Half sister," she said. "I mean, we called ourselves sisters, and we were. But no, I'm not over her." She sighed. "I don't know if I ever will be."

. . .

She got Maya showered and into pajamas, and fixed her a grilled cheese sandwich for dinner. By six o'clock, she willingly allowed herself to be tucked into bed with Ellie clutched in her arms.

Once the child was asleep, Letty poured herself a glass of wine and took a seat on the metal lawn chair in the breezeway outside her room, leaving the door open in case her niece awoke.

A soft breeze rustled a pale pink hibiscus in a nearby flower bed and carried the scent of burning charcoal and the sound of laughter, coming from the rec room beside the pool. Letty turned her chair sideways, so she could see the sky turning a vivid orange.

Sunsets had quickly become her favorite time of day here, a time to pause and be still, but tonight there would be no stillness. She looked down again at the torn magazine page, the one she'd found in Tanya's go-bag the night her sister was murdered. She ran her fingers over the colorful photo of the Murmuring Surf, and pondered its significance.

Rooney. Tanya's "boyfriend," who she claimed had abandoned her, left her high and dry five years ago in Atlanta, with nothing but her car and the clothes on her back. Rooney was the name of the con man who'd bilked old ladies. Right here at the Murmuring Surf. And he'd had an accomplice, a charming redhead, whom he'd abandoned when the law closed in. Joe said he couldn't remember her name, but it had been five years ago, and her name "might" have started with a *T.*

This could not be a coincidence. There were no coincidences where Tanya was concerned. Her beautiful, lovable, charming half sister lied with effortless ease. She was a chameleon who could go from redhead to blonde, victim to criminal, in the blink of an eye. And now those lies had drawn Letty right back here, to the scene of the crime.

The question was why.

"Hey." His voice startled her. She turned around. Joe DeCurtis was holding an overflowing paper plate, covered with foil.

"Hey yourself," she said. She quickly tucked the magazine page into the pocket of her shorts.

"Am I interrupting something?"

"No. Just enjoying what I can see of the sunset."

He held out the paper plate. "Ava insisted. You gotta eat, right?"

"Well, I don't know," Letty said. "There's a tantalizing bag of microwave popcorn inside with my name on it."

"Popcorn for dinner?"

"And wine," she said, holding up her glass.

"I've got a much better idea."

He pulled up a nearby metal side table and placed the plate on top, removing the foil with a dramatic flourish.

"Chicken DeCurtis," he said, pointing to a slightly charred chicken breast glistening under a coat of reddish-orange sauce. "Arlene's baked beans. Alice Sheehan's macaroni and cheese. Trudi Maples's coleslaw. And the pièce de résistance, day-old store-bought rolls from Oscar Jensen."

Her stomach growled, loudly and unmistakably.

"Oh my God," she said. "Please pretend you didn't hear that."

"Hear what?" He cupped a hand to his ear. "I didn't hear nothing."

He shifted awkwardly from one foot to the other. She sensed he was waiting for something. Like an invitation to join her. Part of her desperately wanted to let down her guard, invite him to stay and share a glass of wine. But to what end? Better not to encourage him.

"Thanks for this," she said, gesturing at the plate. "You're a life-saver. I'm just going to put it inside for now, because it's still a little early for dinner for me."

The last thing she saw as she closed the door to her room was the baffled, hurt look on his face.

~~~~~~~~~~~~~~~

16

LETTY PICKED AT THE FOOD on the paper plate. The barbecued chicken had a tangy-sweet sauce, and the lukewarm macaroni and cheese reminded her of Mimi's, cheesy and buttery with a thick oven-browned crumb topping, and the vinegar-brined coleslaw made a nice contrast to the chicken. She tapped at the dinner roll with her fingernail. Rock-hard.

She glanced over at Maya, who was asleep in the middle of the double bed, on her tummy, with both arms and legs spread out, pajama-clad rump in the air. Her gaze traveled to the window, where she was hoping to catch one last glimpse of the sunset. But the sky had turned plum-colored. The moment was gone. She pushed away the plate of half-eaten food and picked up her phone.

It was surprisingly easy to find the Florida Department of Law Enforcement's website, which included a helpful dashboard to search the state's criminal-record database. All she had to do was type in her sister's name, age, date of birth, sex, and race. She left blank the spaces for Social Security numbers and aliases.

There was a price for all this efficiency, she discovered—a twenty-five-dollar processing fee, payable only by credit card. She chewed on her bottom lip as she debated the problem. She had Tanya's American Express card, but didn't dare use it. Finally, she fished her billfold from her bag and extracted the Visa debit card she'd bought at a nearby convenience store. She typed the credit card information into the payment field using the address of one of the units she'd managed for Evan, and hit SUBMIT.

The speed of the search took her breath away. In an instant the phone screen lit up with the damning details.

Letty looked away from the phone. She got up, bent over the bed and listened to Maya's steady breath, kissed the damp ringlets at the base of her neck, then pulled the sheet up over her shoulders.

Then she went back to the official State of Florida Criminal Records report. She didn't want to know. But she needed to know, if not for herself, then for Maya.

Tanya Michelle Carnahan, age twenty-five, a.k.a. Tanya Cole, a.k.a. Michelle Carnahan, a.k.a. Tanya Rooney, had been arrested in Pinellas County, Florida, in February 2015, on charges of criminal fraud, theft by taking, and operating without a business license. There was an official-looking stamp on the document. CHARGES DISMISSED.

Letty scrolled down the report until she was staring at the booking photo. She hardly recognized her sister. This woman had wild red hair that fell past her shoulders and hollow eyes that glared sullenly back at the camera. She touched the phone screen with a trembling finger, this image of a stranger who was her sister, yet not her sister, a chameleon with a talent for transforming herself into whatever the occasion demanded.

And that was it. There were no other details. For twenty-five dollars, Letty thought ruefully, she hadn't gotten very much, except for the unwelcome affirmation that this time Tanya had apparently gotten in over her head.

And yet, once again, she'd managed to walk away relatively unscathed. CHARGES DISMISSED. Joe said that Ava's ex-boyfriend and Declan Rooney had escaped, and that his accomplice had worked out a deal to avoid prosecution.

AFTER SHE'D ANSWERED her sister's distress call, Letty tried pumping Tanya for details about her relationship with this Rooney, but her sister had been maddeningly vague about the man.

On one of her first nights in the city, they'd stayed in and binge-watched *True Blood*. Tanya was fascinated with vampires.

Tanya was wearing a pair of jeans and a new sweater Letty had bought her—"an early birthday gift," because Tanya had few clothes of her own, and because she'd been living down south in Atlanta, and certainly owned nothing warm enough for February in New York. And Letty had loaned her the money to visit an expensive hair salon and get her hair cut and colored back to her natural blond.

"Tell me again what happened with this guy Rooney?" Letty had prompted.

"He just . . . left. Ripped me off. Everything I owned was in that condo. I went to the store and when I came back an hour later, he was gone."

"Did you report him to the police?" Letty asked.

"Call the cops on Rooney?" Tanya scoffed. "What were they gonna do? Make him come back, hand over my clothes and stuff, and the money I loaned him?"

"I don't understand how you keep getting mixed up with creeps like this," Letty had said.

"He didn't seem like a creep when we met," Tanya said. "He had the most gorgeous eyes, this amazing deep blue, like a mountain lake you just wanted to dive naked into, and long, dark black eyelashes. He reminded me a lot of a young Pierce Brosnan. And oh my God, was he funny. He'd tell these hilarious stories, in that Irish accent of his, and you never knew if they were true or not, but it didn't matter, because that was Rooney."

"Where'd you meet him?"

"I don't really remember," Tanya said airily. "He was just around. And one day, he asked if he could buy me a drink and I said yes, and the next thing I knew, we were a couple."

"Did he have a job? Friends? Other people you knew in common?" Letty pressed.

"Yes, he had a job," Tanya said, clearly pissed off. "God! Do we have to talk about this right now? I came up here to forget about

Rooney, and it doesn't help when you want to interrogate me like I'm on a witness stand or something."

Looking back on it now, Letty realized, someone—the cops, maybe even Joe DeCurtis—really had interrogated Tanya, and once again, she'd managed to talk her way out of a jam.

For as long as Letty could remember, her sister had gotten into what their mother affectionately termed "youthful scrapes"— shoplifting a tube of mascara from the drugstore, getting kicked out of school for selling diet pills stolen from a friend's mother, and once "borrowing" an elderly neighbor's Buick for a weekend-long drunken joyride with her boyfriend that had ended when she'd smashed the car into a telephone pole. But Tanya had always walked away from those youthful misdemeanors by batting her eyelashes and placing the blame solidly on someone else's shoulders.

What, Letty wondered, was the truth about Tanya and Declan Rooney? The date on her arrest record showed that she'd been right here, at the Murmuring Surf, ripping off old ladies when she claimed to be living in Atlanta and working as a model. Obviously she'd lied. Were they really married?

Once again, she was grateful for Florida's "sunshine law," which made public records so readily available. This time, she found what she was looking for on the state's Bureau of Vital Statistics website. She typed in Tanya's name and Declan's name and waited a moment, holding her breath as she waited for results.

She finally exhaled when the red letters appeared on screen. NO RECORD FOUND.

Letty thought about it. This didn't necessarily mean they weren't married. Tanya had been using an alias at the time of her arrest, so maybe Declan Rooney had one, too?

The lies, she thought. So many, many lies. And why? She downed the rest of the wine in her glass. She was ashamed of how gullible she'd been, at how easily she'd bought into Tanya's tale of woe.

"No, no, no!" She looked over to see Maya, batting her arms wildly in the air, although her eyes were still tightly closed. "Nooooo!"

Letty pulled back the covers and climbed into bed with the little girl, snugging her close against her chest, inhaling the sweet scent of baby shampoo.

"It's okay," she whispered. "I'm here. Go to sleep, baby," Letty said, stroking her back and smoothing the hair from her damp forehead.

"Letty?" Maya sat up in bed, rubbing her eyes. "I got a bad dream."

Not again, Letty thought. They'd had three good nights in a row without the night terrors.

"Can you tell me what happened?" Letty asked.

"The bad man came," Maya said tearfully. "He tried to get me."

"That was just a dream, sweetie. There is no bad man here. I would not let a bad man come in here. Okay? I promise you. Never, ever will I let that happen."

Maya snuffled and buried her nose in Letty's shirt. "Okay." She looked up at her aunt. "Will you do the bunny song?"

Letty rolled her eyes but began to sing, letting her fingertips trail along Maya's back. "Little Bunny Foo Foo, hoppin' through the forest, scoopin' up the field mice and boppin' 'em on the head . . ."

Maya giggled and chimed in on her favorite part, wagging her finger at her aunt. "Down came the Good Fairy, and she said, Little Bunny Foo Foo, I don't wanna see you scoopin' up the field mice and boppin' 'em on the head."

Letty lost count of the number of choruses she repeated until Maya finally drifted back to sleep. When she was sure the child wouldn't stir, she crept into the bathroom, brushed her teeth, undressed, and crawled back to bed.

She'd opened the windows earlier, and now she heard laughter and music coming from the direction of the pool.

"B-10," she heard a man's voice call. "G-59." She recognized the voice as Joe's. "O-74." Ironic, she thought. It was eight o'clock on Sunday night and she, the youngest guest at the Murmuring Surf, was already in bed, while the Murmuring Surf's elderly regulars were still chowing down on free barbecue and a hot bingo game.

Maya let out a long sigh and threw an arm across Letty's chest. The child was a whirling dervish while she slept, spinning this way and that, like Tanya that way, Letty thought. In their childhood days they'd frequently shared a bed in whatever mobile home or cheap apartment Terri was renting. Tanya thrashed around in her sleep, what Mimi called "starfishing," with both arms and legs spread wide across the bed, driving Letty, many nights, to sleep on a sofa, or even on a pallet on the floor.

She gingerly removed the child's arm and rolled over on her side, facing the window. She was almost asleep when the thought struck her with such intensity she sat bolt upright in the bed. She tiptoed over to the table, picked up her phone, and reread her sister's arrest report from five years earlier, this time paying closer attention to the date. Tanya had been arrested, here in a unit at the Murmuring Surf, on February 2, 2015. According to Joe DeCurtis, Declan Rooney, her accomplice-slash-boyfriend-slash-husband, was already in the wind.

Tanya's urgent distress call and subsequent move to New York had come only days later. Early February, and before Valentine's Day, because Letty remembered feeling sorry for her heartbroken sister and buying her a tiny heart-shaped Whitman's candy sampler as a joke. How long after that had Letty taken up with Evan? And how soon after that had Tanya announced her "surprise pregnancy"?

Maya had been born seven months later, a tiny but surprisingly healthy preemie with blond curls like her mother's, and blue eyes, not the same pale blue as Tanya's, or their mother's, but eyes that Tanya described as "the deep blue of a mountain lake you wanted to dive naked into."

Letty scrolled back to the Florida Department of Law Enforcement's website, punched in payment information, then typed in the name Declan Rooney.

The screen lit up with citations. There were warrants out for Declan Rooney in Palm Beach, Broward, and Dade Counties, for fraud, theft by taking, wire fraud, and more. The only photo she found of Rooney was a booking photo taken in Jacksonville. It showed a man with shoulder-length, dark wavy hair, a square jaw, and a prominent nose. He did have lush, dark eyelashes, but nobody, thought Letty, would ever mistake him for a young Pierce Brosnan. Nobody except Tanya.

She clicked the phone for a screenshot of the booking photo, then put the phone on the nightstand. Maya burrowed into her side and sighed softly in her sleep.

~~~~~~~~~~~~~~~~

17

"WELL?" EVAN PUSHED THE PLATE with his half-eaten breakfast away.

"Well, what?" Vikki Hill asked. She'd eaten her egg-and-bagel sandwich as soon as it arrived at the table, and now she was sipping coffee.

"What have you found out? That police detective keeps showing up at my door, asking questions about the day Tanya was killed and my past relationship with Letty. Which is nuts—because Letty is the one who killed Tanya and abducted my kid. What's taking so damn long?"

"They haven't come out and accused you of killing your ex, right?" Vikki asked.

"Not in so many words, but the implication is there, and I don't appreciate it," Evan said. "I don't understand why they're not concentrating on finding Letty. And Maya."

"Seems like Letty Carnahan is off the grid," Vikki said. "The cops didn't get any hits from the Amber Alert. Zero. Let me ask you this, Evan. How much do you think Letty knows about your Airbnb business?"

He waved the question aside. "She worked for me, for over a year, but that was ages ago. Letty wasn't involved in the financial side. She was more like guest relations. Why? What's that got to do with anything?"

Vikki raised one eyebrow. "Motive? That's what the cops are looking for."

"I keep telling that detective, and I'm telling you too, Letty was jealous of Tanya. And she was obsessed with Maya. There's your motive. Maya."

"Maybe." Vikki looked dubious. "How much did Tanya know about your business?"

"More than she goddamn should have," Evan muttered. He stared at her. "She knew about you. About our . . . arrangement."

"What?" She set her mug down, sloshing coffee onto the table-top. "You never told me that. How could she know?"

"I'm still trying to figure that out. But she did. The day she died, when I was at her apartment, Tanya threatened me. Said she knew I'd bribed an investigator working for the city to look the other way. Concerning the uh, the Astoria thing. And the other properties. She knew about the *Hamilton* tickets and the Vegas trip. . . . She knew your name. Hinted that we were having an affair."

"Shit!" Vikki Hill looked around the diner, then lowered her voice. "You don't think Tanya actually talked to anybody about our arrangement, do you? I mean, it's my ass that's on the line here, Wingfield."

"Relax, okay? She threatened to go to the IRS, you know, to blab about the different business entities, but there's no way she would have. I was her meal ticket, and no matter how many threats she made, down deep, she knew that. She was pissed, that's all, because she knew I had the upper hand."

"How so?"

"Let's just say I had the goods on her, and leave it at that. Can we get back to finding Letty and my kid now?"

"I'm working on it," she said. "You have no idea where she might have gone? Friends or family who might be helping her hide?"

"No."

"Wonder what she's doing for money? I called her former boss, but he wasn't any help. Said she was a good worker, blah, blah, blah. My source at the police department says her bank account hasn't been touched, not that there's much there. I've got more money under my sofa cushions than she had in her checking account. Could Tanya have given her money?"

He'd been knotting and unknotting a rolled-up paper napkin, but at the mention of money he looked up. "Maybe. Or maybe Letty stole from Tanya, before she took off with Maya."

"Would Tanya have ready access to cash?"

"She had the child support I paid, and whatever she might have saved on her own from her acting gigs, but Tanya burned through money. She was like a child that way."

"Was anything missing from her apartment?"

He scowled. "The cops won't let me in. Even though I own the place. They say it's a crime scene. I'm supposed to get an inventory of the apartment at some point, but I'm not holding my breath."

"Do you think Tanya told Letty about our arrangement?"

Evan blotted his lips with what was left of the paper napkin. "Who knows? Find Letty. And then we'll figure out exactly how much she does or doesn't know."

18

~~~~~~~~~~~~~~~

ISABELLE SHOVED THE LAUNDRY CART through the swinging doors. Letty stood at a table in the middle of the room, folding an unending mound of towels and sheets.

"Letty, have you seen Maya?" she asked.

"No, I haven't seen her," Letty answered in a high, loud voice. "Where could she be?"

"Maybe she swam off on the back of a dolphin," Isabelle said. A faint giggle escaped from the pile of linens in the cart. "Or maybe she became a mermaid."

"Or maybe she climbed to the top of the coconut palm and she's eating coconuts with a monkey," Letty said. "Which is okay, because if she's eating coconuts, she won't want any chocolate chip cookies, right? I guess you and I will have all the cookies to ourselves."

The linens erupted and Maya popped her head out. "Here I am!" she declared. "I was hiding."

"*What?*" Letty said, feigning shock. "I never would have guessed." She scooped up her niece and deposited her on the floor of the laundry room.

Maya looked around the room. "I want cookies, Letty. Where the cookies at?"

"Miss Ava just baked them, and she said she would save some for you," Letty said. "Can you go over to her apartment all by yourself?"

"I'll take her," Isabelle volunteered. "Then I'll come back and give you a hand."

"I go by myself," Maya said. "I'm a big girl."

Letty and Isabelle stood in the door of the laundry room, watching, until Maya reached the motel office and was greeted by Ava.

"*How's* school going?" Letty asked, as Isabelle helped her fold an unwieldy fitted sheet.

"Kinda boring, to tell you the truth," Isabelle said, smoothing her hands over the folded sheet. "Graduation is in two months, but I've already finished most of the stuff I was supposed to do. School seems so lame right now. I'm ready for summer, and then college."

"Senioritis," Letty said. "I remember it well. But you've got so much exciting stuff still ahead of you yet. Take it from an old lady like me, don't wish it all away."

"You're not that old," Isabelle said, cocking her head. "You're what, like, twenty-five?"

"I wish," Letty said. "I'm thirty-three, but some days I feel like twice that old. Especially nights when Maya isn't sleeping, or has one of her meltdowns."

"She's super smart, you know," Isabelle said. "When I'm reading to her, she can sound out a lot of the words. And she can totally read the menu in the McDonald's drive-through."

"She's got it memorized, unfortunately," Letty said. "But I agree, she is pretty smart." She sighed. "I guess I need to start thinking about kindergarten in the fall."

"Here?" Isabelle asked. "I mean, do you think you'll still be living here at the Surf?"

"I'm not sure," Letty said. "Your mom has been so great to me, but living in a motel room isn't an ideal situation for raising a child. Maya needs some stability. A room of her own. Maybe a backyard."

"I get that," Isabelle said. "I always used to wish we lived in a real house. My friends all think it's so cool, living in a motel, with a pool right here and the beach and everything. They don't really get that we live, like, above the store. Like, my mom is on call, twenty-four seven. If one of the guests' air-conditioning isn't working, they'll wake her up at two in the morning to bitch her out about it. And all the regulars think that they're the boss of me. And Joe."

"They think the same thing about me, if it makes you feel any better," Letty said.

Isabelle nodded. "Where would you go, if you leave the Surf?"

"I'm not sure. I'm taking it a day at a time. I need to make plans, but right now, I feel sort of frozen."

"Like Elsa," Isabelle said, laughing at her own joke. "Well, I know I'm being selfish, but I hope you don't leave anytime soon. My mom really, really likes you, and of course, she freakin' adores Maya. I think it's great that she can leave here for a few hours every day and have a life, knowing that you're here and have things under control. I've been kind of worried, you know? About what will happen when I leave for school in the fall. I mean, Joe's around, but not really around all the time like I am. I love my brother, but he's kinda clueless when it comes to family stuff."

"I envy you your relationship with your mom," Letty said wistfully. "We didn't really have that with my mom, growing up."

"You and your sister? Maya's mom?"

"Yeah," Letty said.

"Is your mom around?" Isabelle asked. "I mean, she's not dead, right?"

"No, she's just not in my life. Hasn't been for a long time," Letty admitted. "She wasn't what you'd call a traditional mom. She shipped us off to live with our grandparents when we were bratty teenagers and she was in the process of splitting up with her husband. We finished high school in West Virginia, then Tanya and I both kind of did our own thing."

"Tanya?" Isabelle looked startled. "That's your sister's name? The one who died?"

Letty knew instantly, from the look on Isabelle's face, that she shouldn't have let Tanya's name slip. But it was too late to take it back now.

"Yes," she said.

"Oh my God," Isabelle said slowly. "That's why I keep thinking Maya looks so familiar. Why you look vaguely familiar." She studied Letty's face. "She was taller, and her hair was red. Your hair is darker, and you've got brown eyes. Different mouth, too."

"We're half sisters," Letty said. "Irish twins, my mom used to like to say. She split from my dad right after I was born, and got involved and pregnant, with Tanya's dad on the rebound. They never actually married, which was just as well, so she just gave Tanya my dad's name. It was easier that way. For her."

"Oh my God," Isabelle repeated. "Tanya was your sister. Maya's mother. I can't believe it. Does my mom know? Does Joe?"

"No!" Letty said. She gave Isabelle a pleading look. "Are you going to tell them?"

"No. But will you tell me what's going on? Why you're here?"

Letty folded and unfolded a top sheet, trying to make up her mind. She desperately wanted to confide in someone. Maybe saying Tanya's name wasn't an accident. Maybe it was the universe's way of letting her know it was okay to trust.

"You have to swear not to tell anybody," she said, her voice stern. "You can't tell anyone. Not your mom or Joe or any of your friends. I mean it. My life depends on it, Isabelle. Maya's too."

The girl's eyes grew wide. She crossed her heart. "Holy shit! I won't. I swear it, Letty. I won't tell a soul. I can't believe it. Is Tanya really dead? Are you guys really in trouble? From who?"

"Yes," Letty said. "It's a long story, but it's true. Tanya's ex-boyfriend killed her. He'd been fighting her in court, trying to get custody of Maya, but she was determined not to let that happen. She told me, about a month before . . . she said if anything bad ever happened to her, it would be Evan. Tanya begged me—she made me promise, if anything happened, that I would take Maya and get as far away from Evan as possible. So that's what I did."

She told Isabelle a condensed version of the story. About how she'd worked for Evan, and how Tanya became involved with him, and the details of their bitter breakup.

Letty recounted the day her sister showed her the canvas tote bag she'd hidden in a boot in her closet, her "getaway stash" with the enormous diamond ring push present and the magazine article about the Murmuring Surf.

She left out only one detail—the amount of cash in Tanya's go-bag.

Letty had been thinking about the money, nineteen thousand dollars, ever since she'd learned about Tanya's involvement in Rooney's gold-and-silver-buying scam. Knowing her sister, she'd been naïve to believe her story about "saving" money.

"So that's why you came here? Because of that magazine article?" Isabelle said. "She never told you about living here at the Surf, or about what happened here?"

"Oh, Isabelle," Letty said, with a long sigh. "I'm not sure I can explain my sister, because I'm just now realizing how little I really knew about her. Tanya was . . . complicated. All her life, she had secrets. Big ones and little ones. And I know this sounds terrible, talking about my dead sister like this, but she wasn't always truthful. For instance, five years ago, she called me out of the blue. She said she'd been living in Atlanta and that her 'boyfriend'—Rooney—had stolen all her clothes and money and abandoned her. She was crying and so pathetic. She asked if she could come stay with me in New York, to get a fresh start."

"But that part was a lie," Isabelle said. "She was right here. On Treasure Island. At the Murmuring Surf."

"So it seems."

"And they weren't really married after all?"

"I can't find a record that they were married in Florida," Letty said. "But maybe they got married somewhere else." She hesitated. "There's more, though. Almost as soon as Tanya moved to the city, while she was still living with me, she got involved with Evan. At the time, I worked for him. And we were . . . sort of dating."

"She stole your boyfriend?" Isabelle said indignantly. "Wow. That's cold."

Letty allowed herself a sad smile. "The next thing I knew, they were living together. And then Tanya got pregnant. Maya was born seven months later."

"Wait," Isabelle said, doing the math in her head. "Oh my God. Maya's eyes. They're just like Rooney's. That dark blue. And her eyelashes. Oh my God!" She pounded the top of the folding table. "Rooney is Maya's father. I can't believe I didn't figure it out earlier."

"I only figured it out myself after your brother told me Sunday about the scammers who'd been living here at the Surf. He mentioned a man named Rooney, and I remembered that was the name of Tanya's boyfriend. The one who ripped her off. The only other time she ever mentioned him to me was when I was asking her how she always got involved with losers. And she said he had deep blue eyes—like a mountain lake you wanted to dive naked into."

Isabelle absorbed that piece of information. "But Tanya told Evan he was Maya's father."

"I'm sure that in Tanya's mind, it all made sense. She was pregnant, Rooney was gone. Evan was available, sort of, and he was rich. Why not let him think he was her baby's daddy?"

"And even after they broke up, she didn't tell him Maya wasn't his?" Isabelle asked. "Even when he was trying to get custody of a kid that wasn't his, she still kept it a secret? Why?"

"Money, for one thing," Letty said. "As long as Evan believed Maya was his daughter, he'd support them both, even if they weren't married. Even after things got really, really ugly between them, she never hinted to me that he wasn't Maya's father. Typical Tanya."

"I can't believe Tanya is dead," Isabelle repeated, blinking back tears. "I'm so sorry, Letty. I really liked her. Everybody here liked her, even the Feldmans, and they don't like anyone."

"Yeah," Letty said, nodding. "That sounds like my sister. Our mom used to say Tanya could charm the birds out of the trees."

"I was just a goofy kid, but she was always super nice to me. Rooney was nice too, but I guess that was just so he could rip people off."

"What can you tell me about him, Isabelle?"

The teenager shrugged. "He had that sexy Irish accent, you know? But I think Mom must have sensed he was up to no good. Back then it was my job to deliver clean sheets and towels to everyone's room every week, but she made sure she delivered them to Rooney and Tanya, not me. Come to think of it, she acted weird around Tanya too. But maybe that's because she was worried her asshole boyfriend might get too friendly with her."

"You're talking about Chuck?" Letty asked.

Isabelle shuddered. "That old dude was totally sketchy. The day she kicked him out of our place was the happiest day of my life."

"Joe told me a little bit about their scam, and how when the police came to arrest them, Chuck and Rooney were gone, along with the money and gold coins and jewelry," Letty said. "Were you around when that happened?"

Isabelle shook her head. "No. I don't remember where I was, just that when I got home, there were all these cop cars in the parking lot, and all the regulars were standing around, trying to figure out what was going on. Mom made me go up to the apartment, but I was looking out the window when they brought Tanya out in handcuffs. It was so messed up, you know? Rooney and Chuck took off and your sister ended up in jail."

"But not for long," Letty mused. "Somehow, she talked her way out of it. The cops dropped all the charges."

"I didn't know that," Isabelle said. "Mom never talks about Chuck around me. I think she's embarrassed that she fell for his bullshit."

"And nobody has any idea where the two men went?"

"It's not something Mom would ever discuss with me," Isabelle said with a shrug. "And Joe thinks I'm still a little kid. He never tells me anything."

"They're trying to protect you," Letty said, reaching out and tugging at Isabelle's ponytail. "Be glad you have a big brother and a mom who cares. Tanya and I never had that. All we had was each other. And now she's gone."

"But you've got Maya," Isabelle pointed out. "Hey Letty, couldn't you just call the cops in New York and tell them what happened? How it was Evan that killed her, not you?"

Letty ripped a plastic bag from the large roll on the table. She placed a set of sheets, four bath towels, two face towels, and two washcloths on a stack, then slid them into the bag and knotted it.

"I wish it were that easy. But I can't prove a negative. I can't prove I didn't kill my sister. And in the meantime, what happens to Maya? If I went back, Evan's lawyers would either get a judge to award him custody, or they might put her in foster care. I can't let that happen to her."

Isabelle was bagging up linens, too. She took her stack and placed it in another laundry cart and added the stack Letty had just finished. "So what are you going to do?"

"I don't know how, but I guess I'm going to have to prove Evan Wingfield killed Tanya," Letty said. She put the last stack of linens into the cart. "But first I've got to deliver all this laundry."

"I'll help," Isabelle said. "With both. I'm good at figuring stuff out."

"Absolutely not," Letty said. "I never should have told you anything. Don't even think about trying to play detective, Isabelle. You don't know Evan. You don't know what he's capable of."

19

~~~~~~

"UGH," AVA SAID, PUSHING AWAY from the computer monitor. She'd been working with the new booking software all morning, mumbling and cursing under her breath. "That's enough of that for today."

Letty came in from the storeroom, where she'd been reorganizing the shelves, and looked over her boss's shoulder at the spreadsheet. "This looks great, Ava. You've uploaded all the upcoming reservations. Don't be so hard on yourself."

"It was a lot easier when I just had a paper calendar and a registration book," Ava groused. "Why is progress always such a royal pain in the patootie?"

"You're getting there," Letty said. "Okay, I've cleaned out a bunch of shelves in the supply room, and labeled everything, so I'd say that's progress. Hope it's okay that I threw out all the old outdated rate cards, promotional flyers, and motel stationery. I found stacks and stacks of brochures that were so old they didn't even have our area code."

"Good work," Ava said.

"Letty, look what I did," Maya said proudly. "I do good work too."

She'd assembled a large wooden puzzle that was a map of the United States.

"That's great, ladybug," Letty said. "Where'd you find the puzzle?"

"I gave it to her," Ava said. "That used to be Joe's. And then Isabelle's. I know I promised to clean out every closet in the place, and I did get rid of most of their old books and toys, but there were a few things I just couldn't part with."

Maya placed her hands protectively over the puzzle. "Mine."

"What's next on my list for today?" Letty asked, wiping her dusty hands on a paper towel.

"Can you get the rec room ready for tonight's Ping-Pong tournament and then pick up my grocery list at Publix?" Ava asked. "Maya can stay here with me."

"We're having a Ping-Pong tournament?" Letty asked, laughing. "Really?"

"Oh yes. Everybody here is dead serious about Ping-Pong. We've got folks coming over tonight from the Islander, the SeaBreeze, and the Michigander."

"Those are motels?"

"Yeah. Ruth and Al Zofchak, they're gone now, God rest their souls, organized the first tournament, I guess maybe fifteen years ago? They were retirees from outside of Pittsburgh. We used to have folks from seven or eight motels up and down the beach playing, but a lot of those places are long gone, torn down for condos, and of course, so are a lot of our regulars from back then. The tournament rotates among the four motels left, and this year we're hosting."

"What do you need me to do?"

"Set up the refreshment tables and the bar, and make sure the rec room bathrooms are clean. Anita's supposed to hit them every day, but she skips them when she thinks I'm not paying attention. The girls will be in there watching television, so just work around them. You'll find a couple of folding tables in the closet over there. And there are some plastic tablecloths on the top shelf. Joe's going to bring over extra folding chairs when he gets off work this afternoon."

The Murmuring Surf's recreation room, Ava had told her, had originally been the motel's coffee shop. It was a low-slung concrete-block building with a fifties-era zigzag cement tile roofline and large plate-glass windows facing the parking lot.

Friday morning, she found the group Ava called "the girls" watching a taped episode of *Wheel of Fortune* in the lounge area, which consisted of two aging turquoise vinyl sofas, a mosaic-tile-topped coffee table, and a flat-screen television.

"Hi ladies," Letty called out, as she pushed through the heavy glass door.

Wilona Wilson, a retired African American schoolteacher from Cleveland, was the de facto leader of "the girls," the group of regulars who congregated most mornings to watch television together before drifting together over to their assigned lounge chairs by the pool.

Billie Feldman was one of the girls, although her wife Ruth rarely joined the group. Alice Sheehan, whose silver-white bob contrasted with her deep tan, was the third, and Arlene Finocchia made up the fourth. Today they were joined by Trudi Maples, but Letty noticed that Louise Schmidt—another retired schoolteacher, from Akron—was absent.

Wilona was hopping up and down on the sofa, clapping her hands. "I knew it! I knew it was 'Sugar and Spice Girls.'"

Billie Feldman snorted. "You're the only one here who ever even heard of the Spice Girls."

"I've heard of them," Alice Sheehan said. "I think my daughter used to listen to their CDs."

"I'll try to stay out of your way," Letty said, "but Ava wanted me to get everything ready for tonight's Ping-Pong tournament."

She began straightening the coffee cart, mopping up spilled grounds, wiping down the sugar and powdered creamer containers and replenishing the supply of cardboard cups. She emptied the trash and began sweeping the terrazzo floor.

While Letty worked, the girls chatted among themselves, gently ribbing each other over missed clues.

She was setting up the refreshment table during a commercial break when Trudi turned to Arlene. "Doesn't Letty remind you of someone?"

Letty ignored the comment, spreading out the red-and-white-checked tablecloth, smoothing out the fold marks. She went back to the closet for the second table. Arlene was sitting forward on the sofa, staring at her.

"Now that you mention it," Billie said, "she does have one of those familiar faces."

"It's been driving me crazy," Trudi said. "Letty, did you ever do any acting?"

Here it comes, Letty thought, trying to stay calm. "Yes, I tried acting. I wasn't very successful at it. Every girl who goes to New York thinks they're going to be the next Jennifer Lawrence. And then they end up working in a diner. Like me."

"Were you ever on television?" Arlene asked.

"That's what I said," Trudi agreed. "She reminds me of someone I've seen on television."

Wilona got up and refilled her coffee cup, stopping to study Letty's face up close. "Trudi's right. You're sure pretty enough to be in show business."

"I did some tiny bit parts," Letty admitted, "but it was so long ago, I didn't even keep track."

"We don't mean to pry," Wilona said, "but you're not exactly a senior citizen like all the rest of us who've been coming here for years. So, Letty dear, how did you end up here at the Murmuring Surf?"

Uh-oh, Letty thought. *Here it comes.* She needed to end this discussion.

"I had a bad breakup with my boyfriend, and I just wanted to get out of town, so I got in my car and started driving." This was all true, if you stretched a point, which she didn't mind doing.

"Isabelle tells me the little girl is your niece," Alice said. "I think it's wonderful that you're raising her. I have a grandniece up home in Traverse City that I'm very close to. She usually flies down in April and drives back home with me at the end of the season."

"She's quite the little swimmer, your niece," Billie commented. "Shouldn't she be in school, though?"

"That child isn't old enough to be in school yet, Billie," Wilona said. "Not even five yet, isn't that right?"

"That's right," Letty said. "Maya's only four."

She found an old-school aluminum Coleman cooler in the closet and set it on top of the table for the bar, then headed into the bathrooms with a roll of paper towels and spray cleaner.

When she emerged, the girls were intently critiquing Vanna White's outfit, which today consisted of a short, slinky red halter dress. "I liked it better when she wore those pretty long formals," Trudi said. "But these young girls today, all they ever want to wear are those awful yoga pants and hoodies."

"Vanna isn't exactly a young girl," Billie said. "I bet she's fifty if she's a day."

"That can't be right," Arlene protested. "I read in *People* magazine that she's got grown kids."

"Okay, ladies," Letty said, pausing at the door. "Have a nice day!"

She felt giddy but guilty, wheeling a shopping cart full of groceries around the supermarket without Maya, sipping a Starbucks latte and breezing past the aisle of sugary cereals without having the child clamor for Froot Loops.

Motherhood, Letty reflected, was the most exhausting thing she'd ever done. She adored her niece, but bearing sole responsibility for another human's well-being was overwhelming. Not to mention terrifying.

For once, she thought wryly, she'd discovered something Tanya had not overexaggerated.

"You have no idea how tired I am. I can't remember the last time I had an uninterrupted night of sleep," Tanya would exclaim on Sunday mornings when Letty arrived for her regular playdate with Maya. "You have her for three hours, but the rest of the time it's just me."

"And the help," Letty pointed out. "A nanny, a once-a-week housekeeper, and preschool."

"You try it sometime," Tanya had shot back. "Now I get why Mama was only too happy to ship us off to Mimi every chance she got. If I never have to wipe another snotty nose or poopy butt, I will die happy."

The thought of her sister brought sudden tears to Letty's eyes, but she shook them off. Crying wouldn't bring Tanya back and it wouldn't help Letty figure out how to bring Evan to justice. She'd been scared and powerless long enough now. It was time to fight back, she decided. Just as soon as she figured out how.

An hour later, she was unloading groceries when the door to unit 11 opened and Sheila Bronson emerged. "Help!" she cried, spotting Letty. "Come quick. I think Harry's having a heart attack."

Letty dropped the sack of groceries she'd been toting and raced to the unit. The bedroom door was open and the first thing she saw was Harry Bronson, stretched out on the bed, clutching his chest and groaning. "I'm okay," he protested, rolling onto his side. "I'm okay." He didn't look okay to Letty. His face was pale and flecked with perspiration. He was a beefy man, built, Letty thought, like the beer trucks he'd driven before retirement.

"Did you call 911?" Letty asked.

"He won't let me call," Sheila said, wringing her hands.

"No," Harry growled. "I'm fine. . . ." His face contorted in pain. "Shit, it hurts."

Letty reached for her phone. "Then I'll call."

"Goddammit, I said I'm fine!" Harry tried to sit up, but sank back down onto the bed. "Just leave me alone."

"Harry! You don't have to yell. She's just trying to help," Sheila said, starting to weep.

Letty backed out of the motel room, followed by Sheila. "He's so stubborn, but he's been having these chest pains since lunch. He swore it was just heartburn, because he ate kielbasa, and it always gives him heartburn. . . ."

Ava came out of the office and trotted over to where the two women stood in the breezeway. "Sheila? Is everything okay?"

"Well, not really," Sheila said, her voice trembling.

Letty spoke up. "Harry might be having a heart attack. He's been having chest pains for over an hour, and he's pale and sweating, but he won't let her call for an ambulance."

"He doesn't trust doctors down here," Sheila said, glancing over her shoulder into the unit, where they could hear the husband softly moaning.

"I'm going back to the office and calling Joe," Ava said. "Letty, stay here with Sheila, please."

Letty reluctantly went back into the darkened bedroom. The nightstand beside Harry was littered with pill bottles and the remnants of a messy sandwich.

"Aspirin," Letty said, remembering something she'd read somewhere about first aid for heart-attack patients. "Sheila, do you have any aspirin?"

"Y-y-yes," the older woman stammered. She scrabbled around on the nightstand, shook out a capsule, and offered it to her husband.

"I think you're supposed to chew it, not just swallow it, to make it work faster," Letty said.

"Leave me alone," he muttered, but after a moment, he took the tablet and chewed.

"Has he had chest pains before?" Letty asked.

"I told you, it's just heartburn," Harry said. "Can't you just leave me alone?"

Joe DeCurtis looked down at the stricken man on the bed, while Ava, Sheila, and Letty hovered nearby. "I called 911," he announced.

He sat on the bed next to the patient. "Don't think I'm getting fresh," he said, "but I'm gonna unbuckle your belt and unfasten your shirt."

He touched the side of the man's face. "Come on, Harry," he said, grabbing his arm. "Let's get you sitting up. It'll make it easier for you to breathe." He helped the older man to a sitting position, then slid a pillow under his knees. "Now lean forward if you can," he said, his voice calm. "That'll help pump blood to your heart."

He looked over at Sheila. "Does he take nitroglycerin? Any kind of heart medication?"

She shook her head. "He had an episode like this last summer, when we were at the lake in Wisconsin. The doctor there prescribed it, but then the symptoms went away, and we never got it filled."

"We had him chew an aspirin right before you got here," Letty volunteered.

"Good idea," Joe said. He kept his hand on the stricken man's back. "Hang in there, Harry. The dispatcher I talked to said the EMTs were five minutes out."

Right on cue, they heard the high-pitched sound of an ambulance drawing near. Letty stood outside in the parking lot, waving it toward the unit.

Ten minutes later, the paramedics wheeled the patient out of the room on a stretcher, an oxygen mask strapped over his face. "They gave him nitro because it looks like it actually is a heart attack," Joe said, touching Sheila's arm. "They're going to take him to the emergency room."

"I'm going too," Sheila said, but Joe pulled her back. "They won't let you ride in the ambulance. I'll take you myself." He glanced back inside the room. "Why don't you grab all his medications? The doctors are going to want to know everything he's taking. And don't forget his ID and yours and your insurance cards."

"Okay," Sheila said. "I will."

"We'll lock up here," Ava told her. "You just go with Joe. And let us know what the doctors say."

The ambulance pulled away, lights flashing and siren screaming. Sheila buried her face in Ava's shoulder for a moment. "Thank you," she said.

20

~~~~~~~~~~~~~~~~

A SMALL KNOT OF MOTEL GUESTS had begun to gather in the parking lot, drawn outside by the sight and sounds of the ambulance.

"Who was it?" Ruth Feldman asked Ava. "What happened?"

Ava and Letty exchanged a worried glance. "We think Harry Bronson might have had a heart attack," Ava said reluctantly.

"Who?" Merwin Maples walked up, a beach towel wrapped around his waist. "Is he dead?"

"No!" Ava said. "It was Harry. He had some chest pains after lunch. He was insisting it was just heartburn and wouldn't let Sheila call 911."

"Stubborn old fool," Wilona Wilson said, shaking her head. "That's the same thing that happened with my Barrett. Wouldn't let me call a doctor, didn't want to make a fuss. By the time I got him to the hospital, it was too late."

Oscar Jensen strolled up, a lit cigarette in hand. "Did somebody say Harry Bronson died?"

"Oscar, put that thing out," Ava snapped. "Nobody died."

By now the crowd of regulars had grown to more than a dozen people, worriedly murmuring among themselves.

"Everybody, listen up," Ava said. "Here's what happened. Harry Bronson was having chest pains. He didn't want Sheila to call 911, so I called Joe, and he called 911. In the meantime, Letty got him to take some aspirin, which is the best thing to do. The EMTs told us they think maybe Harry did have a heart attack. They gave him some nitroglycerin, and took him to the hospital. Joe took Sheila over there in his truck. He'll call me as soon as they have news, and I'll let everyone know."

Oscar Jensen stubbed out his cigarette on the pavement, and when Ava glared at him, picked up the butt.

"That's it. We're screwed," he told Merwin. "Might as well call off the tournament if we don't have Harry. He's our ace."

"Damn," Merwin said. "I thought we might have a chance this year. That guy from the Michigander, the one with the wicked forehand spin? I heard he got prostate cancer. Didn't even come down this year."

"We're not calling off the tournament," Ava said. "It's too late for that. Joe will keep us updated on Harry's condition, but we've got other players. And anyway, I already bought all the food and beer and wine. We'll see you all at six o'clock in the rec room," she said, loudly enough for everyone to hear.

One by one, the regulars drifted back to their rooms. It was three o'clock.

The door to her unit was slightly ajar. Isabelle was sitting at the tiny kitchen table in Letty's motel room, reading a paperback mystery from the rec room's lending library. "She's asleep," she whispered, nodding in the direction of Maya, who was tucked under the covers in the bed. "We swam in the pool for a while, and I gave her lunch."

"Thanks," Letty said, sinking down onto the bed. "What a morning!"

"I heard what my mom said about Mr. Bronson," Isabelle said. "Is he going to be okay?"

"I hope so. Poor Sheila. The way he yelled at her—and at me, was awful. I felt so sorry for her. She was just trying to help."

Isabelle dog-eared the page of her book and stood up. "He can seem pretty grouchy sometimes, but my mom says he's actually a nice guy. He knows a lot about gardening, and every year he brings her plants and seeds from his garden up north. He planted all those flowers around the pool, and down by the beach walk. And he drives Miss Wilona to church every Sunday, because he said he doesn't want her taking the bus."

"Sheila was so scared," Letty said. "I felt helpless, and I know she did too."

"I'm gonna go on home and do a little homework," Isabelle said. "You still want me to watch Maya tonight, right?"

"Unless things change, yes," Letty said. "I promised your mom I'd help out with the food and the bar at the tournament tonight."

Ava bustled around the food tables in the rec room, bringing in foil chafing dishes of pigs in blankets, potato salad, and chicken wings. There were bowls of chips and pretzels and a supermarket fruit and cheese platter. The centerpiece was an enormous platter of cookies.

"Wow, that's a lot of food," Letty commented. "How many people are we expecting?"

"We usually get fifty or sixty people," Ava said. She pointed toward the kitchen. "Can you get the bags of ice and dump them into the cooler? I've got white wine and beer to go in there. And there's a jug of iced tea on the counter that you could bring out too."

Letty was icing down the jug wine and beer when she heard tapping on the front door. She looked up to see three older women, standing expectantly on the doorstep.

"Here we go with the early birds. Not even five o'clock yet," Ava said, rolling her eyes. She turned to the door. "Sorry, ladies," she said loudly. "We're not ready for you yet."

Letty followed her into the kitchen to bring out paper plates and cups. "Seems like a lot of excitement for a Ping-Pong tournament."

"It's not the Ping-Pong they're excited about. It's the all-you-can-eat buffet for five bucks and wine and beer for a buck," Ava said. "Plus, like I said before, it's kind of a tradition. A lot of our folks know the regulars at the other motels. They go to church or do water aerobics at the community center or play golf or shuffleboard together. It's a real community, you know?"

"I've been meaning to ask, what happens when the snowbirds fly back north in the spring? Does your business see a big drop?"

"Not really. We fill up with families over spring break and Easter. There's a little bit of a lull until school gets out, then we stay busy all summer long until September. That's our slow time, 'shoulder season' we call it, until things pick up again close to Thanksgiving."

"Interesting," Letty said. "What do you want me to do now?"

Ava pointed to a folded-up card table. "You can put that outside by the door. I'm gonna let you sell tickets tonight." She glanced up at the clock. "Joe should be here any minute with the folding chairs, and you can help set them up before it's time to man your post. We'll open the doors at five thirty."

"Did you find someone to take Harry's place in the tournament?"

"I had to twist his arm, but Joe finally agreed to step in." There was another tap at the door. "Good. That's him now."

"*How's* Harry?" Letty asked. She was setting up the folding chairs around the perimeter of the Ping-Pong table.

"Better than he deserves to be," Joe said. "The docs said the aspirin you made him take probably saved his life. Sheila asked me to let you know how grateful she is."

He gestured toward the Ping-Pong table and handed her a paddle. "How about you warm me up? Ava guilt-tripped me into filling in for Harry, and I haven't played in ages."

"Me? I don't think I've played Ping-Pong since I was twelve."

"It'll come back to you. We'll just volley a couple minutes. Those oldsters are gonna break down the doors to get at the pigs in blankets if we don't let 'em in pretty soon."

He held the ball in his left hand and the paddle in his right and gave it a thwack. The ball bounced once on Joe's side of the table, then skipped over the net and caromed off Letty's side. She swung but missed.

But the "pong" sound of the ball hitting the table took her instantly back to Camp WeLoJe, the sleepaway camp where she'd spent two weeks the summer she was twelve. Somehow, Terri had wangled a "scholarship" for both her and Tanya to the camp, which was a moldering collection of cabins sprinkled around the edge of a dank-smelling lake in the mountains of North Carolina. WeLoJe stood for We Love Jesus, and it was run by an ultraconservative Christian church that forbade watching television, wearing makeup, and chewing gum, the three activities that were twelve-year-old Letty's personal Holy Trinity.

Tanya had cleverly faked a case of stomach flu on the day of departure and had stayed home, much to Terri's annoyance.

The campers had mandatory Bible study every morning and afternoon, campfire "sing-alongs," archery, arts and crafts, and the only thing Letty remotely enjoyed, a Ping-Pong table. She was an outcast from the beginning, because all the other girls in her cabin attended the same church together. At the end of the two most miserable weeks of her childhood, when the church bus dropped her off at home, the only thing Letty had to show for her stay was a leather belt stamped with WeLoJe and her initials, and a wicked case of poison ivy. But she knew how to play Ping-Pong.

Letty retrieved the ball and lobbed it over the net. Joe hit it back, she managed to return his serve, whiffed the next two serves, then, to her amazement, managed to sustain a volley for four or five exchanges.

Someone was pounding on the plate-glass door. "Open up! We need to practice too." Merwin Maples and Oscar Jensen had their faces pressed to the glass.

"Okay," Ava said. "The food's ready. Letty, you get out there and start selling tickets. Let's get this show on the road."

People streamed into the rec room. A van pulled up and disgorged eight elderly guests from the SeaBreeze Motel, all dressed in matching aqua SeaBreeze T-shirts and sun visors. Letty sold tickets, made change, and politely but firmly refused (per Ava's instructions) to accept personal checks or Canadian currency.

She could tell from the noise from inside that the tournament had begun, but she was too busy to get up and spectate. At some point, Ava brought her a plate of chicken wings and a glass of the worst white wine she'd ever tasted. Cheers and boos erupted from the rec room. At eight thirty, Joe came outside, dragging a folding chair with him. His hair was damp with sweat and his MURMURING SURF MARAUDERS T-shirt stuck to his chest.

To Letty's surprise, she thought he looked cute. Hot even.

"I thought you were playing in the tournament."

"I got skunked," he said, looking chagrined. "By an eighty-year-old retired gym teacher from Milwaukee." He shook his fist in mock indignation. "Damn those professional Ping-Pongers at the Michigander!"

Letty cocked her head. "Will you ever get over the disappointment?"

"No. The worst of it is, the SeaBreeze guys didn't even want me to play. They said I was a ringer because I don't live here."

"Then why did you get to play?"

He laughed. "When your mom runs the tournament, your mom makes the rules."

"So who won?" Letty asked, craning her neck to look inside the door.

"Not us. Merwin's playing now. We're doomed. Looks like the coveted golden Ping-Pong paddle will once again be awarded to our archenemies."

He jerked his head in the direction of the beach. "Come on, let's blow this pop stand."

"I can't," she said. "I'm on duty."

"So clock out," Joe said. "Merwin's going down and people will be leaving here in droves in five minutes." He tugged at her hand. "Come on. Ava told me to tell you it's okay. You've been working all day, with hardly a break. The Feldmans are going to help her clean up."

"I shouldn't," Letty said reluctantly. "If Maya wakes up and I'm not there . . ."

"Isabelle's there," he said, pulling her to her feet. "For God's sake, Letty. It's not even nine o'clock yet. You haven't even been here three weeks and you're already turning into an early bird."

Where are we going?" They were walking along the beach, headed south. A silver sliver of a moon splashed its reflection on the Gulf, and the stars looked like pinpricks in the dark sky. Letty stopped momentarily in the ankle-high surf, letting the gentle waves roll over her feet. "Water's kind of cold," she said, surprised.

"It cools off fast when the sun goes down," Joe said, staying where he was at the edge of the waterline. "But you wait 'til July or August. It's like bathwater. Hurricane season."

"I'll skip hurricane season, if it's all the same to you," Letty said.

"What? You're leaving?"

She joined him on the sand. "I'm not sure. I mean, I can't keep living indefinitely in a motel room with an almost five-year-old child. I've got to figure out school for her in the fall."

"We've got schools right here at the beach," he pointed out. "And they're pretty good. I mean, look at Isabelle. She's a product of the public schools here, and she's headed to Emory on a full scholarship."

"We'll see," Letty said. "You still haven't told me where we're going."

"And you haven't told me where you're going," Joe said.

He pointed north, up the beach, where strings of party lights outlined a sprawling beach bar with an outdoor patio and rows of lounge chairs facing the water. They could hear the strains of a Jimmy Buffett song drifting across the dunes. "Wanna grab a drink at Sharky's?"

She considered. "Not really. Too crowded. Too noisy. I've been around people all day. Can't we just walk?"

He shrugged. "Sure."

She spotted a low-slung motel nestled into the dunes. The concrete-block buildings were a faded aqua. "Is that the SeaBreeze? It looks different from the beach."

"That's it," Joe said, with a sigh. "For now."

"What's that mean?"

"Eleanor Triplett told Mom tonight that this is probably their last season. A developer has been hounding her to sell for years now. Doug died three years ago, and her kids aren't interested in running a cheesy motel. I'd be surprised if it doesn't get bulldozed before Christmas."

"That's sad," Letty said.

"Happens all the time."

"I've been wondering," Letty said. "What will happen with Harry Bronson? Will he be okay?"

"Maybe. The doctors want to do surgery, but he's dead set on seeing his doctors at home. Their daughter is going to drive down here this weekend to help Sheila drive them back north."

"I can't believe what a sexist pig he was today," Letty said. "He wouldn't listen to his own wife—or me—about calling 911, but as soon as you showed up and took over, he was meek as a lamb."

"He's a hardheaded old bastard, that's for sure," Joe said, chuckling. "You shouldn't be offended. It's a generational thing. Guys like him, they're not used to having to listen to—or obey—a woman. And it didn't help matters that the cardiologist on call at the hospital today was a woman. Or maybe it's just the uniform. Guys who're Harry's age, they're used to respecting a uniform."

"Did you always want to go into law enforcement?"

"Hell no. Growing up at the Surf, hauling trash and raking

seaweed and cleaning the pool, I was convinced that wearing a suit
and tie and carrying a briefcase would be the life. I had a high school
buddy whose dad was in insurance and financial planning. They had
a nice house on the water and a pool. I thought that's what success
looked like. Ava didn't have money for me to go away to school, so I
lived at home and worked my way through the University of South
Florida and got a business degree. My friend's dad gave me a job
right out of college.

"I sat in a cubicle all day and cold-called clients, trying to sell them
whole life policies or annuities. Hated every minute of it. Turns out
I'm no good at sales."

"You went from insurance to being a cop?"

"Not quite. One of our regulars, Bob Wilhite, was a retired FBI
agent from Charlotte. He and his wife Shirley stayed at the Surf for
probably twenty years. He became sort of a surrogate dad to me.
We used to go hit golf balls at the driving range, or go fishing on a
charter boat. He bought me my first legal beer at the VFW lodge
down the beach here. I had a lot of different jobs back then. Assistant manager at a bank, dispatcher for a trucking company . . ."

He stopped walking and looked over at Letty. "Why am I boring
you with all of this?"

"Because I asked," she said. "Keep going."

"Long story short, Bob kept bugging me, telling me I should go
into police work. He'd even send me job postings every summer, after
he and Shirley went back home to Charlotte. Seven years ago, Shirley
called to tell me Bob was gone. He'd played eighteen holes of golf,
came home, sat down in his recliner, and just never woke up again."

"Oh," Letty said, touching Joe's shoulder. "I'm sorry."

"Me too. A couple weeks later, I got a package in the mail from
Shirley. It was Bob's FBI retirement plaque with his badge mounted
on it. They never had kids, and she wrote that he wanted me to have
it. It was his way of nagging me from the grave. Funny thing is, I'd
just quit my job. I was at loose ends, so I thought, What the hell? I'll
go to the police academy."

"You didn't think about leaving the area? Maybe going to a bigger city?" Letty asked.

"Not really. I like it here. Close to the beach, and yeah, I'm around if Ava or Isabelle need me. Now it's your turn."

"For what?" Letty asked.

"I've just told you my whole life story. And you haven't told me a damn thing about you. All I know is you showed up at the Murmuring Surf out of nowhere, and even though I told you we didn't have a vacancy, you wouldn't take no for an answer."

"I'd been driving for hours, and I was exhausted. And Maya needed to pee," she said.

"There you go again, avoiding answering my questions," Joe said. He leaned in close, until she could feel his breath in her ear. "Who are you really, Letty?"

A shiver went down her back. "I'm nobody."

He slid an arm around her waist. "You're not married, right?" His lips grazed the skin of her collarbone, and then her neck, and then her earlobe. She felt warmth radiating out from all the places his lips skimmed. Just as his lips met hers he repeated the question. "Married?"

The kiss she returned gave him the answer. She slipped her arms around his neck, fully committed. "No," she murmured a few seconds later, as he slowly ran his hands under her T-shirt, grazing her nipples with his thumbs.

"No?" He stopped what he was doing, looking puzzled. "You mean, no, don't do that?"

"No, I'm not married," she said, kissing him again. "And no, please don't stop."

~~~~~~~~~~~~~~~~

21

VIKKI HILL STARED DOWN AT the screen of her laptop. She blinked. She'd run the search on a whim, with zero expectations. But damned if she didn't get a hit.

Tanya Michelle Rooney, real name Tanya Michelle Carnahan, had been arrested down in Florida almost exactly five years ago, on charges of fraud and conspiracy to commit fraud.

She read the arrest report with interest. It looked as though the woman was mixed up in a scam, along with two male associates. The three of them had set up shop in a motel room and duped their unsuspecting victims into selling gold and silver coins and estate jewelry for far below their actual worth. One report she read put the amount the trio had earned in excess of $150,000. Not a bad profit for less than two weeks of work.

But when an elderly victim complained to a local cop that she feared she'd been cheated, the authorities closed in. A sting was organized with an undercover agent, but by the time the cops moved in, the two male associates had fled, leaving only Tanya behind holding the bag. But not the profits from the scam, or any of the gold or silver, which had apparently vanished.

"Ain't that the way?" Vikki mused aloud.

The woman had been booked and arrested, but eventually released. Vikki wondered why, until she pulled up Tanya Carnahan's booking photo.

"Ahhh," she said. She'd seen other, flattering photos of Tanya in the New York tabloids, and she'd even seen the police photos taken at the murder scene. But even dirty and disheveled in a police mug shot, the woman was strikingly beautiful. Vikki could see what Evan Wingfield had seen in Tanya. And she could understand how even a devious crook like Wingfield had been taken in. The snake had been charmed, and he still didn't know to what extent.

She read the arrest report again and laughed at a detail she'd over-looked earlier. Tanya Carnahan had been arrested in a small beach town called Treasure Island. *You couldn't make this shit up if you tried,* she thought.

Several different jurisdictions had been involved in the sting op-eration, including the Florida Department of Law Enforcement, the FBI, the Pinellas County Sheriff's Office, and, of course, the locals.

The feds and the state cops probably weren't all that invested in the incident, especially since the men had slipped through their grasp, but this would have been a big deal to a small police depart-ment. Vikki figured the arresting officer, a man named Joe DeCurtis, would know the most about the incident. She glanced at the clock. It was after six, but she put in the call anyway. As expected, her call went straight to voice mail, so she left a message.

Returning to the arrest report she found the name of the other two suspects in the scheme, both of whom had slipped away be-fore the authorities closed in. One, a Declan M. Rooney, age forty-two at the time of the incident, was apparently the mastermind and founder of the ring. And, it seemed, he was married to Tanya Car-nahan. Or so she claimed.

Rooney's driver's license photo was included in the report. Vikki had a theory that you should never trust a man who took a good driver's license photo, and Declan Rooney's photo only reinforced that belief.

He had dark, wavy, shoulder-length hair combed back from a high forehead, and piercing blue eyes. He looked, Vikki thought, like a goddamned pirate.

"Good stuff," Vikki said out loud. She did a quick search and discovered that Declan Rooney had an impressive arrest record, with stops around several Florida towns, like Fort Lauderdale, Palm Beach, and Sarasota. He was a small-time thief with ambitions for the big time.

She widened her search to the NCIC database and found a more extensive rap sheet, dating back to Rooney's teen years in Boston. His juvenile arrest record was blocked, but starting at seventeen, he'd been booked for shoplifting, breaking and entering, drug possession, auto theft, and aggravated assault. The last charge piqued her interest, because his other arrests were mostly nonviolent property crimes.

After a little more digging she found the incident report for the aggravated assault charge. After some short jail stints up north, Rooney, like so many other ambitious crooks, had decided to take his talents for the grift down south, to Florida, specifically.

Declan Rooney had advertised a phony ten-thousand-dollar Rolex Oyster Perpetual watch on Craigslist in Boca Raton, but when the buyer whipped out a jeweler's loupe to examine the watch, Rooney pulled a gun and beat the man so badly he'd broken his jaw and fractured an eye socket. Unfortunately for Rooney, the victim had snapped a quick photo of his license plate when he'd pulled into the shopping center where the transaction was set to take place. He'd done six months in a county lockup for the assault.

Vikki scrolled back to the photo of Tanya. She took a screenshot of her booking photo, then clicked over to compare it with the photo of Letty Carnahan that Evan Wingfield had provided.

There was a definite family resemblance. The older sister had the same nose and mouth, but her face was fuller, the features softer and the cheekbones not nearly as prominent as her younger sibling's. Letty's hair was almost a chestnut brown, and the way she parted it down the middle accented her widow's peak.

When and how, she wondered, had Rooney hooked up with Tanya? She had no other arrest record that Vikki could find. According to Evan Wingfield, his ex had done some modeling and acting in Atlanta, immediately prior to her move to New York to live with her sister. Had that been a lie, too?

According to Evan, the sisters, estranged after he dumped Letty for Tanya, had only reconciled after his breakup with Tanya. "After that they were thick as thieves," Evan claimed.

But if that was true, what would have prompted Letty to kill her sister, accidentally or not?

She needed to find Letty to answer that question. And she needed to find her before Evan Wingfield did.

22

～～～～～

LETTY SIGHED.

Joe lifted his head and gave her a quizzical look. "What's that supposed to mean?" He kissed her deeply. "You just said 'Don't stop.'"

She kissed him back. "I know, but this is a public beach. Maybe we should slow things down a little. Go get a drink somewhere and chill out?"

"I know a place. It's not far from here."

"What's it called?"

"It's called Joe's Place. And it's only a block away. The atmosphere ain't much, but the drinks are free and the bartender is a *very* friendly guy." He leered at her with this last statement.

She raised an eyebrow.

"Come on. I'm harmless."

"I sincerely doubt that," Letty said.

"And yet you went for a moonlit walk on the beach with me, and you'll notice I didn't grab you and rip your clothes off."

"Yet," Letty said. "I'm sorry, Joe, but I don't think going to your place is a good idea."

"Because you're afraid you'll grab *me* and rip *my* clothes off?"

She looked away for a moment. "Yeah, that's part of it."

He took a half step away from her. "What are you so afraid of? I don't think I've ever been around you when you were completely relaxed. I like you, Letty. And I know you like me. Can't you turn off your brain and your self-control for an hour or so and relax and enjoy yourself?"

"You don't understand," Letty said quietly. "I wish I could be like you and do whatever I want, but I can't. My life is too complicated right now."

"Complicated how? You're essentially a single mom now. I get that. Remember, I was raised by a single mom. But Ava never walled herself off the way you're trying to do."

"I can't explain it." She walked to the water's edge and looked out at the sky. A jagged bolt of lightning flashed on the horizon, and the wind picked up, creating whitecaps on the water.

"I've got to get back to the motel," she told him. "Maya's afraid of lightning."

"And what are you afraid of?" Joe stalked away.

First it was the wind. From nowhere, it seemed, it swept off the Gulf, nearly knocking her down in its intensity. The temperature seemed to plummet, and then the rain started when she was halfway back to the Murmuring Surf, slashing at her face and clothes. Letty broke into a run, head down, stumbling in the soft sand, and she didn't slow until she saw the lights of the motel. Lightning crackled over the water as she made her way up from the beach path, drenched and shivering from the cold.

She found Isabelle sitting on the rusty chair in the breezeway in front of her room, with Maya wrapped in a blanket and curled up in a ball in her lap. The child was asleep, with Ellie hanging limply from one hand.

"What are you doing out here?" Letty asked, trying to catch her breath. "Maya is terrified of lightning."

"When it started, she got really upset and was crying," Isabelle said, smoothing the sleeping child's hair. "But then I told her what Mom used to tell me when I was little, that the lightning was just angels laughing. So we came out here to watch it. And she reminded me that her mama was an angel, and she wanted to watch her laugh. She just now fell asleep."

"That's amazing," Letty said. She held out her arms. "Here. I'll take her."

"I can do it," Isabelle said. She looked Letty up and down. "I didn't expect you back so soon. What happened to Joe?"

"How did you know we were . . ."

"He texted me to say you guys were going out for a drink, and could I hang out with Maya for a while. Must have been a short drink."

"It didn't really work out," Letty said. "And then it started to rain. I'm gonna go inside and get dried off. Can you tuck her in for me?"

By the time she came out of the bathroom in dry pajamas, Isabelle was sitting in the room's only chair, reading her paperback, and Maya was softly snoring from her side of the bed.

Letty tried to hand the teenager a wad of cash, but Isabelle shook her off.

"No way. Maya and I had fun."

"But you gave up a Friday night to stay with her," Letty protested.

"I didn't have anything else going on. It's cool." Isabelle went over to the bed and dropped a kiss on the top of the little girl's head. "Night night, Maya Papaya." She picked up her book and went out the door.

The rain drummed against the breezeway's metal roof outside and the wind rattled the unit's jalousie windows. For the first time since she'd arrived in Florida, Letty was cold. She burrowed under the covers and tried not to think about her ill-fated stroll with Joe De-Curtis.

But the genie was out of the bottle. How long had it been since she'd been kissed like that? When she closed her eyes she could still feel the delicious, unsettling sensation of his lips and his hands.

And she could still feel the sting of his accusations. He couldn't know how close she'd come to completely letting go.

"Letty, Letty." Maya pressed her face against hers and used her thumb to pry open one of her aunt's eyes. Letty opened the other one. The room was bathed in a murky gray light. It was still raining, and according to the clock radio on her nightstand, it was only seven o'clock.

"Go back to sleep, baby," she said, yawning and rolling onto her side. "It's Saturday. Letty's day off."

"Where's Ellie?" Maya asked. "I want my Ellie."

Oh Lord, Letty thought. She sat up and looked around the bed. No sign of Maya's beloved companion. She lifted the covers.

"Look under the bed," she told Maya. "Maybe Ellie's hiding under there."

The child giggled and crawled under the bed. "She's not here."

"Check the bathroom. Maybe she needed to go pee-pee."

Maya wandered away. "Ellie," she called. "C'mere, Ellie."

A moment later Maya was standing by the side of the bed wailing. "Ellie's not there! I want my Ellie."

"We'll find her," Letty said grimly.

Not finding Ellie was not an option. She could remember other incidents when the stuffed elephant had gone missing. There was the time Tanya's new housekeeper had made the mistake of tossing it into the toy box and piling other toys on top, which had resulted in an epic meltdown from Maya, and the unsympathetic housekeeper's subsequent sacking. Once, shortly after Evan and Tanya separated and Evan had Maya for her first visitation, Tanya had "forgotten" to pack Ellie in the child's overnight bag.

Maya's resulting case of hysterics had led to a series of frantic late-night emergency calls to Tanya, who, Letty always suspected, had rather enjoyed the spectacle of seeing Evan, exhausted and unshaven, having cut his weekend plans short, drive back from the Hamptons to deposit Maya back on her doorstep at six o'clock the next morning.

Of course, he'd accused Tanya of deliberately leaving the toy behind in order to sabotage his visitation. Thereafter, Evan managed to track down the exact same elephant to keep at his place, but Maya would have nothing to do with Ellie 2.0.

For the next fifteen minutes Letty and Maya searched every corner of the small motel room, but to no avail.

"I want her," Maya sobbed.

Letty tried to remember the last time she'd seen the love-worn stuffed elephant. And then it came to her—last night, when Maya was curled up with Isabelle outside on the breezeway. Maybe Maya had dropped the toy?

She opened the door, but a gust of wind pulled the knob from her grip and blew it all the way open. "Stay here," Letty warned her niece, closing the door behind her. Outside, an inch-deep torrent of rain—overflow from a nearby stopped-up gutter—gushed past, carrying leaves and twigs, cigarette butts and a stray coral-colored hibiscus blossom. But there was no sign of the elephant.

Grimacing, she waded out the door and down the breezeway. At the end of the concrete walk she spotted a telltale lump of gray with a gold-studded red leatherette collar wedged up against a large plastic trash bin.

Rainwater streamed from the sodden stuffed animal.

Maya was standing right inside the doorway, sucking her thumb when Letty returned. "Look who I found!" Letty said.

"Gimme," Maya said, stretching her arms out for her toy.

Letty shook her head. "Ellie stayed outside in the rain all night and she's soaked. We need to let her dry out."

"Bad Ellie," Maya scolded, shaking her finger at the elephant. "You runned away from me."

Letty fetched a towel and her hair dryer from the bathroom. She held the elephant over the small kitchen sink and did what she could to squeeze out some of the rainwater, then placed her on the towel and began to blot her dry. When she switched on the hair dryer and began running it over the toy, Maya stood right beside her, one hand patting the toy, as if to reassure herself that the elephant would not stray again.

It was slow work. She was running the dryer over the elephant's head when she felt something hard and solid beneath the plush fur covering. She switched off the dryer and examined Ellie closer. Part of the toy's leatherette collar formed a headdress that mimicked the kind worn by circus elephants. Several of the brass studs that decorated the headdress had been lost over the years, but now, she realized, there was something hard beneath the hole left by a missing brass stud located squarely between the elephant's eyes.

Letty fetched her eyebrow tweezers from the bathroom and poked at the hole. There was definitely something there, metal or maybe plastic?

"What you doin', Letty?" Maya asked.

"I'm, uh, fixing Ellie. She's got a boo-boo right here on her head," Letty said.

The rain continued all day. Her plans for grocery shopping followed by a beach day with Maya were put on hold. Instead, they sat on the floor of the motel room and had a peanut-butter-and-jelly-sandwich pretend picnic, followed by watching what seemed like endless episodes of Nick Jr. shows.

At four, Maya yawned and put herself down for a nap.

As soon as she was convinced her niece was sleeping, Letty picked up the still-soggy elephant. She probed again at the object beneath the plush, then retrieved a pair of nail scissors from the bathroom. Working slowly, she moved aside the leatherette harness, then carefully cut a slit in the fabric just large enough to insert her fingers through to extract the object.

The hidden object was small, maybe an inch square, and made of black plastic with what appeared to be a tiny lens in the center.

"My God," Letty breathed, turning the object over in the palm of her hand. Ellie, it seemed, had a secret. And it was yet another of Tanya's secrets, hidden in plain sight.

She glanced over at the bed.

Ellie had been Maya's constant companion since the day she'd received it as a birthday gift. The elephant went wherever Maya went. Always.

"*Oh Tanya,*" Letty thought, placing the camera aside. "*What have you done now?*" After some thought, she texted Isabelle.

Are you busy?

Isabelle's response was immediate.

No! So freaking bored. What's up?

I could use some electronics tech support. And a needle and thread.

Isabelle texted back a series of question marks and a wink emoji.

I'm not so good with tech, but I'll call my friend Sierra. Total computer nerd.

Thanks, Letty texted. She put the phone down and waited. Ten minutes passed.

Sierra's coming over. See you in fifteen.

23

~~~~~~~~

ISABELLE'S FRIEND ARRIVED ON A lime-green Vespa scooter. She shook the rain off her helmet and left it on the chair in the breezeway.

"Hey, Letty, this is Sierra," Isabelle said, ushering the girl into the room.

Sierra was a slight-figured African American girl with enormous dark eyes hidden behind steel-rimmed granny glasses with pink-tinted lenses and hair that had been dyed fuchsia and cropped close to her skull. She wore an oversize army fatigue jacket and had a shiny vinyl backpack slung over one shoulder.

She didn't look old enough to ride a Vespa, or drive a car, Letty thought, but her opinion of the teenager soon changed.

Sierra held the plastic object in the palm of her hand and looked up at Letty.

"It's a nanny cam," she said. "Where'd you find it?"

Letty nodded toward Maya, who was now stretched out on the bed watching *PAW Patrol* with Isabelle, the still-damp and newly mended Ellie tightly tucked beneath her arm.

"It was in Maya's stuffed elephant," Letty said quietly.

"Genius!" Sierra exclaimed. "Who put it there?"

"Maya's mom. My late sister."

"Oh, man. Sorry. Isabelle told me the little girl's mama was dead. So she was spying on someone? Like, literally the nanny?"

"No," Letty said. She checked to see if Maya was listening, but the child was still enraptured by her favorite television program.

"More likely Tanya was spying on her ex. They were fighting over custody of Maya, and things had taken a nasty turn. I'm sure she was trying to get the goods on him."

"So, she didn't tell you the nanny cam was there?"

"I had no idea. My sister . . . liked to have secrets. Any idea how it works?"

Sierra held the camera inches from her nose. "Okay, so the brand name is TriCommCo. I'll have to look them up to see the specs for this camera, but I can tell you most of these things are usually motion and sound activated. Battery operated. Some of 'em have a little flash card, but this one looks like maybe it's Wi-Fi enabled."

"Do you think the camera could have been ruined when Ellie got left out in the rain last night?"

"Only one way to find out," Sierra said.

"So . . . where does the video, or whatever you call it, end up?"

Sierra gave Letty the exasperated look every teenager gives any technically challenged person over the age of twenty. "It's uploaded. Like, to the cloud, or a phone or a laptop."

"And how would I retrieve it?"

"You'd have to hack into her account. And you'd need your sister's phone or laptop. And the username and password."

"Sierra can hack anything," Isabelle said proudly. "She hacked into our school's database to figure out who had the highest GPA."

"I didn't change anybody's grades or anything illegal like that. I just wanted to know, in case our dipshit administration named one of the cool kids valedictorian," Sierra said. "It wasn't me, obviously. I only made a B in AP English."

"And she hacked her boyfriend's phone . . ."

"Ex," Sierra said.

". . . and figured out he was out there on Tinder trolling for cougars," Isabelle said.

Sierra allowed herself a small smirk. "Busted!" She looked over at Letty, whose expression answered her next question. "So, you don't have her phone?"

"No," Letty said, her shoulders slumping.

"Hmm."

Sierra sat down at the postage stamp–size table, unzipped her backpack, and brought out a slim silver laptop. "You've got Wi-Fi here, right?"

Letty nodded and told her the name of the network— "'MURMURING SURF,' all caps"—and the password.

Sierra's slender fingers danced over the keyboard with lightning speed. "A lot of people don't bother to come up with a unique username for all their apps and devices. Big mistake, but it happens. Worse than that, lots of times they just leave the factory-set default password on their device. Like, a password that's 1–2–3. How dumb can you get?"

As dumb as me, Letty thought, silently vowing to change the password on every app and device she owned.

"Okay," Sierra said. "I'm on the TriCommCo website." She held the nanny cam next to the laptop. "Looks like this is their most-expensive-model camera, which isn't great news, because the cheapest cameras are usually the ones with the worst security lapses. We need to log on to her TrimComm website and they will ask for verification from her email. Tell me your sister's email address."

"It was Tanyaterrible, all one word, at gmail dot com," Letty said.

Sierra snickered as she typed. "Okay. Let's try obvious passwords in email first. How do you spell the little girl's name? And what's her birthday?"

Letty spelled out the name. "M-A-Y-A. And her birthday is 09–23–2014."

"Nope," Sierra said a moment later. "Too easy. Give me all the clues you can think of. Your sister's birthday, her phone number, street address, nickname?"

"Our grandmother called her Terrible Tanya, that's where her email address came from," Letty said. She supplied three combinations of the other ideas the girl requested, but nothing worked.

"Crap," Sierra said. "We can't try another password, or we'll get locked out of her account. We'll give it forty-eight hours and try again. In the meantime, think about other possibilities like her husband's birthday? Or their anniversary?"

"I'm not sure of either one, but they weren't married, and they were definitely not on friendly terms," Letty said. "So it probably doesn't matter."

"Street where you grew up? Your high school mascot?" Sierra asked. "Any pets?"

"No. Tanya was allergic to cats. We had a beagle when we were kids, named Snoopy, but Evan thought dogs were dirty. He didn't allow pets in any of his properties."

"Wow, what a creep," Sierra said. "Hey, what about an old boyfriend?"

Isabelle overheard the suggestion and sniggered. "Would you use Farber's name as your password?"

"Shut it," Sierra said. "Farbs is dead to me."

"Tomorrow let's try Declan, or Rooney, or both," Letty said.

"Sorry," Sierra said, closing her laptop. She picked up the nanny cam and examined it again. "Would it be okay if I took this and showed it to one of my friends from school?"

Letty hesitated.

"Never mind," Sierra said. She took her phone from a pocket of the backpack and began photographing the camera. "He might not even know anything about nanny cams, but I'll show him these pictures anyway."

"Thanks," Letty said. "In the meantime, I'll keep trying to think of other possibilities for the password."

"Cool." Sierra hitched her backpack over her shoulder and looked around the motel room. "Do you guys actually live here? I mean, like Isabelle and her mom do?"

"For now."

"That's so awesome. We live in a boring old house that looks exactly like everybody else's in the world," Sierra said. "I always wanted to be like those Boxcar Children, you know? Live in an old caboose or something, out in the woods, with just a dog and a bunch of junk you find at the dump."

"Yeah, just as long as the caboose had Wi-Fi and a microwave and cable," Isabelle retorted. "You're so crazy, Sierra." She stood up and ruffled Maya's hair. "Okay, Maya Papaya, gotta go now. See you later, alligator."

Maya rolled over and flashed the babysitter a conspiratorial grin. "After a while, you big fat crocodile!"

24

~~~~~~~~~~~~~~

AVA LOOKED OUT THE PLATE-GLASS window of the motel office and sighed. Letty followed her gaze. It was Monday morning and Sheila Bronson and her daughter were loading luggage into the cargo hold of a silver minivan.

"I sure hate to see them go like this," Ava said. "Sheila is worried sick about making that long drive home so soon after Harry got out of the hospital."

"You'd think their daughter could help her talk sense into him," Letty said.

"No. Once a man that age has his mind made up, you can't talk him out of nothin'."

Sheila Bronson leaned up against the registration desk. Her face was pink and slick with perspiration. "I guess that's it then," she said, placing the key with the plastic tag on the glass-topped counter. "I'm sorry to leave you in the lurch like this, Ava. Harry wanted me to ask you to refund us for the six weeks' rent left for our unit, but I told him no. It's his own damn fault we're leaving early."

Ava grasped Sheila's hand in hers. "I appreciate that. You all take care driving home, and let us know how things are going after Harry sees his regular doctor up there. We'll all be thinking about you."

A horn beeped from outside. Sheila swiped at a tear rolling down her cheek. "I better get going before he gives himself another heart attack."

"Bye, Sheila," Letty said, going around the counter to hug the older woman, who squeezed her tightly.

Five minutes later, Merwin Maples was standing at the registration desk. "Ava, since the Bronsons have moved out, Trudi and I want their old unit. Trudi's already started packing up our stuff, so as soon as you get Anita in there to clean it, we can be ready to move over there."

"Sorry, Merwin, but the Bronsons' unit is already spoken for," Ava said pleasantly.

"What's that? Spoken for by who? That's outrageous. Trudi and I have been coming here longer than anyone else here at the Surf. We should have first priority."

"That's actually not how it works around here. I'll let you know if anything else comes available, but in the meantime, maybe you better tell Trudi she can stop packing."

Letty waited until he'd stomped angrily out of the office. "Wow. He didn't even wait an hour before coming in here to demand the Bronsons' unit. And Harry is his best buddy. That's what I call cold."

"He's used to getting his way," Ava said. "But unfortunately for Merwin, I'm not so easy to bulldoze anymore."

Letty craned her neck to see the Murmuring Surf sign out by the road. "Who did you rent the Bronsons' unit to? I didn't even see the vacancy sign lit up until just now."

"I thought I'd move you and Maya over there," Ava said. "After all, it's paid for until after Easter, and that little efficiency you're in is way too small a space for you to be trying to raise a child. The good news is, since you cleared out the old storage room and it's a viable room again, I can easily rent it at market rate."

A slow smile spread over Letty's face. "For real? You'd let us move into the Bronsons' unit? That place is twice the size of ours."

"You've earned it," Ava said. "I honestly don't know how I've been running this place all this time without you. I called Anita, and she's going to come in early today to turn their unit. You should be able to move over there this afternoon."

"But what about Merwin? Won't he be pissed you're letting me have the Bronsons' room?"

"You let me worry about that old goat," Ava said. "In the meantime, why don't you run back over to your place and take some photos of it all neatened up and cute? The sooner we get it listed on our website, the sooner I can get it rented for the rest of the season. I'm always getting inquiries from singles who want a smaller, cheaper efficiency."

Letty rolled her suitcase across the threshold of unit 11, stopped, and exhaled. The tile floor sparkled and smelled of Pine-Sol. She was standing in the combined living and dining room, which held a sofa, armchair, and coffee table, as well as a table with four wooden chairs. A counter-height bar separated the dining area from the compact kitchen alcove, with a full-size refrigerator, stove, and dishwasher. On the other side of the room, an open pocket door revealed the bedroom, with a queen-size bed, a double dresser, and a closet. She poked her head in the bathroom, which had obviously been updated. The white tile floor gleamed, as did the combined tub and shower.

"Look, Letty," Maya said, pointing to the far side of the bedroom, where a small rollaway bed was made up with fresh linens and a pink flowered bedspread. "That's where I sleep!" She ran to the bed and placed Ellie on the pillow. "Ellie sleeps here too!"

The very best aspect of their new home was a set of sliding glass doors that let out on a tiny courtyard garden.

Letty opened the sliders and stepped out onto the courtyard. The space held a pair of wrought-iron patio chairs with a small table between them, but every other inch of free space was a lush green garden.

Harry Bronson's hobby was in full flower. A pair of tall potted palms were planted on either side of the low garden gate, and other pots held blooming hibiscus plants, a fragrant gardenia shrub, and feathery ferns. Huge staghorn ferns grew from boards that had been hung on the fence, which was nearly covered with sweet-smelling jasmine. Pots of blooming white and pink orchids hung from the low branches of a shade tree. There was a dwarf citrus tree whose limbs drooped with almost ripe lemons, and there were terra-cotta pots growing parsley and chives, and cherry tomatoes in various stages of ripening.

"You like it?" Ava stood in the doorway with a bundle of fresh towels in her arms.

"I can't believe we get to live here," Letty said, gesturing toward the patio. "I didn't even know we had a space like this."

"We've got three courtyard units, but this is by far the nicest. And that's because of Harry. He grew a lot of these plants from seed in his greenhouse back home, and the rest he bought at a nursery down here. Every year he added something new." Ava pointed to a small concrete birdbath in the shape of a seahorse in the right corner of the garden. "He just bought that birdbath last month."

"I've never had a garden before," Letty said. "Unless you count a Chia Pet. I don't know how to take care of any of this. What if I kill it all?"

"You won't." Ava handed her two sheets of paper. "Harry left you detailed instructions. I'm not supposed to tell you this, but it was his idea to move you over here. He knew some of the others would be lining up to get this unit, and he thought you and Maya should have it. He didn't say as much, but I think this is his way of thanking you for saving his life."

"I didn't save his life," Letty protested. "Joe's the one who got the ambulance here, and the doctors at the hospital did the rest. All I did was give him some aspirin."

Ava arched an eyebrow. "Are you saying you don't want this place after all?"

"No! I mean, yes, I want it, but I don't exactly deserve it. That's all I'm saying. And thank you. Thanks so much, Ava."

"You're welcome. Just don't kill the lemon tree, okay? I count on those for my iced tea."

Letty uploaded the last of the photos of the efficiency unit onto the Murmuring Surf's website and allowed herself a tiny, self-congratulatory pat on the back. Even she had to admit the efficiency had undergone an amazing transformation. She'd convinced Ava to replace the nasty old shag carpet with a boring but unobjectionable indoor-outdoor carpet that *almost* looked like seagrass. With Ava's permission she'd painted the battered dresser and the mismatched nightstands with a homemade chalk paint she'd created with a quart of flat turquoise enamel mixed with non-sanding grout mix from the hardware store.

Letty had "borrowed" from Maya's stash of seashells and hot-glued them in a mosaic pattern around the frame of the dresser mirror.

Then she'd raided the motel's linen supply and found four white cotton chenille bedspreads, and used clip-on curtain rings to transform three of them into drapes, while the fourth bedspread was actually used for its intended purpose.

There wasn't much she could do with the dated dusty-pink bathroom except scrub the tile and style the photos with a pile of folded towels on top of the closed commode and a vase of hot-pink hibiscus blossoms plonked into a water glass on the sink.

"Okay, done!" she said, closing the lid on the laptop.

She poured herself a glass of wine and took it out to her new patio garden. Isabelle and Maya were baking cookies together at Ava's, so she had a rare and precious hour all to herself.

If she turned her chair in just the right position, she could see a patch of the Gulf through the row of palm trees lining the Murmuring Surf's swath of beach. The sky was the color of an orange Creamsicle, and tourists were perched in chairs at intervals along the sand, awaiting the nightly sunset ritual.

It was a ritual Letty could get used to, sitting in her private little paradise, with the smell of jasmine and gardenias and a tiny plot of velvety grass beneath her bare feet. Today, as the last of her clothes were folded and placed in the dresser, and her toothbrush and Maya's were lined up on the bathroom sink, it occurred to Letty that she was finally in a good place.

Maya seemed happy. The meltdowns and night terrors were fewer and farther between, and the new routine—working along-side Letty in the mornings, then spending late afternoons with Isabelle—seemed to suit her.

Letty liked her job, liked the feeling that she had something to contribute to here. She'd grown fond of her employer, and of her daughter, and even the regulars seemed to grudgingly accept her presence at the Murmuring Surf. Maybe, she thought, she could relax here, let down her guard, live in the moment.

Out of the corner of her eye, she saw a familiar figure strolling down toward the beach, fishing rod in one hand, with a cast net looped over his shoulder and a bait bucket in the other hand.

There was no way Joe DeCurtis could see her here, through the tangle of greenery, but just in case, she slumped lower in her chair. He was dressed in a long-sleeved white T-shirt that clung to his mus-cled back, and baggy neon-orange board shorts. Joe planted the butt of the fishing rod in the sand, then waded out into the surf. He held one edge of the weighted net between his teeth, then folded a sec-tion of the net over his outstretched right arm. While she watched, fascinated, he grabbed the weight line with his right hand, reached back, and flung the net out in an elliptical arc. After fifteen seconds, he drew the net in, wriggling with hundreds of minnows flashing silver in the fading sunlight.

He made a handsome sight, silhouetted against the glittering tur-quoise water. A postcard: WELCOME TO FLORIDA.

She heard a ping coming from inside the apartment and got up to fetch her phone.

It was a text from Zoey.

Girl—I hope you're okay. A lawyer came here today, looking to see if I knew where you're at. I acted dumb and said I hadn't heard from you, but don't think she bought it. She says she's your sister's lawyer and needs to talk to you. Wouldn't say what it's about. Here's her card. Take care, you hear?

The next text message contained a screenshot of a business card.

Samiya Chritesh, attorney-at-law. There was a phone number and an email address. Written in neat block letters on the bottom of the card was a note.

Ms. Carnahan. I represent your late sister's estate. It's urgent that I speak with you. Please call.

25

~~~~~~~~~~~~

LETTY DIDN'T KNOW WHETHER TO laugh or cry. Tanya had an estate? She didn't recognize the lawyer's name, but knew this Samiya woman was not the attorney who'd represented her sister in her custody battle with Evan.

She'd met that lawyer, a sharp-eyed older man recommended by one of Tanya's Mommy-and-me friends, when she'd been deposed in the court fight.

Was this some kind of trick? Letty typed the name Samiya Chritesh into the computer's search engine.

A moment later, she was reading the woman's online biography. Graduated top of her class at Northwestern, NYU law school, sole practitioner at Samiya Chritesh LLC, specializing in trusts and estate planning.

Letty studied the photo accompanying the bio—of a thirty-something woman with smooth brown skin dressed in a sedate lawyer-lady blazer—and realized she'd met her before.

Could this be Sammi? Tanya's yoga friend? That was how both sisters always categorized Tanya's eclectic roster of friends and acquaintances. There was Vida, no last name, her modeling-agency friend; and Heather and Jenn and Portia and Liza, her ex-friends, because they were married to Evan's friends; and Demetria, her nutritionist, whom she'd met through Portia, but who'd stayed loyal to Tanya because Demetria wasn't married to any of Evan's friends. And then there was Sammi.

Letty had steadfastly resisted Tanya's pleas to accompany her to yoga class, because she didn't want to become a clichéd yoga-practicing kombucha-drinking Manhattanite, but she'd once, in a moment of weakness, agreed to meet Tanya and a new friend for coffee after class.

At the time, she'd been instantly intimidated by Sammi, so sleek in her Lululemons, her glossy dark hair totally unmussed, even after an hour of what Tanya described as "excruciating" hot yoga. Letty hadn't known that she was a lawyer.

Letty paced around the living area, debating the pros and cons. She went back out to the patio, watched the sun sink lower toward the horizon, watched Joe DeCurtis, patiently casting and recasting his line again and again. He was a man who didn't give up, she concluded.

It was nearly dusk when she picked up her phone. First, she tapped *67, to hide her own number. Then she called the number on Samiya Chritesh's business card. She'd expected the call to go directly to voice mail, had even practiced the message she'd leave, but was startled to hear a voice at the other end of the line.

"Hello. This is Samiya. Who's calling please?"

Letty was momentarily stunned into silence. "Um, this is Letty Carnahan. Tanya's sister."

"Oh! Oh my goodness. Letty. I didn't think you'd call."

"I didn't think so either," Letty admitted. "My friend texted that you need to talk? What's so urgent?"

"Where are you? Is Maya with you? Is she all right?"

"Maya's fine. You don't need to know where we are. Have you talked to Evan?"

"I've talked to his lawyer. Very unpleasant man. But I don't represent Evan. I represent your sister Tanya, or your sister's estate."

"What does that even mean?" Letty asked. "Are you telling me Tanya actually had a will? Because I find that hard to believe."

"Yes, of course she did," Sammi said. She paused. "Oh, I see what you're getting at. You're right. Tanya was a free spirit, wasn't she? But when she found out the kind of law I practice, she asked me if she should have a will. And I told her, as the parent of a small child, especially because she was not married to that child's father, she should definitely do some estate planning."

"And Tanya did as you suggested?" Letty was still unconvinced.

There was a long silence at the other end of the phone.

"Did Tanya ever tell you anything about me?" Sammi asked.

"Not really. I know that you met at yoga."

"We didn't meet at yoga," Sammi said finally. "We met at AA. I mentioned one night that yoga really helped, when I was trying to become sober, and afterward, your sister asked me about yoga. She joined the studio I attend. That's where we became friendly."

"Is that allowed?"

Sammi's laugh was low and throaty. "Of course. When we met, we were both struggling. Tanya helped me as much as I helped her. I was grateful, so I agreed to assist with some legal matters."

"I just . . ." Letty was at a loss for words. "Did she talk to you about Evan, about her fears, for herself and for Maya?"

"She did," Sammi said. "I'm sorry, Letty. Sorry for your loss. And even sorrier that I couldn't do something to save your sister."

"You know Evan did this, right?"

"From what Tanya told me, yes, it seems he must bear some responsibility. I know Tanya was desperate because she did not want him to have custody of the child. And she was insistent that he wanted to harm her. I thought, well, to be honest, I suspected she was overreacting. Your sister was very . . . theatrical in that respect."

"'Theatrical.' That's a good word to describe Tanya. She was that in almost all respects," Letty said bitterly. "But this one awful time, she was right to be worried."

"I still can't believe she's gone," Sammi said. "We'd meet for coffee—well, I had coffee, she had that vile herbal tea—about once a week, at the same place where you and I met that time. I still go, after yoga. And every time I walk in, I expect to see her waving at me from the corner table, calling 'Yoo-hoo! Sammi!'"

"You said you needed to talk about Tanya's estate," Letty said,

interrupting. She was still paranoid about using this phone, paranoid about talking to anyone at all about her sister.

"All right. I see your point. Tanya did have a will. She named you
as a secondary beneficiary, and Maya's legal guardian. The will is
very specific on that point. All of her assets are to be put into a trust
for Maya, until she reaches the age of twenty-one."

"What assets are we talking about?" Letty asked. "I mean, Evan
owned the brownstone she was living in, and supported her. She had
some nice clothes and jewelry, but that's it. Right?"

"Not quite," Sammi said with a slight chuckle. "She had quite
a large life insurance policy. Three million dollars. Again, Maya is
the primary beneficiary, but those funds will be held in a trust. As it
turns out, there were other assets too. A large ring? Do you know
about that?"

"Yes." Letty left it at that.

"The ring is to be sold, and the funds distributed to you," Sammi
said. "And then, of course, there's the real estate."

"Excuse me?"

"Your late sister holds title to several parcels of extremely valuable residential real estate properties in Tribeca, the East Village, and
Brooklyn."

"You mean, Evan owns them," Letty said.

"Actually, there are seven apartments, including the one where
Tanya resided, that were purchased over the past three years, by an
LLC controlled by Evan Wingfield. It appears that he then transferred title of the entities to your sister, while they were still domestic partners," Sammi said. "Strictly a tax dodge on his part."

Another long pause.

"Letty? Are you still there?"

"I'm here," Letty said finally. "I'm just floored. I knew about the
ring, of course, because she showed it to me when Evan gave it to
her, after Maya was born, but did Tanya know about the real estate?
She never mentioned it to me, and we talked all the time."

"As far as I know, she wasn't aware of the real estate," Sammi

said. "I only discovered it myself after I began the process of pro-
bate. All of this is complicated, as you might guess, by the nature of
Tanya's death."

"You mean her murder," Letty said. "Evan murdered Tanya."

Letty couldn't stop thinking about Declan Rooney, the con man
whose deep blue eyes were the same distinctive shade as Maya's.
"Did Tanya ever hint to you that Evan wasn't the father of her child?"
she asked.

"No!" Sammi said sharply. "Are you telling me that Evan isn't
Maya's father?"

"I'm not telling you anything," Letty said. "As you've already
noted, Tanya was complicated. She liked secrets and she was really
good at keeping them."

Sammi exhaled loudly. "Let's set that aside for a moment, please.
Evan's attorney has notified me that he'll fight any attempt by the
estate to claim those real estate assets. What I need from you . . ."

"No," Letty said. All this talk about Evan Wingfield was making
her feel panicky and cornered. "I can't talk about this, Sammi. You
do what you have to do. But you can't tell anyone that we talked. Especially Evan. You have no idea what he's capable of. This isn't just
about me. It's about Maya. If something happens to me, Evan will
get custody of Maya."

"Wait," Sammi said.

She heard voices approaching outside, from the breezeway. Maya
burst in, holding a foil-lined shoebox in both hands, followed by Isabelle.

"Lookit, Letty," Maya crowed. "Cookies!"

Letty disconnected the call.

26

~~~~~~~~~~~~~~~~

"GOOD NEWS," AVA SAID, AS Letty settled herself behind the registration desk on Wednesday. "I've booked your old room."

"Already? That was fast." Letty sat Maya down at her table, and unpacked her crayons and markers and the new reading workbook Isabelle had bought for her, and the child went right to work.

"Those photos of yours did the trick," Ava said. "I'm thinking, when it slows down in the fall, or maybe sooner, right after the spring breakers leave, I'll get you to style and photograph all the rooms. You could sprinkle some seashells around and freshen things up. I bet I could raise prices by at least ten percent, and nobody would even notice."

"Merwin would notice," Letty said. "But Ava, about fall . . ."

Ava waved away her objections. "I realize, you said you weren't sure if you'd hang around 'til then, but I'm just gonna pretend I didn't hear that. You know, with Isabelle going off to college in August, I'll need all the extra help I can get around here."

Letty nodded in Maya's direction. "Can we talk about this later, please?"

"Oh. Right. Anyway, we've got a guest checking into the efficiency this evening. She's coming down from New York, and wasn't exactly sure of her arrival time, so I told her if it's after six she can just call my phone and I'll meet her here and check her in."

"How long is she staying for?" Letty asked, pulling up the

Murmuring Surf's booking page on the computer monitor. She clicked over to the page she'd designed for her old unit.

"She paid in advance for four days," Ava said.

Letty frowned. "I thought we had a one-week minimum stay during the season."

"Well, yeah, but since we just added the efficiency, I thought it would be okay to take a shorter stay. Just this once."

Letty shrugged. "You're the boss, but seems to me we'd be better off waiting for the weekend and booking a guest who'll be here at least a week."

"Now you sound like Joe," Ava said. "It's just four days. After this, yes, I'll absolutely apply the one-week minimum stay."

Ruth Feldman was not happy. "Ava, would you please look at this?" She held up a piece of faded and frayed plastic webbing. "Billie sat down on one of the lounge chairs by the pool just now and the thing collapsed. She could have been killed!"

Ruth and Billie were both dressed in their modest one-piece bathing suits and matching terry cover-ups. Ruth's swim goggles were pushed on top of her still-damp steel-gray hair.

"Oh Lord," Ava said. "I'm sorry, Billie. Are you okay?"

Billie Feldman turned around and displayed a mildly scraped ankle. "It could have been much worse," she said. "I managed to catch myself or I might have broken a hip or something."

"Okay," Ava said. "Thanks for letting me know." She looked over at Letty. "Could you please go over to the pool and drag the broken lounger over to the dumpster? I don't want anyone else getting hurt."

"We already took care of that," Ruth said. "But Ava, the webbing on all those chairs is in the same condition. You need to do something before someone gets seriously injured."

"I will," Ava promised.

Maya peeked around the corner of the reception desk and gave a shy wave to the two older women.

"Hello there, young lady," Billie said, leaning down. "What are you working on today?"

"I write my name," Maya said. She held up the workbook sheet where she'd laboriously traced the letters of her name, and then wrote the letters freehand, wobbly, but legible.

"Look at that, Ruthie," Billie said, pointing to the worksheet. "Isn't that good? And she's what? Five years old?"

Maya held up her hand with her thumb tucked behind her palm. "I'm four. How old are you?"

Ruth snorted. "She's seventy-two. Eleven months younger than me."

"My birthday is in September. And I will be five and I will go to big-girl school. When is your birthday?"

"Actually, Ruth's birthday is next week," Billie volunteered. "But we're both all done with big-girl school, thank God."

"Will you have birthday cake?"

"No," Ruth said quickly. "Grown-ups don't have birthday cake."

"I'm sorry," Maya said politely. "You can come to *my* birthday party and have some of *my* cake."

"Awww," Billie said. "That's the sweetest thing I ever heard of." She nudged her wife. "Isn't that sweet? Maya invited us to her birthday party."

Ruth managed a smile. "That is sweet. Thank you, Maya." She turned to Billie. "Okay, time to hit the pool again."

"I like to go swimming," Maya said.

Billie nudged Ruth, who gave her a questioning look.

"Letty," Billie said. "Would it be all right if Maya went swimming in the pool with us for a while? We'd be very careful. You know, I used to be a Red Cross lifesaving instructor."

Letty could hardly believe the offer on the table. "Really? That's awfully kind, but I wouldn't want her to interrupt your lap swimming."

"We did our laps earlier," Billie said. "It'll be fun to have an excuse to just splash around. Won't it, Ruthie?"

"I suppose," Ruth said.

"Obviously, Maya would love to take you up on your offer," Letty said. "If you're serious, I'll just run her back to our place and get her bathing suit and towel. And I'll meet you at the pool. Okay?"

"Yes! Swimmy, swimmy, swimmy," Maya said, hopping up and down with excitement. She grabbed her aunt's hand. "Letty, hurry. I want to go swimming."

"That sounds fine," Ruth said stiffly. "We'll see you at the pool."

"Will wonders ever cease," Ava said, as soon as the older women left the office. "Ruth came this close to cracking a smile at Maya just now."

"I'm glad you were a witness, because I wasn't sure if it was a smile or just gas."

"See, they're really not that awful, once you get to know them," Ava said. "Now you better get Maya over there before Ruth changes her mind. When you get back, let's talk about ordering some replacement lounge chairs."

Bad news," Letty told her boss when she returned to the office. "Ruth was right. Every single one of those loungers is on its last legs. All the webbing is rotted out. And if one of the oldsters does fall through one and get injured, I'm afraid we'll have a lawsuit on our hands."

Ava smiled at Letty's use of the word "our" but didn't make mention of it. She pointed to the computer screen, where she'd been pricing lounge chairs from a commercial furniture company.

"Those don't look much better than what you've got now," Letty said. "What about something a little sturdier? Like cast aluminum, or better yet, teak?"

"Like this?" Ava scrolled down to a photo of a grouping of teak outdoor furniture. "See the price of them?"

"Wow. Twelve hundred dollars?"

"And that's wholesale. And it doesn't include cushions," Ava said.

Letty was reading the product description. "Plus, the delivery time is at least six weeks. We'll have a mutiny on our hands if we don't have lounge chairs for the pool. Couldn't we just buy something locally?"

"There's that factory-outlet patio place up on US 19 in Clearwater," Ava said. "I've never been in there. . . ."

"I see their television commercials all the time," Letty said. "Maybe we should check it out."

"Agreed. And I'm putting you in charge of this little project," Ava said. "You could run up there now. If you see something that will work, go ahead and buy it."

"Really? You trust me to make a big decision like that? We need what? At least a dozen chairs?"

"Make it sixteen," Ava said. "I'm tired of listening to guests bickering over who gets the 'good' chairs. Price out some drinks tables to go between the loungers while you're there. You can take pictures of what you've chosen and text me. Okay?"

Letty glanced out the window.

"Don't worry about Maya," Ava said, anticipating Letty's concern. "I'll walk over there in an hour, get her into some dry clothes, and feed her lunch. Isabelle will be home from school around one, and then she can take over."

"You're the boss," Letty said.

"Stop somewhere and buy yourself a nice lunch," Ava said, handing her a credit card. "It's on me."

Letty sat under an umbrella on the patio of a French bistro just up the beach road from the Murmuring Surf, and after her lunch arrived—steamed stone crab claws with a tangy mustard sauce and a crisp green salad—she sat very still for a moment, feeling alternate waves of guilt and giddiness.

It was, she thought, the first real restaurant meal she'd eaten alone since that awful Sunday afternoon back in New York. She picked up the tiny fork provided by the café and nibbled at the sweet crabmeat, savoring the opportunity to taste her food, rather than wolf it down in order to help feed her niece.

Meals with Maya were simple affairs: cereal, peanut butter and jelly sandwiches, grapes or strawberries or orange slices, spaghetti, chicken fingers, steamed carrots or broccoli, hot dogs or hamburgers, and her default dinner choice, grilled cheese sandwiches and tomato or chicken noodle soup.

It wasn't as if she'd never spent time with her niece, or fed her or taken her places, while Tanya was alive, but living with and raising a four-year-old required a vast adjustment, both in her standards and her attitudes.

As she sipped her iced tea she once again pondered the issue of Maya's future—and hers. According to Tanya's lawyer, her sister's estate had the potential to provide security for Maya—but only if Evan didn't sue to retain control of the property he'd placed in Tanya's name.

She was positive that Evan would also fight to keep Letty from becoming Maya's legal guardian—unless, maybe? She could prove that Evan wasn't Maya's biological father. And that Evan had murdered Tanya. To do that, she'd need to stay out of jail.

Letty had already vowed that she wouldn't return to New York until she could prove her own innocence—and be sure that Maya wouldn't be placed either with Evan or in foster care.

Foster care was the dark, terrifying bogeyman in any consideration of what would become of Maya. Letty and Tanya had agreed, long ago, never to speak again about their own experience in foster care.

A month—thirty days—was all they'd spent living in a foster home in West Virginia. It happened the summer they were thirteen and fourteen. Terri's latest boyfriend, a mean drunk who was also a local sheriff's deputy, had confiscated Tanya's Game Boy, after she'd flunked summer school. Tanya had persuaded Letty to run away with her. After stealing the Greyhound bus fare from Terri's purse, they'd gotten as far as Paducah, Kentucky, before the bus driver, sensing trouble, called the authorities, who in turn called Terri.

When they returned home, Terri's boyfriend told the local child welfare authorities that the two girls were ungovernable, wildly out of control, and petty thieves.

Thirty days. They'd spent the time living with a sour-faced older couple, Mr. and Mrs. Boggs, who dragged them to a fundamentalist church three times a week. They weren't allowed to attend the local school, which the couple considered "ungodly," and instead were forced to work in the couple's garden for hours in blazing heat. Tanya had taken a beating when she refused to give up her beloved pierced earrings. It wasn't until they'd managed to call their grandmother one night, when the couple was out of the house, that they'd been returned home to Terri, who reluctantly kicked her boyfriend to the curb.

Maya, Letty vowed, would never go through what she and Tanya had endured.

The server brought her check and offered her a to-go cup of iced tea. Remembering her own not-so-long-ago waitress days, Letty left a big tip and headed off to the patio-furniture clearance center.

She wandered around the enormous showroom in a daze. There were more picnic tables and umbrellas, lounge chairs, swivel chairs, sectionals that seated twelve, entire outdoor kitchens, and firepits than she'd ever seen in one place. The selection was overwhelming.

Finally, she found a display of lightweight but sturdy aluminum-frame lounge chairs. They had heavy plastic strapping in pastel-candy shades of yellow, coral, aqua, mint, and pink, almost the exact colors of the units at the Murmuring Surf. She flipped the tag on one of the chairs and winced. They were 150 dollars apiece.

"Too much," she muttered, anticipating her employer's reaction to such a hefty price tag.

Just around the corner from that display she found the warehouse's Last Chance clearance center. Shoved in the corner were two stacks of the same chairs she'd just spotted—but in an unfortunate shade of brown. A bright orange starburst sticker was handlabeled with the price. Eighty-five dollars. She found a salesman and asked about delivery options, then texted photos of the chairs to Ava.

"My God, those are ugly," Ava said, when she called back. "But I guess they'll do. When can they deliver?"

"Not until next Monday," Letty said. "And there's a pretty hefty delivery fee."

"I'll call Joe," Letty said. "He's off this afternoon. Can you hang around there until he arrives?"

"Is that necessary?" Letty asked. She wasn't looking forward to seeing Joe this soon again after their awkward parting on the beach. "I should probably get back to Maya."

"Maya's right here, stringing beads with Isabelle. Please just wait for Joe and make sure those folks load everything you've bought."

Joe pulled the truck up to the clearance center's loading dock, where Letty was waiting.

"These?" He pointed at the stacks of lounge chairs on a shipping cart. "You bought these butt-ugly chairs for the Surf? Has Ava seen them?"

"Yes," Letty said. "I texted her a photo. They're half the price of the pretty ones, so she said to go ahead and buy them."

"No," Joe said flatly. He gestured to the stock clerk who was standing by, waiting to help load the chairs. "Take these back inside, please. We've changed our minds."

The guy in overalls shrugged and grabbed the cart.

"Please don't do that," Letty said. The guy retreated to the far side of the loading dock.

Her carefully controlled temper flared. "What the hell do you think you're doing? They're ugly, but they're sturdy, and they're all we can afford. Your mom approved those chairs. I've already put them on her credit card."

He bounded up the steps to the loading platform and grabbed her by the elbow. "Lesson one in dealing with Ava DeCurtis. She always thinks cheaper is better. That's why we ended up with those crappy broken-ass chairs we've got now. Some guy came by with a truckload of 'em and made her a deal she couldn't refuse."

Letty wrenched her arm away from him. "I'm not getting in the middle of an argument between you and your mom. She's my boss, not you. And anyway, I don't appreciate your second-guessing me."

Joe pointed at the mud-colored loungers. "If you owned the Surf, would you want potential guests seeing those when they pulled up to the motel?"

"Well . . ."

"Aren't you the one urging Ava to bump up the room rates so she can spend a little money on updating and improving the place?"

"The other chairs cost twice as much as these," Letty argued. "That's a big investment."

Joe crossed his arms over his chest and shook his head.

"What?"

"Are you fighting with me because you disagree, or because you're still pissed at me for kissing you the other night?"

She felt the blood rising in her cheeks, but ignored his taunt. "There's a right and a wrong way to be right, you know."

"Huh?" He glanced over at the warehouse worker, who rolled his eyes and sniggered.

"Maybe you could stop being Joe the cop and Joe the authority on everything and try thinking about your approach to other people," Letty said.

"That makes no sense."

The sun was beating down on her head, and the store guy was now stretched out on top of the stack of loungers, making no effort to hide the fact that he was vastly amused by the heated exchange he was witnessing.

Exasperated, she threw her hands in the air. "Okay. I give up. You're right. These chairs are hideous. So I'm wrong. But you're an asshole. Every day I get another chance at being right, but tomorrow and the day after that? You'll still be an asshole."

Letty flipped the credit card toward Joe, but it fell to the concrete loading dock. "There are plenty of these same chairs in pastel colors inside. You want pretty chairs at twice the price, be my guest. I'm done here."

The warehouse worker scrambled to his feet and stopped her as she was about to leave the loading dock. "Uh, ma'am? Does your husband want these chairs or not?"

"That man," Letty said, through clenched teeth, "is *not* my husband."

27

"HOW WAS YOUR FLIGHT?"

Vikki Hill looked up from scribbling something illegible on the registration book. "Okay. They put me in the middle seat between two smelly old men. And they didn't serve any food. Not even a lousy Biscoff cookie."

"That's terrible," the motel manager said. "I can recommend some local restaurants if you're hungry. Do you like seafood?"

"Not particularly." Vikki Hill looked around the office. It was cluttered in the way of a business that had been around for a while. Racks of brochures for tourists. A shelf full of well-thumbed paperback books with a sign that said NEED ONE? READ ONE! There were a pair of cracked plastic chairs on the wall by the front door.

The manager was older, matronly, wearing a bright pink polo with the motel's logo stitched over the breast. Her name badge said MURMURING SURF. MANAGER. AVA DECURTIS.

Vikki tried not to stare. DeCurtis wasn't a common name. She had to be related to the cop.

"There's a really good pizza place just up the beach road," Ava said. "Even our guests from New York say it's good pizza. Gianni's." She pushed a pamphlet-size booklet across the counter. "There's a coupon for a free drink in here. If you're too tired to go out, they deliver."

"Thanks," Vikki said. "I am kind of beat."

"Can I ask you a question? How did you find us?"

"Why?"

Ava's face flushed. "Well, uh, you know, we mostly get repeat business here this time of year. I mean, we hope our website is drawing in new business, but I'm always trying to improve. For instance we just redid the unit you're staying in. So I was wondering if you found us through one of the search engines, or. . . ."

"I thought the name sounded cute. Murmuring Surf. Like an old song or something." Vikki looked over the manager's shoulder. An open door behind her led to an office and storage area. And there was a small red child-size table and chair in an alcove directly behind the reception desk. But no sign of a child, or the child's aunt.

"It was called that when we bought the place," Ava said. "My ex thought it sounded cute too. I wasn't too sure, but you wouldn't believe what it costs to get a new neon sign. Even back then. So we kept the name. It's grown on me over the years. And of course, our regulars like it. They hate change. If I so much as bring in a new kind of coffee maker in the kitchens, they raise hell about it."

"You've owned this place for a while then?"

"Oh yeah. Over thirty-five years. What kind of work do you do, Ms. Hill?"

"Nothing too exciting. I'm a civil servant. I punch a clock."

"Just looking for a little sunshine, huh? I bet it's still cold back up north. I'll tell you, I don't miss those winters."

"Yeah, it's nasty cold," Vikki said. The sun was starting to go down. There was a large palm tree in the middle of the courtyard, and she could see a small group of people gathering there in lawn chairs. "What's going on out there?"

The manager craned her neck to see. "Oh, that's just the happy hour group. I don't allow smoking anywhere else on the property, but they'll gather out there and have a drink. Strictly BYOB. You're welcome to join them. I can introduce you."

"Maybe later," Vikki said vaguely. She picked up her key. "My room is where?"

"Right down at the end of the breezeway," Ava DeCurtis said. "Turn left when you walk out the door here. Let me know if there's anything you need. And welcome to the Murmuring Surf."

The room was nothing to write home about. It was clean, though, and there was a palm tree right outside her door. She stripped off the heavy black sweater and jeans she'd worn on the plane. It was seventy-two degrees outside, and she'd been roasting since she stepped out of the airport in Tampa.

Telling herself she needed to canvass the area, she dressed in shorts and a T-shirt, and put on the rubber flip-flops she'd bought at the airport gift shop, and a pair of oversize sunglasses.

She walked toward a strip of palm trees that divided the motel property from the beach. There was a row of lounge chairs facing the water, and just beyond were the sparkling turquoise waters of the Gulf of Mexico.

Vikki Hill gasped. She'd been to the beach, lots of times, mostly the Jersey Shore back home. But this was different. She left her shoes on the grass and walked out onto the sugary white sand, letting her toes sink into it. The water was like a magnet. She drew closer, stopping to study the waves lapping at the shore. Huh. She ventured closer, bracing herself for the shock of cold, but the water was surprisingly warm. She wiggled her toes, and something beneath them wiggled back. She stooped down to see that there were millions of tiny multicolored clamlike seashells strewn along the waterline. She smiled despite herself.

"They're called coquinas." She jumped, startled. An elderly man, shriveled and bald with skin like an old Samsonite suitcase, stood only a foot away on the hard-packed sand. His white T-shirt was shrunken with age and he wore baggy knee-length shorts, black socks that came to his mid-calves, and white tennis shoes.

"Excuse me?"

"Those shells you're looking at. They're co-qui-nas." He pronounced it slowly, like she was hard of hearing, or stupid, or both.

"Huh. So these are like what, babies? Do you eat 'em?"

"Only if you've got a really tiny knife and fork." He guffawed at his own joke, then stuck out his hand as if to shake. "Oscar Jensen. You're new here, aren't you?"

She ignored the outstretched hand. "Yes."

"Just come in, did you?"

"That's right."

"Couldn't pick better weather."

He was a chatty old bastard. So far, everyone she'd encountered down here was overly friendly and super chatty. Annoying. Her usual tendency would have been to blow him off, but since he seemed to be the self-appointed welcome committee here, maybe she should break her own rules.

"The weather's pretty good," she said. "Have you been coming here very long?"

"Oh yeah. Started coming down in the nineties, I guess, me and my wife, Sue. She passed, so now it's just me. We don't get a lot of new folks here at the Surf. All us regulars, we've been coming here for a real long time. I'm guessing you're staying in the efficiency?"

"That's right. How'd you know?"

"Like I said, I know everybody here, and we all always stay in the same place. Until somebody dies or quits coming. I figure you're here because Harry Bronson had a heart attack. Him and the wife headed home Monday, which meant their unit was available. It's one of the nicest ones here, got a great little patio with a Gulf view. Merwin, he thought he and Trudi would move over there, but Ava went and gave it to Letty. So she moved out of the efficiency, which meant that was vacant. See?"

Vikki tried not to act too eager. "Who's Letty?"

"Oh, she's the newcomer. Been here two, three weeks. Her and the little girl. Just showed up out of the blue, looking for a place to stay, so Ava moved her into the efficiency, even gave her a job working in the office."

"Where'd she come from?" Vikki asked.

"I think maybe she said New Jersey? She's all right. Mostly keeps to herself. But it caused kind of a stir, like I said, because it wasn't really fair, Ava giving her that room when it should have been Merwin's. I think Ava felt sorry for her, what with the little kid and everything."

"I see." Vikki nodded. "Well, nice to meet you. Guess I'll go up to the room now."

The pizza at the joint from down the street, she begrudgingly admitted to herself, was half decent. Nice crisp crust, definitely homemade sauce. Who knew they had good pizza in Florida? She was eating a slice, sitting in the chair by the window, watching the happy hour under the palm tree. She figured the median age of the congregants at seventy-five. No sign of anyone who could be Letty Carnahan, or of the kid.

At seven thirty, her phone rang. She smiled and answered.

"Officer DeCurtis. Thanks for getting back to me."

"Sorry for the delay. What's this about?"

"A woman named Scarlett Carnahan. She calls herself Letty. Do you know her?"

There was an extended silence on the other end of the line. While she waited, Vikki picked a pepperoni off the last slice and nibbled at it.

"Why are you asking?"

"She's a fugitive. Wanted for questioning in the murder of a woman in New York, and the abduction of her child. The victim was her own sister."

Another long silence. "You flew down here from New York today and checked into my mother's motel a couple hours ago, right?"

It was Vikki's turn to be surprised. She didn't much like the sensation.

"How'd you know that?"

"I make it my business to know who's staying at the Murmuring Surf. Ever since the incident with Declan Rooney. Your message didn't mention the fact that you were coming down here."

"It was a spur-of-the-moment decision. So, when can we talk?"

"There's a bar just down the beach from the Surf. Called the Ka-Tiki."

"For real?" Vikki asked. "Is the bartender named Don Ho?"

"I can meet you there in an hour," DeCurtis said. "I'm wearing a red Atlanta Braves T-shirt and blue board shorts. How will I know you?"

"I'll be the one not in a Hawaiian shirt," Vikki said. "See you then."

Maya held out a handful of tiny red cherry tomatoes. "Look, Letty!" She crammed one in her mouth, the juice oozing down her chin. "I picked them!"

"They're yummy, right?" her aunt asked.

Their new routine was to sit in the courtyard garden after dinner, watching squadrons of pelicans soar past on the darkening horizon. A wind-down time.

"Where they goin'?" Maya had asked, pointing to the birds in flight.

"I guess they're going home," Letty said.

"Where's home?"

"Good question," her aunt said. She'd been pondering that for weeks now. Living day to day as she had could not continue, but what was the alternative?

Maya picked up her worksheet. She loved playing school. Writing names was her new passion.

"Spell Letty," she commanded.

"L-E-T-T-Y," her aunt said, and Maya laboriously used a red crayon to form her idea of what the letters should be.

"How you spell Ellie?" Maya asked, holding up her stuffed toy.

Letty looked over and smiled. She'd done a sloppy job of stitching the elephant's wound back together, but Maya didn't seem to care.

"E-L-L-I-E." As soon as she'd spelled the word, the light bulb switched on.

"Ellie!" Letty said, sitting upright. Why hadn't she thought of that before? It was so simple. So obvious.

Ellie. It had to be the password for Tanya's nanny cam. She reached for her phone and texted Isabelle's teenage hacker friend, Sierra.

I think I figured out the password!!! Plz call me ASAP.

28

~~~~~~~~~~~~

THE KA-TIKI WAS AN OPEN-SIDED, palm-thatched throwback. *Kinda like the Murmuring Surf,* Vikki Hill thought. She walked into the bar and spotted the cop instantly. He was sitting at a high-top table, sipping a draft beer.

"Joe?" she asked, walking up.

He nodded. "That's me. You're Vikki Hill?"

"Agent Hill," she said, sitting down.

"No offense," he said, "but could I see some ID? This is kind of a sensitive matter we're here to discuss, and I'm not comfortable telling a stranger who walks in off the beach anything about Letty Carnahan."

She pulled a leather badge holder from her purse and handed it across to him. "Satisfied?"

He shrugged.

The server, dressed in skintight shorts and a violently patterned tropical shirt showing off plenty of cleavage, appeared, and Vikki Hill ordered a Michelob Ultra. Joe grimaced and held up his plastic cup. "Try one of the local beers. They're pretty good."

"No thanks," she said. "I know what I like. Now, let's get down to it, shall we? First off, I don't want to have to point out that you're knowingly harboring a fugitive at that motel of yours. I'm meeting with you as a courtesy, but if I want, I can arrest Scarlett Carnahan tonight and turn the kid over to child welfare authorities."

"What the fuck?" Joe leaned forward, his jaw muscles tensed. "I only agreed to talk to you because you said that was not your intention."

"It's still not my intention," Vikki said.

"Then . . . what?"

"Let me talk please," she interrupted. "You know about Scarlett's connection to a man named Evan Wingfield, correct?"

"Correct," Joe said tersely. "Letty worked for him, when she first arrived in New York, right? It wasn't clear to me what her job was."

"Wingfield owns dozens of Airbnb units all over the city. Mostly Manhattan and Brooklyn, and most of them illegal. From what we can tell, he hired Scarlett as a sort of concierge. He put her up in an apartment in a building where he owns several units. Her duties included making sure the Airbnb guests got into his units quietly, without raising attention from the other tenants in the building. At some point, it appears they began a romantic relationship. But after Tanya moved to the city, Wingfield dumped Letty and took up with the younger sister. She moved in with Wingfield and had his kid."

"Maya," Joe said.

"Right. The sisters, naturally, were estranged for a couple years after the kid was born, but then they reconciled—right around the time Wingfield and Tanya broke up. Tanya Carnahan, by all accounts, had some serious substance-abuse issues, a fact that Wingfield tried to use against her when he sued for custody."

"Wingfield and Tanya weren't married, right?" Joe asked.

"Correct. But they were domestic partners, and he was listed as father on the kid's birth certificate."

"Maya," Joe interrupted. "Her name is Maya. I still don't understand how the FBI got involved in all this."

"I'm getting there," Vikki Hill said. "The bureau's public corruption unit has had an ongoing investigation into Evan Wingfield's illegal Airbnb business activities for the past eighteen months, which we initiated after we learned that he'd bribed a New York City housing inspector, as well as two members of the city's zoning appeals board and a city council member. At that point, the bureau sent me in undercover, posing as a new inspector. And within minutes of meeting with me, Wingfield made not-so-subtle references to 'arrangements' he'd made with other inspectors."

"The guy wasted no time," Joe said.

"He's efficient, I'll say that about him. In my subsequent meetings with Wingfield he complained bitterly about his estranged girlfriend and what their custody battle was costing in legal fees," she said. "But he didn't mind the money he spent bribing me with cash, Broadway theater tickets, and trips to Vegas."

"Why didn't you just arrest him then? Maybe Tanya Carnahan would still be alive."

"Because we knew that what we had on him was just the tip of the iceberg. We knew he'd bribed others, he bragged about it to me. But then Tanya started threatening to report him to the feds. Somehow, she knew about me, even knew my name, although she didn't know I was actually undercover law enforcement. We didn't know where she was getting her information. Wingfield was worried. He told me he'd begun thinking of ways to shut her up. . . ."

"And yet you still didn't think it was time to pull the plug?" Joe shook his head. "Christ!"

"The bureau acts at its own speed," Vikki said. "We were getting closer, and then, well, out of the blue, Tanya was killed and her kid vanished."

"Murdered by Evan Wingfield."

"We assume so, yes. He was there that day. Told the detectives they'd argued, but she was alive when he left. He's been proclaiming his innocence very loudly and very publicly. And blaming Letty Carnahan."

"I hope you're not buying that bullshit," DeCurtis said.

"The NYPD is investigating the murder aspect. But we know that Letty was at her sister's brownstone the afternoon Tanya was killed. Witnesses placed her there. Security cameras placed her there. She grabbed the kid, took her sister's car, and fled. Why didn't she come to the police with her suspicions? You gotta admit, the optics aren't good."

"I don't know about the optics," Joe said. "I only know when she arrived here, she was clearly terrified. I was suspicious at first, sure. I'm a cop."

"You knew that authorities were searching for the kid. And you also knew Scarlett Carnahan was wanted for questioning in her sister's death, but you still didn't notify police in New York?" Agent Hill's voice was sharp. "Ever hear of obstruction of justice? Or doesn't that count down here in Florida?"

"I didn't know she was a fugitive at first," Joe said. "That morning she arrived here, all I had was suspicions. Anyway, my mother was not going to turn away a woman with a little kid in tow. As for Letty, we've gotten to know her. My mother trusted her enough to give her a job at the motel. She saved one of our guests' life, when he was having a heart attack. She actually jumped on a meth head I was trying to arrest, kept the woman from cracking my skull with a baseball bat. Take it from me, that woman is not a murderer. She's just not."

"Has she said anything to you about what brought her down here?"

"No," he admitted. "She's intentionally vague about those kind of details, but who can blame her? Anyway, a few days after she arrived I put two and two together. Now I've got a pretty good idea of why she showed up at the Murmuring Surf."

"Agreed," Vikki Hill said. "Once we started looking into Tanya Carnahan's past we found her arrest record. We figured it out by the process of elimination. The sisters were close and there were no other family connections that we could find. In fact, we know that Tanya drew up a will in the months leading up to her death. It names Letty as the child's legal guardian."

Joe sipped his beer. "Have you considered another suspect in Tanya's murder? I mean, other than Letty, or even Wingfield?"

"You mean Declan Rooney? Tanya's old boyfriend? Kind of a

reach, don't you think? I know he's still at large, but what would his motive be for killing her?"

"Money, for one thing. We never recovered any of the jewelry or gold or silver they'd been buying—an estimated hundred and fifty thousand dollars that's never been accounted for. When we arrested Tanya, she claimed Rooney and his partner, Chuck Sheppard, had absconded with all of it," Joe said. "But what if she actually did have the loot—and was supposed to meet up with him but didn't?"

"That's an extremely far-fetched scenario you've cooked up," Agent Hill remarked. "Any proof to back it up?"

"Nope." Joe leaned back on his barstool, his eyes drifting toward a wall-mounted television over the bar. "Is the bureau aware that Evan Wingfield probably isn't the child's biological father?"

"What?" Her voice was sharp. "How can you know something like that?"

"If you saw Maya, especially in person, you'd agree. Declan Rooney had very distinctive, piercing blue eyes and thick black eyelashes. Maya has them too. The resemblance is unmistakable."

"If Tanya knew Wingfield wasn't the baby daddy, why didn't she just tell him that after the breakup, before all the hassles of the custody battle?" Agent Hill demanded.

"Did you ever meet Tanya?" Joe asked. "I did. She and Rooney lived at the motel for two weeks while they were grifting senior citizens. She was a piece of work. Beautiful, loaded with charm and street smarts and as gifted a liar as I've ever met. My guess is that it had to do with money. I mean, Rooney was in the wind, and then she finds out she's pregnant. From what you've told me, Wingfield is rich. Maybe Tanya saw a sugar daddy opportunity and went for it."

"That's an interesting theory, but it's got nothing to do with me," the agent said. "It's not why I came down here."

"Why did you come? As you said, you can arrest Letty Carnahan at any time. What do you want from me?"

Vikki studied him over the rim of her beer. "Letty has a relationship with you and your mother. She trusts you, otherwise she wouldn't have hung around here."

"I'm not sure Letty trusts anybody," he said.

"Okay, here's what I want. Shortly before Tanya was killed, Evan was ranting that he'd deeded over several of his most valuable residential properties, put them in Tanya's name, as a tax dodge. We're talking several million dollars' worth of real estate. And now, with Tanya's death, the property goes to her child. Letty is the child's guardian, which puts her in control of what Wingfield regards as *his* property—meaning both his kid and his real estate."

Joe raised one eyebrow. "You're telling me, what?"

"Wingfield's solution is hiring me. To find Letty, get rid of her, and bring Maya back."

Vikki motioned to the server, pointed at her empty glass, and waited for Joe's reaction.

"You're shitting me," he said finally. "He's put out a hit? On Letty?"

"Afraid so."

Joe pointed at his own empty glass and nodded at the server.

"Let me get this straight. Evan Wingfield hires a woman he thinks is merely a corrupt civil servant—to kill his former girlfriend? I'm sorry. I can't wrap my brain around that. I mean, he bribes you to look the other way when it comes to some illegal apartments, and then next thing you know you're a contract killer? Why would he trust you like that?"

The server set the refills on the table and whisked away the empties. Agent Hill tasted hers and grimaced. "Gross. This is yours. How do guys drink that craft beer shit?"

"How do you drink those piss-weak sorority beers?" Joe countered.

She pushed the plastic cup away. "Never mind. Look. I've been dealing with Wingfield for eighteen months, flattering him, fending off his not-so-subtle advances, giving him what he wants. When we met, I told him I was a former NYPD officer, who left the force under shady circumstances. The former-cop part is true. Anyway, he's a narcissistic sociopath. He surrounds himself with people who feed his ego. Because he's a crook, he assumes everyone else is a crook."

Joe DeCurtis looked dubious.

"Okay. I don't have time to screw around trying to convince you that I'm for real. I need you to introduce me to Letty Carnahan. Like, right away. Wingfield is not a patient man. He wants her dead, and he wants it done right away. If I'm gonna pull this off, I need her to trust me. I need you to trust me. Otherwise, this whole thing falls apart. And Wingfield literally gets away with murder."

"You're asking a lot," Joe said.

"Yeah, I am. But consider the alternative."

"Which is what?"

"We've been over this already. If Letty Carnahan doesn't cooperate, I take her back to New York with me, and hand her over to the New York cops. Maya goes to child protective services. And you, Officer DeCurtis, will face charges of obstruction of justice, harboring a fugitive, and whatever other crimes I can come up with. Even if the charges don't stick, your law enforcement career is over."

Joe exhaled slowly and pushed his chair away from the table. "I'll talk to her," he said.

"You do that," Agent Hill said. "I need an answer by noon tomorrow."

29

~~~~~~~~~~

THE LIGHTS WERE STILL ON inside unit 11. Joe tapped lightly at the door, and a moment later she opened the door a crack with the chain lock still engaged.

Letty didn't look happy to see him. "What now?"

"I know you're still pissed at me about the pool furniture, but we really need to talk," he said, keeping his voice low.

She glanced backward into the apartment. "Can't it wait until morning? I just got Maya to sleep."

"Sorry, it really can't. This is important." He paused. "We need to talk about Evan Wingfield."

Her eyes widened. "Okay, come on in. We can sit out on the patio and talk without disturbing Maya."

She was dressed in loose-fitting pajama pants and a T-shirt, and her hair was mussed. She clasped her hands around both knees, perched uneasily, like a bird, on the rusty metal chair.

"How long have you known?"

"I knew something was up with you the first night you got here. But I didn't figure out that you were her sister until later that first week. That's when I found out about Tanya's death and the fact that Maya was missing."

"Why didn't you arrest me, or turn me in?"

"I would have, at first. But Ava insisted you were good people, right from the start. She would have kicked my ass. Plus there was Maya. And then you jumped Mrs. Ben Dover in the parking lot and kept her from splitting my head in half. And you saved Harry Bronson's life, making him chew that aspirin. I decided to wait and see what happened. Mostly, I guess, I was trying to figure you out."

"Let me know when that happens. I'm still trying to figure me out too." She paused. "I didn't kill Tanya."

"Can you tell me what happened?"

"Back in New York, I had a standing Sunday-morning playdate with Maya. We'd go to the park, or out to breakfast. Just the two of us. But that morning, Tanya texted me that Maya'd had a rough night, and she wanted her to sleep in. She also mentioned Evan was coming over."

"Was that unusual?"

"Very. Things had gotten really bitter between them, with all the lawyers and everything. He'd made some nasty threats. But she said he wanted to talk things over between the two of them, to get things settled. Tanya thought that meant he was going to give in and let her take Maya with her to California."

"She was moving to California?"

"Yeah. She wanted to get away from Evan, restart her acting career. She'd rented a house, found a new agent out there . . . she was begging me to move with her."

"Okay, so what happened next?" Joe asked.

"She was supposed to text me that morning, to let me know he was gone. But when I didn't hear from her, I got worried. I called and texted, then finally went over there. I had a key, so I let myself in. And that's when I found her. . . ."

Letty ducked her head and began to cry. "She was . . ."

Joe leaned forward and grasped her hands. "It's okay."

Her chest was heaving as she struggled to get the words out. "Blood. Around her head. And then I looked up, and oh God. Maya was standing at the top of the stairs, crying."

"Do you think she saw what happened?"

"I don't know," Letty said, her voice catching. "It all happened so fast."

"Okay," he said. "But why didn't you call the cops, when you found her?"

"Because I knew, right away. It was Evan. Tanya told me, if anything bad ever happened to her, it would be Evan. She made me promise, swear, that if anything happened, I would take Maya and go."

"Go where? Did she tell you to come down here, to the Murmuring Surf?"

Letty shook her head. "Not exactly."

"How exactly?"

She dabbed at her eyes with the hem of her T-shirt. "You had to know Tanya. She was . . . complicated. She liked secrets. You never knew the whole truth with her. A few months ago, when things were really bad between her and Evan, she told me she was afraid of him. Because he wouldn't ever let go of Maya. Not because he actually loved her, but because Evan thought she was, like, his property."

"Did Wingfield physically threaten to harm her?"

Letty shrugged. "With Evan, it was more intimidation. Like, 'You can never win against me. I'm rich, and I'll mow you down.' So she had a plan B."

"Which was?"

"A few months ago, after Christmas, when I was at her place, she took me into her closet. She had this bag, hidden in one of her boots. She called it her 'go-bag.' It was stuffed with cash, and this big diamond ring Evan gave her as a push present when she had Maya. And she told me, if anything ever happened to her, to grab the bag and Maya and get the hell away from Evan and New York.

"I thought it was just Tanya, overreacting. Being dramatic. Turns out this one time, she was right. I didn't even have a plan. I threw some clothes for Maya and me in a suitcase. I took Tanya's car, the Mercedes. I drove it to Newark, and just left it in a parking lot near the airport with the keys in it. Then I rented a car at Hertz, and eventually dropped it off in Raleigh. I bought the Kia there, and paid cash, then I started driving down here. Maya cried most of the way. We spent the night in a motel along the way, and then I ended up here. You know the rest."

"Why do you think Evan didn't grab Maya, after he killed Tanya?" Joe asked.

"He didn't know she was there. Evan knew about our Sunday playdates. It's probably why he went over there that morning, because he figured Maya wouldn't be around."

Letty started to weep. "But she was there the whole time. Oh my God. Maya was there when he killed Tanya."

"Maybe Maya was asleep," Joe said, hoping it was true. "Maybe she didn't see it."

"I wish I hadn't seen it," Letty said, rubbing her arms and shivering. "It was awful."

Joe stopped her. "Go back to the money Tanya had hidden. How much?"

"A lot. Nearly twenty thousand."

He let out a low whistle. "Did she say where she got the money?"

"Just that she'd saved it. I know what you're thinking. That she stole it. I still have most of the cash. In the back of my mind I probably knew it was dirty money."

"You still haven't told me how you knew to come to the Surf," he prompted.

"It was that old magazine article your mom mentioned. Tanya had a copy of it, in the go-bag. At the time, I didn't know what it meant. I just figured it was as good a place as any. Turns out, it actually was a good idea."

"You didn't know Tanya had stayed here? That I'd arrested her?"

Letty shook her head vigorously. "I didn't know about any of that. Tanya told me she'd been living in Atlanta during that time, doing some modeling. She told me Rooney, her boyfriend, had ripped her off, taken everything and left her stranded in Atlanta. She never mentioned this motel."

"Which was another lie," Joe pointed out. He studied her face. "I kept thinking you looked like someone I'd seen before."

"You and Trudi Maples," Letty said, chagrined. "I kept waiting for the other shoe to drop, especially once you told me that story about Declan Rooney and his associate. I almost left right then."

"Why didn't you?"

"I'm not sure. Where else would I go? Your mom was so good to me, gave me a job and a place to stay. My stomach has been in knots since the day I left New York. But here, I started to feel safe. I guess I was fooling myself."

Joe took a deep breath. "You're not safe. Not yet."

Alarmed, she half rose from her chair. "You're turning me in?"

"No. But there's been a development. That's why I had to talk to you tonight."

"What is it?"

"Evan Wingfield has put out a contract on you."

Letty felt her breath leave her body. Her brain buzzed with what felt like static electricity, and once again, she felt trapped and helpless.

"He knows I'm here? In Florida? Oh my God!"

Joe grabbed her hand again. "No. He doesn't know where you are. But he hired a woman he thinks is a corrupt housing inspector to track you down and . . . take care of things. Fortunately, the woman is actually an undercover FBI agent. Her name is Vikki Hill. She flew down here from New York today and checked into the motel."

"That's crazy. Nobody else knows I'm here. Nobody."

"The FBI knows. After Tanya was killed, they found her arrest record and put it together."

Letty looked around wildly. "Why would Evan want to kill me? I'm no threat to him."

"Money. And Maya. He wants both," Joe said.

"I've got to get out of here. Tonight."

"No," Joe said firmly. "You can't do that."

"I can't stay here. You don't know Evan . . ."

"Letty. Wait. Listen to me. You can't keep running. Not with a four-year-old in tow. I know you're scared. Hell, I'm scared for you. But I honestly think this is the only way you and Maya will be safe."

She buried her head in her hands. "We'll never be safe. Not as long as Evan is walking around."

"That's why you've got to do what this FBI agent wants. You've got to help us put Evan in prison, for what he did to Tanya."

Letty looked up at him. "How?"

"Agent Hill wants to meet with you. Tomorrow. She'll explain everything."

"I don't know . . ." Letty said. "What if this is some kind of trick? Evan knows people."

"It's not a trick," Joe insisted. "Everything she told me checks out." He let out a long sigh. "Anyway, you really don't have any other options. You've just got to trust me on this."

Letty stood up and fixed him with a cold stare. "You turned me in to the FBI. How else would they find out where we were?"

"You know that's not true. If I'd wanted to, I could have turned you in weeks ago." He touched her cheek lightly. "I care about you, Letty. You and Maya. You've got to believe me. I'm on your side. Meet with Agent Hill tomorrow and hear her out. Okay?"

She brushed his hand away. "What other choice do I have? If I try to leave here tonight, you'll arrest me, won't you?"

"Try to get some sleep," Joe said, opening the patio gate. "She wants to meet with you tomorrow."

30

~~~~~~~~~

"JOE!" HIS MOTHER'S VOICE STARTLED him awake. He opened his eyes and when he struggled to sit upright his cramped back muscles screamed in protest.

Ava was standing beside the driver's-side window, both hands on her hips. "What do you think you're doing?"

He yawned and opened the truck door. "I was sleeping. Until you started screeching at me." He started walking toward the office. "And now I'm gonna go take a pee inside. Unless you want me to whip it out right here in the parking lot of your motel."

He took his own sweet time washing his hands and splashing water on his face. Ava was waiting when he walked out of the bathroom.

"Why were you sleeping in your truck in my parking lot? Were you drunk last night? And aren't you supposed to be at work right now?"

He yawned again, then headed for the coffee bar. He poured himself a mug and gulped half the cup down.

"I wasn't drunk. I'm taking PTO today. Anything else?"

"When are you going to tell me what's going on with Letty?" Ava asked. Her arms were crossed over her chest. He should have known she'd figure something was up.

"You're right, there is something going on. But I'm not really at liberty to discuss it right now."

"That woman who checked into the efficiency yesterday. Vikki something. Who is she really? And don't tell me it's none of my business. She's staying at my motel. I have a right to know."

Crap. He didn't need this. He'd been awake half the night, sitting in the front seat of his truck, wedged tightly behind Letty's Kia, just in case she decided to make a run for it. He'd finally dozed off around three.

"Vikki Hill is an FBI agent. From New York. I really can't talk to you about this right now, Mom."

Ava would not be deterred. "Just tell me this. Does it involve Maya? Is she in some kind of danger?"

"Maya is involved . . . indirectly," he admitted. "But I'm going to make damned sure she'll be okay."

Isabelle came bounding down the stairs from the apartment. "Hey, bro," she said, kissing his cheek. "Aren't you supposed to be out chasing criminals?"

"Aren't you supposed to be at school?" he countered. "Why is everybody so worried about my work schedule?"

"He slept in his truck out in the parking lot last night," Ava told her daughter. "Because Letty and Maya are in some kind of trouble with the FBI."

"Oh, shit!" Isabelle breathed. "For real? Do they really think Letty killed her sister? I mean, that's cray-cray. Letty would never."

"What do you know about any of this?" Joe asked sternly.

"That's what I'd like to know, too," Ava said pointedly. "Young lady?"

Isabelle took a half step backward. "I promised Letty I wouldn't talk about it. To anybody. She's in big trouble, okay? That's all I really know."

"Who is Letty's sister?" Ava asked. "Why is there an FBI agent staying here? And why am I always the last to know anything?"

The office doorbell chimed and Maya and Letty walked in.

"Maya Papaya!" Isabelle exclaimed, as the little girl jumped into her arms.

Letty had dark smudges under her eyes and now she warily regarded the assembled family.

"This is about me, isn't it?" she asked Joe. "You told them?"

"I didn't say anything, Letty," Isabelle volunteered. "I kept my promise."

"Nobody's told me nothing," Ava said. "Don't you think it's about time you filled us all in?"

Letty silently nodded in the direction of her niece.

"Come on, Maya," Isabelle said, understanding the unspoken cue. "Let's go upstairs and play school before it's time for me to go to real school."

Joe poured a mug of coffee and handed it to Ava, then poured one for Letty, who waited until she heard the two girls' footsteps ascending the stairs. She took a sip of coffee, then put the mug aside. "I'm sorry I lied to you, Ava."

Her coffee grew cold while the whole story poured out, a torrent of jumbled words and emotions, betrayal, regrets, grief and fears. Letty held nothing back. Nothing, with the exception of the object she'd found sewn inside Maya's stuffed elephant. For reasons she didn't really understand, she decided to keep the nanny camera's existence to herself, at least for the time being.

Ava listened without interrupting, until Letty mentioned the name Declan Rooney.

"Him!" she said, scowling. "That man was the devil. I should have known he was bad news the minute Chuck brought him and your sister to this motel. I guess that Irish accent of his had us all fooled. That and those damned blue eyes of his."

"Not all of us were fooled," Joe said. "And as it turns out, Rooney's accent was as fake as the rest of his story. He grew up outside Boston."

Her tone softened. "Letty, I still can't believe I didn't notice until right now the resemblance between you and Tanya."

"I guess it's a good thing you didn't figure it out, or you never would have rented me a room," Letty said.

"I probably would have anyway, though. Because of Maya. And also, because I sensed you were a good person," Ava said. She turned and gave her son a pointed look. "What happens now?"

"That depends on Letty," Joe said.

"I'll meet with the FBI agent today. Then I guess I'll do whatever she wants," Letty said. "I'm out of options, and I'm tired of running."

They heard footsteps clattering down the stairs, and the discussion was suspended.

"Letty," Maya said, running into the office. "Isabelle says she has to go to school now."

Isabelle was a step behind the little girl. "Unless Mom writes me a note so I get an excused absence. Then we could go to the beach."

"Nice try," Ava said. "You go on to school. Maya will be here waiting after lunch, and so will the beach."

Joe's phone pinged to signal an incoming text message. "It's from Agent Hill," he told Letty. "She wants us to meet her for breakfast at the Seahorse."

"The diner down in Pass-a-Grille? Now?"

"Maya can stay here with me," Ava offered. "We'll have our own school."

"I can write my name," the child boasted. "M-A-Y-A."

Ava clapped her hands in appreciation. "That's great. Let's see if you can write my name. A-V-A. Hey, did you know my name is spelled the same backward and forward?"

"Nice parking job," Letty said, as they approached his truck in the motel lot.

He opened the passenger door and she climbed into the truck.

"Did you really think I'd run?" she asked, as they pulled into traffic.

"No, but I didn't want to take a chance," he said. "The FBI isn't fooling around with this stuff, Letty. They want to nail Evan Wingfield, and as I understand it, you're their best shot at doing that."

It was early and traffic was light. They passed tourists and retirees out walking or jogging along Gulf Boulevard, the road that strung the beach towns together, going south to St. Pete Beach and Pass-a-Grille.

The Seahorse Restaurant was a low-ceilinged wood-frame building sitting on a corner lot facing Tampa Bay across the street. It had cheerful green-and-red awnings and flower boxes spilling over with red geraniums. Joe pulled over to the curb. Letty sat very upright, looking straight ahead. Only her hands moved, clutching and unclutching in her lap. She'd hardly slept, and her stomach was in knots.

"I'm scared."

"I know." He placed his hand atop hers. "I swear, Letty, no matter what, I won't let anything bad happen to you, or Maya. We've got this."

She took a deep breath. Nodded. "Okay. Let's go."

"That's her," Joe said in a low voice, indicating a lone woman seated at a table in the corner of the covered patio.

The agent was dressed in a black knit tank top and white jeans. Letty was surprised to note that Vikki Hill looked younger than the photo Zoey texted from the diner, maybe early forties? Her sunglasses were pushed up into her dark, shoulder-length hair. Her skin was coffee colored, in contrast to the vivid red lipstick she wore. She was studying the menu, but looked up as Joe and Letty approached.

"Agent Hill," Joe started, as he pulled Letty's chair away from the table.

"Just Vikki, please," the agent corrected him. "Hi, Letty. Thanks for coming." She gestured at the coffee carafe, but Letty shook her head. "I've been up since three, and I've already had enough caffeine."

"How about some food?"

"Not hungry," Letty said.

"You sure? The bureau is buying. I've already eaten. Shrimp for breakfast! Crazy, huh? I could get used to being in Florida this time of year."

"You probably wouldn't like it in July, though," Joe said.

"I don't like July, anywhere," Agent Hill said.

Jittery from all the coffee, Letty kept looking around the room.

"It's just me," Vikki Hill said, noticing her unease. "No backup agents, no plainclothes cops dressed as waiters or other tourists or hidden cameras. Just me. So, I understand Joe here has filled you in on what's going on?"

"He tells me Evan Wingfield hired you to kill me. Right?"

"Well, not me personally. You know Wingfield pretty well, worked for him, dated him, so you probably realize he doesn't really have a very high opinion of women. I mean, he likes them for some things, but he doesn't really trust them to do the heavy lifting, if you get my drift. He actually wants me to act as a sort of broker, to find him someone else to kill you."

Letty swallowed hard. Her head was throbbing and she felt sick. She took a tiny sip of water.

"No offense, or anything," she said finally. "But I find all of this hard to believe. Even for Evan Wingfield."

Agent Hill nodded. "I get it."

She placed her phone on the table, studied the screen, and paused before tapping an icon. "This is a recording of a conversation I had with Evan Wingfield last week. Remember, he thinks I'm just a greedy, crooked city housing inspector."

The recording quality wasn't stellar. It sounded tinny, with a bit of echo, but Letty recognized Evan's voice instantly.

"Listen, ah, there's something I need you to do for me."

"What's that?" It was a woman's voice.

"You know they still haven't found my daughter, right? I mean, it's nuts. Maya's only four, and as far as I know, that crazy bitch Letty could have taken her anywhere. She could be in real danger."

"Uh-huh."

"I was thinking, you have a lot of contacts, like in the city. You used to be a cop and you still know a lot of cops, too, right?"

"I know a few."

"Somebody has to know where Letty is. I mean, she's not some criminal mastermind, for Christ's sake."

The woman's voice sounded bored. "Maybe you should hire a private detective or something."

"I have. It's like flushing money down a toilet. Nobody can tell me anything. That's why I thought of you."

"Really? Because I am a criminal mastermind?"

Evan got a laugh out of that.

"No, seriously. I want you to ask around. Talk to her friends at that diner. You have the kind of face people trust. I bet people tell you stuff all the time."

"And then what? What if I were to find out where she is? I tell you and then you tell the cops and they arrest her and bring your kid back home?"

"Something like that . . . Or . . ."

"Or what?"

"Or we deal with Letty ourselves. You know what the courts are like. She's a woman. Some guys probably even think she's hot. She'd probably get off with a slap on the wrist—even for killing her own sister. No. She should have to pay for what she did to my family. Like, really pay."

Letty felt a chill run down her spine. Joe had been watching her face carefully. He reached across the table and gave her hand a reassuring squeeze. Vikki Hill saw, but said nothing. She tapped the phone and the recording stopped abruptly.

"It goes on like that for a few more minutes. He dances around, blames you for killing Tanya, blames her for wrecking his business. He has some not very nice things to say about you, Letty. I tell you, he's pretty paranoid right now. Apparently, Tanya told him she knew he was paying off city inspectors, and she threatened to take what she knew to the police."

Letty's voice was hoarse from anxiety and lack of sleep. "About a month before she was killed, Tanya told me Evan was going to have to agree to giving up custody of Maya, and that he'd have to agree to her move to LA because she had the goods on him. But she never told me what she knew, or how she knew it."

"Your sister was full of secrets, wasn't she?" Vikki Hill asked.

Letty stared down at the tabletop, at the greasy, yolk-streaked remains of the FBI agent's breakfast. It reminded her of the thousands of dishes she'd cleared in her years of waiting tables at the Lazy Daizy. And of sitting down, that first time, across from the polite, generous customer all the waitresses referred to as Table Two.

What if she'd blown him off, told him to take a hike that day, when he invited her to see the apartment he suddenly had available? What if she'd never met Evan Wingfield, or allowed Tanya to guilt-trip her into allowing her to move in with her? The what-ifs were relentless. They woke her up every morning, came to her in her sleep, or at odd moments when she was reading with Maya.

"Yeah," she said softly. "Secrets within secrets. That was Tanya."

Joe drummed his fingers on the tabletop. "So far, all we've heard is Wingfield blowing off steam, which is not the same thing as asking you to find somebody to kill Letty. Did he eventually stop dancing around?"

Vikki Hill picked up the phone and tapped the fast-forward button on the recording. "Give a listen," she said.

It was her voice, midsentence.

"Why don't you tell me the real reason you want Letty dealt with?"

"I told you already. Call it frontier justice."

"No. I call it bullshit. I know you, Evan. It all comes down to money, doesn't it?"

"That crazy Tanya had a will. Who knew? Some Indian woman she met at AA. Who hires a drunk lawyer for estate planning? Tanya

Carnahan, that's who. Long story short, she left everything to Maya, in a trust with Letty named as Maya's guardian."

"So?"

"So, when we were together, before things went bad, I put a bunch of my holdings in an LLC and transferred it into Tanya's name, which I never mentioned to her."

"As a tax dodge."

"It's perfectly legal. Now though, with Tanya dead, my four-year-old kid and her crazy aunt hold title to, like, twelve million dollars' worth of prime New York real estate. My apartments. And my lawyers tell me I can sue, but unless I can prove Letty killed Tanya, the apartments are held in a trust that Letty controls."

"But you're Maya's legal father, right? Can Tanya just cut you out of the kid's life like that?"

"Maybe, maybe not. But we don't need to go into that right now. Let's get back to Letty. Can you find her, or not?"

"Maybe? I mean, what's it worth to you?"

"Ten thousand."

"Bwhahahaha. Seriously. I've got a job, you know. I'll have to take time off, call in some favors, that costs money. Plus, travel, if it comes to that. Plus, if you want me to hire someone to take care of Letty, that ain't free. I mean, I don't even know how much it costs to hire a hit man."

"Christ! Will you quit saying that word?"

"What should I call it instead? A consultant?"

"Whatever. Just get it done."

"Fifty thousand. And don't even try and dick around with me. I know you've got the money, Evan."

"Okay. Do it. I don't want to know any of the details. Just take care of it."

"And what about the kid?"

"Yeah. Of course. Maya. You'll see that she's not hurt, right? Look, I gotta go. Text me when you know something."

31

~~~~~~~~~~~~~~~~~~~~~~~

THE FBI AGENT TAPPED THE phone and the recording ended abruptly.

"Take care of it," Letty said, her tone bitter. "That's what Evan used to tell me when I worked for him. If the cable was out in an apartment, he'd say 'Take care of it.' If one of the tenants in a building was making waves, or a mattress needed replacing, my job was to 'take care of it.' I'm just another messy inconvenience to him. And Maya? She's an afterthought."

Vikki Hill nodded in agreement. "Wingfield sees her as an asset. Like one of his apartments."

"Do you think he knows he's not really Maya's father?" Joe asked.

"Doubtful." Vikki motioned for the server to refill her coffee. She turned to Letty. "You heard the man, in his own words."

"We all did. He was hiring you to hire a hit man to kill me. So arrest him. That's a crime, right? Why do you need me?"

Joe and Agent Hill exchanged a knowing look. "Because it's not enough," Joe said gently. "Solicitation for murder is difficult to prove. Even when you have the accused on tape. And Wingfield is careful. He never actually says he wants you killed. Even though that's clearly his intent."

"What are you telling me?"

Agent Hill leaned across the table, locking eyes with her. "This sucks, I know. But if you want to put Evan Wingfield in prison, make sure he never threatens you, or your niece or anyone else, ever again, you need to help us, Letty." She glanced over at Joe, who reluctantly nodded.

"Here's what we're gonna do. I'm gonna text Wingfield today and tell him I found a guy who'll 'take care of things.'" She pointed at Joe. "Officer DeCurtis is that guy. It's going to be tricky, because Wingfield is cautious, and he's paranoid. But on the plus side, he thinks I'm just another dumb broad. I'll play along with that, ask for specific directions. We have to get him on the record, directing the hit on you. And after, after he's convinced I've done my job, and he pays me, we drop the net. He's trapped and can't get out."

"This won't work," Letty said. "I've known Evan way longer than you. He always covers his ass. He has layers of people around him, doing the dirty work."

"Okay, what do you suggest? I'm listening."

"I don't know," Letty admitted wearily. "I feel like I'm living in a nightmare. When does this go away?"

"After we put Evan Wingfield behind bars," Agent Hill repeated.

"Maybe we do something to spook Wingfield. Make him believe it's urgent to get Letty out of his hair once and for all?" Joe said. "What if we let him think she has proof that he killed Tanya? He'd come after her then, right?"

"But I don't have proof," Letty objected.

Vikki Hill nodded slowly. "He doesn't know that. I could contact one of the NYPD detectives investigating Tanya's murder. Get him to pay Wingfield a visit, yank his chain a little, maybe hint that they've been in contact with Letty, and she's cooperating. Which is true. That would light a fire under him, right?"

"Maybe," Letty said.

"I think it's worth a shot," the FBI agent said. "I'll text Wingfield, tell him we need to talk. When he calls, I'll tell him I've found a guy who can do the job. If he balks, I'll turn up the heat. Okay?"

"Are you absolutely positive Evan doesn't know where I am?" Letty asked.

"No way. I've covered my tracks," Vikki Hill insisted. "I promise you, he's never heard of the Murmuring Surf. He's clueless."

"Well? What did you think of Agent Hill?" Joe asked. They were in his truck, driving back to the motel.

"She's okay. I guess. For an FBI agent."

"Yeah. Not very likable. But she seems to know what she's doing."

Letty stared out the window at the passing scenery, chewing on a ragged bit of cuticle. "You really think this scheme of hers will work?"

"I wouldn't have brought you to meet her today if I didn't."

"And she would have arrested me anyway and dragged me back to New York."

"No," he said, turning to look directly at her. "I would not let that happen."

"What happens if Evan doesn't bite? If they can't prove he killed Tanya and tried to have me killed? What then?"

"We'll figure it out," Joe said.

"We?"

Without slowing down he veered sharply right into the parking lot of a strip shopping center. He slapped the gear in park.

"Yeah," he said, solemnly. "We. You and me. And maybe Ava and Isabelle will help too, but I'm thinking it will mostly be you and me. Unless you've got a problem with that."

Letty chewed her bottom lip. "I don't know what to say. I'm grateful, but Joe, I'm not . . . I'm not in a place where I can do this right now. Not with everything that's hanging over my head. And with Maya. When and if we ever get this mess with Evan straightened out, she's got to be my priority. I'm all she's got. And I promised Tanya . . ."

"Did you promise her you'd never have a life for yourself?" he asked.

"I promised I'd keep her daughter safe."

He laughed. "What's safer than hanging out with a cop?" He reached under the passenger seat and brought out a set of handcuffs. "I've got a nightstick under the seat too, but I can't reach it right now."

She managed a smile. "You know what I mean."

"Okay, set aside all that stuff. Just tell me, yes or no. Are you at all attracted to me?"

"A little."

"One thing you don't have in common with your sister? You're a terrible actress, Letty Carnahan."

He leaned over and kissed her on the lips before she could disagree.

She returned the kiss, but reluctantly pulled away from their embrace after only a moment. "You sound like my last agent."

An elderly woman pushing a shopping cart with a dachshund strapped in the child seat stopped as she was passing the truck and wagged her finger at Letty in disapproval.

"We should go," Letty said. "I've got work to do and it's not fair to leave Maya with your mom when she's trying to work too."

"You're still avoiding my question. What about us? Me and you? Anything?"

"Let's keep things strictly professional for now, please? My life is too complicated."

"What if I told you I don't mind complications?" Joe said.

"Okay," she said, relenting. "You're right. I am attracted to you, and more than a little. But here's the thing, Joe. I don't want a relationship based on being rescued by you. You're sweet and I appreciate that you're so good to Maya, but that can't be all there is to us. Years ago, I stupidly got involved with Evan because I let him 'rescue' me. It's the same damn trap my mother fell into, over and over again, relying on a man, instead of figuring out how to make it on her own. That's where Tanya learned it, you know, to use her 'charm' and feminine wiles—which really meant to lie and keep secrets. I don't want that for me, and I don't want Maya to think that's how she needs to live her life."

Joe sat, speechless.

"Rescue you? That's what you think I'm trying to do?"

"Yes. You're a cop, and I know that's what cops are trained to do, but I don't want to be a victim anymore. I won't be a professional victim for the rest of my life."

He pounded the dashboard with his closed fist. "Dammit, Letty. Yeah, I'm a cop. I can't turn that off and on. But that's not why I'm trying to help you, not because it's my job. Hell, if I were doing my job, I would have turned you in as soon as I figured out you were a fugitive. But I didn't. Because I knew you couldn't have done what you're accused of. I care about you, and I want to be with you. Is that a crime?"

"No," she said quietly. "Not a crime. Just not right for me. Not now anyway."

He pulled the truck back into traffic, steering with one hand, the other braced on the open driver's-side window. "What now, then?"

"We get through this, as best we can," Letty said. "No emotional attachment though. Please?"

Joe shrugged. "You're the boss."

32

~~~~~~~~~~~~~~~~~~

As soon as Letty walked into the office, Ava pounced. "How did it go with the FBI?"

"I'm not sure," Letty said.

She bent down and kissed the top of her niece's head. "Have you been having fun with Ava, lovebug?"

"I made a puzzle," Maya said proudly. "And now I'm making you a necklace."

Letty pulled her chair up to the reception desk and powered up the computer, and began checking the reservation portal. "This is good," she said, looking over at her employer. "April is really starting to fill up. The efficiency is totally booked, all the way into mid-July. I wonder if we should have bumped up the rates a little more?"

"Letty!" Ava exclaimed. "What happened with that woman? You can't just waltz in here and clam up like that."

"I'm not sure I'm supposed to talk about it." Letty glanced meaningfully over her shoulder at Maya, who was stringing wooden spools on a length of red yarn.

"Does she believe your story?" Ava asked in a near whisper. "She's not going to arrest you, right?"

"Yes, I think she believes me. And no, I don't think an arrest is imminent," Letty said.

Ava craned her neck, looking out toward the parking lot. "Where'd Joe go? I thought he had the day off?"

"He said he had some stuff to take care of," Letty said. Anxious to divert Ava's laser focus, she pointed at the screen of the computer.

"According to the portal, you've got guests checking into unit twelve the Monday after Easter. But I thought you told me the Sheehans aren't driving home until that next weekend."

"What?" Ava peered over her shoulder at the screen. "This dog-gone new booking software has me so confused, I don't know who's coming and who's going. Does that mean we're double-booked?"

"You were supposed to input all that data into the new spread-sheet," Letty said, trying to sound more patient than she felt.

"I was trying, but then Merwin interrupted me, complaining about the damned shuffleboard cues, and I guess I lost track of what I was doing," Ava said. "What do we do now?"

Letty clicked over to the bookings for the rest of the motel. "Hmm. The Feldmans are checking out on Easter morning. Can you turn the unit that quickly? Will Anita come in to clean on Sunday, or Monday morning?"

"We'll have to get it turned, even if I have to do it myself," Ava said, sounding resigned. "I don't want to disappoint new guests. Especially since they're booked for ten days. And at the new rate."

Letty nodded. "Okay, I'll email the guest and tell them we've had a slight hiccup, but the unit they'll be in is just as nice. Maybe we can give them a free breakfast coupon for Sharky's, as a consolation prize."

"You're a natural at this, you know it?" Ava said, beaming at her assistant manager. "If I didn't know better, I'd think you'd been in hotel management your whole life."

"Not my whole life," Letty said modestly. "But I was doing residential property management, which is sort of the same thing, back in New York, before I came down here."

"Since you're here, I'm going to go run my errands. I should be back around three, if anyone comes looking for me," Ava said.

Once her boss was gone, Letty threw herself into work, imputing all the existing motel reservations from Ava's handwritten logbook into the new software. It was arduous, mind-numbing work, just the thing she needed to keep from thinking about Evan Wingfield.

Maya contentedly colored in her workbook, humming under her breath, pausing occasionally to show off her work.

Isabelle arrived in the office after lunch. She slung her backpack onto the reception counter and launched a stream of questions at Letty.

"How was your meeting with the FBI agent? What's she like? I mean, did she have a gun and stuff like that? What happens next? You're not under arrest, right?"

"Whoa!" Letty said. "And lower your voice, please. The meeting went okay. Agent Hill is pretty businesslike. If she had a gun, I didn't see it. I'm not under arrest, yet." She motioned toward Maya, who was beaming at Isabelle, pointedly waiting to be greeted.

"Hiya, Maya Papaya," Isabelle said, picking up the workbook to examine the child's work. "Wow, this is awesome coloring!"

"I know," Maya said, tugging at her babysitter's hand. "Now we go to the beach, right, Isabelle?"

"I'll tell you the rest later," Letty promised.

Letty was puzzling over one of Ava's nearly illegible scrawls when the office-door bell chimed. She looked up to see Vikki Hill, dressed in running shorts and a sports bra, her hair gathered into a ponytail. Her nose was smeared with white sunblock and her sunglasses dangled from a strap around her neck.

"Did you hear from Evan?" Letty blurted.

"No. And I hate to say it, but you might be right. I texted Wingfield to tell him I'd found someone to do the job, and now he's gone dark on me."

"Is that unusual?"

"Up until today, he was texting and calling me every day, sometimes twice a day, wanting to know what I was doing about finding you. But now, I'm a little concerned. I don't want to text him again, because I don't want to seem overeager."

"What can you do?" Letty asked.

"The one thing I'm terrible at. Wait. In the meantime, I'm going to go for a run on the beach to keep from going crazy. But I've got my phone with me." Agent Hill looked around the office. "Where's DeCurtis?"

"Home, I guess," Letty said. "You'll let me know if you hear from Evan, right?"

"Definitely."

The afternoon and early evening dragged on. She was thankful that Maya was tired after her day at the beach, and by seven thirty, she'd fed her and tucked her into bed.

Letty tidied up the kitchen, then went out to her tiny patio garden. She watered the plants, clipped dead leaves and spent blooms, then went back inside and tried, in vain, to immerse herself in a yellowing paperback Mary Higgins Clark mystery plucked from the Murmuring Surf lending library.

When her phone dinged to signal an incoming text, she was so rattled she dropped both the book and the cup of tea she'd been sipping.

The message was from Sierra, Isabelle's hacker friend.

R U home? I've got something!

Letty grabbed a towel and mopped up the spilled tea, then texted back.

Yes. Home. Come now.

She heard the buzz of the Vespa approaching, and walked out onto the breezeway to wave the girl inside.

"Maya's asleep," Letty cautioned as they entered the unit. She gently closed the bedroom door.

"Oh man," Sierra said, as she removed her helmet and began to unload her backpack onto the table. "This was a blast. I mean, it was crazy complicated, but I was totally into figuring it out, once

I got started. It's definitely high-tech, but it was WiFi enabled, like I thought. Normally these cameras only sync up to the network where the camera was installed. Because, like, if you're watching your nanny, you're not watching her everywhere. You're just watching her at your house, right?"

"Oh-kay, I guess that makes sense."

"But this camera—it was uploading to your sister's iCloud."

Sierra flipped the top of her laptop and powered it up. "I didn't watch all of it," Sierra said, as she clicked some keys and brought up Tanya's iCloud. "Here's one of the video clips. I think Ellie must have been sitting on a table nearby, because the video quality is better than a lot of the other stuff."

To Letty's surprise, the video was in color. The image was blurry, but as soon as Sierra tapped the arrow on the film clip, she immediately recognized Evan's voice, and saw him, in soft focus, sitting at a table, drinking a glass of red wine.

"Maya!" His voice was sharp, irritated. "Stop dropping food on the floor. You're a big girl now. Big girls don't do that."

Letty heard but couldn't see Maya, who began crying. "I'm sowwy Daddy."

A woman's voice came from off camera. "Evan honey, leave her be. It's a few Cheerios. I'll sweep it up when she's done."

"That's not the point, Juliette. She's turning into a little slob, because Tanya lets her get away with crap like that."

Evan's girlfriend moved into camera range. She was lovely, slender with long hair and dressed in a flowing, gauzy green caftan. *Just his type,* Letty thought. Juliette began massaging his shoulders. "You're still cranky because of your meeting with the co-op board. Can't you let it go?"

"No! You don't understand. They've hired a lawyer, and they're threatening to take me to court over my units in that building. I haven't been able to rent them out for nearly two months now. Do you have any idea what that's costing me in lost income, not to mention the legal fees I'm looking at?"

"Well, what are you going to do about it?"

He sighed. "The debt service on those units is killing me. Looks like I might have to sell."

"Oh no," she laughed. "The great Evan Wingfield is going to sell? I thought you only bought."

"Not funny," he snapped. "The good news is, my girl Vikki is working out great. That last city inspector was a pain in the ass. Every time I turned around, he had his hand out. Lucky for me, I heard he got canned. Vikki's gonna work out just fine."

"How do you know you can trust her?" Juliette asked.

"I just know. I get vibes from people. Vikki's vibe is mellow. She's not greedy. Realizes she'll make more in the long run if she works with me."

"And what kind of vibe did you get from Tanya?"

He turned to look at her. "Don't start. She was an unfortunate, temporary lapse in good judgment."

Juliette leaned down and kissed his neck. "Oh, Evan. Relax. I'm just teasing you. If it weren't for Tanya, we wouldn't have Maya now, would we?"

"That's true," he said, pulling his girlfriend onto his lap. "And if we ever get done with all this custody shit, we'll have Maya full-time, and get her crazy mother out of my hair once and for all."

Maya's voice chimed in from off camera. "All done! JuJu, I want grapes."

"Grapes, please!" Evan yelled. "Jesus, she's just like her hillbilly mother. No manners."

Letty winced at the mention of her late sister's name. It was jarring, hearing Evan's voice after all these months, and even more disturbing hearing the way he interacted with Maya.

"There's a lot of this kind of stuff," Sierra told her, pausing the video. "It's a ton of data, so I broke it up into individual files and put them on a thumb drive for you. The original files are date-stamped, by the way, so it looks like your sister put the nanny cam into the elephant back in November. The most recent date on any of the files was from February twenty-eighth."

"Sierra, this is amazing," Letty said, sitting back in her chair. "I don't know what to say. I never actually expected you to be able to get anything from the nanny cam. Isabelle said you were a genius, and she wasn't kidding."

The teenager grinned. "Not a genius. Lots of people are way better at this than me. One thing though. Some of the video is pretty crappy quality, and you can't quite make out what they're saying on the audio. Maybe that's because Maya was holding Ellie, or moving around, or whatever. Not really sure."

"Doesn't matter," Letty said. "I can't thank you enough. This was a lot of work. You have to let me pay you."

"No way," Sierra said. "It was fun. Like solving a mystery. Real James Bond spy stuff."

Letty got her billfold. "I'm serious. How many hours did you spend working on this?"

"Not that many."

"Stay there." Letty tiptoed into the bedroom, pulled Tanya's go-bag from its hiding place, and extracted five twenty-dollar bills.

She took Sierra's hand and pressed the bills into it, closing her fingers around the money.

"Take it," she said. "It's not as much as you earned, but it's not fair to ask you to work for free."

Sierra's eyes widened when she fanned out the bills. "For real?"

"Absolutely. I forgot to ask Isabelle. Are you headed to college next year? Where are you going? MIT?"

"No way," Sierra said, giggling. "I'm taking a couple college classes at University of South Florida, but that's just for fun. I want to go to Caltech, but my mom has a fit every time I mention it, because she says she doesn't want her baby going so far from home."

She began packing up her laptop. "In fact, I gotta go. My parents bought a smart TV, and I promised I'd help them figure out how to use the remote control tonight. My dad is pretty hopeless with techy stuff."

Letty stood in the doorway and watched Sierra zip out of the parking lot and into traffic on Gulf Boulevard. When the green Vespa was out of sight she went back to the living room and set up her laptop. She fixed herself another cup of tea and settled in to watch Ellie's video secrets unfold.

33

~~~~~~~~~~~

LETTY OPENED THE BEDROOM DOOR to check on Maya. The child was sleeping on her side with Ellie tucked beside her on her pillow.

The videos did not make for riveting entertainment. The first few were herky-jerky motion-sickness-inducing views of the various rooms in Tanya's apartment, clearly the result of Ellie being dragged around the house by an active four-year-old. Letty heard and saw Angelique, Tanya's on-again, off-again Dominican housekeeper/babysitter, vacuuming and folding laundry, in between singing songs and reading to Maya.

Tanya herself was a constant presence in the videos. At first, Letty found herself tensing each time she heard her sister's voice, with its lingering Southern accent. Tanya had never bothered to try to erase her drawl, even exaggerating it on occasion, claiming that casting agents—and men—found it alluring.

Letty felt a thick cloud of melancholy descending over her as she realized she would never again hear the sound of her infuriating, intoxicating, darling, damaged sister's voice.

There were lots of blurry views of Tanya, talking in hushed tones on the phone, watching television or practicing her yoga poses, dancing around the living room to her favorite Taylor Swift song as Maya laughed and, with Ellie in hand, spun around in dizzying circles until mother and daughter collapsed, breathlessly, onto the floor.

Mostly the videos were of a toy's-eye view of Maya's world, going from trips to the grocery store with Angelique to Mommy-and-me exercise classes with Tanya, with weekly cameo appearances by Letty herself, strapping Maya into a stroller for trips to the park or the zoo during their weekly playdates.

Letty had almost dozed off watching one of the videos, which, because of Angelique's presence in the apartment, must have been a weekday morning. As she watched, Tanya came into the living room, dressed in her yoga clothes, carrying a cardboard take-out container from the corner deli.

From the camera angle, Letty guessed that Maya must have left Ellie on the bookshelf that held her stash of favorite picture books.

"Angie," Tanya called. The housekeeper bustled in, carrying an armful of folded towels.

"You can go home early today. See you tomorrow, okay?"

Angelique looked surprised, but a little while later she hurried out the door. Maybe five minutes after that, Tanya reappeared in the living room, dressed in jeans, a low-necked black sweater, and thigh-high black suede boots. She'd combed her hair and applied makeup. *Camera-ready*, Letty thought.

The door buzzer sounded, and Tanya spoke into it, although Letty couldn't hear what she said. A moment later, her sister stood, holding the door open, as a tall man in a knit ski hat and bulky leather jacket appeared. Tanya took a half step backward, then threw herself into the man's embrace.

"What the hell?" Letty whispered aloud. She couldn't see the man's face, or hear their conversation. A moment later, her sister closed the door and led the man into the living room, still holding his hand. She pointed at something just out of camera range. "Isn't she precious?" Tanya cooed. The man hung back, though, and Letty still couldn't get a good look at his face.

Without any warning, Letty heard Maya burst into tears, and Ellie, and the camera, beat a hasty retreat up the stairs, toward her bedroom. All Letty could see at this point was the pricey leopard-print runner on the stairway.

"Maya!" Tanya called. "Come on back, baby! Don't be scared."

"Noooo," Maya's voice cried. "I don't wanna. I don't like that man." The video footage was dizzying as the stuffed elephant was dragged behind on the stairs, and then down the hallway and into Maya's nursery. Letty heard the door slam. More crying from Maya, and then, eventually, views of the ceiling of the nursery, with its commissioned painting of clouds and treetops. Soon, she heard her niece's soft snores.

Letty backed up the video, freezing it at the point the stranger entered the apartment. She studied the frame, but Tanya stood between the man and the nanny camera, so tall in her high-heeled boots that she totally obscured him from view. She tried enlarging the frame, too, but only got a fuzzier image of a man—at least she thought it was a man—in a knit cap.

Whoever he was, he wasn't a stranger to Tanya, who was clinging to his hand like a junior high school girl.

She knew she shouldn't have been surprised that Tanya had already moved on to seeing a new man, because she couldn't remember a time, since her younger sister reached puberty, that she didn't have a boyfriend.

Letty tried to think back to the conversations she'd had with Tanya in the months leading up to her death. She remembered Valentine's Day—walking into Tanya's apartment to find a huge arrangement of pink peonies. "Secret admirer?" she'd asked, teasingly.

"No!" Tanya had exclaimed. "I'm done with men. I bought these for myself. Just because."

Letty watched more of the nanny-cam video for two more hours, reliving the tedium of life with a preschooler. Winter in New York City meant that Maya, and by extension Ellie, didn't leave home much.

The camera captured Tanya, seated at her kitchen table, having several heated telephone exchanges, with, Letty guessed, her lawyer.

"How much longer 'til we get all this settled?" Tanya raged. "I don't understand why he gets to hold me hostage here. He's the one who walked out. Not me. Plus, he's richer than God. Anytime he wants, he could get on a plane and fly out to see Maya, if that's what he really wants. But he doesn't. He just wants to jerk me around."

Letty began fast-forwarding through the videos, but each time the frames flashed by she was afraid she'd missed seeing something important.

In one of the videos in late January, mother and daughter were clearly having a no good, very bad day. Tanya struggled to get the little girl dressed, yanking Maya's tights up as she protested that she wanted to wear pants. "Noooo!" Maya screamed as Tanya pulled a dress over her head, trying to bat her mother's hand away as she fastened the buttons up the front. Each time Tanya managed to buckle one of the leather Mary Janes onto her child's foot, Maya would grab the shoe and toss it across the room, laughing spitefully as Tanya, cursing under her breath, retrieved the shoe and repeated the process two more times. "Fuck it," Tanya said, tucking a shoe in each of her back pockets. "Come on, we're late."

Letty watched in dismay as Tanya dragged Maya by the arm. "Nooo!" the child yelled, "Ellie, I need Ellie," then darted away to grab the stuffed elephant. Next they were in Tanya's building's dimly lit garage, where the film quality was poorer than usual, but where Maya's voice echoed loudly. "I don't wanna go see Daddy. I don't like Daddy." But Letty had to chuckle when Tanya's voice snapped, "I don't like him either. But a girl's gotta do what a girl's gotta do."

The nanny cam's view of the Mercedes's back seat was limited, but Letty could see Maya's legs as she struggled against being buckled into her car seat, and she soon heard the rhythmic kicking of Maya's feet against the back of her mother's seat.

"Stop that!" Tanya hollered at one point, turning around to ineffectively slap at her daughter's feet.

"I'm hungry," Maya whined, after they'd been in the car less than five minutes. The next moment, a plastic baggie of snacks and then a pink plastic sippy cup flew past the camera lens. Goldfish and apple juice, Letty guessed, her niece's most favored car snacks.

For the next fifteen minutes, the nanny cam recorded traffic sounds, and Maya sounds, as she chomped on the Goldfish and sucked at the plastic straw in her cup.

Finally, the car's engine idled. Letty had to believe they were parked at the curb in front of Evan's building. Someone tapped on the car window, and Letty heard it slide it down. "I'm waiting for my little girl's father. He's supposed to be right down."

"Mommy. I need to pee-pee," Maya whined.

"I know, sweet girl. Can you please hold it? Daddy will be here any minute now."

Minutes ticked past. Letty could picture her sister fuming, as she heard Tanya cursing her ex under her breath. "Come on, dammit. I don't have all day to sit here in the cold and wait for you."

After another few minutes, the nanny cam picked up the sound of Tanya's voice, obviously calling her ex. "Goddammit, Evan! I'm tired of your games. If you're not down here in two minutes, we're leaving. I've got a life too, you know."

Finally, the sound of a car door opening. Evan's face came into camera view as he stuck his head in the car and began unbuckling Maya's seat belt. "About damn time," Tanya griped. "That cop was about to give me a ticket for being in a no-parking zone."

"I don't wanna go to Daddy's house," Maya wailed.

"Maya, hush," Tanya said.

Evan started to lift the child from the seat. "Jesus, Tanya. She's covered in crumbs. And she's wet her damn pants again. You did this on purpose, you bitch."

"It's your own fault for making us wait," Tanya said. She turned around in the seat. "Oh, don't forget Ellie." Evan's hand snatched up the stuffed elephant.

Tanya's voice sounded strained. "Bye, baby, be a good girl for Daddy and JuJu."

"Nooooo," Maya cried. "I want Mommy."

Letty clicked STOP on the video. She'd watched all the disturbing images of the wreckage of her late sister's life that she could take for one night, and she was weary from the day's roller-coaster events.

She went to the front door, locked it and engaged the safety chain, then retreated to the bathroom, washed her face and brushed her teeth, checked on Maya one more time, and gratefully climbed between the sheets in her own bed. Right before she fell asleep, she checked her phone to make sure she hadn't missed any messages from Vikki Hill. Nothing.

34

By NINE O'CLOCK, VIKKI HILL could feel the walls of the Murmuring Surf's efficiency closing in on her, so she walked down the beach to Gianni's, the Italian joint Ava DeCurtis had recommended.

It was a small place, located at the end of a strip shopping center with a nail salon, a dry cleaner's, and a liquor store. She opened the heavily carved wooden door and was welcomed with the scent of garlic, onions, and red sauce.

The hostess was busy, so Vikki looked around. It was a narrow room, fairly dark, with a wall of red leatherette booths facing the bar. The décor ran to heavily stuccoed walls with cheesy frescoes that she guessed were supposed to be Italian villages. The arched entrance to the crowded dining room was framed with a pair of gigantic fake olive trees draped with straw-wrapped Chianti bottles and clumps of green plastic grapes. The tables were topped with red-and-white-checked vinyl tablecloths and more Chianti bottles with candles stuck in them.

It was like a scene straight out of *Lady and the Tramp,* and she halfway expected to see a cocker spaniel and a mutt sharing a plate of spaghetti and meatballs.

The hostess, a rail-thin woman with fake eyelashes like dead spiders, approached. "Sorry, hon, we're awful busy tonight. There's a thirty-minute wait, unless you want to sit at the bar."

"The bar's fine," Vikki told her.

She actually always preferred to eat at the bar when she was out of town, not because she was such a big drinker, but because it felt less awkward than sitting at a table for two or four and explaining to the servers that she'd be dining alone tonight. Again.

"Get you a drink?" The bartender was Hispanic and twenty-something.

"Yeah. Do you have a really dry red Merlot?"

"So dry you'll spit dust," he said. "Will you be dining with us to-night?" He offered her a menu, she took it, glanced at it, and nodded.

"I'll have the pasta with bolognese and a house salad with vinai-grette dressing. No black olives, okay?"

"Never."

He came back with the wine and a setting of flatware, and she was taking her first sip when the door opened. Joe DeCurtis stood there for a moment, looking around. He spotted her and walked over.

"Eating alone?"

She nodded.

"Me too. Mind if I join you?"

"Okay by me," Vikki said.

The bartender was back. "Hey Joe, what's shakin'?"

"Nothing much. What's the special tonight?"

"Baked snapper. Just came off the boat this afternoon. Sautéed zucchini and tomatoes, and gnocchi. Sound good?"

"Perfect. And a glass of the Barolo I like in the meantime, okay?"

Vikki raised an eyebrow. "Barolo. I don't know too many cops who know anything about wine. I'm impressed."

"I wasn't always a cop. I worked for a wine distributorship for a year or so, after college."

"Good for you."

The waiter brought his wine; he sniffed, tasted it, then nodded his approval. "I take it you didn't hear from Wingfield today?"

"No." She frowned. "I don't like it."

"I don't like it either. Did you reach out to that detective back in New York?"

"Yeah. He said he'd show up at Wingfield's place first thing in the morning and rattle his cage. Nothing else I can do, right?"

He sighed. "Yeah."

"How's Letty holding up? She looked pretty tense this morning."

"'Tense' is one word for it," Joe said.

"You two have something going on?"

He gave her a sheepish grin. "Not as far as she's concerned. I like her, but she says she wants to keep it strictly professional. Probably just as well."

The bartender slid a napkin-wrapped basket of warm bread-sticks in front of them.

"Tell me about Evan Wingfield," he said, as she broke one of the sticks in two and slathered butter on it.

"He's not your typical entitled asshole. He grew up in New Jersey, upper-middle-class family, but not rich, got a business degree from Rutgers, moved to the city, and by the time he was twenty-two, he'd borrowed enough money from his grandfather to buy his first apartment. He lies about his background, by the way," Vikki Hill said. "Tells people he's Ivy League, inherited money, blah, blah. It's all bullshit."

Joe swirled the wine in his glass. "How'd he get rich so fast?"

"He's smart. He got a job working for a bottom-feeder real estate investor, and that guy taught him some stuff, eventually began loaning him money to make his own deals. When the real estate market tanked in 2007, he scooped up several distressed properties." Agent Hill nibbled at her breadstick. "And he's so crooked, if he ate a nail, he'd shit a corkscrew."

Joe DeCurtis snorted, then dabbed his face with his napkin. "If he's so smart, how did he get on the FBI's radar?"

"He bribed some low-level civil servants who weren't so smart," she said. "And when he paid off a couple of city council members to vote his way on zoning issues, that got our attention, and the bureau's public corruption unit, where I work, got involved. We've had a secret grand jury empaneled, and they've indicted the council members. Now we're gunning for Wingfield."

"Okay. We know he's smart, and usually careful. Do you really think he's gonna fall for this fake hit-man scam you've cooked up?"

Vikki Hill rested her elbows on the counter and considered the question. "Yeah," she said finally. "The stakes are higher than they've ever been for him before. Bribes are one thing, murder's a whole different ball game. Letty is a loose end he can't afford to ignore."

"Have you considered what happens if he decides to take his business someplace else?"

"He won't."

"But what if he does?"

The bartender arrived with their food. "Hot plate," he said, pointing to the platter of pasta. Agent Hill attacked it with her fork, spearing the pasta noodles, then winding them around her fork. She chewed rapidly, nodded her approval, then turned to her companion.

"You've got it bad for this chick, don't you?"

He stared down at his own plate. "Maybe I do. Or maybe I'm not used to losing control of a situation to an FBI agent I just met twenty-four hours ago. I mean, Letty is living and working at my mother's motel. She's got a four-year-old child. I'm just pointing out that a lot could go wrong."

She rolled her eyes. "Oh Christ. Here it is. The girl thing again. I bet you'd trust me more if I was Agent *Victor* Hill. Right?"

"No!"

Vikki patted his arm. "Keep telling yourself that, DeCurtis. It's okay. I'm used to it by now." She pointed at his plate. "Eat your dinner before it gets cold. And then I'll tell you how I think this thing is gonna go down. And you can go back to sleeping in your truck outside her motel room."

"You saw that, huh?"

"I see everything. It's my job."

·   ·   ·

Agent Hill polished off her entrée and pushed her plate away. "Okay. Let's talk. If I don't hear back from Wingfield in the next twenty-four hours, obviously we have to assume something went wrong and regroup. We've applied for a wiretap for his phone, but judges are moving slower these days on electronic surveillance. If it comes to that, we'll probably move Letty and Maya, out of an abundance of caution."

"Are you talking about protective custody?"

"It probably won't come to that," she said. "Let me remind you, this is a huge step for Wingfield. We don't think he actually planned Tanya's murder. It seems like more of a crime of passion, or opportunity. Yeah, he wanted her off his payroll, but at no time did he ever mention violence to me. As far as we know, he doesn't have a lot of acquaintances in the criminal world."

"As far as you know," Joe said pointedly. "There's a wild card in this situation, you know."

"You mean Declan Rooney?"

He nodded. "I ran a search on him. There are still warrants out for him in a couple different jurisdictions around Florida, but he seems to have flown off the radar. Do the feds know anything about his whereabouts?"

Vikki Hill chewed on the end of a breadstick. "No."

"Does that mean you don't know, or the feds don't know, or you know but can't acknowledge that you know where Rooney is?"

"Sometimes, Joe, a no is just a no," she said. She glanced at her phone, which was sitting on the bar top beside her, then drained her wineglass and gestured to the bartender for her check. "Gotta go. See you back at the motel, right?"

"Maybe. You'll call me as soon as you know something, right? I'm taking PTO for the next couple days, so I'll be around."

Letty awoke with a start. It was still pitch-black outside. Ten after two in the morning. She got out of bed and checked on Maya, who

was still sleeping. She heard it then, a faint sound, like metal scraping on metal. Her heart thudded in her chest.

She crept into the living room, moved the curtain aside, and peeked out the front window. The breezeway outside the unit was empty. Beyond, in the parking lot, Midnight, the motel's pregnant resident black cat, slunk into the shadows. She exhaled slowly and stood still, listening.

The faint *skriiiiccch* sound repeated, and her heart beat even faster. Letty stepped into the darkness and moved slowly toward the sliding glass door, her legs trembling so badly she was amazed she couldn't hear her knees knocking together. It was nothing, she told herself, a leaf scraping against a window screen. The curtains were partially open, allowing a sliver of light to fall onto the floor, and she silently cursed herself for forgetting to draw them before she'd gone to bed.

Had she remembered to lock the slider? She took two steps forward and stopped in her tracks when she saw something move on the patio. She leaned forward again and peeked outside.

Someone was there! A dark figure, barely moving, reclining on one of the metal patio chairs, his long legs resting on the seat of the other chair. In the moonlight she saw that he had a baseball cap tipped forward, nearly covering his face. But she recognized the jeans-clad legs and the silhouette.

Damn Joe DeCurtis. He was determined to save her, one way or another. She exhaled slowly and felt her pulse drop back down to normal. Her fingers found the latch for the door. She fastened it, then walked briskly back to the bedroom.

Maya mumbled something inaudible, then turned and drifted back to sleep. Letty hesitated, then climbed in beside the child, spooning close to her comforting warmth. She closed her eyes, felt her shoulders relax, and then her neck, and then her legs. She grudgingly admitted that for the first time that day, she felt safe.

35

~~~~~~~~~~~~~~~

FRIDAY MORNING, LETTY SET THE mug of coffee on a table, unlatched the sliding glass door, and pushed it aside. She poked her head outside. The patio was empty. He was gone. The two chairs were pushed back into their original position. An empty can of Red Bull rested in a nearby flowerpot.

Maya was sitting at her red table behind the reception desk, quietly placing stickers in the new sticker book Isabelle had given her. Letty was on the phone with the pest-control company when the office door chimed and Oscar Jensen raced inside, followed by Merwin Maples. "Where's Ava?" Merwin demanded.

"Right here. What's the problem?" Ava emerged from the store-room where she'd been spring cleaning. She had a bundle of thread-bare beach towels under her arm and was holding a plastic bucket full of half-used bottles of sunscreen.

"There's your problem," Oscar said, pointing at Merwin. "He thinks he owns the place just because his wife uses a walker."

Merwin's voice shook with anger. "He parked in the handicapped space in front of our unit. That's where we always park. I came back from the store with a trunkload of groceries—and he was parked in my space!"

"It's not your space. Does it have your name on it? No, it doesn't. It's a handicapped space, and as of yesterday, I am handicapped." Oscar held out a square white decal with a blue wheelchair stenciled on it.

"Your only handicap is that you're out of your damned mind!" Merwin yelled. He snatched the decal out of his former pal's hand and examined it. "This thing isn't even real." He waved it at Ava. "Tell him he's got to move his damned car. Trudi's out there in the van right now, baking in that hot sun."

Maya looked up at the adults, her face puckered with concern.

Ava studied the decal, then looked up at Jensen, her expression dubious. "Oscar? Since when are you handicapped?"

"I told you, since yesterday. I have a very painful bunion situation and my doctor says I should try to stay off that foot if at all possible," Oscar said.

"What doctor? Dr. Scholl's? Dr Pepper?" Merwin grabbed the decal, ripped it in half, and threw the pieces onto the floor. "That handicapped sticker is as phony as your doctor."

"Did you really just do that?" Oscar poked him in the chest, and Merwin slapped his hand aside.

"No fighting!" Maya whimpered. "I don't like fighting."

"Hey!" Ava said sharply, stepping between the two men. She patted the little girl on the shoulder. "She's right. Cut it out, you two. No fighting in the office." She picked up the torn sticker pieces and handed them to Jensen.

"Oscar, you and I both know this thing isn't real."

"It is real," the old man insisted. "The guy at the flea market said it's totally legit. He's a doctor, and he should know."

"The flea market?" Merwin cried. "You've got to be kidding me. You think a licensed physician sets up a booth at a flea market? What? Between the tube socks and eight-track tapes? Or is he over on the aisle with the discontinued Avon products and the voodoo candles?"

"Dr. Jerry happens to see patients in his space by the Asian produce," Oscar said. "He's a very gifted healer. He gave me some ointment and my foot already feels a lot better."

Merwin stuck his face in Oscar's. "Quack!" he quacked.

"Merwin . . ." Ava sounded a warning.

Oscar took a step backward, but Merwin kept advancing, flapping his arms like a deranged duck. "Quack! Quack! Quack!"

The shorter man made a fist and reared back, ready to land a punch.

"Nooo!" Maya screamed. "No hitting!" She clamped her hands over her ears and buried her face between Letty's knees.

Ava sprang into action. She spritzed Oscar in the face with a stream of sunscreen, then turned and aimed a spray at Merwin.

"Owww!" Oscar howled, clutching his hands to his eyes.

"I'm blind!" Merwin cried, staggering backward.

"You'll both live," Ava said, handing them each a tissue. "Now let's settle this once and for all. Oscar, that alleged bunion of yours didn't keep you from playing shuffleboard for two hours yesterday. And anyway, you don't buy a handicapped sticker at the flea market. Merwin, that handicapped space is reserved for loading and unloading only. Says so right on the sign. It's not your personal space. So after Oscar moves his car, you can pull up in your van and unload Trudi and your groceries. And then you move your car into the space in the parking lot that's marked with your unit number. Understand?"

Oscar mopped at his face with the tissue and blinked rapidly. "My eyes! I think you burned my corneas."

"Tell it to Dr. Jerry," Ava snapped. She pointed at Maya, who was sobbing in Letty's arms. "Look how you've upset this little girl. Now both of you need to quit your bickering and get out of my office before I evict your bony old asses. We're trying to run a motel in here."

"Oh," Merwin said, properly chastised. "Well, I didn't mean to upset the kid. It's just that . . ."

"Out!" Ava bellowed.

"*Shhh,* ladybug," Letty said softly, rubbing Maya's back. "They weren't really fighting. They were just mad and talking too loud."

Maya lifted her tear-streaked face. "I don't like fighting and hitting. It's not nice. Mommy and Daddy had a big fight."

Letty and Ava exchanged shocked glances. Had Maya actually witnessed a physical altercation between Tanya and Evan? She'd been plagued by that question since the day she'd discovered her sister's body and looked up to find Maya crying at the top of the staircase. Her fears had only grown since watching the painfully hostile handoff captured on the nanny-cam video she'd watched just the night before. Up until now, she hadn't had the heart to question the traumatized child about what she had or hadn't seen.

"Mommy and Daddy weren't mad at you, sweetie. They were probably just upset," Letty said. "Whatever they said, I'm sure they didn't mean it."

"That's right, Maya," Ava said, her voice low and soothing. "Sometimes grown-ups say things they don't mean. Like Mr. Oscar and Mr. Merwin. They're really friends, but they both got upset today and said things they shouldn't have. But they're sorry now. And I promise, I won't let them fight again."

"No hitting," Maya said, rubbing her face against Letty's shoulder. "I don't like hitting."

Letty took a deep breath. "Maya, did you ever see Daddy hit Mommy?"

The child lifted her face, still damp with tears and snot. She nodded. "Hitting is not nice. It's very, very bad."

Vikki Hill was in her motel room, typing up her field notes, such as they were, when her phone rang. UNKNOWN CALLER.

She tapped ACCEPT.

His voice was muted by the background noise of street traffic, but she knew instantly that the caller was Wingfield. She tapped the record icon on the phone.

"Hey, Vikki," he said casually. "I've been trying to call you for two days. Where you been?"

"I didn't have any messages or missed calls on my phone. Doesn't sound like you were trying very hard, Evan. What's up?"

"Just responding to your last text. Where'd you say you are now?"

"I didn't say. Because you don't really want to know. But I did manage to locate your missing friend, just in case you're still interested," Agent Hill said.

"Yeah. Huh. That is interesting. Well, what did you have in mind?"

"Are you still playing games?" Vikki said, making her annoyance clear. "Like I told you, I found a guy who can take care of things. He checks out. But he doesn't work for free, and neither do I."

"How do you know he checks out? That he isn't a cop?"

"He *used* to be a cop. That's how I know him. But there were some . . . unfounded accusations, shall we say, of excessive force. Now he works private security at some clubs, and he does some freelance work."

"What's his name?"

Vikki's laugh was low and unamused. "Listen, Evan. I've put some time and effort into this, you know. I do have an actual job, despite what you think about civil servants. I tracked this guy down, told him a little bit about the job, negotiated terms. You're dicking around, and it's making me look bad. I'll tell you what. Forget it. I'm done."

She tapped END CALL and waited. She tried to go back to her notes, but was too antsy to concentrate. She went to the tiny kitchen and poured herself another mug of coffee. By the time she got back to the table that served as her desk, the phone was ringing again. Another unknown caller.

She was about to hit ACCEPT when the phone alerted her to an incoming text from Joe.

Heard anything?

The agent typed as quickly as she could.

He's playing hard to get. Two can play at that.

The phone rang a second time.

Now someone was knocking on the door of the efficiency. "Housekeeping!" The door opened and a woman's head popped in. "Oh, I'm sorry. . . ." She held out a stack of clean towels.

"Not now!" Vikki yelled.

"Sorry!" The woman left, and the agent got up and slammed the door, securing the security latch this time.

She rushed back to the phone, then tapped ACCEPT. "Hi. What's it gonna be?"

"Okay, yeah," Evan said. "Let's do it." His voice was clearer now. No traffic noise. He'd gone inside somewhere.

"Do what?" Vikki said a silent prayer that Wingfield would spell out his intentions.

"What we discussed. But I want it done right. She should just . . . disappear. Like, for real. I don't want anything showing up that could be traced back to me. Is your guy capable of something like that? Is he smart enough not to get caught?"

"He's not exactly Snow White. From what I've heard, it's not his first rodeo," Vikki drawled. "What about the price? He won't budge, and neither will I."

"You know what they say about greediness, right?" His tone was ominous. "Pigs get fat. Hogs get slaughtered."

"Is that a threat?" Her voice grew shrill. "Fuck you, okay? I'm going out on a limb in a major way here. Setting up a hit on somebody is a lot more serious than looking the other way when you set up another illegal Airbnb in a building in Brooklyn. How do I know you won't turn around and blame this whole thing on me once this girl is dead? For all I know, you could be ratting me out to the city right now, you creep. . . ."

"Hey, chill, Vikki," Evan said hastily. "Nobody's ratting anybody out. This is a negotiation, right? It's nothing personal. It's just how I do business. You made an offer, I made a counter, which you rejected. Jesus! Doesn't mean the deal's off the table. Calm down, okay?"

"You know what?" she said heatedly. "I am so *over* guys telling me to calm down, I could puke. Just tell me, do we have a deal? Fifty thousand. Final offer."

"Yeah. It's a deal. Couple things. I'm gonna need proof that the deed is done."

"That's crazy. You want her disappeared, there won't be any proof."

"A photo's good. But I want to be able to tell it's Letty, not some homeless bag lady you snatched off the street. I've seen that episode of *Law & Order*."

"Okay. That sounds doable," Agent Hill said. "What else?"

"My daughter. I don't want her hurt. Make sure she's nowhere near Letty when it happens. You understand? And then, I want you, personally, to deliver her back to me."

"Me? I'm not a child welfare worker, Evan. I don't even like kids."

"You'll get over it. She's a sweet kid. Nothing like her mother. One more thing. I want this done. Now. Like, this weekend. Maya's been gone almost a month. No telling what she's been through. I'll probably still be paying for a shrink when she's in college."

"I don't know," Agent Hill objected. "My guy might not be ready. He's gonna have to do some legwork to set up everything. Also, he's gonna want half up front."

"This weekend," Wingfield repeated. "Or the deal's off. Also, half won't work. I'll transfer ten thousand dollars into your account this afternoon. You'll get the rest when I get proof."

He hung up before she could offer any more lame objections.

Agent Hill disconnected, too. She went back to her text chain with DeCurtis and began typing.

GAME ON.

~~~~~~~~~~~~~

36

MELTDOWN OVER, MAYA SAT AT her red table, contentedly sucking on the cherry Popsicle Ava had fetched from her apartment above the office.

"Letty, is there any way you can go to the grocery store this morning and pick up the stuff for Bingo Night?" Ava asked. "I want to be here when the pest-control guy arrives. There are ants all over the pool patio, and the Feldman girls said they've seen some of those damned German roaches in their unit. I need to walk him around and point at every place I want sprayed."

"Happy to do the shopping. I don't want Maya around when the spraying happens anyway," Letty said. "Anything else you want me to get while I'm out?"

Ava handed her the shopping list. "This is all for now, but I'll call you if I think of anything else. Are you sure you don't want to leave Maya here with me?"

At the mention of her name, Maya looked up. Her face and hands were smeared with sticky red Popsicle juice. "I go to store."

"Thanks, I appreciate the offer, but she's been pretty clingy all morning," Letty said. "I'd better take her along."

She turned and held out a hand to her niece. "Let's go home and get you washed up before the store. Okay?"

"Okay," Maya said.

·   ·   ·

Letty was in the produce aisle at Publix, picking through a bin of avocados, trying to find the elusive—not hard as a rock, not on the verge of rot—when the man on the other side of the display nodded and smiled in her direction.

Letty gave him a curt nod. She chose four avocados, bagged them, and placed them in her shopping cart. Maya was sitting in the bottom of the cart, leafing through the pages of her sticker book.

"How many avocados did we choose?" Letty asked. She'd read somewhere about teachable moments, and had already gotten her niece started with counting, an activity Maya loved almost as much as spelling.

Maya touched each of the dark green fruits. "One. Two. Three. Four!"

"Good job!" The man was beside her now, smiling down at Maya. "What a smart little girl you have."

He was in his early forties, good-looking, deeply tanned, with a square jaw and a baseball cap with the brim pulled low over his face, and in his black jeans and black pullover, he looked totally incongruous among the usual crowd of tourists, snowbirds, and retirees. His shopping cart held only a six-pack of beer and a bag of chips.

Letty instinctively moved her cart away from his. "Thanks," she said.

"How old?" he asked, rolling his cart toward her.

"I'm four!" Maya piped up. "I'm a big girl."

"I've got a little girl just your age at home," the stranger said, staying right alongside Letty's cart. "She likes to count and spell too. Can you spell your name?"

Maya beamed. "M—"

Letty shook her head emphatically at her niece, then lightly tapped her index finger across her lips.

"I don't mean to be rude," Letty said, stopping in the middle of the aisle. "But I'm trying to teach her not to speak to strangers. So I'd appreciate it if you'd just move along. Okay?"

"Wow!" the man said with a smirk. "Sorry if I was trying to be pleasant. Excuse me!"

Letty felt a chill run all the way down her spine. She was sure she'd seen this man before. In fact, just the night before in the nanny-cam video, not to mention his booking photo. She rolled the cart out of the produce section, nearly running in her haste to get away from him. The store was crowded with people getting an early start to their weekend shopping, so she had to dodge and weave and swerve.

When she got to the next aisle, she turned around and saw that the stranger was at the back of the store, leaning over, pretending to examine a display of ground chuck. She whipped out her phone, snapped a couple of photos of him, then hurried to the front of the store. She left her cart outside the women's bathroom and took Maya inside.

Her hands were shaking as she called the motel. She started speaking as soon as Ava picked up. "Ava, is Joe around?"

"Haven't seen him this morning," she said. "What's up?"

"I'll explain later," Letty said. "Can you please text me his phone number?"

"Doing it right now."

As soon as the number popped up on her phone screen, Letty texted him. *Call me back, please. Important.*

Her phone rang a moment later. "Letty? What's wrong?"

"I'm at the Publix in Madeira Beach, and Maya's with me. We were in the produce department when I noticed this strange man staring at us. It creeped me out. He wanted to know how old Maya was, and said he had a four-year-old at home too. Then he tried to get her to say her name, but I stopped her, and basically told him to back off. Joe, maybe I'm being paranoid, but I think it's Declan Rooney. I think he was stalking us. I took a couple photos of him when he was pretending not to watch us."

"Text me the photos. But what makes you think this isn't just some garden-variety perv? Rooney's never seen you or Maya."

"Maybe it is just some random creep. He was wearing a baseball cap that obscured his face. But Joe, I think he has seen Maya before. I'll explain it later."

"Where is this guy now? And where are you?"

"I'm hiding out in the ladies' room. He was trolling around in the meat department. He's wearing black jeans and a black zip-neck pullover, and some kind of navy-blue baseball cap. I'd say he's about six-two."

"Okay, sit tight. I'm headed your way."

He called Vikki Hill on his way to Publix. "Hey. We might have a complication. Letty just called me from Publix. She thinks she saw Rooney. He was stalking her. I'm going there right now."

"Aw, shit," Agent Hill moaned. "How does she know it's him?"

"Not sure. But she texted me some pictures she took, and although he's got a ball cap pulled down over his face, the build and profile fit. It looks like this could be our guy."

"You want backup?" she asked. "That store's just a mile from here, right?"

He hesitated. "I guess it couldn't hurt. See you there."

"Letty, I don't wanna stay here," Maya whined. "I want my goldfish crackers. And my sticker book."

They'd been in the bathroom for ten minutes. They'd washed their hands, watched a cartoon on Letty's phone, and sung "Let It Go" twice. Letty was tired of hiding in a locked bathroom stall, and she was tired of being afraid, and she was tired of listening to bathroom noises.

"Okay, ladybug," she said. "Let's go."

She was placing Maya back in the shopping cart when her phone dinged with a text from Joe.

Here.

She texted back. *We're right inside the front doors.*

Letty scanned the front of the store, but didn't spot any tall men dressed all in black.

Joe sprinted through the door. "Is he still here?"

"Not up front," Letty reported.

A moment later, Vikki Hill joined them. "Any sign of him?"

"Not up here," Letty said.

"Let's split up," Joe said. "You take the right side of the store, I'll take the left."

"I'll go with Vikki," Letty said.

The agent gave Maya a tentative smile. "Hey there. I'm Vikki."

Maya ducked her head. "I'm not s'posed to talk to strangers."

"Exactly right," Vikki Hill said. "Do *not* talk to strangers. Ever."

They were rolling at a fast clip through the frozen food aisle, then past the wine and beer, then the pharmacy, dodging senior citizens who were perusing lists on their phones or just chatting in the middle of the aisles.

"Jesus! Aisle cloggers are the worst," Hill said under her breath.

"It's the coupon clippers who drive me nuts," Letty said.

"And don't get me started on people writing checks. Who does that? You see him anywhere?" Vikki asked.

"I think he's gone," Letty said. "I'm so pissed at myself for hiding out in the bathroom like some chickenshit. I should have at least tried to follow him out to the parking lot to see what he was driving."

"With a little kid in your cart? No. You did the right thing." Hill pointed at Joe, who was standing in front of the customer service counter, chatting with a man in a short-sleeved dress shirt and tie and Publix name badge.

"We think he's gone," Vikki Hill said, as they approached.

"I didn't see him either," Joe said. "Agent Hill, Letty, this is Craig Hoffman. He's the manager here. I've asked if we could take a look at the store's security cameras. Maybe we can get a better look at this guy's face that way."

"And I was just explaining that I'd have to get my district supervisor's approval for that kind of thing," Hoffman said. "Sorry. Company policy."

Vikki Hill frowned. "Mr. Hoffman? How long would that take? The man we're looking for is a felon and a fugitive. He's a suspect in an unsolved homicide in New York. We won't disrupt business or hassle your customers. All we want to do is look at the video for the past hour."

Hoffman shrugged. "And as I said, it's company policy. We like to assist law enforcement in any way we can, but . . ."

The FBI agent waved aside his apology. "Never mind." She turned to Joe. "Let's roll. We're getting nowhere here."

"I'll meet you back at the motel," Letty said, brandishing Ava's grocery list. "I've got to finish shopping. . . ."

Agent Hill plucked the list from her hand. "Now," she said quietly. "I heard from our friend this morning. We leave now."

~~~~~~~~~~~~

37

AVA AND ISABELLE MET HER in the parking lot at the motel. "Are you okay?" Ava asked. "Joe called to tell me what happened."

"I'm a little shook," Letty admitted, lifting Maya out of her car seat. "Sorry I didn't get your groceries."

"Hi, Isabelle!" Maya reached out her arms to her babysitter.

"Hi, Maya Papaya," Isabelle said, giving the child a quick hug before setting her on the ground.

"Was it really Rooney?" Isabelle whispered, leaning into Letty.

"I don't know. Remember, I've never seen him in real life. But when I looked up and saw him staring at us, and then when he tried to talk to Maya, the hair on the back of my neck stood up. I couldn't get away from him fast enough."

"If it was him, he'd better not show his face around here again," Ava said, her expression fierce. "I would just as soon shoot him as . . ."

Letty cut her eyes toward her niece.

"Anyway," Ava said. "You're okay, and that's all that matters."

"Isabelle, let's go to the beach," Maya said, taking her babysitter's hand as they walked slowly toward the office.

Letty shook her head slightly and Isabelle caught her meaning.

"Not right now. My mama is going to fix us some lunch! And after that, we can play dress-up."

"I wanna go to the beach," Maya said, her lower lip pooching out.

Letty shook her head again.

"Maybe we'll bake some cookies," Ava offered. "Do you know anyone who likes cookies?"

Maya held up her stuffed elephant. "Ellie loooooves cookies."

"I'm probably being super paranoid, but please tell Isabelle not to let her out of her sight today," Letty whispered in Ava's ear. "I know it's a lot to ask, but keep her inside, away from the pool or the beach. Just in case."

Ava patted her arm. "Don't you worry. We're not gonna let anything happen to that little one. Or to you. And that's a promise."

"*First* off," Vikki Hill asked Letty, "how is it that you were able to recognize Declan Rooney? It was my understanding that you never met the man."

They were sitting in the living area of Letty's unit.

Letty turned to Joe. "After you told me about Rooney's connection to Tanya, I looked up his booking photo online. But there's something else . . ."

She clasped her hands in her lap. "I was going to tell you guys. First thing this morning. But then stuff was happening so fast . . ."

"Tell us what?" Joe asked.

"About the nanny cam. In Ellie. Tanya must have sewn it there. So she could snoop on Evan when Maya was with him. She never said a word about it to me. I only found it by accident. . . ."

"Whoa! Who's Ellie?" Agent Hill looked from Letty to Joe. "A nanny cam?"

"Ellie is Maya's stuffed elephant. Like, her security blanket. Right? But this is the first I'm hearing about a nanny cam," Joe said. "Letty?"

"The other night, after the barbecue, Isabelle was babysitting and Maya fell asleep and we were carrying her inside to put her to bed, and she must have dropped Ellie out in the breezeway. It was the night it rained so hard. Anyway, I found her out there, Ellie, that is, not Maya, in a puddle, and I was drying her off with a hair dryer, and I felt something hard—inside, like, her forehead. So I got some scissors, and dug around, and I pulled out this *thing*. It turns out it was a tiny video camera. I didn't know what to do with it, but I asked Isabelle, and she has a friend from school who's sort of a hacker, so Sierra came over, and . . ."

"You told my seventeen-year-old sister about this nanny cam? But not me?" Joe interrupted.

"Yeah. I did." Letty was unrepentant. "Turns out Isabelle had already figured out that I'm Tanya's sister. This was before Agent Hill showed up. While I still wasn't sure I trusted you. Can I keep going now?"

"Be my guest."

Letty quickly filled them in on how she'd figured out her sister's password, which allowed Sierra to access the nanny-cam videos on Tanya's iCloud. And she gave them a description of the content that she'd watched the night before.

"We need to see that video right now," Vikki Hill said. "Did you watch all of it?"

"No. There are hundreds of hours of footage, starting from November. A lot of it is whatever you can see while Maya drags Ellie around the apartment. Or in the car. It's mostly life from the viewpoint of a four-year-old."

"Tell us again about the part where Rooney shows up," Joe said.

"It might not even be him," Letty repeated. "It's a guy in a knit cap and a puffy jacket. He walks into the apartment, and Tanya looks a little surprised, but then happy to see him. They kiss, and Tanya points out Maya, who's across the room holding Ellie, which is why it's hard to make out the guy's face, or hear any of what the grown-ups are saying. Then, Maya freaks out and runs upstairs, taking Ellie with her. And that's it. I watched more of the footage after that, but the mystery man doesn't show up again."

"And you can't hear what Tanya and the man are talking about?" Agent Hill repeated.

"No."

"Where's this camera now?" she asked.

Letty fetched the camera and thumb drive Sierra had given her from her nightstand and placed it in the FBI agent's hand. "This is it. Can you copy it and return it to me?"

Vikki nodded. "Okay. We'll get it back to you. When was the most recent video shot?"

"February twenty-eighth was the last date," Letty said. "I probably only got through a couple weeks' worth before I finally fell asleep last night."

She looked down at her hands, and then up at Vikki Hill. "I think the battery must have run down . . . before Tanya was killed. I fast-forwarded to the end, which takes place three days before. It's nothing special. She takes Maya to the dentist, and the pediatrician. Tanya was getting ready to move to LA, you know, so she wanted to have all Maya's records for when she started school out there."

Letty's eyes filled with tears. "I know my sister wasn't a model mom. She could be self-involved and impetuous and so, so self-destructive. And yes, she struggled with drugs and alcohol. She and Evan had these awful knockdown fights, right in front of Maya. There's one on the video, and it was so tough to watch. But she loved her daughter. Really loved her. And she was trying to do what was best for Maya. To get away from Evan, and start over."

Letty found herself remembering the last bit of footage she'd watched the night before. The video showed Tanya giddy with excitement in anticipation of the move. She found herself choking up as she described the video.

"They went to Old Navy. It was snowing outside. She bought Maya a bathing suit, because the house she was going to rent out there has a pool. . . ."

Vikki Hill nodded. "It's okay. We get it. I'll take a look at the videos on the thumb drive, and I'll send the one with Rooney to the bureau's tech guys. Maybe they can amplify the sound or something."

She glanced over at Joe DeCurtis. "How the hell would Rooney know where to find Tanya? And how—and why—would he show up back down here, following Letty and Maya around?"

"I'm wondering the same thing," Joe said.

"We can't get sidetracked by that right now," the FBI agent said. "There's no evidence Rooney was anywhere near Tanya's apartment that day."

She pointed at Letty. "Wingfield wants you 'disappeared' as he put it. This weekend. I've got to show him proof that you're dead. And then he wants me, personally, to deliver Maya back to him."

Letty crossed her arms over her chest. "Over my dead body."

"That's the idea," Vikki agreed. "As far as Wingfield knows."

Agent Hill placed her phone on the table and played the first phone conversation she'd recorded with Evan Wingfield.

Joe frowned when the conversation ended. "He doesn't really commit to anything here. I'm not telling you how to do your job, but why cut him off, just as he's starting to come around?"

"I needed to make him fish or cut bait," Vikki said. "And sure enough, he did come around, not more than five minutes later." She looked down at the phone again, and her face froze.

"Oh no. Tell me this did not happen." She slapped her forehead with the palm of her hand and groaned. "Nooooooo."

Joe and Letty waited, exchanging worried glances.

The FBI agent's face reddened with embarrassment. "Jesus, what a rookie move! Right when Wingfield was calling back I got a text from you, Joe, and then the maid was knocking on the door and trying to leave towels, so I chased her away and got up to lock the door . . . and I was in such a hurry to pick up, I must have forgotten to push the friggin' record button when he called back. There's no excuse for this. And the worst thing is, when Wingfield called back, he actually did commit. He negotiated the price, agreed to fifty thousand and promised to wire a ten-thousand-dollar deposit to my bank account this afternoon. He explicitly said he wanted Letty 'disappeared' and said he wanted photographic proof that she was dead."

Letty shuddered.

Vikki stood up and paced around the room. "I screwed up. That phone call directly ties him to the murder-for-hire plot. Now we got no proof. Jesus, what a fuckup!"

"Maybe not," Joe said. "How did you leave it with him?"

"He was adamant that the job had to get done this weekend. I told him my guy needed more time, but he pushed back hard on that."

DeCurtis nodded. "Can you check your bank account? To see if the money has landed?"

"Yeah." The FBI agent picked up her phone again, scrolled through the apps on the screen, then tapped one. She studied it, then nodded, her expression hopeful.

"It's here. Ten thousand. Wired fifteen minutes ago."

Joe held out his hand. "Give me your phone."

"Why?"

"I'm gonna call him and turn up the heat. And this time, I'll record the conversation."

"Screw you," Vikki said, but she gave him the phone.

Wingfield answered after the first ring and Joe put the phone on speaker.

"You again? I don't like all these calls. I thought we had a plan. You got the money, right? Just do your damn job now."

"Hi, Evan. It's not Vikki, it's Vikki's guy," Joe said easily. "How ya doin'?"

"I've had better days. What's your name, anyway?"

"You can call me Joe. So we don't get our signals crossed, tell me exactly what it is you want me to do."

"I told Vikki already," Wingfield said. "Talk to her."

"Screw that. I don't know or care what you told her. She's only the middleman. I need you to tell me exactly what you expect."

Silence at the other end of the line.

Wingfield cleared his throat. "I don't feel good talking about this on the phone. How do I know this isn't just a giant rip-off? That you even know where they are?"

"Watch your phone, and then call me back here," Joe said. He disconnected, then took his own phone from the pocket of his jeans. He scrolled through the photos, found a candid shot he'd taken recently of Letty and Maya, at sunset, sitting on the beach, and AirDropped it to Vikki Hill's phone before texting it to Evan Wingfield.

The FBI agent's phone rang a minute later and Joe picked up.

"Satisfied?"

"They're at the beach? Where is this?"

"They *were* at the beach. Can we cut the bullshit now?"

"Yeah. Listen up, because this is the last time I'm talking to you. Or her. I want Letty gone. As in permanently. I don't want her body turning up in a week or a month. And I want proof that she's gone. Like I told Vikki, I've already seen the *Law & Order* episode where the bad guy snatches a bag lady off the street to phony up a hit. When it's done, send me a photo. You'll get the rest of your funds— after my daughter is returned to me."

"What?" Joe said. "No way. That's not what Vikki said. I'm not dealing with a kid. . . ."

This time, it was Wingfield's turn to disconnect.

Joe turned to Vikki Hill. "What do you think? Is that good enough to get him arrested and charged with conspiracy to commit?"

"It was pretty good," the agent admitted. "The photo of Letty and Maya was a nice touch. I need to touch base with the AUSA I've been working with. I'll send her both the recordings and fill her in on where we're at." She glanced at her phone again.

"I'm going back to my place. I'll grab a bite, then circle back to you. Hopefully no later than three. In the meantime, DeCurtis, maybe you can start thinking of places to 'dispose of' Letty's body."

When she was gone, Letty collapsed back into the sofa cushions. "How is this even real?" she asked. "When does it end? When do Maya and I get to have a normal life?"

Joe sat on the sofa beside her. "Soon. But I won't lie, Letty. The hard stuff's still ahead of you. Hopefully, you'll be cleared of Tanya's murder, and the NYPD will prove Wingfield did kill your sister. But if the feds make a case against Wingfield, you'll be their star witness. It could be a long, dragged-out process."

"And in the meantime, I just know Evan's going to fight me to try and get custody of Maya. Especially now that he knows he stands to lose control of all that real estate he deeded over to Tanya."

She slumped down even farther into the cushions. "I should have dumped that pot of hot coffee in his lap the first time he sat down at table two."

~~~~~~~~~~~~

38

VIKKI HILL WALKED SLOWLY OVER to Letty's unit, finishing off the last of her lunch, which had consisted of a prepackaged cellophane sandwich from the convenience store down the block and a bag of Cheetos. She pushed through the partially open door and found Joe DeCurtis, slumped over in an armchair near the front window, obviously dozing.

"Where's Letty?"

Joe yawned. "She went back over to the office, to get some work done. Said she couldn't stand sitting around here all afternoon, waiting on us to decide how her life's gonna turn out. Can't say I blame her."

Obviously frustrated, Agent Hill ran a hand through her hair. "Okay, well, I don't have good news. I played the recordings of Wingfield to Cheryl Shapiro, she's the assistant US attorney I've been working with, and unfortunately, she says we need more."

"You've gotta be kidding me," Joe said. "We've got him on tape, saying he wants Letty disappeared, and doesn't want her body showing up a month from now. That should be more than enough for an arrest, and an indictment."

"It might be enough for a district attorney in a state court," Vikki pointed out. "But I work for the federal government. Our standards are different. An arrest isn't enough. An indictment isn't enough. We need solid, incontrovertible evidence for a conviction."

"Which means what?" he asked.

She shrugged. "We need Wingfield paying you off after he sees what he thinks are photos of Letty's body. And we need him meeting you—in person, when you hand off his daughter to him in exchange for your payoff."

"Letty will never go for that," Joe said. "You heard her. She's not going to let me take Maya back to New York."

"Okay, I just had a genius idea. What if you tell Evan he has to come to you if he wants Maya?"

"You mean here? Like, Florida?"

"Right here at the Murmuring Surf. The more I think about it, the better I like it. If Wingfield has to cross state lines to get her, that strengthens our case. It's interstate commerce, possibly furthering the racketeering enterprise. The AUSA will love it."

"And Wingfield? Seems to me he's already pretty skittish."

"Yeah, he is. I've been dealing with Evan for eighteen months now. He's a cautious guy. He's been blaming Tanya's murder on Letty, but he has no idea exactly what Letty—or Maya—knows about Tanya's death. As long as Letty's alive, she's a threat to him.

"The other thing that motivates him is greed. He's still beside himself that he was dumb enough to put those real estate assets in Tanya's name. Now? He tells himself that he's a great dad, just looking out for the welfare of that little girl, but the truth is, it's all about the money. If Letty's alive, he's fighting her in court over that guardianship, and there's no guarantee he'll prevail. I'm sure he thinks fifty thousand dollars is a reasonable investment to protect his own interests. Hell, he'll probably find a way to make it a tax write-off. Cost of doing business."

Joe leaned forward and braced his hands on his knees. "But first we gotta convince Wingfield that Letty is dead, and that she won't be found. I think we stage it so that it looks like I dumped her body in the Gulf. Weighted down with chains and an anchor."

Vikki nodded thoughtfully. "So . . . sharks would take care of the rest. I like it."

"We can take her out on my boat. I've got a twenty-two-foot Pathfinder. We wait until right before sundown. It's more convincing that way. I'll truss her up, fake up some blood. Take a photo and send it to him."

"Chains and anchors? 'Truss her up, fake some blood'?"

Joe and Vikki turned to see Letty standing in the apartment's open doorway. "When were you two going to tell me about your plan? Before or after you threw me to the sharks?"

"It's just for show," Vikki Hill said. "You know Wingfield. You know how careful he is. We need to convince him you're really dead."

"I literally just came up with this idea," Joe said, knowing it sounded lame. "We don't have to do it that way if you don't feel comfortable."

Letty flopped down onto a chair at the dining table. "How exactly am I supposed to feel comfortable about posing as a corpse before becoming shark bait?"

"You're not," Vikki said. "No way around it, the next few days are going to be brutal for you, and that's if we do everything right. Okay? But remember, we're doing this so that you and Maya can be safe."

"And so that Evan rots in prison for what he did to my sister," Letty said. She sat up straight in the chair. "All right. Tell me the plan. I'm ready."

Vikki cast a dubious eye about her as the Pathfinder bobbed in the water at the end of the boat ramp. "Are you sure this thing is safe to take out on the water? It looks awful small for three people."

"Yes, it's safe," Joe said, annoyed. "This isn't the S.S. *Minnow,* and we're not going for a three-hour tour. From here, it's a twenty-minute ride out to Egmont Key, tops." He pointed at the bow of the boat. "The life jackets are in that locker up front. Feel free to put yours on."

The FBI agent scowled, then opened the locker hatch, found an orange life vest, and tied it over her windbreaker.

He glanced at Letty, perched on the seat next to him on the center-console, and softened his tone. "Do you want a life jacket?"

She shook her head. "Let's just go."

He backed the boat slowly away from the concrete ramp, raising his voice over the din of the outboard engine. "Okay, the wind's picked up some, and we've got a light chop, which means I'm gonna need to run the boat pretty fast to get out to the ship channel and back before dark. I'm warning you, we could get bounced around a little, but again, it's perfectly safe."

"Ready?"

Vikki shrugged, Letty nodded.

He pushed the throttle and the Pathfinder surged forward. Letty grasped the console and gritted her teeth as the boat rose up on a wave, then slapped down hard. Water splashed over the gunwales, and Vikki let out a muffled screech before scurrying toward the bench seat in the stern of the boat.

The wind whipped her hair and clothes, and she could feel her sneakers and pant legs growing wet and cold from water being splashed into the boat, but Letty felt weirdly energized by the boat's motion. She couldn't remember the last time she'd been out on the water—maybe as a teenager, when a boyfriend had taken her waterskiing on a lake? She'd loved the freedom, the sense of watching land recede as they moved across the horizon.

Gradually she got accustomed to the Pathfinder's pace, bending her knees to absorb the shocks of the teeth-jolting ride. The sun was starting to dip toward the horizon, and the late-winter sky was streaked with gradations of orange and purple and blue.

Joe nudged her in the side and pointed off to the boat's port side. "Dolphins!"

A pair of the sleek curved-back creatures dove in and out of the waves beside them, seemingly racing to keep pace with the boat. Letty watched, entranced, wishing that Maya could have seen them, too.

He must have read her mind. He leaned in close to be heard over the din of the engine. "When this is all over, we'll bring Maya out dolphin-watching. Okay?"

She nodded.

The boat thudded and rocked, the wind howled, and waves slapped at the bow. Finally, Joe pulled the throttle back and the Pathfinder slowed and then stopped.

"This is the ship channel," he said. "It's ninety feet deep here. Perfect place to bury a body."

Letty turned and saw Vikki, leaning over the back of the boat, hurling her guts into the swirling green water.

"Aaaarggghhhh." The FBI agent straightened and sank down onto the bench, wiping her mouth with the hem of her windbreaker.

"Are you okay?" Letty asked, sitting beside her.

"No," Vikki said, closing her eyes. "I will never be okay until this voyage of the damned is over."

Joe reached into the cooler at his feet and handed over a bottle of water. "Here. Take a sip. Slowly." He pulled a small foil packet from a compartment in the console. "You want a Dramamine? You didn't tell me you get seasick."

"You didn't tell me we were heading out to sea in gale-force winds," Vikki shot back. "If I'd wanted a roller-coaster ride I'd have gone to the county fair and ordered a corn dog. Now give me the damned Dramamine and let's get this done."

He pointed to the sandy, tree-lined shoreline in the distance. "This ain't out to sea. That's Egmont Key right there. But whatever."

He went to the Pathfinder's stern and lowered one anchor, then climbed onto the bow and dropped a second.

When he returned to the two women he was carrying a lidded plastic five-gallon bucket and a third anchor attached to a long length of chain.

He lightly touched Letty's arm. "Vikki's right. Let's get this over with. Ready?"

She swallowed hard and rose unsteadily to her feet. "Yeah. Just tell me what to do."

"Come on up to the bow with me. I'll get you posed, and then Hill, once you're done tossing your cookies, you can play photographer."

Joe hefted the lidded bucket onto the bow, alongside the third anchor, which was attached to a long length of chain.

He offered Letty a Dramamine. "You might want this. Even though I've got us on the backside of Egmont, facing into the wind, I can't completely stabilize the boat."

She shook her head.

"Okay, then. I need you to stretch out here with your feet together. I'm gonna wrap this chain around your ankles, then your middle, then your shoulders. It's kinda damp and rusty, but there's nothing I can do about that."

The sun had slid even lower in the deepening purple sky and the wind picked up again, making whitecaps on the water's surface. Letty crawled onto the bow and assumed the position. Joe worked quickly, winding the chain around her body. She felt the dread and nausea rise in her throat as he worked his way toward her torso, and she arched her back to let him slip the wet metal links beneath her body.

"Almost done," he said. She turned her head and saw that he was kneeling beside her. "Try and breathe out of your mouth. It's fixing to get ugly now." He lifted the lid of the bucket and she gasped as the fetid smell of dead fish assaulted her nostrils.

"I'm sorry, but this was the best I could do on such short notice," Joe said, as he dipped a rag into the bucket and brought it out, dripping with deep red blood. "Probably best if you close your eyes so you don't see what happens next. And keep breathing through your nose."

She did as he suggested, and flinched as she felt him dabbing her forehead, cheeks, and neck with the bloody rag. She heard the sound of liquid pouring from the bucket and gagged out loud as she felt the wet fish blood seeping into her hair and the collar of her shirt.

He patted her shoulder again. "Almost done, Letty." Her eyelids fluttered open and she saw the flare of a match lighting and saw him touch it to the tip of a cigar. "What are you doing?"

When the cigar had burned down half an inch, he pinched the flame with his forefingers, then, holding the cigar in his left hand, he tipped his right pinky finger into the ash, then delicately tapped it onto her forehead and right shoulder.

"Bullet holes," he said.

"Not too shabby," Vikki said, leaning over to inspect. "But to be completely convincing, we could use some brain tissue."

Joe rolled his eyes. "I'll tell Wingfield I did the deed in a dark alley, then moved the body to the boat. Like any self-respecting hit man would."

"Could you two quit admiring your handiwork and take the damned picture before I pass out from the smell?" Letty said, gritting her teeth.

"Turn your head to the side," the FBI agent ordered. She held out her phone and began clicking the shutter, moving slowly around Letty's body, photographing it from a dozen different angles.

"All done," she said, after what seemed like an eternity to Letty.

Joe worked quickly, freeing her from the chains. She sat up and moved from the bow to the bench seat Vikki had vacated. He handed her a clean wet towel with the Murmuring Surf's logo stamped in green on the hem. She wiped her face, neck and hands.

"Here," he said, holding up another towel. "I can get the back of your hair."

"Yes, please," she said, desperate to remove the smell from her body. He blotted the blood from her hair, then took the used towels and mopped the blood from the boat's bow. He raised the bucket and tossed the remains of the bloody fish into the water, then leaned over the gunwale, filled the bucket with water, and splashed it around the bow three more times before he was satisfied that the last traces of the gore were gone. Then he put the used towels in the bucket, replaced the lid, and stowed the extra anchor and chain in one of the front lockers.

"All done," he announced.

"Oh my God," Vikki cried, pointing to the water's surface a few yards from the Pathfinder. The water boiled and a trio of dorsal fins circled the floating fish remains.

"Quick. Take a picture," Joe said. "It's the pièce de résistance."

The agent clicked the shutter six more times. "Got it. Wingfield will really get off on a shark feeding frenzy."

Letty choked back the bile rising in her throat. "Now can we please go home?"

As soon as the sun set they heard the rumble of thunder. The temperature plummeted by what felt like ten degrees, the wind picked up even more, and the rain began, huge, cold droplets.

"Let's run for shore," Joe announced, as he scrambled to raise the anchors.

"Yes, let's," Vikki Iill agreed.

The rain slashed at their faces as the Pathfinder plowed through the rising waves. Vikki huddled, wet, shivering, and thoroughly miserable, in the stern of the boat. "Come on up here and get behind the windshield," Joe beckoned.

Letty edged closer beside him in the pilot's seat, and the three of them crowded in behind the console's windshield as the boat rose and buckled back down. "Oh God," Vikki moaned. "Just get me back on dry land and I'll never leave again."

"Are you gonna puke again?" Joe asked, peering through the rain-splattered windshield. "Don't puke on my GPS, okay?"

She nodded wordlessly and squeezed her eyes shut. "I can't watch."

Ten minutes passed and then the Pathfinder's running lights

illuminated the looming boat launch. Joe nosed the boat forward until it was parallel with the dock. He jumped onto the dock and tied the boat to cleats at the bow and the stern.

"Hey Letty. I'm gonna jump out and back the trailer down. You guys can go get in the truck too. I'll take it from here."

He reached a hand down and helped Vikki and then Letty onto the dock, and they ran, splashing, through the rain.

"Okay," he said, ten minutes later, as he climbed behind the steering wheel. "Who wants to go get dinner? I'm starved."

Letty shuddered and cut her eyes toward Vikki Hill, whose head rested on Letty's shoulder, her mouth open, softly snoring. "I think her Dramamine finally kicked in," she murmured. "I can't think about anything—especially food. I just want a hot shower. And maybe a good stiff drink."

Joe reached under the seat and pulled out a pint bottle of Knob Creek. He passed it to Letty. She took a swig, swished it around in her mouth, then felt the slow, comforting burn as the bourbon trickled down her throat.

He pulled the boat slowly away from the launch, then casually stretched his free arm over her back, resting his hand lightly on her damp shoulder. She nestled closer to his side. "Let's go home."

39

Friday Night

"MAYA IS SOUND ASLEEP," AVA reported, when Letty unlocked the door to her unit. "I fed her some supper, and we read some stories, and then she took herself to bed."

"Thanks again for watching her," Letty said. "I'm headed for the shower."

Ava wrinkled her nose. "Good idea. No offense, but you smell like the bottom of a bait bucket."

When she emerged from the bathroom, dressed in clean, dry clothes, Ava was gone, but Letty found Joe and Vikki Hill sitting in the dining area, with a half-full bottle of red wine and a cardboard pizza box on the table.

"Sorry for the intrusion, but we really need to get these photos sent off to Wingfield," Joe said. He gestured at the box. "Want some?"

"No thanks. I'm just going to have some hot tea and toast."

"How quaint," Vikki said. "Like something from an Agatha Christie novel."

Letty shrugged. "My grandmother used to fix me tea and cinnamon toast when I was upset or anxious. It calms me down."

"I find Xanax calms me down," Vikki said. "But I had to quit."

Letty brought her mug of tea over to the table and stood, looking down at the screen of Vikki's phone.

One glance at the gruesome images was enough. She sat at the opposite end of the table and nibbled at a slice of toast.

"This one," Vikki said, passing the phone to Joe. "Good work. If I hadn't seen it with my own eyes, I'd swear she was dead in this one. And I've seen a lot of murder scenes in my time."

"Really? I thought the feds only investigated nice, tidy white-collar crimes."

"Wrong. We get called in on homicides, especially organized crime. Remember, I work in New York," Agent Hill said.

She scrolled through the photos again, bookmarking two more. "I like these two. The wide-angle shot, where you can see the tip of the boat, and her with the chains and anchor, and then that first close-up of her head, with the blood, and then the shark shot."

"Your call," Joe said. "I'm just the muscle."

Vikki Hill typed the text message into the phone.

Mission accomplished.

Next, she texted the three photos.

Consider this your invoice.

Joe helped himself to a gooey slice of pizza, then sprinkled red pepper flakes on it. "Now what?"

"Now we wait," the agent said.

He looked over at Letty. "Are you okay? You look pretty pale."

She managed a wan smile. "I thought that was the idea. I'm supposed to be a corpse, right?"

"That part of the charade is over," he said.

"You did great," Vikki said. "A real trouper."

"I might never eat seafood again," Letty said. "I must have used half the bottle of shampoo, trying to get that smell out of my hair."

"Sorry . . ." Joe started to say.

Vikki's phone pinged. She grabbed it up and read the text message out loud.

Where's Maya? Is she okay?"

Vikki typed a quick reply.

She's fine.

Wingfield texted back immediately.

Proof?

Vikki looked expectantly at Letty. "What should I say?"

Letty got up and went into the bedroom, where her niece was turned on her side, clutching Ellie to her cheek. She shut the door and went back to the dining area.

"Point out that it's after nine o'clock, and she's asleep."

"Should we take a photo of her, to prove it?" Vikki asked.

Letty's reply was sharp. "No. I don't want her to wake up and think something is wrong. If Evan doesn't like it, too bad."

"Good idea," Vikki said.

It's after 9. She's asleep. Long day.

Wingfield's text was to the point.

No proof, no money.

Joe peered over the agent's shoulder, reading the text as it appeared. "What a douche. Tell him your guy doesn't like getting stiffed. No money, no kid."

Vikki texted Joe's message, verbatim.

They waited.

"Okay, I'll take a very small glass of wine," Letty said, after fifteen minutes of pacing the room. "Otherwise, I'll never sleep tonight."

She took the glass of wine and stood at the sliding glass doors, looking out at the rain. What would they do if Evan balked at completing the transaction? Would the FBI have enough evidence to arrest him? How could she prove she hadn't killed her sister? Would Evan ever face charges for killing Tanya? Would she and Maya have to return to New York? The questions swirled around in her head as the minutes ticked slowly past.

"It's been thirty minutes," Joe said. "Should we ping him again?"

"No," Vikki said, standing up. She yawned loudly. "Let Wingfield stew about it overnight. I'm going to bed. If I hear from him, I'll let you know."

She went to the sliding glass doors and stood beside Letty for a moment. "Don't worry," she said softly. "We'll nail this guy. I promise you, Evan Wingfield is not going to get away with this. Okay?"

"Okay."

Joe gathered up the pizza box and the paper plates and placed them in the kitchen trash bin. He corked the wine bottle and placed it on the counter.

"I'm gonna shove off too," he told Letty.

"No more sleeping on my patio, or in your truck out in that parking lot," Letty said, trying to look severe. "Go home. You heard Vikki. They're gonna get Evan. Maya and I will be fine."

He cocked one eyebrow and studied her. "Will you? Seems like you've been through a lot. Especially today. I get that you're physically okay. But what about up here?" He tapped her forehead.

"Truthfully? I'm a mess, emotionally. I need a good night's sleep, and then Maya and I will get up in the morning, and we'll somehow get through this. Because we don't have a choice."

He took her hand and squeezed it. "You're a ballsy chick, Letty Carnahan. You know that?"

She leaned in and kissed him on the cheek. "I'm going to take that as a compliment."

He placed the flat of his hand on her back and it lingered there, for a moment. "I have lots of real compliments. You know, when you're ready to hear them."

Letty walked him to the front door and locked it behind him.

"Don't forget the security latch," he said, his voice muffled by the door that stood between them.

"Go home."

When she heard his footsteps echoing outside in the breezeway, she stood with her back to the door, feeling a mixture of relief and regret. She had come so close to caving in, to asking him to stay, to allowing herself to give into her growing attraction to Joe DeCurtis. For tonight, anyway, she'd managed to dodge that bullet.

40

~~~~~~~~~~

"HEY, JOE."

He opened one eye. Oscar Jensen stood in the breezeway outside Letty's room, unlit cigarette in hand, looking down at him with a bemused expression.

Joe yawned. It was just past daylight. He stood up and stretched. His back was killing him.

"What's going on?" Oscar whispered, glancing around furtively. "You staking out Letty's room, or what?"

Joe plucked the cigarette from Oscar's fingers. "You gotta quit smoking out here, Oscar. Also, you didn't see me. Understand?"

He was just emerging from the shower when he heard the phone ringing on his nightstand. He dove for it, stubbing his toe on the metal frame of his bed. "Goddamn!" he howled, tapping ACCEPT.

"Excuse me? I'm looking for Officer DeCurtis?" It was a man's voice. Joe looked at the caller ID screen and saw a South Florida area code.

"Oh, sorry. This is Joe DeCurtis. Who's this?"

"This is Chief Deputy Warren Davis, down here in Collier County. I'm just following up on a lead and I see your department has an outstanding warrant for a Charles Sheppard?"

"Who?" Joe sank down on the bed, examining his little toe, which was bleeding.

"Charles Sheppard. White male, age sixty-three. Wanted for theft by taking, fraud, conspiracy to commit fraud. Your warrant is from 2014. Sound familiar? Looks like he and a couple associates had a racket going at a motel up there in Treasure Island. Buying estate silver and gold and jewelry and bilking senior citizens."

"Chuck!" Joe exclaimed. "You mean Chuck Sheppard?" His toe was bleeding all over the floor. "Don't tell me you caught up with that piece of shit."

"Yeah, I guess you could say we caught up with him. Or what's left of him," the deputy said, chuckling at his own joke.

Joe padded into the bathroom, tore a piece of toilet paper off the roll, and wrapped it around his toe. "He's dead?"

"Oh yeah," the deputy drawled.

"When was this? What happened?"

"We found his remains four days ago, but we couldn't identify him until yesterday. We were able to lift his fingerprints from the vehicle he was driving, and that's when we found out his name and discovered the outstanding warrants."

"How was he killed?"

"Somebody wanted us to think that he was killed in a car fire. His body was discovered on a county road down here, in a stolen vehicle, a 1998 Jeep Cherokee. The Jeep was smashed up and partially burned. We found your guy in the driver's seat."

"But he wasn't killed in the wreck?"

"Probably not. Our medical examiner found a bullet lodged in his cerebellum."

It took a moment for the finality of Chuck Sheppard's death to sink in for Joe. "Does your medical examiner have any thoughts on when he was killed?"

"The body was in pretty bad shape. That road's in a remote part of the county, way back in the swamp. It was discovered by a couple of hog hunters. Doc says rough estimate, death occurred about a week ago."

"Well, damn," Joe said, toweling his hair dry and looking around for his clothes. "I don't suppose you have any suspects?"

"I was hoping you could help us with that," the deputy said. "Since he had no ID on him, we don't know where he was staying or what he was doing here."

Joe thought back to where his mother had started her ill-starred acquaintance with Chuck Sheppard. "Do y'all have any Indian gambling casinos in your area?" Joe asked. "That's where he liked to hang out when he was living up here, at the Seminole casino in Tampa. That is, when he wasn't ripping off old people."

"The Seminole tribe has a casino here in Immokalee," the deputy said. "I'll look into that. But from what I can tell, the last time Sheppard was detained, he was working with a couple of associates. A woman named Tanya Carnahan and a Declan Rooney. Do those names ring a bell?"

"They do," Joe said. "Tanya Carnahan died about a month ago."

"Natural causes?"

"No. She was murdered."

"Well, damn. How about this Declan Rooney? I see he's got a record. Any idea of his whereabouts?"

"Funny you should ask," Joe said. "Rooney may have returned to the scene of the crime. I've got a witness who spotted someone who looked like him at a Publix right here on Treasure Island, yesterday."

"That's interesting," the deputy said. "You think this witness is reliable?"

"If it was Rooney, he was wearing a baseball cap, so his face wasn't very visible, but I think we're going to go back to the store and ask for footage from their security cameras," Joe said.

"Seems pretty surprising this Rooney character would resurface in a place where he just barely escaped the law the last time around," the deputy said.

Joe pulled on his jeans and a clean shirt. "I think maybe Rooney left behind something the last time he was here. And he's just getting around to looking for it."

His phone beeped and he saw he had an incoming call from Vikki Hill. "Tell me your name again?"

"Warren Davis. Collier County Sheriff's Office."

"Okay, Warren. I've got to take another call. Text me your contact info, and any other pertinent info you have. I'll get back to you about Rooney. And thanks for calling."

Joe disconnected and clicked over to Vikki Hill. "Hey," he said. "What's up? Any word from Wingfield?"

"He wants proof that Maya's with me. Then, he says, he'll be in touch."

"Okay, great. Did you call Letty?"

"I did, but she didn't answer. So I walked over to her unit and knocked on the door. No answer. And her car's gone too."

"Dammit. I just left there, not thirty minutes ago. I'll head back now," Joe said. He shoved his feet into a pair of flip-flops and grabbed the keys to his truck.

"Okay, don't panic. Maybe she went to the store or something," Vikki said. "You haven't heard from her this morning, right?"

"No." He was reluctant to admit to the FBI agent that he'd spent the night on a chair outside Letty's door. "I'll call my mom. Maybe she sent Letty out on an errand or something. But in the meantime, I just had a call from a sheriff's deputy in Collier County. That's south of here, down by the Everglades. Chuck Sheppard's body was found in a stolen Jeep. Somebody set it up to look like the Jeep had crashed and burned, but the medical examiner found a bullet in his brain."

"When was this?"

"Some hunters found the remains four days ago, but they think it had been there a few days. They identified the body from fingerprints they recovered from the Jeep."

"How did they know to call you?"

"Same way you did. They researched his criminal history, saw that we had warrants out up here for him, and for Declan Rooney."

Vikki Hill let out a long breath. "That's some coincidence.

Sheppard's killed, and then Rooney turns up—how far away is this Immokalee?"

"Not sure. I think it's in central South Florida. Maybe two and a half hours from here? Okay, we can talk about this, after I find Letty."

"Keep me posted," the FBI agent said.

Hey Mom, have you seen Letty and Maya this morning?"

Ava was sweeping sand from the office floor when her son called. "No. Why?"

"Vikki and I need to talk to her. She's not in her unit and doesn't answer her phone. We thought maybe you'd sent her out on an errand or something."

"I didn't send her for anything. You sound kind of worried, son. Is something going on that I should know about? It's not Rooney, is it?"

For a moment he debated not telling her about her ex-boyfriend's fate. But she had a right to know, didn't she? And given that Declan Rooney might actually be lurking in the vicinity, they all needed to be on high alert.

"I promise, I'll fill you in later," Joe said. "But in the meantime, can you and Isabelle kind of scout around and see if anybody's seen Letty?"

"Sure thing."

His apartment was only five minutes from the motel, but he covered the distance in record time. He slowed and checked the parking lot for the silver Kia, but it wasn't there. He drove past, headed south, and scanned the parking lot of every business he passed, hoping to glimpse the Kia. He tried calling her, but each time he was sent directly to voice mail.

When he reached St. Pete Beach, he turned around and headed back north, slowing as he passed through Treasure Island, Madeira Beach, Redington, Redington Shores, and Indian Rocks Beach.

Joe was stopped at a traffic light a couple of miles from the Murmuring Surf when he spotted the silver Kia as it pulled out of a McDonald's parking lot and into traffic. The light turned, but he had to wait while a bedraggled-looking homeless man shuffled across the street pushing a shopping cart loaded down with bags of plastic bottles and aluminum cans for recycling. By then, the Kia was three cars ahead. He accelerated, pulled up next to her, and lightly tapped the truck's horn. Letty glanced over, looking surprised, and gave him a wave. Maya was seated in the back seat, contentedly sipping on something in her plastic cup. His shoulders relaxed and he called Vikki Hill. "Found her," he reported, pulling into a convenience store parking lot. "They were at McDonald's." He exhaled slowly and headed back to the Murmuring Surf.

When they reached the motel, she got out of the Kia and waited for him to park. Letty knew something was up from the serious look on his face.

"Something wrong?" she said, as he walked up to her.

"You scared the crap out of me, taking off like this without telling anybody," he said.

Letty leaned into the car, lifted Maya out of her car seat, and set her down on the pavement. "Hey Mr. Joe," the child said. "I got a Happy Meal."

He forced a smile. "Good for you."

Letty started walking toward her unit. "We need to talk," he said, hooking his hand around her elbow. "Vikki got the call this morning. When she couldn't reach you, and you weren't at your place, yeah, we panicked."

"Well, we're back now," she said.

"There's more." He pointed toward the office, where Ava and Vikki Hill stood waiting in the open doorway.

"I need some coffee," Joe said. "And then we talk."

The four of them sat around Ava's kitchen table while Maya parked herself in front of *PAW Patrol* in the living room.

"I got a call from a sheriff's deputy down in South Florida this morning," Joe said. "They found Chuck's body in a car, back in the swamp, with a bullet in his brain."

Coffee splattered over the side of Ava DeCurtis's mug. "Oh?"

Letty jumped up, fetched a paper towel, and began cleaning up the spill.

"Sorry to break it to you like that, but I didn't know how else to tell you," he said.

"It was only a matter of time, I guess," Ava said, scowling. But her hands shook as she sipped what was left of her coffee. "I guess he got what he had coming to him. Does that deputy know who did it?"

"That's why he was calling me," Joe said. "The car was stolen, and they were only able to identify him from fingerprints. When they ran them through the state's criminal records system they found the warrant we had out on Chuck. He wanted to know about Chuck's pals. Tanya and Declan Rooney.

"I told him we think Rooney was spotted up here yesterday," Joe continued. "We need to see that security-camera footage from Publix. I'll call the manager back today and lean on him."

Vikki spoke up. "That's why I freaked this morning, when we couldn't reach you, Letty."

"Sorry," Letty said. She looked around the table. "Really. I am sorry. I gave Maya my phone so she could watch a cartoon. And the battery ran down. I didn't mean to worry everybody."

"We're all gonna be on edge until this thing is over," the FBI agent said. She handed her phone to Joe. "I think it's time to take that photo of me with Maya. Don't want Wingfield to start having second thoughts."

Vikki went into the living room and sat beside Maya, who was lolling on the sofa cushions, softly singing to herself.

"Maya, Mr. Joe is going to take a picture of us together. Is that okay?"

"Okay," the little girl agreed.

"Wait." Letty took a hairbrush from her pocketbook and hurried to her niece's side. "Let's get rid of that bird's nest in your hair." She gently combed the child's hair and clipped the sides with plastic barrettes that she fished out of the pocket of her shorts. She tugged at the hem of Maya's pajama top so that it covered her exposed tummy. "We've got to get you some new clothes," she said. "You've just about outgrown everything I packed for you."

As Vikki posed the little girl on her lap, Letty felt another pang of guilt. Tanya would have died if she'd seen her daughter happily eating junky fast food in public, with uncombed hair and bare feet, dressed in her pajama top and a pair of shrunken leggings. She'd always taken such care with Maya's appearance. "I can't have her going around looking like some poor little street urchin," she'd tell Letty, as an excuse for spending exorbitant amounts of money for a designer outfit her child would outgrow in three months. "And I won't have Evan's friends' bitchy wives judging me and calling me white trash behind my back."

Vikki stared straight ahead at the camera, unsmiling, while Maya kept watching television. Joe hovered a few feet away from the sofa, clicking the shutter. "Okay, I think I've got something we can use," he said, handing the phone back to its owner.

The FBI agent studied the frames. "Yeah. This one will work. It's the only one where Maya is looking directly at the camera." She tapped the photo, typed something on the screen, then handed the phone over to Letty.

She's fine. I need to get back to my job. Let's do this.

Vikki tapped the phone and the message transmitted with a soft whooshing sound.

41

~~~~~~~~~~~~~~

"HE'S PLAYING GAMES AGAIN," VIKKI Hill said, after fifteen minutes had passed with no response from Evan Wingfield. She stood up and looked over at Joe. "Screw that. I've got calls to make. You'll be around today?"

"Yeah. I want to go back to Publix and talk to that manager again." He patted his back pocket. "I printed out Rooney's most recent mug shot. It's an old one, but I thought I'd show it to the cashiers to see if anyone recognizes him."

"Let me know what you find out, and I'll ping you if I hear back from Wingfield."

"Guess I'd better get to work," Letty said, taking the coffee mugs and setting them in the kitchen sink. She poked her head around the corner and called to her niece, who was busily coloring at Ava's coffee table, along with Isabelle.

"C'mon, lovebug. Time to punch the clock."

"If it's okay with you, Letty, she can just hang out with me for a while this morning," Isabelle said.

"Are you sure?" Letty asked. "I know she adores you, but it's not fair to saddle you with a four-year-old all day."

"I'm sure. I went to the Goodwill with one of my friends yesterday, and I found a cool dress-up princess dress for her, but I left it out in my car. We can hang out for a while, and then I'm supposed to have study group at the library with some kids from school."

"Princess dress-up!" Maya said. "Bye, Letty."

Letty sat back down at the table beside her boss. "Ava, I thought I'd get back to working on the new software this morning. Unless there's something else? Do we have any check-ins today?"

"Just one," Ava said, looking up from the morning newspaper. "Anita is over there now, but she should be done by noon."

"Okay. I'll take a look to make sure everything's ready. Did the plumber fix that leaking shower head yesterday?"

"He said he did, but if you would, check that too."

Joe followed Letty downstairs and into the front office. He took the sheet of paper from his pocket and smoothed it out on the reception desk.

"Just to be sure. Does this look like the guy you saw at Publix?"

She'd seen the mug shot before, but once again Letty was struck by Declan Rooney's impossible-to-ignore appeal. The dark hair that flopped over his forehead, the sullen, glaring deep blue eyes with their impossibly thick, long, dark lashes, the high cheekbones and prominent hawklike nose. Tanya's daughter shared her mother's round face, pointed chin, Kewpie-doll lips, and fair coloring, but Maya's eyes were unmistakably Rooney's.

"One thing," Letty said. "Now that I think about it, the guy I saw in the store had a beard. He was sort of scruffy-looking."

Joe took a pen and began drawing facial hair on the photo, starting with the suggestion of a narrow mustache and neatly trimmed goatee.

"Like this?"

"Mmm, the beard was a little fuller than that. Not really hipster scruff, more like hobo."

He sketched in more hair. "That's it," Letty said.

She tapped Declan Rooney's photo. "I can see why Tanya fell for him. He looks—dangerous and unpredictable, and okay, sexy."

"Like your sister?"

"Yeah," Letty said softly. "I still wonder where and how they met."

"I'll be sure and ask when I arrest him," Joe said. "I'm going back to Publix, to show this to some of the cashiers, and then I thought I'd hit some of the other nearby motels and restaurants, to see if anybody has seen him."

Letty bit her lower lip. "So you really think that was Rooney? And he's watching me—and Maya?"

"Now that we know what we do about Chuck, I'm afraid it's safe to assume that Rooney could be in the area," Joe said.

"Here's a thought," Letty said. "The Surf is part of a LISTSERV of motels and hotels from Clearwater south to St. Pete Beach. Managers put out advisories and alerts, you know, like if they want to warn the other motels about someone stealing from cars, or whatever. I can post a message to the list with Rooney's photo, asking people to contact you if he's staying there or if he's spotted."

"Perfect," Joe said. "I'll email you the photo with the beard drawn on. I'd forgotten about the LISTSERV. The good news is, Rooney probably won't come near the Murmuring Surf. Too many people know him here. Still, it'd be best if you don't leave again without letting one of us know where you're going."

Ava emerged from the back office area with her car keys in hand. "Yes, please. I don't need another panic like we experienced this morning. I'm off for now."

Isabelle and Maya pushed through the office door. "Letty, Letty!" Maya cried. "We found Midnight's kittens."

"Where were they?" Ava asked.

"You know that big concrete pipe, at the edge of the parking lot?" Isabelle asked.

"That old drainage culvert?" Joe asked.

"Whatever you call it. Yeah. It's full of a lot of old weeds and trash and stuff, and she made herself like a little nest in there. Maya heard them mewing just now when we were getting my book bag out of my car and we followed the sound to that pipe."

"Four little kitties," Maya reported, holding up four fingers. "I want a kitten, Letty."

Letty knelt down beside her niece. "Those kittens need their mama right now. Midnight is feeding them and taking care of them, so we can't take them away from her. They're her kittens, not ours."

"I would feed my kitten," Maya protested. "And I would take care of it and it could sleep in my bed with me."

"I'm afraid not," Letty said, shaking her head. "It's Midnight's job to take care of her babies. Just like it's my job to take care of you. Besides, Miss Ava doesn't allow pets in the motel, do you, Miss Ava?"

"She doesn't," Isabelle volunteered. "My whole life I've wanted a dog, and my whole life she's said pets don't belong at motels." She glared at Ava. "Super unfair."

Maya's lower lip began to tremble. "But I waaaaaant a kitten!"

Letty tried to put her arms around her niece, but Maya pushed her away. "No! I don't like you, Letty. I want my mama to take care of me. Not you."

"Maya!" Ava said. "That's not very nice."

Isabelle sat down on the floor and pulled Maya onto her lap. "Letty's right, Maya Papaya. We can't take those kittens away from Midnight, or they might die."

Letty winced at the teenager's reasoning, but Maya's deep blue eyes widened at the mention of death. "Do kittens go to heaven when they die? Like my mama?"

"I don't know," Isabelle replied. "But if heaven is where everyone is happy, then yeah, I bet there are kittens and puppies and all kinds of animals in heaven with the people we love."

"Oh. But I still want a kitten now."

"Someday," Letty said. As soon as she made the vague promise she recognized it as the same lame response her own mother gave over the years whenever she and Tanya begged for a pet, or a house with a real yard, or a trip to the beach. "Someday."

She stood up and dusted off the seat of her shorts. "Someday," she said, "I promise we will have a house of our own and you will have a pet. But in the meantime, you and Isabelle could help Midnight by putting out some extra cat food for her, couldn't they, Miss Ava?"

Ava sighed. "That cat's supposed to be earning her keep chasing rats away from the dumpster. But I guess I could pick up a bag of food when I go to the store."

The Publix bag "boy" leaning against the shopping-cart corral and taking a smoke break was a wizened seventy-something white man dressed in a green apron and wrinkled khaki pants. His name badge said TOMMY. He looked down at the photo Joe offered and nodded.

"I think he's been in here a couple times lately. He kinda stands out, ya know, dressed like that?"

"Like what?"

"Black shirt and black pants and the ball cap and beard. He reminded me of Zorro."

"Did you ever see what kind of car he was driving?"

"Nope." Tommy dropped the cigarette butt into the Styrofoam coffee cup he'd been holding. "He don't buy much. Maybe a sub sandwich, chips."

"When was the last time you saw him?" Joe asked.

"He come in here this morning." The bagger tossed the coffee cup into a nearby trash can. "Sorry. Gotta get back to work."

"Wait," Joe said. "How long ago did you see him?"

"Hmmm. We open at eight, it was right after that. You know what? I think he's using our men's room to wash up in."

"What makes you say that?"

"That bathroom gets cleaned and restocked last thing at night. But this morning, right after that guy was in there, a customer complained it was a mess. I went in there, and it looked like someone had taken a shower in the sink. Soap and paper towels all over the place."

"So maybe he's living in his car or something," Joe mused. "No access to a bathroom."

"Or he sleeps on the beach," Tommy said. "Until the cops run him off. But that's mostly young kids doing that around here."

"Hey, thanks. That's really helpful," Joe said. He pulled some bills from his pocket and tried to press them into the bagger's hand, but the old man shook him off. "Not allowed," he said.

After he left the shopping center, Joe drove to the Treasure Island police station. He went inside and tapped on the glass separating the desk officer from the lobby.

Serafina Suarez looked up from her computer monitor and smiled. "DeCurtis! Where've you been? We missed you."

"Just taking some comp time," Joe said. "Can you do me a favor, Fina? I'm interested in recent arrests or citations for public vagrancy. My suspect is white male, late thirties to forties."

"How recent?" she asked.

"The past week."

Suarez started typing. "How are things at the motel? Your mom doing okay?"

"She's fine, thanks," Joe said.

"My aunt and uncle loved staying there this past fall. They want to come back next year too. And they really appreciated the friends and family discount."

"Tell 'em to book early," Joe said.

She nodded and tabbed down through the incident reports for the past week. "I'm not seeing any vagrancy reports for white males," she said, and then laughed. "Oh, here's something you'll love. You know Driscoll? The new recruit? He caught Sweaty Betty sleeping on one of the benches at Sunset Vista Park Friday morning."

"Bet I know where this is going," Joe said. Elizabeth Schockle, whose street name was Sweaty Betty, was a mostly harmless, if smelly alcoholic who drifted in and out of local homeless shelters. He himself had transported her, more than once, to the emergency room after she'd been found unconscious behind a convenience store or on the beach.

"Driscoll, being Driscoll, woke her up to tell her to move along, and of course she cussed him out, so he slapped cuffs on her and put her in his cruiser to take her to lockup."

Joe raised one eyebrow. "And?"

"Betty, being Betty, took a dump and pissed all over the back seat of his unit," Fina said, chuckling. "He had to spend half the morning hosing it down and disinfecting it."

"No fun," Joe commented. "Hey, are there any new hobo camps around the beaches where I might look for my guy?"

"Not since the local chamber started pressuring us to close down the camps," Fina said. "Homelessness is bad for tourism, in case you haven't heard. It's mostly a case of solo guys sleeping on a park bench or in the bushes a night here or there, and then moving along. You want me to check if your guy's been arrested? What's his name?"

"Might as well," Joe said. "Declan Rooney."

"Really?" Suarez looked startled. "I remember his name coming up in that gold-and-jewelry-buying scam at the Surf a few years ago. You're still looking for him?"

"I am, only this time we think he's moved up to bigger and better crimes. He's been linked to a homicide down in Immokalee. He was spotted at Publix yesterday, and again today."

"I can put out a BOLO on him if you want," Suarez offered.

"Yeah, do that," Joe said. "And put my phone number as the contact. Thanks, Fina."

From the police station, he cruised north on Gulf Boulevard. Tourist season was still in full swing, with cars bearing license tags from as far north as Canada and as far west as Missouri. Every few blocks he slowed or stopped to allow beachgoers to cross the road from motels on the east side of the road toward the beaches on the west.

This was not the Gulf Boulevard of his youth, when, as recently as the eighties, modest family-owned motels and restaurants lined the north-south beach road. Now, the Murmuring Surf was a distinct minority among the flashy condominium and time-share towers and chain hotel resorts.

He turned the truck in at every public-beach parking lot, scanning to look for any clues of a homeless encampment. But the parking lots were mostly asphalt and concrete—not a really welcome spot to spend the night. All Joe saw were happy, sunburned beachgoers, trudging to and from their cars in the late-morning sunshine.

It was an exercise in futility, he decided, but then he remembered Tiki Gardens. It had started as a family-owned gift shop with a small adjoining garden, and then morphed into an improbable but typical Florida tourist trap—a Polynesian-themed attraction complete with monolithic carved tiki gods and a tropical bird show. The original owners sold out to out-of-town developers in the late eighties, but when Florida's roller-coaster boom and bust economy took a nose-dive, the property was eventually sold to the county in 1990.

Joe could remember wandering the palm-lined paths of the gardens on school field trips, tossing peanuts to the caged monkeys and listening to the unearthly screeches of the peacocks that roamed the grounds. After the gardens were plowed under and the birds and monkeys rehomed and the Polynesian kitsch was sold off, he'd never forgotten the sight of the largest tiki god, Ku, being carted away on the back of a flatbed truck.

The county had kept a toned-down facsimile of the original Tiki Gardens roadside sign, but now the place was just a public-beach-access parking lot.

He drove a couple of miles down the beach and turned in to the lot. He'd grudgingly admit the county had done a decent job of landscaping the entry—if you didn't know better, maybe you'd actually expect to see a howler monkey hanging off one of the co-conut palms.

But you'd be sadly disappointed, Joe thought. Small islands of land-scaping were spotted throughout the property, but mostly the place was a sea of late-model cars with out-of-state license plates.

Even the hardiest homeless man would find it tough to find enough cover to camp out at Tiki Gardens these days. Feeling de-jected, he pulled back onto Gulf Boulevard and headed north.

~~~~~~~~~~~~~~~~~~~~

42

As SOON AS VIKKI HILL walked into the office, Letty could tell by the grim expression on her face that she had bad news.

"Just tell me," she said quietly, closing out the reservation form on the computer monitor.

"Wingfield is balking at our terms. He wants Maya delivered to him. My people think it's too risky to try to do this down here. They want us to go back to New York for the exchange. Hate to say it, but I agree. I've booked tickets on a flight for tomorrow morning. We'll have tighter control of the situation. . . ."

"No."

Vikki blinked. "It's not really your call."

"Actually, it is," Letty said, her tone much calmer than the roil in her gut.

"According to my sister's will, I'm Maya's legal guardian. And I am *not* going to allow you people to traumatize a four-year-old child by picking her up and taking her right back to the place where her mother was killed a month ago."

"Come on. You know we won't take her to Tanya's apartment. We're not monsters."

"The answer is still no."

"I can get a court order," Vikki threatened.

Joe DeCurtis strode into the office. "Get a court order for what?" he asked.

"Vikki's bosses are saying I have to send Maya back up to New

York for the exchange with Evan," Letty explained. "And I told her no. Hell, no."

"I thought we already had this all worked out," he said.

"Wingfield balked. And my supervising agent and the AUSA agree that it should happen in New York, where they can control the situation. Letty doesn't agree," the FBI agent told him.

Letty leaned across the reception desk, her palms sweaty as they flattened on the Formica surface. "If you manage to get a court order, I'll get a lawyer and fight you. What will you do? Handcuff Maya and drag her kicking and screaming onto a flight full of alarmed snowbirds heading home to Long Island after spending the winter in Florida? Snowbirds with cell phones?"

Vikki Hill did not back away from Letty's cold fury. She was not used to having her authority challenged. "You're technically a fugitive from justice, Letty. I could take you into custody right now, lock your ass up . . ."

Letty held out her arms, fists clenched together. "That's what you'll have to do. Maya's upstairs with Isabelle in Ava's apartment. You gonna go up there and lock her up too?"

"Whoa!" Joe said. "This is getting pretty extreme, don't you think?" He turned to Vikki Hill. "Last I heard, Wingfield wanted me to be there for the handoff. But I'm not going to New York."

The FBI agent started to say something, but changed her mind.

Letty decided to press her point. "You both know I'm right about this. Text Evan and tell him what I just told you. That Maya is too emotionally fragile to travel right now. Which is the truth. Tell him she's asking questions about what happened to me, and her mother. If he wants her, he'll have to come and get her."

"You don't get it. It's not just Wingfield. It's my bosses."

"Are you telling me you never buck The Man?" Letty asked.

"In this case, 'The Man' is Cheryl Shapiro, who is an extremely ballsy assistant US attorney, who is also calling the shots on this investigation."

"Ballsier than Vikki Hill?" Joe said mockingly. "I seriously doubt that."

The FBI agent knew she'd been beaten. "You're gonna get me fired," she said with a groan. "If this thing blows up, I'll end up working as a school crossing guard."

She pulled her phone from her pocket and started to type.

Your kid is a basket case. On verge of hysteria about Tanya and Letty. Too risky to bring her to New York. You'll have to come get her. Bring cash.

"That should work," Joe said, looking over the agent's shoulder as she typed.

The three of them stood motionless in the office, waiting for Evan Wingfield's reply.

"What will you tell your bosses?" Letty asked.

"Just what you said. Anyway, the deed is done. They'll have to either back me up or fire me."

"I hope they don't fire you. You'd be a terrifying school crossing guard."

The agent's phone dinged with Evan Wingfield's response.

Tell me where and when.

"Tomorrow," Joe urged. "Tell him tomorrow. Have him fly into Tampa. Get his flight info and tell him we'll text him details as soon as he lands."

"That could work," Vikki said, nodding.

"You pick him up at the airport. We set up a meeting at a safe place. I'll be there, waiting. We tell him he doesn't get to see Maya until we get our money. When he does that, you arrest his ass and charge him with conspiracy to commit murder," Joe said.

The FBI agent shook her head vigorously. "You don't know Wingfield. He's no pushover. He's going to insist on seeing Maya. Tell him, Letty."

"Oh, God." Letty rested her forehead on the reception desk. "I just can't put her through this. Seeing Evan again? It's too confusing for her."

"This'll be the last time," Vikki said, awkwardly patting Letty's shoulder. "The minute he transfers that money, the act is complete. He'll be arrested and put into custody. It'll be quick and clean. Surgical."

Letty looked up at Joe. "You'll be there?"

"I will."

"And we'll have backup," the FBI agent said. "I'll put in a call to the Tampa field office. They'll give us whatever assistance I request. What about locals?"

Joe nodded. "Pretty sure my chief will cooperate. I'll ask Shauna to give us a hand."

"Is she the officer who showed up when you were arresting the meth heads?" Letty asked.

"Yeah. Shauna's good people."

Letty ran her fingers through her hair in a gesture of frustration. "I know you'll do your best to keep Maya physically safe. But I just can't stop worrying about what kind of long-term effect this will have on her emotionally. Maya's just now getting to the point where she doesn't have night terrors. This is going to dredge up all the horrible stuff she witnessed when Evan and Tanya were fighting over custody. And we still don't know what or how much she saw when Tanya was killed. Will she freak out when she sees Evan?"

"I don't honestly know," Vikki admitted. "I can spot a psychopath at fifty paces, but I never wanted a kid, so I don't know how their evil little minds work."

"Look," Joe said. "I was twenty when Isabelle was born, and her shitbird dad took off when she was only three. God knows, I can't take any credit for how great she turned out, but I think me being around maybe helped a little. Mostly, it was my mom. You've met Ava, but you don't know all she's gone through over the years. She's a fighter, and she's a survivor. And so are you, Letty. Give yourself credit for that. Maya will be okay. Because she's got you."

His eyes searched hers. He was waiting for her to say something. She opened her mouth, then clamped her lips together, fighting for composure.

"Okay," she said, when she could finally trust herself to speak. "Okay."

"Glad that's settled," Vikki said briskly. "Joe, did you turn up any Rooney sightings while you were out?"

"A bagger at that Publix said he thinks he saw Rooney in there this morning," Joe said. "He thinks Rooney was using the bathroom there to clean up, which tells me he's probably either sleeping in his car or on the beach somewhere. I asked the duty sergeant, Fina Suarez, to put out a BOLO for him, and she promised to keep me posted, but if Rooney is sleeping out in the rough, he's keeping a low profile. All the cops in the local beach towns have marching orders to run off vagrants, because it's bad for tourism."

"Speaking of tourism, I posted that photo of Rooney on the hotel-motel LISTSERV, but I haven't seen any responses," Letty said.

"Look, for now, let's concentrate on the big picture—which is Evan Wingfield's imminent arrival," Vikki said impatiently. "We need to lock down a location for the handoff, and since you're the local, DeCurtis, I'm thinking you need to come up with that."

"What'd you have in mind?"

"Obviously we want it to be someplace where our people can be nearby, but unobtrusive. Is there, like, a mall anywhere around here?" the FBI agent asked.

"There's a mall about ten miles from here," Joe said. "But what about here?"

"Here? In the motel office?" Vikki frowned. "With people coming in and out to bitch about broken Ping-Pong paddles?"

"Here, on the property. Maybe on the beach. Why not?" Joe asked. "Our people will just look like tourists, picking up sand dollars, soaking up some rays. And it won't be as weird as taking Maya to a mall where she's never been before. I could be sitting with her, on a lounge chair, under a beach umbrella. Wingfield sees her, hands over the funds, and that's when we drop the net on him. We could maybe even have Letty nearby, so Maya won't be too freaked out."

"Maybe," Vikki said slowly. "If we did it late in the afternoon, it won't be so crowded. But what if Wingfield decides to cross us up, or gets violent? I don't like the idea of an innocent civilian stumbling into our little drama."

"I thought you said he isn't a violent type," Joe said.

"Evan hit Tanya," Letty said.

Both cops turned to stare at her. "He did?" Vikki said.

"I had no idea until this week," Letty admitted. "Tanya never even hinted that he'd gotten physical with her. Maya was here in the office, with me and Ava, when two of our regulars, Merwin Maples and Oscar Jensen, got into a knock-down, drag-out fight. I thought they were going to actually come to blows. Over a parking spot! When the fighting got heated, Maya lost it. That's when she said it. That she'd seen her daddy hit her mama."

"Dear God," Vikki said, her face paling. "Wingfield never struck me as that kind. I mean, I always knew he was a crooked, scheming sociopath, but I never saw him as the kind that would hit a woman."

"In front of her kid," Joe added.

"We won't give him the chance to get physical tomorrow," Vikki vowed. "He's flying down here solo, has no idea where the handoff is taking place until he gets in the car with me. And I'm not gonna tell him where we're headed. If he tries anything with me, he'll live to regret it."

"And I'll help you make that happen," Joe said.

The office door chimed and Ava struggled in, burdened down with two armloads of groceries. Her neck was ringed with a dozen brightly colored plastic leis, and she wore a straw islander hat.

"Aloha!" she greeted the trio. "Who wants to help me get ready for bingo, Hawaiian style?"

"I was just heading back to the efficiency," Vikki said. "Really? Hawaiian bingo?"

"The regulars love it," Joe told her.

"I can help," Letty said.

"Good. The rest of the stuff goes over to the recreation room. You can start blowing up the inflatable palm trees while I get the sweet-and-sour meatballs going in the Crock-Pot." She gave her son a meaningful look. "You're coming tonight, right? Isabelle already has plans, but I'm expecting a big crowd. Maybe fifty people."

"Do I have to?" Joe tried to look aggrieved.

"Yes. I need you to call numbers, and you can also work security, just in case we have any more dustups over who called bingo first." Ava reached into one of the shopping bags and pulled out a shirt with an oversize print of green palm fronds and hot-pink hibiscus blossoms. "Here's your uniform."

"Gaaaaah," Joe groaned.

"Try it on," Ava ordered, thrusting it at him.

"No way." He let it drop onto the countertop.

"Joseph?"

He knew that tone. It was the same tone Ava used when she guilt-tripped him into following Isabelle's date's car in a city police unit when she went to the junior prom.

"Shit," he muttered, pulling the shirt over his own T-shirt, leaving the front unbuttoned.

"You look ad-ore-able!" Vikki said, getting ready to leave. "Ava, can short-timers play too?"

"Absolutely," Ava said. "Bring your money and take your chances. A dollar a card, a dollar a drink."

"Hope you like Hawaiian Punch with lime-sherbet floaters," Joe warned.

43

"WHOOPS! LETTY, I ALMOST FORGOT." Ava reached into another shopping bag and pulled out a grass skirt. She waved it in the air. "Here's your outfit for tonight."

"That's it?" Joe asked, waggling his eyebrows.

She batted at her son with the skirt. "She's supposed to wear it over her bathing suit."

"Oh, Ava, I don't know," Letty protested. "Can't I just wear shorts and my Murmuring Surf shirt and a lei?"

"No, no," Joe said. "You don't get off that easy. If I go native, you go native."

"He's right, for once," Ava said. "We all get dressed up for Aloha Bingo. It's everybody's favorite night. Even the Feldman girls come in costume." She gave Letty what Joe called her patented Mom stare, then pulled a miniature grass skirt and a toy ukulele from the shopping bag.

"I got this for Maya. Isn't this the cutest thing you've ever seen?"

Letty smacked her forehead. "I forgot Isabelle's going out tonight. But Ava, I'm not sure about taking Maya to bingo."

"Nonsense. It'll be an early night. You know these old geezers. We start at six and play the jackpot game right at nine. You can have her back at your place and in bed by no later than nine fifteen. And tomorrow, you sleep in. Right?"

Joe and Letty exchanged an uneasy look, which Ava didn't miss.

"What? What's going on?"

"Tomorrow's the day Evan Wingfield is flying down. He thinks he's picking up Maya."

The color drained from Ava's face. "You won't really let him get near her. Right?"

"Right," Joe said. "But let's not talk about it right now. I'm gonna run home and shower, but I'll be back in time for bingo." He started for the door, but Ava grabbed his arm.

"Don't forget your shirt."

Maya danced around the living area, twitching her hips and delighting in the way it made her ankle-length grass skirt swish against her bare legs. She strummed the plastic ukulele.

"Look at me, Letty. I'm Moana!"

Letty grabbed her phone and snapped a photo of her niece. Maya cheesed for the camera and twitched her hips again. Her niece loved playing dress-up, and she was particularly excited tonight, because Letty was also dressed up.

It had taken gulping down two glasses of wine for her to get up enough courage to don her most modest bikini and then slide the grass skirt down over her hips. She piled on three sets of beads from Maya's junk jewelry trove and added two plastic leis in order to cover most of her cleavage, and then topped off the costume with an unbuttoned flowered blouse.

She was draping a plastic lei around Maya's neck when she heard the putt-putt just outside in the breezeway.

When she opened the door, Isabelle's friend Sierra was leaning the green scooter against the wall.

"Come on in," Letty said.

"Hi, Sierra!" Maya called, twitching her hips and twanging her ukulele. "I'm a hula girl!"

"You're both hula girls," Sierra said, grinning at Letty and her niece. "You guys look totes adorbs. Aloha Bingo Night, right?"

"That's right," Letty said. "Where are you and Isabelle headed?"

"We're just gonna hang out with some kids from school," the teenager said. "We might go to the movies later. But what I wanted to say is, I emailed you something."

"Really?"

"Yeah. You know that piece of video where the dude in the ski hat comes into your sister's apartment and they're talking, but you can't hear what they're saying?"

"Right. The FBI's tech guys are working on it, trying to figure out how to turn up the sound," Letty said.

"Hah! Screw them," Sierra said. "I figured it out. I mean, my friends and I did. I'm on this tech nerd loop with this kid in Albuquerque, he calls himself KDawg, and I think he's in a band or something, so he knows about sound. He's always messing with video and digital enhancement. I was mentioning on the loop about the problem I was having with the nanny-cam video, and he said if I sent it to him, maybe he could fix it. Anyway, I hope you don't mind, but that's what I did. I don't really understand what or how he did it, but you can definitely hear more of what they're saying now. Not all of it, but a lot."

Letty threw her arms around the petite girl's neck and gave her a hug. "Sierra, that's amazing!"

"I didn't really do anything. It was KDawg. Okay, so I gotta go. See ya!"

Letty watched the video once, then texted Joe. *Better stop by my place before bingo. I've got something you need to see. ASAP.*

Joe gave a low wolf whistle when he saw Letty standing in the doorway in her bikini top and grass skirt. "I take it back. I wish every night was Aloha Bingo Night."

She flushed and tugged at the flower garlands around her neck. "Stop. I'm self-conscious enough."

He was wearing navy board shorts and a T-shirt, with the Hawaiian shirt unbuttoned over it. With his dark hair and tan, he made a believable, even desirable islander, and he was brandishing two dinner plate–size hot-pink hibiscus blossoms.

"This one's for you," he said. Letty reached out to take it.

"Allow me," Joe said, taking a step closer and tucking the flower behind her left ear. He trailed his fingertip lightly down her neck. "You smell good," he whispered.

"Hi, Mr. Joe," Maya said, brandishing her ukulele. "I'm Moana."

"You are?" Joe feigned surprise. "I thought you were Elsa?"

"No. Tonight I am Moana." She twanged the ukulele strings for emphasis.

"I'm gonna kill Ava for giving her that thing," Letty said.

Joe knelt down beside Maya and fastened the other hibiscus behind her right ear. "Now you're a real island girl."

"Ladybug, why don't you go in the other room and draw a picture of Moana for Mr. Joe?" Letty said. "He doesn't even know what she looks like."

"Okay," the child said, swishing her grass skirt as she walked away twanging her ukulele.

Letty gestured at the laptop computer on the table. "Pull up a chair." She tapped some keys, and the first frame of the problematic video clip appeared.

"I've already seen this," he objected.

"Isabelle's friend Sierra shared this with one of her tech friends who's good with audio. He somehow managed to amplify the sound. It's still pretty patchy, but give a listen."

At the start of the video clip, Tanya seemed hesitant, and almost alarmed at her visitor's arrival. "Oh my God, Rooney!"

Letty looked at Joe. "So it was him."

Rooney pulled Tanya to him, and after a brief hesitation, she crushed herself against him, and their kiss was so long and passionate, Letty wanted to look away.

The next bit of video was inaudible.

They finally separated. He looked around at the opulent surroundings, the marble floors, the massive rock-crystal chandelier, the floor-to-ceiling windows hung with silk draperies, and the over-the-top furnishings. He said something that was garbled, and then, ". . . you really lucked into a sugar daddy."

Tanya pretended to pout. The first part of her sentence was inaudible, but it ended with her saying, ". . . worked hard for everything here. I damn well deserve all of it."

Rooney's laugh was low and somehow menacing at the same time. "Define 'work.'"

"You're still such a dick. You know that? How did you even find me?"

He was slowly walking around the room, taking it all in, mentally adding up the cost of such a place. His back was to the nanny cam hidden inside the stuffed elephant, and his answer was inaudible.

"No. Seriously," Tanya insisted. "I need to know who else might try to find me up here."

When Rooney turned around and smiled, Letty shuddered. He had the smile of a python. Even though she'd already viewed the video earlier, she leaned forward again to hear his response. The first part was garbled, but then: ". . . checked your IMDb page. Found out your agent's name."

"I don't believe you. He'd never just give some random stranger my phone number."

There was that same closed-mouth smile again. "You forget how good I am at what I do."

Rooney caught Tanya's hand in his and brought it to his lips. He kissed her open palm, and then she abruptly pulled away, walking far enough from the nanny cam that they could decode only part of her response.

"I'm still furious . . . And Chuck . . . leave me like that? . . . a week in jail! . . . threatening . . . federal prison . . . sick . . . puking up my guts every morning. It was the worst experience of my life."

Rooney's deep voice was much clearer as he spontaneously laid on the Irish brogue. "Aah, well, darlin', we had no choice. Chuck and I, we've got a little history with the criminal-justice system, but you, on the other hand, had none. We knew with your pretty face and acting abilities, you'd find a way out of a jam."

Tanya walked back into camera range. "Don't start that phony Irish crap with me, Rooney. I know better."

"And yet, here you are today." He gestured around the room. "Not exactly a shitty motel room at the Murmuring Surf, is it, Tanya, my love?"

In the video, Maya darted into the room then, but stood staring, with her thumb in her mouth, at the stranger.

"Now who would this be?" Rooney asked. He bent down to touch the child, but Maya cowered behind Tanya's legs.

"My daughter." Tanya's mood changed to belligerent. "What do you want, Rooney?"

"She's darling," Rooney said. "And a dead ringer for her beautiful mother. Who's the father?"

Tanya, looking flustered, backed away. ". . . go now. Evan's spying . . . finds out a man came to see me, he'll use it against me in court."

Rooney was circling the room. His next statement was so quiet the microphone didn't pick it up. Joe and Letty leaned closer to the laptop, straining to hear.

". . . loot. I want what's mine, Tanya."

He clamped his hand around her wrist, but she jerked it away from him. "Loot? You and Chuck took it all and left me behind, holding the bag."

Rooney said something else inaudible. He stood inches away from Tanya, his jaw tight with tension.

"Goddammit, I told you, I don't have it!" Tanya screamed.

Maya began to cry. "No, Mommy!" She clawed at Tanya's leg and raised her arms to be picked up, but Tanya ignored her daughter's cries.

Rooney said something, but Maya's howls drowned it out. She ran toward the stuffed elephant, and from the dizzying camera angles it was obvious she was running up the stairs, dangling Ellie by one ear.

Letty closed the laptop and looked at Joe DeCurtis.

"A high school kid managed to make the audio work—when the FBI couldn't?" he asked, shaking his head. "I don't know whether to be frightened or annoyed."

"You know what this means, Joe," Letty said. "Rooney's here, and he's looking for that loot. He seemed pretty convinced Tanya had it. How much are we talking about?"

Joe rubbed his jaw. "We estimated it could be close to a hundred and fifty thousand dollars' worth of stuff that they bought here. We do know they'd worked the gold-and-jewelry-buying scam over in Orlando and down in Lauderdale before moving up here when the cops there started investigating them. We searched the unit Tanya and Rooney were living in at the time. We found some odds and ends of sterling silver, a couple gold coins, but nothing of any real value, and definitely no cash. Chuck was living in the efficiency after my mom kicked him out, and we searched that too. Tanya swore up and down that she didn't know Rooney and Chuck were swindlers, and that they'd actually victimized her."

"You didn't believe her?"

"Hell no," Joe said. "I know she's your sister and she's dead and all, but I don't think anybody ever victimized Tanya Carnahan. Unfortunately, she was able to sweet-talk an assistant district attorney into dropping the charges against her. The minute that happened, she was gone. And of course, she skipped out on her motel bill."

"Oh God. I'm sorry . . ."

"It was almost worth it," Joe said. "To get that son of a bitch Chuck away from Ava. If he'd hung around any longer, he would have bled her dry."

Letty's thoughts immediately strayed to the suitcase hidden under the bed that contained Tanya's go-bag, and the wad of cash she'd stashed in it. Tanya had claimed it was her savings, but Letty had never really believed her sister had managed to save that much money from her faltering acting career.

Was the cash part of the loot from the gold-and-silver-buying scam? Whose money was it? Should she admit to Joe what she'd been hiding? Her head was starting to throb—either from the wine or the prospect of admitting to the crime of omission.

"Remind me again of how you figured out they were fleecing people?" she asked.

Joe toyed with the plastic lei around his own neck. "One of our guests here—a regular—pulled me aside one night, I think it was after a barbecue. She was mad and at the same time embarrassed, because she'd sold a piece of jewelry she'd inherited—her grandfather's antique gold watch—to Rooney, who'd told her it was only worth the value of the gold, maybe three thousand dollars. Later on, after she confided to a friend what she'd done, the friend helped her look up the value of the watch on eBay. Turns out, it was a rare collector's piece that was worth at least ten times what Rooney paid her. She didn't dare tell her husband what she'd done, because the guy's a real tight-ass, but the friend convinced her to tell me about the way she'd been fleeced."

Letty considered the roster of Murmuring Surf regulars she'd come to know over the past month. "You're talking about Trudi Maples, right?"

Joe's silence convinced her she was right.

"I can just see Merwin throwing it up to her about getting ripped off," Letty said. "He'd never let her live it down."

"I can neither confirm nor deny," Joe said. "I promised the victim that I'd keep her identity confidential."

"Tanya told Rooney that she didn't have the money. She pointed the finger at Chuck," Letty said.

"And now Chuck's dead," Joe said, his expression grim.

Maya came skipping in from the bedroom, holding a piece of paper with a childish stick-figure drawing of a girl with long flowing hair and something approximating a grass skirt. "Here's Moana, Mr. Joe," she said, flourishing her picture.

"This looks just like you," Joe exclaimed. He glanced at his watch. "Uh-oh. We're late. If we don't get over to the rec room this minute, Ava's gonna be the one putting out a BOLO."

"Joe?"

"You're still worried about Rooney," he said flatly.

Letty nodded toward Maya, who was standing in front of the mirror on the closet door, preening at her reflection as she plonked at the ukulele strings. "Do you think he knows he's her father?"

He rubbed his jaw again. "I don't think it's a coincidence that he ran into you at Publix."

"You don't think he'd try . . ."

"No! I know this guy, Letty. He's not looking to become Father of the Year. I think he's here for the money. Maybe Chuck told him where to find it—before his unfortunate accident."

Letty shuddered and pulled the blouse tighter around her shoulders.

"I think you need to think about moving, at least until we track Rooney down and lock him up for good."

"Where would I go? Do you know what first and last month's rent, plus utility deposits, cost for an apartment around here? I do, and I don't have that kind of money. Besides, what would Ava say? Part of my deal with her is living on the property makes me accessible any time she needs me."

"Okay. Hear me out. You and Maya could stay with me. Just for the short run. And I'm totally not trying to get in your, er . . . grass skirt."

"You're not?"

He grinned. "Okay, well, yeah, I mean, I am kinda trying, but I'm not a pig. My place is five minutes from here and it has two bedrooms. You and Maya could have my room, and I'd stay on the pullout in the room I use as an office. And I would totally respect your boundaries."

Letty was watching Joe's face as he made his case. He was so earnest, so . . . so unexpectedly kind. He was, she concluded, that rare thing. He was a good man. And he was damn fine-looking, too.

"Can we not do this tonight?" she asked. "After tomorrow, after you've dealt with Evan, I promise I'll think about moving in with you for a few days."

"Letty! Mr. Joe." Maya was standing by the door. "Let's go!" She swished her grass skirt. Joe swished his hips in imitation, and Letty swished hers. She went to the sliding glass door and checked the lock. She locked the window that led to the breezeway, and finally, after they were outside, she locked the front door.

~~~~~~~~~~~~~~

44

"ALOHA!" AVA CALLED, WHEN SHE spotted Letty and Joe approaching the rec room with Maya. "Oh, if y'all don't look too stinking cute!" She whipped out her phone. "Joe, stand right there with those girls, and for God's sake try to smile. Put your arm around Letty. No, closer. Maya, sweetheart, look at me now." She quickly snapped half a dozen photos.

The motel owner was dressed in a floor-length fuchsia flowered muumuu, with a flower crown balanced on her graying blond curls and half a dozen leis draped around her neck.

"You look pretty cute yourself," Letty said.

"Are we done yet?" Joe asked, deliberately baiting his mother. "This shirt itches. What the hell is it made of? Aquarium gravel?"

"Quit your bitching and get inside and start working the bar," Ava directed. "We're gonna have a full house tonight. Letty, can you sit by the table and sell bingo cards?" She looked over at Maya and smacked her forehead. "Oh Lord. I am getting senile in my old age." She leaned in closer to Letty and lowered her voice. "I'm so sorry, hon. I completely forgot. We can't let Maya stay. It's illegal for a minor to be on the premises when gambling is going on."

"She's right," Joe admitted.

"But it's only bingo," Letty protested. "Who's going to mind?"

"Vanita Dunn," Ava said promptly. "The bitch who owns the Islander. A couple years ago, Joe arrested Vanita's son for stealing from her hotel guests, and ever since then, she's always trying to make trouble for me. I wouldn't put it past her to have one of her spies here tonight. She'd rat me out in a heartbeat. It wouldn't be so bad for me, but Joe's a cop. It could look bad for him."

"I'll keep Maya tonight."

Letty turned to see that Vikki Hill had joined the small group clustered around the four-year-old.

The FBI agent was dressed in jeans and a pale pink button-down blouse, with a plastic flower stuck behind her ear as her only concession to the evening's theme.

She nodded at Joe. "Nice shirt, DeCurtis."

"Oh no, Vikki, I couldn't ask you to babysit," Letty said, uneasily. "You're sweet to offer. . . ."

"What? You don't think I could keep a kid alive for three hours? I'll have you know I had a pet goldfish in a bowl on my kitchen counter for three years. That's longer than either of my marriages lasted."

"You don't want to play bingo?" Ava asked.

"Nah. I just came out because those four walls in the crummy efficiency were starting to close in on me—no offense, Ava. Plus I was hungry."

"If you're really serious, you could watch her at my place," Letty offered.

"And you can eat dinner from the buffet," Ava added. "We won't start the first game for another fifteen minutes."

"Good deal." Vikki squatted down until she was at eye level with the four-year-old. "Hey Maya. Wanna hang out with me tonight? We can eat some sweet-and-sour meatballs and, uh, watch *Hawaii Five-O* on television, okay?"

Maya focused her huge blue eyes on the agent for a moment, considering the offer. "*PAW Patrol?*"

"Huh?" Vikki wrinkled her nose.

"It's sorta like *Five-O*, but with cartoon dogs," Joe advised.

"Okay, cool. But let's eat first." Vikki extended her hand and Maya took it.

As Ava predicted, the motel's regulars were already streaming toward the rec room, and the parking lot was filling with cars. "Big crowd, huh?" Letty observed.

"Word gets around," Ava said, showing her the metal cash box containing stacks of one-, five-, and ten-dollar bills. "Of course, it's mostly snowbirds and retirees. Where else are folks gonna go for a night out where they maybe spend ten or twenty dollars for an evening of entertainment like this—they get as much food as they can eat, cheap drinks, and maybe even win a jackpot."

"And it's legal to gamble like this?" Letty asked.

"As long as you do it for a nonprofit," Ava said. "We partner with the Legion of Mary, from the Catholic church. We don't make any money on this. After we pay for our operating costs, all the rest of the money gets paid out in jackpots. Good clean fun, right? Our regulars look forward to this all year long. It's a tradition, and lesson one here at the Murmuring Surf is, you don't mess with tradition."

"And it looks like everyone is really into the aloha theme," Letty said, marveling at the array of loud flowered shirts, plastic leis, and muumuus flowing through the door.

"There aren't any costume prizes, but still, it's a real cutthroat competition," Ava said. She nudged Letty. "Even the Feldmans want to play."

"Ruth! Billie!" Ava called, as the couple approached the table. "Where on earth?"

The two women wore matching traditional Hawaiian women's long muumuus, with wide puffed sleeves and gathered, ruffled necks, along with flower crowns woven with bits of palm fronds, vines, and yellow frangipani blossoms. They wore necklaces of cowrie shells and puka beads.

"Billie designed and made our dresses herself," Ruth said proudly. "I only made the necklaces."

"Those are works of art," Letty said. Before she could say anything else, Billie handed her two twenty-dollar bills. "How many cards?" Letty asked.

"Forty," Billie replied, hefting a large straw bag onto her shoulder. "We came to win."

More players crowded into the room. Trudi and Merwin Maples arrived, he dressed as a beachcomber with tattered shorts and straw hat, she in a blouse with a pattern of golden pineapples. The guests swarmed the food table, and Ava was kept busy, ferrying more platters of meatballs and fruit trays from the kitchen.

Joe stood at the front of the room on a makeshift plywood platform with a bar-top table and a large lit-up screen where the bingo numbers would be displayed. He tapped the microphone, resulting in an eardrum-piercing static squawk. "Five minutes, everybody!" he boomed. "Get your cards and take your seats."

People rushed her table, holding out money, and Letty dealt out the bingo cards as fast as she could.

"One-minute warning," Joe called. "Letty, go ahead and close the doors. Anybody not in the house sits out the first game."

She was in the process of closing the door when a slight figure in a grass skirt came barreling down the breezeway in her direction.

"Wait! Don't lock me out," Oscar Jensen yelled.

She looked at Joe for approval. He shrugged. She held the door ajar.

Had there been a costume prize, Oscar Jensen, Letty thought, should have won it. His *South Pacific*–inspired costume consisted of a crudely made bra constructed of coconut halves strung together with duct tape and bungee cords, the grass skirt, and a sailor hat worn at a rakish ankle. He'd smeared his pasty-white chest, face, and torso with a cheap orange bronzer, and was barefoot. He thrust a handful of bills at Letty, still out of breath from his dash to the door. "Gimme twelve cards."

Ava edged Joe away from the microphone. "Aloha everyone, and welcome to our twenty-eighth annual evening of Aloha Bingo at the Murmuring Surf. I'm Ava DeCurtis, sole owner and proprietor of the Surf, and my handsome son Joe here is your caller tonight. That beautiful young lady at the back of the room, my assistant manager

Letty, will be circulating the room and checking numbers and solving any issues. I assume y'all know the rules, but let me repeat—the first person I recognize as calling out bingo will be the winner of that game. Prizes will not be awarded until the numbers of each card are verified and approved by me. Also, and please remember this point, don't piss me off. Play nice, or go home."

Joe reclaimed his place. "Okay, we're gonna start off the evening with a straight bingo. First to cover five numbers horizontally, vertically, or diagonally wins."

Ava spun the wire cage holding the numbers, and the game was off.

"O-72," Joe called.

Letty circled the room, greeting the regulars and smiling at newcomers.

"Hey Letty." Merwin Maples summoned her to the table where he and Trudi were seated. He and his wife had four cards assembled on the tabletop.

Ruth and Billie Feldman sat across from the Mapleses. They had twelve cards neatly lined up in rows. Billie Feldman presided over a colorful village of rubber troll dolls. She had an array of fat plastic felt-tip bingo markers and was glaring at Merwin, whose plastic cup of Hawaiian punch was bumped up against the troll village.

"N-43," Joe called.

"Got two, Billie," Ruth said, pointing to the card with those numbers.

"What's up, Merwin?"

He gestured at the dolls. "Can you tell her to move those creepy damn dolls? She's taking up the whole tabletop. I can't even concentrate on my cards with all those things."

Billie Feldman didn't look up. She was using a marker to slash N-43 on her cards. "Shove it, Merwin," she said. "You don't like it, move to another table."

"G-54," Joe intoned.

"Bahahahaha," Ruth chuckled, pointing at the corresponding number on one of the cards Billie had just colored.

"There are no other tables," Merwin complained. He gestured around the room. "It's a full house."

"O-63," Joe called.

Trudi stabbed at one of their cards with her forefinger. "We got one, Merwin. Pay attention."

Billie colored numbers on her cards. "Yeah, Merwin. Quit yer bitching and pay attention. Not that it'll do you any good." She pointed at her cards. "I got the winning combination right here."

Letty peered over her shoulder. She saw three cards that only lacked one more winning number.

"Come on B-7. Or G-48," Ruth chanted, rubbing her hands together. She held out one of the troll dolls to Billie, who kissed the top of its head for luck.

"I-29," Joe called.

Oscar Jensen erupted from his chair the next table over. "*Bingo!*" he yelled, waving his hands in the air. "Bingo, bingo, bingo!"

With one hand, Billie swept her losing cards off the table, knocking over Merwin's half full cup of punch in the process. The sticky red liquid dripped off the table and onto his lap.

"Oh, sorry," she said, dabbing ineffectively at the mess with a paper napkin.

Letty hurried away from the simmering feud to check Oscar's card, matching the numbers on the screen against the numbers on his card. "We've got a winner!" she called to Ava.

"Oscar, you get a six-pack of Sprite and a free round of putt-putt at Island Golf," Ava said.

"What? I don't want no stinkin' Sprite," Oscar griped. "What about the cash?"

"Sorry, you won the warm-up game. Next game is a cash prize," Joe answered. "Ten dollars and a genuine Murmuring Surf souvenir tote bag. This one is a postage-stamp game. Cover any four numbers in a contiguous block on your card. Okay, let's roll. O-75."

The next hour passed in a flash. The bingo players were a raucous, rowdy bunch. They cheered and booed and played blackout, four corners, black diamond, and half a dozen other variations of the game that Letty had never heard of before. In between games they bought cards and claimed prizes and argued (in vain) with Ava over who was first to call bingo.

At eight, Joe called for a fifteen-minute break, and people surged toward the buffet and the bar.

"How's it going out there?" Joe asked, offering Letty a glass of lukewarm white wine.

"It's crazytown," Letty reported. "I never knew people could get this worked up over winning a Pancake House gift card. Merwin and Billie Feldman almost got in a fistfight because Merwin bitched that Billie was invading his territorial imperative."

"Bingo is serious business," Joe said. He looked up and grinned as Oscar Jensen approached. "Speaking of loony tunes . . ."

"Joe, Joe," Oscar said. He tugged at the cop's arm. "I was taking a smoke break just now, and I saw some guy, skulking around outside, peeking in windows."

"Where?" Joe said.

"Out there. He was looking in the window of the office. I saw him."

"Show me," Joe said. He looked over at Letty. "Tell Mom she needs to take over calling numbers. It's probably nothing, but stay here, and don't let anybody leave."

He bolted out of the room, with Oscar trailing behind.

Letty looked out at the darkened parking lot, where the Murmuring Surf's cheerful neon sign blinked off and on, spilling pink and green and blue reflections onto the pavement. She retrieved her purse from beneath the card table and called Vikki Hill.

"Hi," she said, keeping her voice low. "Just checking to make sure you guys are okay."

"We're fine," Vikki said. "Your kid's still alive. We've had Popsicles and popcorn, and watched a lot of *PAW Patrol*. I tried to convince her of the moral superiority of *Scooby-Doo*, but she's a stubborn little thing. Just put her to bed and she's already snoring. How's it going with Aloha Bingo?"

"It's okay." Letty hesitated. "One of the regulars thinks he saw somebody lurking around outside, peeking in the window at the office."

"Shit," Vikki breathed. "Does he need me to go out there? Or call the local cops?"

"Not yet," Letty said. "The old guy who reported the prowler is kind of a kook. Easily excited. Joe's out there now, checking things out. I'm sure he'll call you if he needs you. He made me promise to stay in here for now, but the minute he comes back, I'll head home."

With the break over, Ava resumed calling numbers. Letty continued patrolling the room, glancing out at the parking lot every chance she got. Ten minutes later, Joe returned.

"If there was anybody out there, he's gone now," he reported. "I got my flashlight, checked under cars, around the pool, down by the beach. Everything's quiet. I called it in to dispatch too, and they sent a unit by. Nothing. Fina promised she'd have night watch roll through here on the hour tonight."

"Did Oscar give you a description of the prowler?"

"Tall guy, but everybody looks tall to Oscar. He was dressed in dark clothes. And a baseball cap."

"Rooney," Letty said, feeling her scalp prickle.

45

JOE SIDLED UP TO HIS mother as she was escorting the last bingo player to the door of the rec room. "Where was Isabelle going tonight?"

Ava looked startled. "She and Sierra were going to meet friends someplace for burgers, then she said they might go to a late movie. What's going on, son?"

"Oscar thought he saw someone prowling around outside the office about an hour ago," Joe said. He explained about calling for a patrol unit and his fruitless search around the property.

"You think it's Rooney," Ava said.

"Maybe. But I don't want to take any chances. And I don't want those girls coming back here alone, late at night."

"She was planning on spending the night at Sierra's anyway," Ava said. "But I'll text her and tell her to make sure and stay put."

Joe swept the beam of his powerful flashlight around the parking lot, then pointed it toward the office as he and Letty walked Ava back home. He bent down and examined the office door. "Doesn't look like it's been tampered with." After unlocking the door, he motioned for them to stay outside while he checked the interior. "Okay," he said, poking his head around the door. "Doesn't look like anything here has been disturbed."

They followed him back inside. Ava checked the storeroom. "Nothing here."

Joe walked through each of the rooms in his mother's apartment, switching on lights, checking closets and beneath beds. "You okay to stay here alone tonight?" he asked.

She went into the kitchen and reached into the cupboard over the stove and brought down her pistol. She gave it a fond pat. "I moved this out of the office since Maya's around there so much. But I think I'll keep this close by tonight. Just in case."

He frowned. "Mom, I know you think you're a tough old bird, but I don't really think you need to keep a loaded gun under your pillow. I'll be around here tonight. Call me if you see or hear anything."

Ava touched Letty's shoulder. "Maybe you and Maya should stay here tonight. You can sleep in Isabelle's room."

Letty considered the offer, then shook her head. "Thanks, but Vikki said Maya's already asleep. I think we'll be fine where we are."

Vikki met them at the door to Letty's unit. "Shh," she cautioned, pointing toward the bedroom. She gave Letty a mock salute. "I have newfound respect for moms. That kid of yours wore me out. In a good way, but still."

Letty peeked into the bedroom and found Maya curled up in her pillow fort in the corner of the room. She pulled the door shut.

"Any signs of our prowler?" Vikki asked Joe.

"None. But I'm not taking any chances. I asked the night watch supervisor to send patrol units on the regular tonight. And I'll hang around too."

"I can patrol the premises too, you know," Vikki pointed out. "I actually am a sworn law enforcement professional."

"Nah. If it was Rooney, and I'm not convinced it was, he's long gone by now, spooked by the blue lights and all the bingo players tromping around the place. Get some sleep. We've got a big day tomorrow."

"I'm kinda keyed up now," Vikki said. "I might just walk down to Gianni's and get a slice of pizza and a glass of decent wine."

"This late?" Letty checked her phone and gave a sheepish laugh.

"Wow. Almost ten o'clock—which is actually two A.M. in Florida time."

Letty opened the sliding glass doors and stepped out onto the patio. A quarter-moon spilled milky light onto the calm surface of the Gulf, and a slight breeze stirred the palm fronds. She touched the waxy blossoms of the fragrant confederate jasmine clambering over the garden fence.

"Nice night." Joe's arm encircled her waist.

She muffled a startled yip.

He gave her a questioning look.

"Sorry, I guess, like Vikki, I'm keyed up too," Letty said.

"You know what I find helps when I'm keyed up?"

She laughed and rolled her eyes, but after a moment's hesitation, allowed herself to give in to her longing for comfort and to lean against him for a moment. His chest felt warm and solid against her bare back. She closed her eyes. He dropped a kiss on her shoulder. And then her neck. His cheek brushed hers. Slowly, she turned to face him, encircling her arms around his neck. She lifted the cheap plastic leis and threw them aside. He smiled, then removed the ones around her neck.

His kiss was slow and tender at first, and she responded in kind, melting into his embrace as his hands slid over the curve of her hips, cupping her buttocks as he pulled her closer.

Letty held his face between the palms of her hands, exploring his mouth with her tongue, while his hands wandered upward, working his fingers beneath the band of her bikini top, brushing her nipples with his thumbs.

The grass skirt rustled slightly as he worked his knee between her legs.

Letty's hands trailed down Joe's chest, then under his shirt, where she teased his nipples with her fingertips briefly. He inhaled sharply as her palms brushed his abs then rested over the bulge in his shorts.

"Aloha," he whispered.

"I think maybe we should take this inside," Letty whispered back. She took his hand and led him to the sofa, switching off lights as she went, while Joe tugged at the waistband of her grass skirt. She playfully swatted his hand away, went to the front door and flipped the dead bolt, then opened the door of the bedroom by two inches and peeked inside once again, to make sure Maya was asleep.

She's safe, Letty told herself, resting her head against the doorframe. And she realized, with surprise, that at this moment, despite the odds, she felt safe, too.

When she rejoined him in the living area, Joe quickly managed to unsnap her bikini top and fling it to the floor.

Letty crossed her arms over her bare chest, but he frowned and pulled them open. "I just want to look at you, just like this," he said, taking a step backward. "You're like my wildest, horniest teenage dream. A half-naked island girl. In a motel room. All for me."

She laughed and did a slow half turn, swishing her hips in a sensual hula, beckoning him with her outstretched arms. "ComeonIwannalayyou," she teased, pulling him toward the sofa.

He was fumbling with the condom wrapper when Letty froze, naked beneath him. Was that Maya, calling out for her in her sleep? "Wait!" She pulled herself upright, found Joe's discarded shirt on the floor, and clutched it to her chest as she tiptoed toward the bedroom. She held her breath, sliding the door back, but glancing inside, she saw that Maya wasn't stirring. A minute later she was back. "False alarm," she whispered, folding herself into his arms. "Please continue."

With a sweep of his arm he knocked the back sofa cushions to the floor and lifted her atop him. She tried to take her time, as they moved slowly together, she learning his rhythm, he touching, kissing, caressing, teasing. Just as she climaxed she heard a bizarre, hollow, crunching noise from very close by. "What?" she whispered urgently.

"Never mind." He drove himself into her and she moaned as he shuddered beneath her.

"I should get dressed," she whispered, struggling to sit up. Joe ran his fingertip down her spine. "Why?"

"Maya. She has night terrors. Not as often lately, but if she does . . ."

He shifted his weight and this time they both heard the weird crunching noise. Letty pulled him to his feet and examined the sofa. She lifted a cushion and extracted the smashed remains of Maya's ukulele.

"Oh my God," she giggled.

"We made some beautiful music together just now, didn't we?" Joe wrapped his arms around her and pulled her to him.

"Spectacular," she agreed. She handed him his shorts.

"Really? So soon?"

"If Maya wakes up, I can't have her finding a naked stranger on the sofa."

"I don't exactly think I'm a stranger to her. Anyway, how do people with kids ever manage to have a sex life?" he grumbled, stepping into his shorts and retrieving his T-shirt from the floor.

"I don't know," she admitted. "Babysitters?"

"I'm pretty sure Ava doped me up with children's Robitussin back in the day," Joe said. He replaced the sofa cushions and leaned back to watch as Letty scurried around the room picking up her discarded clothing.

"Do that topless hula thing again, will ya?" he asked.

"Not tonight, dear," she said, tossing the Hawaiian shirt at him. She slipped into the bedroom and when she emerged she was dressed in shorts and a T-shirt.

"Aw, man, I was thinking maybe we could take a shower together," Joe groused. "There goes my fantasy."

"Would you settle for a glass of wine?" She went into the kitchen, found the bottle she'd opened earlier, and poured two glasses.

He touched his glass to the side of hers. "Here's to promising beginnings," she said, smiling at him over the rim of the glass.

"Here's to babysitters," he countered.

"Can I ask you something?" he said, a little while later. He was stretched out on the sofa, with his head in her lap.

"Mmm-hmm."

"What changed your mind? About me? I mean, I'm not just another cheap, easy piece of meat, you know."

"What if I said I couldn't resist your boyish charm? You know, girls get horny too."

He picked up her hand and kissed the back of it. "Seriously, Letty. Are we going to be a thing? Or not? I keep getting mixed signals from you. You know, tomorrow, God willing, you're not gonna have to worry about Evan Wingfield anymore. You can pick up the pieces and put your life together—however you want it to be."

"I know," Letty agreed. "But I'm afraid to get too far ahead of myself. What if something goes wrong? I mean, really wrong?"

"Then we'll fix it. And it won't be me rescuing you, I promise. It'll be us fixing it together."

She chewed her bottom lip. "I want to buy into that dream. I want to be able to give Maya the things Tanya and I never had—a home, a real house with a yard and a cat, or maybe a dog. I want her to start school in the same town every year, with friends she won't be ashamed to bring home for sleepovers." She shrugged. "I guess I want stability. But I don't know how to make that happen—especially after all we've both been through these past few years."

Joe swung his legs off the sofa and sat up. He took both her hands in his. "That's a nice word picture you just painted there. Can I ask? Is there a man anywhere in this picture? At all?"

Letty stared down at their joined hands. "You guys—you and Isabelle—you didn't really have a dad. Right? In fact, earlier tonight you pointed out that Isabelle turned out just fine without a dad."

He groaned. "First off, you should never listen to my advice, because clearly I don't know what the hell I'm talking about. I think, if you asked Isabelle, she'd tell you—as long as Mom isn't within earshot—that she got a raw deal, not having a dad. But she might also point out that she had an *awesome* big brother who bitched and moaned—but still took her to the middle school daddy-daughter dance, and taught her how to drive a stick shift, and who, once she turned fourteen, threatened to arrest any little fucker who as much as tried to lay a hand on her without her saying it's okay."

"I wish Tanya and I had had a big brother like you," Letty said, kissing his cheek. "Maybe then things could have worked out differently for both of us. I wish I could wave a magic wand and invent a brother like that for Maya."

Joe pressed his forehead to hers. "You turned out more than okay. You're a good person, Letty. I know you'll make the right decisions for Maya. But don't forget about you. You deserve to have a life too. They don't have to be mutually exclusive."

He kissed her lightly. "You could have a life. And a man in your life. And awesome sex, on the regular with that man, you know, once we find a live-in babysitter."

Letty laughed despite herself. "You're incorrigible. . . ."

Someone was pounding on her door. "Letty? Hey, Letty? Joe?"

She jumped up and unlocked the door. Vikki Hill was grim-faced. "I just got back from Gianni's. Someone broke into my room. It's been ransacked. And my Glock is gone."

46

THE FBI AGENT WAS OBVIOUSLY shaken. "Looks like that prowler was for real. My room's been turned upside down."

Joe grabbed his phone. "I'm calling it in right now. Can you tell if anything else is missing?"

"No. As soon as I saw the lock had been jimmied I went in, saw the mess, and looked for my gun. When I saw it was missing, I backed up and came directly over here. Thank God I had my purse with my badge and ID and credit cards with me."

"Shauna?" Joe spoke into his phone. "Can you get over here ASAP? We've had a break-in at the Surf. No, I don't want to call it in to dispatch. I'll explain when you get here."

Letty wrapped her arms across her chest and looked from Joe to Vikki. "You think it's Rooney, don't you?"

"Who else?" Joe said.

"But why break into the smallest unit here?" Vikki asked. "And what's he looking for?"

"Maybe it's the loot he was accusing Tanya of stealing that day he showed up at her place in New York," Letty said.

"We never recovered most of the jewelry or silver or gold from their scam when we arrested Tanya," Joe reminded Vikki. "At the time of Tanya's arrest, she claimed Chuck and Rooney took it with them. Now, I'm thinking that loot's what got Chuck killed."

"Just how much loot are we talking about?" Vikki asked. "I thought these were a couple of low-rent grifters."

"It was just a guess, but we estimated around a hundred and fifty thousand dollars. But really there's no telling. The operation they set up here at the Murmuring Surf was at least the third we know of, after similar operations around the state. But according to Trudi Maples, the watch they bought from her—just for the value of the gold—turns out to have been worth thirty thousand dollars."

Letty had been pondering the "why" of Rooney tossing the efficiency. "When I first got here, there weren't any available rooms. But Ava offered to let me clear out the unit that she'd been using for storage. It was full of junk—stuff that the maintenance man was supposed to have thrown out or had hauled away, but instead he just shoved it in the efficiency."

"And the alleged maintenance man was Chuck Sheppard?" Vikki guessed.

"Yeah." Joe's phone dinged and he looked down. "Shauna just pulled in."

Letty paced around her living room. She could see the open door of the efficiency if she stood in the breezeway. She saw Joe and Shauna and Vikki standing outside the unit, saw the patrol officer crouch down and examine the doorknob with her flashlight. She saw the flashlight beam sweeping over the roof of the unit, nodded silently as Joe and Shauna walked past, speaking in low voices. She heard Shauna speaking into her radio.

Eventually, she went inside, and after checking on Maya, and re-latching the patio door, she fixed herself a cup of tea. She opened her laptop and rewatched the video clip with the amplified sound that Sierra had sent her, hoping to find some clue she'd overlooked.

Shortly after two, she heard a discreet tap at the door. She unlocked it and Joe walked inside and flopped wearily onto the sofa.

"Anything?"

"No. If it's Rooney, the guy's a damn Houdini. I even got a ladder and went up on the roof. We walked the beach, thinking maybe he's camping in the dunes or something, but there's no sign of him."

Joe's dark hair was damp with sweat and his eyes were ringed with dark circles. "Jesus! I can't stand the idea that creep could still be prowling around here. And now he's got Vikki's gun. I went up to Mom's and told her about the break-in at the efficiency."

Letty curled up next to him on the sofa. "Was she freaked out?"

He shrugged. "Honestly? She's got that loaded pistol on her nightstand and I think she thinks she's Annie Oakley. Whatever."

"What about Vikki? Where'd she go? She's surely not staying in the efficiency tonight, right?"

"Hell, no. We rigged up a temporary padlock on her room and she's bunking in Isabelle's room tonight." He ran his hand through his hair. "Although, given what we've got on our plates for tomorrow, I don't know how much sleep any of us will get tonight." He looked at her hopefully. "Okay if I crash on your sofa tonight? I promise to keep my clothes on."

"Of course." She kissed him, then got up to fetch a pillow and blanket from the bedroom.

"I just had a thought. Maybe Rooney found what he was looking for when he trashed the efficiency. Maybe he found the loot and he's long gone. Right?"

"Let's hope so."

While she was in the bedroom, Letty checked the window locks. She found a folded blanket on the top shelf of the closet, along with an extra pillow. By the time she returned to the living room, Joe was slumped sideways on the sofa, softly snoring. She slipped the pillow under his head, swung his legs onto the sofa, covered him with a blanket, and tiptoed out of the room, turning off the lights as she went.

~~~~~~~~~~

47

MIDNIGHT HAD A GLEAMING BLACK coat, olive-green eyes, dainty white paws, and a white-tipped nose. And four kittens. At dawn, she decided it was time to move. She caught the smallest, most troublesome kitten by the nape of the neck and set out across the parking lot. She skirted the cars and passed along the motel breezeway. At the end of the concrete walkway, she stepped into the dew-drenched grass.

Ahead was a tall palm tree encircled by a thicket of pink bloom-ing oleanders and asparagus ferns. The ferns were bracketed by a circle of large, dusty green bromeliads with sawtooth-edged leaves and ruby-red throats. She darted beneath the thicket, deposited the kitten in a nest of pine needles, and set off again, back to the drain-age culvert.

The other kittens were mewing hungrily. When the largest one, a male, tried to nurse, she batted it with her paw and picked it up in her mouth. She was crossing the parking lot again when a silver se-dan with faded paint and bald tires pulled into the only vacant spot, the handicapped parking space in front of the breezeway. When the engine idled, then stopped, she darted away, hiding in the shadows beneath a van. After a moment, she slunk out and made her way back to the palm tree and her new nest.

She deposited the second kitten beside its sister and paused long enough for both kits to nurse briefly.

·　·　·

Everything was still and dark when Maya awoke. Her aunt was sleeping on her side facing away from the bedroom door, an arm flung across her face. Maya opened the door and went out to the kitchen, where she stealthily removed a juice box and bag of gold-fish crackers from the bottom cupboard.

Mr. Joe was asleep on the sofa and she could not find the remote control for the television. So she crept past him, juice box and crackers tucked under her arm. The sliding-door lock was stubborn. But Maya was a big girl now. She set her snacks on the floor and stood on her tiptoes, her tongue tipped out in concentration until she heard the metallic snick as the lock disengaged.

She slid the heavy glass door aside, picked up her snack, and stepped out onto the patio. The bricks felt cool and damp beneath her bare feet. She pushed the straw into the juice box and took a sip. She was about to open the package of goldfish when she saw something moving beyond the patio gate.

It was Midnight! And she had something in her mouth. A small, wriggling black something. It was a kitten. Maya watched while the cat darted beneath the prickly green bushes. She waited. She opened the bag of crackers and chewed, ignoring the bright orange crumbs that sprinkled down the front of her pajama top. She took a suck of apple juice, then crammed the rest of the crackers into her mouth, dropping the bag onto the bricks.

When Midnight emerged from the bushes without the kitten, Maya smiled. The cat scampered away without looking back. Maya unlatched the patio gate and stepped into the thick, wet grass. It tickled her ankles.

All was quiet outside. She could still see a sliver of moon in the morning sky. She could hear the waves washing onto the beach just beyond the sand dune, and a line of pelicans, those funny birds with the big beaks with grocery bags attached, flew past, low along the surf line.

The world was asleep. She tiptoed toward the palm tree. As she drew closer, Maya could hear soft mewing noises. She got down on her hands and knees and crawled the last few inches until her nose was inches from the circle of shrubbery.

The sawtoothed leaves scratched at her face, but she inched forward. She saw something black and furry curled up in a nest of pine needles. Kittens! There were two kittens. They mewed and wriggled. Midnight had left the kittens all alone. Maya reached out and touched one on its little pink nose. A tiny pink tongue darted out and licked her hand. She giggled with delight. She scratched the kitten's soft black ears and it mewed again.

Her hand was closing on the kitten when she heard footsteps crunching in the wet grass. An arm wrapped itself around her waist and abruptly jerked her up and away. Just before a hand clamped over her mouth she saw the man. It was the man from the store. He had scary blue eyes and a black baseball cap. He smiled. "Good morning, Maya."

Joe awoke with a start, and for a moment, he couldn't figure out where he was. The room was still dark. He yawned and stretched, then remembered. This was Letty's place. He'd fallen dead asleep on the sofa. He stood up and switched on the lamp on the end table and looked around the room and smiled briefly at the memory of what had happened earlier on this very same sofa.

He checked his phone. Nearly seven. He needed to pee, but didn't dare walk into the bedroom for fear of waking Letty and Maya. He went over to the sliding glass door and frowned when he saw that it was slightly ajar. Had Letty left it open the night before? They'd been out on the patio, and then things had gotten intense and they'd come back inside.

Dammit, he'd have to remind her again about keeping everything locked up. He slid the door open wider, went out to the patio, and looked out at the horizon. The morning sky looked clear, the water calm. Joe hoped it was a good omen for the day ahead.

He hadn't wanted to worry Letty, but this whole scheme with

Wingfield could go very wrong, very fast, with just the slightest misstep from any of them. He scowled, considering all the terrifying possibilities, but forced himself to put aside his worries. Vikki Hill was a seasoned federal agent. She would have backup, and he would have backup. And finally, Letty would be freed from the cloud that had been hanging over her head.

Joe yawned again, opened the gate, walked outside, and after making sure he couldn't be seen by any early-morning beach walkers, relieved himself behind a dune.

When he went back inside he locked the slider and went in search of coffee. He found a box of tea bags in the cabinet, but no sign of coffee. Letty's room key was on the end table. He let himself out of the unit, saw that the lights were on in the office, and smiled. If the lights were on at his mother's place, he knew the coffee would be hot. He locked the door behind him and went in search of caffeine.

"You're up early," Ava observed. She was standing behind the reception desk, rummaging through a pile of room keys. They were the old-school variety, with large diamond-shaped plastic tags bearing the Murmuring Surf logo and room numbers.

"You too."

He went to the coffee maker and poured himself a mug, dumping in two packets of sugar. "What are you looking for?"

"The master key. Chuck had one, but I made him give it back when I kicked him out. Or, I thought I did."

Joe scowled at the memory of Ava's relationship with the late Chuck Sheppard. "He could have easily had another key made, you know. Doesn't matter now. He's dead. Anyway . . ."

The office door flew open. Letty was barefoot and wild-eyed. "Is Maya here with you? Is she upstairs?"

"No," Ava said. "She's not here. I haven't seen her this morning."

"She's gone!" Letty wailed. "I just woke up, and she wasn't in her bed or the pillow fort, and she wasn't anywhere in the apartment. . . ."

"The sliding glass door was ajar when I got up," Joe said, setting his coffee mug down. "I assumed we'd left it open last night."

"No, I locked it," Letty insisted. "And I double-checked last night. She must have gotten up while we were still sleeping."

"What's going on?" Vikki Hill emerged from the stairwell. "What's this about Maya?"

"She's gone!" Letty cried. "Oh my God. The pool. What if she wandered over there and fell in?"

"I'll check the pool," Joe said quickly.

"I'll go down to the beach to look," the FBI agent volunteered. "Maybe she's playing mermaid in the sand."

"Mom, can you and Letty check the rec room and the rest of the property? You might have to start knocking on doors. Maybe one of the guests spotted her."

"Rooney. What if Rooney took her?" Letty clamped both hands over her mouth to keep herself from screaming.

Joe touched her shoulder. "We're gonna find her. Okay? We'll find her. If I have to tear this place apart, if I have to tear him apart, we'll find her."

Letty nodded. "I believe you."

Letty's heart pounded in her chest as she ran toward the rec room, and she repeated the only prayer she knew, the one she'd learned during a brief foray to a long-ago Sunday school class.

Our Father, who art in Heaven . . .

Please let Maya be safe . . .

Please keep her safe . . .

Hallowed be Thy name . . .

Thy Kingdom come . . .

Letty rattled the heavy glass door of the rec room, but it was tightly locked, the interior dark. Letty looked down the breezeway toward the bank of motel units on the right. No signs of life. She decided to circle back toward her own place. Maybe Maya had gone

out onto the patio and chased one of the tiny green lizards that fascinated her. Her mind raced with all the dark possibilities. What if . . .

Joe met her at the door of her unit. "The Feldmans were swimming laps and they said they haven't seen Maya, but when I told
them she was missing they got out of the pool and said they'd help
look."

Vikki jogged toward them. "I scouted out the beach. No sign of
her there." She hesitated. "I did see a set of men's footprints in the
sand, leading from the edge of the grass outside your room, Letty,
into the dunes."

"Those are mine," Joe said quickly, shooting an apologetic look
at Letty. "I needed to take a whiz and didn't want to disturb you, so
I went out to the dunes."

"What if she went out into the parking lot?" Letty said, her voice
rising in panic. She knew she sounded hysterical. Because she was
right on the edge of hysteria. "Or out onto the road?"

"I called in to dispatch," Joe said. "They've got patrol cars out
looking for her."

48

~~~~~~~~~~

"SHHH," DECLAN ROONEY WHISPERED INTO Maya's ear. They were crouching in the concrete drainage culvert just a few yards from the motel dumpster. His hand was still clamped over her mouth. She had her eyes tightly closed, but still kicked at his thighs and wriggled in his arms.

He duckwalked toward the end of the culvert, peeking out at the lot. He'd seen the two old ladies in damp, baggy bathing suits trot past, fanning out toward opposite ends of the bank of motel rooms, calling the kid's name. It was full daylight now, and he had a decision to make.

Should he stay? Maybe trade the kid for access to the motel room where that fucker Chuck had stashed the loot from their joint enterprise? Even after four years, he knew the stuff was there: bags and bags of sterling silver, watches, gold and silver jewelry with their gemstones intact, all the valuables they'd bought off the hapless clucks who'd flocked to their motel room convinced they'd hit pay dirt.

Chuck had sworn it was still there. It had to be.

Fucking Chuck. Rooney should have known better. He and Tanya were doing fine on their own, a hit-and-run kind of operation where they'd rent a room in a Holiday Inn, buy some stuff, and then move on to the next town a couple days later. The money hadn't been great, but it was okay. Then they'd met Chuck at the Indian gaming casino in Tampa.

An older guy. Tanya said he reminded her of her granddad. They'd had dinner and some drinks and some laughs. Good old Chuck was quite the storyteller. Probably that's why he and Tanya hit it off so well. Next thing you know, Chuck invited them to stay at his girlfriend's motel on the beach, over in St. Pete.

The beach. That was all Tanya had to hear. A couple days turned into a week, and before Rooney knew it, Chuck was a full partner. They ran ads on Craigslist and in the local shopper papers. Chuck put up flyers in nearby shopping centers, in laundromats and barbershops and nail salons, at the Moose Lodge and the senior center. Rooney had to hand it to him, the old bastard knew their demographic.

Sellers were banging down the door of their motel room, lining up like sheep ready to be fleeced. Things were going so well that a week turned into two weeks, and that, ultimately, was their downfall.

Rooney wanted to move on. The motel owner's son was a cop, a fact Chuck conveniently forgot to mention. Cops gave Rooney the hives. But Tanya was sick and tired of the nomad life. Literally, she was sick. And tired. And Rooney was already remembering his old man's advice: He travels fastest who travels alone.

That last night, he and Chuck decided to hit the greyhound track. Rooney had a hot streak running—every dog he bet on finished in the money. Tanya started calling around eight, but he finally just turned the phone off. They drove across the bridge to Tampa, hit the Seminole Indian casino, where their streak continued. Chuck knew of a strip club near MacDill, the air force base. They were on their way when Rooney glanced down at his phone and saw the text from Tanya that he'd missed hours earlier.

OMG WHERE ARE YOU? THE COPS ARE HERE.

He'd shown the message to Chuck. They drove back to the beach, cruised slowly past the Murmuring Surf, where the parking lot was full of police cruisers. On their second pass they spotted Tanya, being led into the parking lot in handcuffs, by a black female patrol officer.

"Keep driving," Chuck advised.

"But the stuff—all the stuff we were going to take to the refinery. I'm not driving away from my money," Rooney objected.

"Don't worry. I hid it. The cops will never find it. As soon as things cool down, we'll go back."

Rooney had been deeply suspicious. "How are we gonna go back? Everybody there knows you. And me. They'll call the cops the minute they see us."

Chuck patted his pocket. "We'll wait a couple days, go over there late at night. I've got the passkey. I tell you what. Let's go back to the strip club. I know a couple dancers there. We'll get a room, get laid, then tomorrow night, we'll pick up the stuff, right where I hid it." He grinned. "And then we'll move on down the road. A two-way split. It's not like you were planning on staying with Tanya—am I right, partner?"

"Hidden, where?" Rooney demanded, deliberately avoiding the question about Tanya. "I'm not fucking around here, Chuck. You try and cheat me, I promise it won't end well for you."

"Cheat you?" Chuck looked offended. "I would never."

Rooney had started hatching his own plan while they were on the way to the strip club. He'd get Chuck drunk. It wouldn't take long; the guy really couldn't hold his booze. He'd wait until his "partner" passed out, grab the key, and leave him behind in a puddle of piss and regrets.

But he hadn't counted on scoring coke from one of Chuck's dancer friends. Hadn't counted on Chuck getting in a fight with the club's bouncer as they were leaving with the girls and pulling a knife. And he really hadn't counted on watching his "partner" rolling away from the strip club that night in the back of a police cruiser—with the motel passkey securely in his pocket.

In the end, he'd done just what Chuck advised. He kept on driving.

The kid wriggled in Rooney's arms. She was feisty, like her mother. He could feel her jaws working beneath his fingertips. "Shut up," he whispered fiercely. She clamped down and bit his fingers, her sharp little baby teeth digging into his flesh.

He released his hold, only for a moment, but it was long enough. She was off, like a shot, screaming at the top of her lungs. "Stranger! Stranger! Mommy! Stranger!" She ran toward the end of the culvert, toward sunlight.

Rooney hesitated for an instant. Get the kid? Or cut his losses and get out now? He was thinking of all that money, all of it, locked up in that storage room. Fuck it. He'd come back. He was out of the culvert, heading toward his car, blinking in the sudden flood of sunlight.

A champagne-colored van with a handicap license plate was parked directly in back of Rooney's car, blocking it in. The driver laid on the horn. Once, and then twice. The passenger-side door opened and a heavyset elderly woman wearing white surgical hose slowly climbed out. She slid the back door aside and retrieved an aluminum walker.

Rooney ran toward the woman, waving the Glock he'd taken from the efficiency. "Move the van!" he screamed. His ball cap fell off. His voice was hoarse. "Move this goddamn van, or I'll fucking blow your head off."

Trudi Maples turned at the sound of his voice. Her eyes narrowed as she instantly recognized the menacing blue-eyed man charging toward her. It was the man who'd cheated her, who'd bought her grandfather's heirloom watch and cheated her out of thousands of dollars, money she'd planned to use for their fiftieth-anniversary trip. "You!"

He pointed the gun as he came closer. Trudi picked up the walker with both hands. She swung it at his head, sideways, as hard as she could, grunting with the exertion. She would never forget the look on Declan Rooney's face; for months afterward, she would describe it in detail, to Merwin, and then her grandchildren and her bridge partners up home, anyone who would listen really.

It was a look of total astonishment, shock, turning to pain, as the aluminum walker slammed into the side of his face, the sound like the crack of a bat hitting a ripe cantaloupe, knocking him to

the ground. He lay there, clutching his face, writhing in pain on the crushed-shell pavement. Blood bubbled from Rooney's handsome, ruined mouth. She placed the pronged legs of the walker squarely over his body and leaned heavily upon it, effectively pinning the man to the ground.

Finally, Merwin put the van in park and made his way over to his wife. "Jesus, Trudi," he said, staring down at the wounded stranger in horror. "What the hell have you done now?"

49

At the sound of Maya's cries Letty broke into a panicked run, feeling the adrenaline coursing through her blood.

"Maya! Maya, baby, I'm here," she called as she ran. "I'm coming, baby!"

She saw the small pajama-clad figure zigzagging across the parking lot toward her and held out her arms.

Maya rocketed into her embrace and Letty pressed her close to her chest. "The bad man," the child sobbed. "The bad man got me."

"I know, baby, I know," Letty crooned, stroking her back. "But I'm here now. You're safe. Okay? I won't let you go. You're safe."

Doors up and down the breezeway were opening and guests, some still in their nightclothes, poked their heads out of their rooms.

"What's going on?" Oscar Jensen stepped into the breezeway. He was dressed in a cotton bathrobe that barely skimmed his thighs and had a black satin sleep mask pushed up onto his forehead.

Ava rushed across from the office, with Ruth and Billie Feldman trailing in her wake.

"Thank God," Ava said, folding Letty and Maya into an all-encompassing hug. "Thank God she's safe."

Ruth hitched up the bosom of her bathing suit. She gave Letty an awkward pat on the back. "We're so glad," she said. "Aren't we, Billie?"

Billie nodded. "Ruth was about to boost me up and into the dumpster. We were afraid maybe . . ."

Ruth frowned. "And then we heard Maya. She was inside that big concrete pipe. She ran out and that fella came out too. He must've been hiding in there with her."

"Right before that, Merwin and Trudi pulled into the parking lot. Merwin was mad because somebody else parked in that handicap spot," Billie said.

"Yeah, Merwin thinks he owns that handicap spot, but he doesn't," Oscar said. "Ava even told him he can't park there permanent. Supposed to be loading and unloading only."

"We get it, Oscar," Ruth said, giving him a withering glance. "Could you please let Billie finish telling what happened. We were there and you weren't."

"So Merwin had the other car blocked in, and he was really laying on the horn," Billie reported.

"And then Trudi got out of the van, and that guy, the one in the baseball cap, he came running at Trudi."

"The guy in the baseball cap? See? I told you. I told you I saw him creeping around here last night. Nobody believed me, but I saw him peeking in the window at the office." Oscar's pale face was pink with excitement. "It had to be the same guy. I knew he was up to no good."

"It wasn't that we didn't believe you," Ava started to say.

"He had a gun!" Ruth broke in. "And he was pointing it right at Trudi, screaming at her that if they didn't move Merwin's van, he'd blow her bleeping head off."

"Trudi didn't even blink," Billie said. "He kept yelling and pointing the gun at her. I really thought he'd kill her. I even told Ruthie, 'He'll shoot her.'"

Letty began to edge away from the crowd of regulars who'd gathered in the breezeway. Maya's arms encircled her neck. She gently rubbed the little girl's back, crooning the verses to Maya's favorite song in her ear. "Let it go, let it go . . ." Maya's sobs slowed and she took a long, shuddering breath.

"And then Trudi picked up that walker of hers and she swung on him like A-Rod used to swing on a high fastball," she heard Ruth say.

"Ka-pow! She laid him out with one swing. Knocked him clean out of the park."

Joe found Letty curled up in the corner of the sofa in her unit, with Maya on her lap, watching *PAW Patrol* on the television. Letty looked up and smiled when he walked into the room, and he wanted to collapse from relief.

"She's okay," Letty said, before he could ask. "Right, Maya?" She patted the sofa cushion and Joe sat down beside her.

The child turned her face toward Joe. "The bad man got me," she said solemnly. "I was looking at the kitties. Midnight hid them. I only wanted to touch them, but then the bad man got me and put me in the cave. I kicked him and tried to get away, but he was squeezing me. So I bited him, and he let me go and I ran away as fast as I could."

"You were a very brave girl," Joe said. "The bravest little girl I've ever known."

Maya nodded in agreement. "That man yelled at my mommy," she said, her tone matter-of-fact. She shook her head. "I don't like him. He's bad."

"He won't be hurting anybody again for a very long time," Joe told her. "Maya? Is it okay if I talk to Letty in the kitchen? Are you okay to sit here by yourself for a few minutes while we talk?"

"I'm hungry," Maya said, batting her eyelashes in a brazen attempt at extortion. "Can I have a chicken biscuit? With jelly? And French fries? And a milkshake?"

Letty rolled her eyes, but nodded. "In a little bit. Okay? Can you wait until after I've talked to Mr. Joe?"

"Okay. But hurry. I'm hungry."

Joe folded Letty into his arms. "It's over," he said, stroking her hair. "Rooney's on his way to the hospital, and then to jail. He's got a broken jaw, for sure, and probably a shattered occipital. Trudi Maples cleaned his clock but good."

He held her at arm's length and gazed into her eyes. "Okay? I know you're still shook. I am too. But listen. Vikki's headed to the airport."

"Already?" Letty was startled. "It's not even eight o'clock."

"She wanted to get there early, to make sure everything was in place. Just in case Wingfield tries to pull a fast one. There's an FBI agent from the Tampa office who'll be at the gate at every flight arriving from New York."

"That's good," Letty said. "Right?"

"It's called covering all the bases. But here's the thing. We need to get a videotaped statement from Maya."

"Now? Joe, I've just gotten her calmed down. She's only four. I can't put her through this trauma all over again, today of all days. You can't ask me to do that to her."

"It sucks," he agreed. "But if we want to nail Rooney, we've got to do this right. Shauna says she's willing to interview Maya, if you think she'd feel more comfortable talking to a woman, or we can get a social worker from the county's department of juvenile services. But let's get it done and over with, so we can nail this slime to the wall. While it's still fresh in her mind? Please?"

"God," Letty groaned. "What if she doesn't want to talk? She does that sometimes, when she's upset. Tanya told me that during the first few sessions she had with the therapist in New York, Maya would just shut down. She'd sit in the corner with her eyes closed and her hands over her ears."

"If she doesn't want to talk, we absolutely won't make her. How about this? I'll run down to McDonald's, pick up her breakfast, and head back here. Then, Shauna and I can talk to her, and if she's okay, we'll videotape it. You'd be there too, of course. Nobody does anything without you saying it's okay."

50

~~~~~~~~~~~~~~

VIKKI PARKED THE RENTAL AT the curb in front of the Tampa Airport's departure door. She closed her eyes and was about to nod off when she heard a metallic tapping on the passenger-side window. She rolled it down and the cop leaned in. "Ma'am? This is a loading zone only. Need you to move along."

She reached under the front seat and brought out the leather badge holder, flashing it at the cop. "I'm here on police business."

The woman reached for the badge, examined it, then pursed her lips. "For real? FBI? We didn't get word of any kind of an undercover operation here today."

"I'm just picking up a suspect and taking him to St. Pete," Vikki assured her. "But if you don't mind, I need to stay here and wait for my passenger."

The cop shook her head. "Would have been nice if somebody had bothered to give us a heads-up." She muttered something else under her breath, then walked away.

Vikki yawned. Over the past forty-eight hours she'd gotten almost no sleep. She sat up and rubbed at her eyes, realizing too late that she'd smeared her mascara. She pulled down the visor and examined her face in the mirror. Puffy, red-rimmed eyes, blotchy skin, sunburned nose. She found a tissue in her purse and tried to repair the damage. She looked like shit. Maybe she'd put in for a couple of vacation days when this was all over. Just find a lounge chair by a pool somewhere, sip some umbrella drinks, and chill.

A black limo pulled up to the curb behind her rental. She twisted in her seat to get a better look and the leather holster clipped inside the waistline of her slacks chafed at the tender skin there.

Vikki had been forced to pull rank on DeCurtis, who hadn't wanted to return the Glock that Declan Rooney had stolen from her room the night before. But she'd pointed out that the gun hadn't been fired. He'd reluctantly returned her property.

She pulled out her phone and checked for email or messages. Nothing. She sipped at her second cup of convenience-store coffee. Bad plan to add more fire to the acid pit building up in her belly, but without the caffeine she'd be sleepwalking for sure.

"You there?" DeCurtis's disembodied voice drifted from the smart watch on her wrist.

"Where else? How's it going over there? How freaked out are Letty and Maya?"

"Maya's pretty calm now that she's got her Happy Meal," Joe said. "Letty's getting there. How's it look where you are?"

"Surreal," Vikki said. "This Tampa airport is like a Disney invention. So clean. No crowds, no Port Authority buses spewing fumes. I checked in with our field agent, Garcia. He's inside, wandering back and forth between the gates. No sign of Wingfield. Good, right? I hate surprises."

"Agreed. Check ya later."

Shauna clipped the video camera to the tabletop tripod. "All set," she said. "Maya? Are you ready?"

The little girl nodded shyly, tucking her chin into her chest. Letty touched her elbow. "Don't be afraid, ladybug. Okay? I'm right here. Mr. Joe is going to ask you some questions. You're not in trouble, right? You just look at him and tell him what happened. Can you do that?"

Maya picked up her milkshake and sucked at the straw. "Uh-huh."

"Say yes or no, please," Letty reminded her.

Joe scooted his chair next to Maya's and nodded for Shauna to start recording.

"This is Detective Joe DeCurtis of the Treasure Island Police Department. The date is March 28, 2020. Time is nine twenty A.M. Place of interview is the Murmuring Surf Motel. Subject is a minor female, Maya Wingfield, age four. Subject's guardian, Letty Carnahan, has given written permission for this interview and is present as a witness, as is Officer Shauna Arthur."

He looked down at his notes, then back at Maya, giving her an encouraging smile.

"Maya, can you tell me what happened to you this morning? After you woke up?"

Maya nodded.

"Remember? Say yes or no when he asks you a question," Letty prompted.

"Okay. Can you tell us what you saw when you went out on the patio this morning?"

"I saw Midnight! She was carrying one of her kittens in her mouth. She put the kitten under the tree. She was hiding them."

"And what did you do then?" he asked.

"Midnight went away. I wanted to see the kitties. I heard them. They went meeewwww meeeewwwww." Maya looked over at Letty. "They were missing their mommy. Like I miss my mommy sometimes."

"What happened next?" Joe asked.

Maya glanced at Letty for reassurance. Letty nodded, and the child took a deep breath.

"I petted the kitty on the nose, and it kissed my finger. And then . . ."

Her face began to crumple. "And then . . . the bad man got me."

"Did he say anything to you?"

She put her finger to her lips. "He said, 'Shhh, Maya.'"

Letty gripped the edge of the table so hard her knuckles turned white. Her foot tapped nervously on the floor.

"Had you ever seen the man before?"

Maya nodded. "Uh-huh. I mean, yes. At the store Letty took me to. When we hided in the bathroom. I'm not s'posed to talk to strangers."

"That's right. If I showed you a picture of some strangers, could you tell me if one of them was the man you saw in the store?"

"Uh-huh."

Joe held out his phone and scrolled through the photo lineup he'd hastily assembled. White males, age thirty-five to forty.

She studied each of the six photos, finally pointing at one. "That's the bad man."

"Okay." He held the photo up to the video camera. "She's identified a photo of Declan Rooney.

"Is this the same man who grabbed you this morning?"

"Yes."

Letty hadn't realized she was holding her breath, but now she exhaled.

"Good work," Joe said. "What happened after the man picked you up? Where did you go?"

"We went to the cave." She clamped her hand over her nose. "It was stinky in there. Like poo-poo."

"By cave, do you mean the big concrete pipe? The culvert at the edge of the parking lot at the motel?"

"Yes. It was dark."

"What happened next?"

Maya scrunched up her face as she thought back to the morning's events. "He taked my picture with his phone."

Letty leaned forward and exchanged a worried glance with Joe.

"What happened after that, Maya?"

"He said, 'Say "Hi, Daddy." '"

"Dear God," Letty murmured.

Joe motioned for Shauna to stop recording.

"What happened to Rooney's phone? Is it with his effects?"

"It's in the trunk of my vehicle in an evidence bag," Shauna said.

"I'll get it." She rushed from the room and five minutes later handed the phone to DeCurtis.

He thumbed through the camera roll on the phone. The most recent photos were a series of three blurry photos of the little girl, wide-eyed with terror. One was a video. He tapped the arrow. "Hi Daddy," Maya said, choking on the words.

"Look at this," Joe said, handing the phone to Letty. He tapped the text button. A phone number appeared, along with the video of Maya. "Recognize that number?"

"That's Evan's number," Letty whispered. She could hear the roar of blood in her ears. How many times had that number popped up in her own phone logs while she worked for Evan? Hundreds probably. "He was texting a video of Maya to Evan."

Joe shook his head. "But it looks like the text didn't transmit." He displayed the text message to Letty and Shauna. "Maybe because he was still in that concrete culvert."

"I don't understand. How did Rooney know about Evan?" Letty asked.

Maya put her milkshake cup down on the table. "I wanna watch *PAW Patrol*."

"Okay," Shauna said, her tone bright. She unclipped the video camera from the tripod and extended a hand to the child. "Can I watch with you?"

51

"Vikki?"

Her eyelids were heavy from lack of sleep, but she was instantly on alert when DeCurtis called again.

"Yeah?"

"We might have a problem," Joe said. "Looks like Rooney has been in touch with Wingfield."

His announcement was like a splash of cold water to her face. "What makes you think that?"

"We just interviewed Maya, and she told us that while Rooney had her in that culvert, he took a video of her, saying 'Hi, Daddy.' Then he texted it to a number that turns out to be Wingfield's. Or tried to. The video didn't transmit, and right after that, Maya bit Rooney's hand and took off running. But it was definitely Wingfield's number."

"Shit. Shit. Shit." Vikki peered out the window in the direction of the doors from baggage claim where a gaggle of tourists lugging car seats, strollers, and cranky toddlers had just emerged.

"Does Letty have any idea how Rooney could have been in contact with Wingfield?"

"No," Joe said. "But I'm looking at the call history log in Rooney's phone. I found two brief calls to Wingfield's number. One was made four days after Tanya's murder. The other was made Friday."

Letty spoke up. "Right around the time I spotted Rooney stalking us at Publix."

"This is not good," Vikki said, moaning. "How long were those calls? Is there any way Rooney could have spilled the beans about Letty and Maya's location?"

"I don't see how he could have," Joe said.

"Any way we can question Rooney about the calls?"

"Doubtful. Even if he was willing to talk, he couldn't right now, not with his jaw and eye socket smashed all to hell. So what do you want to do?"

"I want to go lay on the beach in the sunshine and fall asleep with my face planted in a frozen margarita," she said. "But instead, I think we just move forward. Garcia checked the Delta flight manifest. Wingfield boarded his flight at JFK, right on time. I think we proceed as planned."

"Agreed," DeCurtis said. "And in the meantime, I'll send Shauna over to the ER. If Rooney wakes up and wants to talk, she knows the right questions."

Vikki's cell phone pinged to signal an incoming text. It was from Garcia.

Your man just deplaned. Headed your way.

Wingfield was dressed in an open-collared pale blue dress shirt with French cuffs, black designer jeans that probably cost more than Vikki Hill's first car, and black suede loafers. Mirrored aviator glasses pushed up into his carefully coiffed hair. Like he was headed for a weekend in Palm Beach instead of paying off a hit man and picking up his kidnapped daughter. He had a leather carry-on bag on his shoulder. Gucci? Prada? Vikki had never been good with designer names.

She tapped the horn as he emerged from baggage claim. He looked around, spotted her, and headed for the rental.

Wingfield opened the passenger door and slid into the front seat.

"How was your trip?" she asked.

He kept the carry-on at his feet, which made Vikki tense.

"I've had worse. How's Maya?"

"You wanna know the truth? She's kinda whiny. I mean, I get that her mom and her aunt are gone, but it's been a couple days now. You'd think she'd settle down, but not so much. You wanna put your carry-on in the back seat?"

He patted the bag like it was a dog. "I'm good. Back in New York, Maya was seeing some bullshit therapist Tanya insisted on. Before all this happened. Once I get her home, Juliette, that's my fiancée, thinks she'll adjust. We'll put her in a good private school. Juliette has already put in applications at Brearley and Chapin. She can make some little friends. The kid just needs normal, you know? Her mom was a whack job, which was part of the problem. Always half drunk or hopped up on pills."

Vikki had to bite her tongue to keep from pointing out that it was always the mother's fault. She pulled the car into traffic and headed for the airport exit, keeping an eye on the rearview mirror. Garcia told her he'd be driving a silver Volvo sedan.

Wingfield kneaded his forehead with his right hand and looked moodily out the side window.

"Something wrong?" she asked, keeping her eye on the side rearview mirror. She felt a tiny spark of relief when she spotted the Volvo two cars back.

"Headache. That coffee they served on the flight was for shit. You'd think they could figure out how to brew a decent espresso for what they're charging in first class. How about stopping at a Starbucks? My treat."

"Oh wow. You'd spring for a grande? For me? Big spender."

He shot her a sour look. "You're a real smart-ass, you know that? No wonder you're not married."

Vikki gave him a bland smile. She was really looking forward to slapping handcuffs on Evan Wingfield. And if he tripped in the sand and fell face-forward and she "accidentally" mashed his face into the ground with her non-designer shoe, that would be icing on the revenge cake she'd been mentally baking since the first day she'd met Evan Wingfield.

"Maybe later," she said. "My guy is gonna get antsy if we're delayed."

"So tell him we're making a coffee stop," Evan snapped. "What else has he got to do today?"

"Lemme just get across the bridge. I think there's a Starbucks on the St. Pete side."

Wingfield stared out the passenger-side window. Tampa Bay was calm, with a light breeze, and sailboats skimmed across the sun-dappled water's surface, but he seemed oblivious to his surroundings. The rank odor of anger and tension radiated off him like cheap cologne.

"That bitch Letty probably filled Maya's head with all kinds of poison against me," he said abruptly. "Have you talked to her since you got down here?"

Vikki shrugged. God, what a narcissist. It was always about him. Never about the child he claimed to love.

"She's a kid. She watches this stupid *PAW Patrol* cartoon show and begs to go to McDonald's."

"Does she ask about me?"

"Sometimes." She deftly slipped the knife between his ribs. "Mostly she asks about her mommy. And Letty."

"Six months from now, she won't remember their names," Wingfield said. "Do you remember anything from when you were four?"

"I remember my dog, Patches."

"Good idea," Wingfield said, snapping his fingers. "We'll get her a dog."

"Super. That ought to fix her right up," Vikki said, keeping her eyes on the road.

When she saw the Starbucks in a strip shopping center, she flipped her turn signal and turned in to the parking lot, hoping that the silver Volvo would follow suit. She turned to Wingfield. "Drive-through?"

"No. I need to go in and use the bathroom. Be right out."

She tried not to stare at the leather bag at his feet, hoping he'd leave it behind. He opened the door, stepped out, and at the last minute, grabbed it and looped the strap over his shoulder.

As soon as she saw him enter the store and head for the men's room, she texted Garcia.

Pit stop. He wants coffee and a piss.

Garcia texted a thumbs-up emoji.

She called DeCurtis from her Apple watch. "We made a pit stop at Starbucks. He's got a carry-on with him that he won't let out of his sight."

"Hopefully it's the money," DeCurtis said. "Has he said anything incriminating?"

"Only if you consider every sentence you utter as being evidence that you are a total shitsicle of a human being," Vikki said. "How's Letty doing?"

"About like you'd expect. Somehow, she's managing to hold it together, probably for Maya's sake."

She saw Wingfield emerge from the bathroom and head for the counter. He paced the restaurant, leaned against a high-top table, pulled out his phone, and made a call.

"I don't like this," Vikki muttered. "He's in there making a call."

"So are you," Joe pointed out.

"He doesn't know that. He thinks I'm out here basking in my own stupidity, waiting for a mocha grande."

Wingfield ended the call, put his phone in his pocket, and walked over to the counter, where the barista handed him his order. He swiped a credit card, pocketed it, and turned to leave.

"Son of a bitch," Vikki said.

"What?"

"He totally stiffed me and didn't get my coffee order. Okay, that's it. He's a dead man."

She ended the call and shot Wingfield an annoyed glance as he slid into the front seat.

"Hey, thanks for that awesome coffee you were gonna buy me."

"Sorry," he said, in a tone they both knew was meant to convey that he was completely not sorry. He glanced at his watch. "Let's get going, okay? We're booked on a four o'clock flight back to New York. Juliette wants to get Maya on a strict schedule right away, so that she'll adapt better."

Vikki backed the car out of the slot and headed for the Starbucks exit. She saw the silver Volvo slowly back out of a slot at the far end of the lot.

"What's your fiancée think about helping raise another woman's kid? Especially one with all kinds of emotional problems?"

"Juliette's cool with it. She wants us to have kids of our own. Someday. In the meantime, Maya loves her. Calls her JuJu."

"Cute," Vikki said.

52

~~~~~~~~~~~~

As soon as Joe ended the call with the FBI agent, Letty cocked her head and looked at him. "You're such a liar."

"What?"

They were in her motel unit. Joe was eating potato chips, shoving one after another into his mouth and chewing noisily. He looked like any other typical Florida beach bum—faded T-shirt, loud orange board shorts, Teva sandals, Ray-Bans—albeit a beach bum with a badge in his pocket and a holstered nine-millimeter Smith & Wesson pistol clipped to his waist and obscured by his T-shirt.

Letty was dressed in the disguise Ava had helped her assemble. Big floppy hat, oversize sunglasses, a flowing poncho-type beach cover-up that brushed her kneecaps.

"You just told Vikki I'm managing as well as can be expected. Which is a ridiculous lie. I'm a complete nervous wreck. What if something happens? What if he tries to grab Maya? What if this plan of yours goes all wrong? He'll get away with it, Joe. Get away with killing Tanya, hiring you to kill me. I'm so terrified I feel like I might barf at any minute."

"Please don't."

He gently removed her sunglasses. "I'll tell you what my sergeant told me when I was in the police academy. Fake it 'til you make it. It's okay to be scared. I'd be lying if I told you I'm not scared. Only an idiot wouldn't be scared. But here's the thing, Letty. We're prepared. We've got the element of surprise on our side. Wingfield doesn't know where Maya is. He doesn't know who Vikki really is, and he's never seen me before."

"You don't know Evan," Letty retorted. "He can sense people's weakness. It's like his superpower. When he spotted me working at the diner, he overheard me tell my friend I was essentially homeless. He could tell I was vulnerable, and he preyed on me. Like Midnight hunting one of those lizards on the patio. He did the same thing with Tanya. I watched it happen, but he still managed to gaslight me, make me think I was imagining things."

"In case you haven't noticed, I'm not a particularly vulnerable kind of guy," Joe reminded her. "But you want me to tell you what I think?"

She nodded.

"You might not like it," he warned her.

"Tell me anyway."

"I think Wingfield met his match in your sister. You've said yourself, she kept secrets, was a liar and an opportunist. She played you, telling you she was homeless so you'd invite her to stay with you in New York, and she played Wingfield, by taking up with him and letting him think he was her baby daddy."

"Is this your way of telling me Tanya was a bad person, as bad a person as Evan? That they deserved each other and she deserved to have him kill her? Is that supposed to make me feel better about this whole nightmare?"

"No. It's me telling you what you actually already know, which is that Tanya was kinda messed up. But she didn't deserve her fate. Evan Wingfield isn't bulletproof. He's no evil genius. You were taken in by him because you, Letty Carnahan, are a good and decent person."

"In other words, a sucker." She smiled ruefully.

He kissed the tip of her nose and replaced the sunglasses. "Not at all. Me, on the other hand? I'm a professional cynic. Ask my mother, she'll tell you. I'm convinced everybody's a suspect, until proven otherwise."

"And yet, when you figured out I was running from the law and wanted in New York, you didn't turn me in."

"I figured you were too cute to be a wanted criminal."

"I'm being serious."

He sighed. "I saw how you treated our guests. Even when they were cranky and hostile, you put up with their crap. Like Harry Bronson. You could have walked away when he yelled at you, but instead you stayed and helped. A murderer wouldn't have done that. And then, there was Maya."

"Maya," she repeated. "Which is why we're doing this. For Maya."

"Yup." He glanced at his watch. "Feeling any braver now?"

"Not even a little," she admitted.

53

~~~~~~~~~~~~~~~~

Vikki Hill pulled into the Murmuring Surf parking lot. The vacancy sign was flashing, which surprised her a little. Which of the regulars was checking out?

"This place?" Wingfield sneered. "Jesus! This is where Letty was keeping my daughter all this time? What a dump."

She gave him the stink eye. "What do you care? She's been sleeping in a bed and eating decent food. She likes to swim in the pool. She doesn't care that it's not the Hamptons. She's four."

"Forget it." He got out of the car. "Now what? Where's this Joe guy?"

"This way," Vikki said, gesturing toward the sparkling expanse of white sand visible in the gap between the office and the motel's north wing.

He slung the leather bag over his shoulder and followed behind her, crossing the parking lot and cutting through the grassy strip dividing the grounds from the beach. He paused at the dune line, looking down at his expensive loafers.

"Christ! You don't expect me to walk out on the beach. Right? These are Belgian loafers. I'll wait right here. Just bring Maya to me."

"Nope." Vikki kept walking, stepping into the sand in her cheap generic running shoes with a malicious sense of satisfaction.

It was not yet noon, and Sunday, and the beach was relatively uncrowded. People were either still in bed or in church, or lining up for the all-you-can-eat brunch buffets at the resort hotels down the road. But there were a few family encampments scattered across the sand, with umbrellas, tents, coolers, and lounge chairs. Half a dozen blue-and-white-striped canvas beach cabanas had sprouted up in the sand along the waterline.

There were even a few hardy souls splashing around in the water. *Canadians,* Vikki thought dismissively. Normal people, even including New Yorkers, did not swim in the ocean when the rest of the world was still bundled up in parkas and mukluks.

She didn't turn around, just kept walking toward Joe DeCurtis, who was standing on the beach, holding a can of beer that she was reasonably sure was empty.

For a moment, Vikki Hill felt a flash of regret. She'd been wrong about Joe DeCurtis. He was no inept local yokel. He was an excellent cop, with great instincts. If circumstances had been different, maybe they'd have had a thing. Too late now, which was probably just as well. Her relationships, even the briefest, always ended up messy.

Vikki turned to check on Wingfield's progress. He was picking his way slowly through the sugar-fine sand, clutching the leather bag to his side.

When he was fifty yards away, he stopped and looked around. "Hey!" he called. "Enough of this charade. Where's Maya?"

"We'll get to that," Vikki said. "But first, meet Joe. He's the guy I told you about."

Wingfield approached warily.

"Joe, this is Evan."

DeCurtis looked the other man up and down in a stare designed to make Wingfield feel uncomfortable.

Evan shifted the bag on his shoulder and looked around. "Where's Maya?"

"She's around," DeCurtis said. "First, let's finish the cash transaction."

Wingfield laughed. "Yeah. No. The deal was, you hand over my daughter, and then you get the cash."

"How about you show me the money?" Joe said.

Vikki was watching the two men stare each other down, each assessing the size of the other's balls. At any moment she expected one to sniff the other's butt.

Out of the corner of her eye she saw someone approaching. It was a scrawny elderly man, who'd just emerged, dripping wet, from the Gulf. With growing horror she recognized the pale, hairless chest, the rubber swim goggles perched atop his bald head. He was fastening a towel around his waist as he walk-trotted toward them.

"Hey Joe," he hailed, waving his arm in greeting. Water was still streaming from his body as he approached the trio standing only a few yards away.

"Hey Joe!" he repeated.

DeCurtis turned at the sound of the old guy's voice.

"Wow, that was some excitement this morning, huh? Did Letty tell you, it was the same guy I spotted creeping around last night? And then he come back here, and he tried to grab Maya. You think that's what he was after? Letty and Maya?" He nodded at Vikki. "I heard that guy broke into your room and stole your gun, too. Did the cops get it back to you yet?"

Oscar Jensen was oblivious to the drama unfolding before him. He greeted Wingfield with a broad smile and extended his hand. "How ya doing? I'm Oscar. So, are you checking into the motel today? Which unit?"

"Hiya," Evan said to Oscar. "So, you know Letty?"

"Oh sure. Everybody knows her," Oscar said. He gave Joe a broad wink. "Especially this guy right here. You think we don't know you're sweet on our Letty?"

Wingfield's eyes narrowed as he looked from the old man to DeCurtis to Vikki. "What the fuck?"

"Huh?" Oscar looked from Joe to Vikki. "Did I interrupt something?"

"Oscar," Joe said, his voice quiet and deadly calm. "You need to go away. Right now."

"Oh. Okay. Never mind." The old man started to scuttle back

toward the water, but Evan reached out and grabbed him by the elbow.

"Oww," Oscar complained. "That hurts. Hey Joe, who is this guy? Don't he know you're a cop?"

Evan grasped Oscar by his right shoulder, twisted his arm behind his back, and shoved him in front of himself, like a frail, shivering human shield.

"Where's my kid?" he demanded.

Joe had worked his gun out of his waistband and was pointing it directly at Wingfield.

"Let him go, Wingfield. And I'll take you to Maya."

"You'll take me to her anyway, or I'll break his fucking neck." He glanced over at Vikki Hill, who'd taken two steps closer and had now drawn her Glock.

Wingfield shook his head as a warning and twisted Oscar's arm so viciously he cried out in pain.

"Back away, Vikki. I just want my kid. That's all. Take me to her. Now."

Joe locked eyes with the FBI agent. She raised one shoulder in a helpless gesture and pointed at one of the blue-and-white-striped tents two hundred yards away.

"She's over there, in that cabana."

"By herself?"

"No." Vikki hesitated. "Letty's with her."

"Give me your gun," Wingfield ordered. He wrapped one arm tightly around Oscar's neck. "Do it now, or I'll snap this old bastard in half."

"How do you think this is going to end?" Vikki countered. She nodded at DeCurtis. "Just to be very clear, this is Detective Joe DeCurtis. Not a real contract killer."

"But the gun's real," Joe said. "Let go of Oscar, or I'll use it."

"Don't think so," Wingfield said. He drove his elbow up and into Oscar's throat and the old man gurgled, his eyes rolling up in his head in terror.

"Take me to my daughter. Now."

Vikki sighed heavily. "Enough already." She pointed the Glock at Evan Wingfield's black suede Belgian loafer and fired a single shot.

Wingfield shrieked in pain and dropped to the sand.

Oscar Jensen stood looking down at the wounded man in disbelief. His throat was red and abraded. "Holy shit. You shot the guy."

Wingfield was rolling around in the sand, clutching his foot in both hands, his face contorted in rage. "You bitch!" he cried.

Vikki knelt down and easily subdued Wingfield with one knee to his chest. She reached into the pocket of her jeans and brought out a set of plastic zip ties, fastening them around the wounded man's wrists, just a little tighter than was absolutely necessary.

"Evan Wingfield, you're under arrest for conspiracy to commit murder, murder for hire, racketeering, bank fraud, bribery, and income-tax evasion."

She stood up and prodded Wingfield's hip with the toe of her cheap sneaker. "Okay. Fun's over. Get up. You're going to jail."

Evan struggled to a sitting position. His foot was bleeding profusely. "I can't walk. You shot me in the foot and I'm losing blood, you fucking bitch."

Joe reached down, grabbed Wingfield's shoulder, and hauled him to a standing position. "I wouldn't piss her off if I were you. That Glock has fourteen more rounds."

54

LETTY STEPPED OUT OF THE shadows of the cabana, and with her left hand, pushed her sunglasses up and wiped the perspiration from her face with the edge of her poncho. Her right hand was still thrust deep into the pocket of the cover-up, clutching Ava's pistol. Beads of sweat rolled down her back and her chest, and the breeze coming off the water gave her a chill. Or maybe it was the scene she'd just witnessed.

Ava had pulled her aside as she was about to walk down to the beach.

"Here," she whispered, pressing the pistol into Letty's hand. "Just in case."

Letty had pulled the canvas door flaps open by mere inches, peeking out to watch as Vikki and Evan walked down the beach to meet Joe.

Evan had his leather messenger bag on his shoulder. Was it full of cash—the payoff for killing her and dumping her body in the Gulf for the sharks to devour? She wished she could hear what was being said, but she knew that Vikki was wired for sound, and that somewhere close, another FBI agent, Garcia, whom she hadn't met, was standing by as backup.

She gasped out loud when she saw Oscar Jensen emerge from the water and start trotting toward Joe and Vikki. What was he doing? He'd ruin everything! Should she try and intercept him, or stay hidden in the cabana, as Joe had made her promise to do?

Letty parted the canvas flaps and was stepping outside when she saw Evan grab Oscar by the arm, and then put him in a choke hold.

After that, everything seemed to happen in slow motion. Joe pulled his gun and pointed it at Evan, and Vikki did the same, and in that moment, time seemed to stand still. Letty's hand clutched and unclutched the pistol Ava had given her, but she felt helpless.

People were walking down the beach. She spotted an older white-haired couple, strolling hand in hand, pointing at the shorebirds skittering along the waterline. A middle-aged man wearing wraparound aviator glasses, loud plaid shorts and a pair of oversize headphones was running a metal detector over a nearby patch of sand. College kids were setting up a blanket and chairs only a few yards away, but they seemed oblivious to the armed standoff happening just a Frisbee throw away.

Seconds later, she saw Vikki fire. The shot echoed in the quiet Sunday morning air.

One of the college guys nudged the other. "Dude! That chick just shot a guy." The older couple stood still and gawked as Vikki fell to her knees and handcuffed the shooting victim. Only the man with the metal detector seemed to realize what was going on. He dropped his instrument in the sand and began running toward the scene.

Letty began to run, too.

"*Joe,* this is Special Agent Alex Garcia," Vikki said.

Garcia removed the headphones and nodded a greeting to Joe DeCurtis. "You had me worried for a minute there," he told Vikki.

"How was the sound?" she asked. "Did you get everything we were saying?"

"I think so," Garcia said.

"Hey!" Evan protested. "I'm bleeding to death here. I need a doctor."

"Relax, Wingfield," Joe said. "Nobody ever died of being shot in the foot. There's an ambulance on the way."

People were beginning to gather in a ragged semicircle around them, gawking at the spectacle. Two of the college kids had pulled out phones and were shooting video.

"Hey, man! What'd that dude do? Why'd you shoot him?" A kid wearing jeans and a Nike hoodie walked toward them, holding out his phone to capture the scene.

"Whoa. Who are you guys even?" the college kid demanded.

Vikki Hill flashed her badge. "We're FBI, assholes. And this dude is a murder suspect. Now why don't you and your friends go film a TikTok dance or something?

"Let's get him out of here," she told the men. Garcia and Joe each took an arm and effortlessly dragged Wingfield back toward the road. Vikki Hill picked up the leather messenger bag.

"That's my property," Evan protested. "You can't just confiscate my property."

"Hold up for a minute," Vikki said. "He's got a point. Joe, let's inventory this douchebag's property, shall we?"

DeCurtis pulled out his phone and she unzipped the bag as he began to video. She carefully removed a folded black windbreaker and set it on the sand. A pair of matching black track pants were wrapped around something else. She unfolded the fabric and revealed stacks of currency.

Vikki looked up at the cop. "Are you getting this? Looks like the balance of the payment due for a murder contract to me. Should be forty thousand, unless he planned to stiff us."

"That's the down payment for a real-estate transaction," Evan claimed. "And you can't prove otherwise."

"Tell it to the judge," Joe said. "Anything else of interest in that bag?"

Vikki held up a bag of goldfish crackers, a juice box, and then, a pair of pull-up diapers and a child-size pale pink dress with matching pink leggings.

"Those are for my daughter, who was abducted by her aunt, Letty Carnahan, who also murdered my daughter's mother, before illegally transporting her down here to Florida," Evan said. "If you check the bottom of the bag, you'll see I have a judge's order, giving me custody of Maya, and a copy of my daughter's birth certificate."

Letty had been standing at the edge of the crowd, unsure of her next move, until she saw Vikki hold up the clothing Evan had packed for Maya.

She'd been with Tanya on what turned out to be their last shopping expedition together. They'd gone into an insanely expensive children's boutique on Fifth Avenue, and Tanya had picked out the ensemble, from a brand called Maisonette.

She remembered the way Tanya had gushed over the organic cotton dress with the Peter Pan collar and a print of pink and white lollipops. "This'll be perfect for Maya to wear when we fly out to LA."

The sight of the lollipop dress made something inside her snap. In a dream state Letty pushed her way through the knot of bystanders, advancing until she was only a few feet away from where Evan Wingfield was being held by Joe and the other man, who she assumed was Garcia, the other FBI agent.

Blood rushed in her ears as she raised the pistol, her hand shaking almost uncontrollably, and pointed it at the man who'd taken her beautiful, broken sister away from Maya.

"Letty?" Joe's voice was a whisper in her ear. "Come on. You don't want to do this."

She was barely cognizant of the sudden stillness that descended over the gawkers.

Evan seemed amused. "What's this, Letty? You're gonna shoot me? In front of all these witnesses? I don't think so," he taunted. "You're just like her. You've never followed through with anything in your life."

Letty glanced at Joe, who was still holding his phone.

"I want you to get this on camera, Joe." She poked Evan in the chest with the barrel of the pistol. "He's going to tell you how he killed Tanya."

"Come on, Letty," Vikki said, her tone even. "Put down the gun. He's going to prison for life."

"Tell them what you did to my sister," Letty repeated.

"Me?" Wingfield looked incredulous. "I gave your sister a career. A home, a kid, clothes, jewelry, everything she ever wanted, until she drank and drugged it all away. That's what I did for your sister."

"Liar," Letty croaked. Her throat was like sandpaper. "You killed Tanya. I know you did. She was getting sober. She was getting better, and she was going to leave and take Maya to California with her, and you told her you'd never let her do that. I heard you threaten her, Evan. And why? You don't really care about Maya. She's just another asset as far as you're concerned."

Wingfield glanced around at the three cops, who appeared more interested in Letty's deranged accusations than they were in his safety.

"Your white-trash sister wasn't fit to raise a gerbil, let alone my daughter," he said angrily. "And you're saying Tanya was sober? That's a joke. She was drinking that morning I went over to her place. Stoned out of her gourd. But you already know that, right? Because after I left, you killed her, and then you grabbed Maya and ran.

"Here's your murderer, right here," Wingfield said loudly. "You see her pointing a gun at me? Threatening my life? Why isn't she in handcuffs instead of me?"

Vikki placed her hand on Letty's shoulder. "Okay, you've said your piece. Come on, Letty. He's not worth the price of a bullet. Think about Maya. You're all she's got left."

Letty looked at the pistol and then at the FBI agent. Her whole body went limp. Slowly, she uncurled her fingers from the trigger and placed the gun in Vikki's outstretched hand. In the distance, for the second time that day, they heard the ear-piercing wail of an ambulance.

55

M AYA WAS BORED. SHE AND Isabelle had colored and had snacks. They'd read all the picture books Letty brought home from the library. Now, Isabelle was curled up on the sofa, looking at her phone, laughing at something she was reading.

The wind ruffled the curtains at the open sliding glass doors, and she stepped out onto the patio, looking over her shoulder to see if Isabelle would object, but the teenager was still absorbed in her own world.

A squirrel sat on the garden gate, with a ripe red cherry tomato clutched between its paws. Maya tiptoed toward it, but the squirrel scampered away, leaping onto a frond of the palm tree that shaded the patio.

She saw a flash of black fur speed past. It was Midnight! Maya unlatched the gate and stepped onto the thick grass. Were the kittens still hidden under the big tree? She looked around to make sure that this time, no bad men were waiting in the shadows.

Emboldened, she ran to the tree and peeked beneath the sawtoothed plants with their bright pink throats. The nest of pine needles was bare, with only a few tufts of black fur left behind.

Maya stood up and dusted bits of grass from her T-shirt. Had Midnight gone back to the scary cave where she'd put the kittens before? No. She must have found a newer, nicer place to hide the kittens. Maybe she would ask Isabelle to help her look. Or maybe she would walk over to the office, to ask Miss Ava if they could bake cookies today.

She was walking toward the motel office when she heard the

whine of the approaching ambulance. It pulled into the parking lot, and two men in blue uniforms got out. People were walking up from the beach.

From nowhere, she saw Midnight streak past again and dive into a big concrete planter of prickly green asparagus fern near the front door of the office. Even from where she stood now, Maya could hear the kittens' plaintive mews. Midnight's babies were hungry and crying for their mama.

Maya was moving steadily toward the planter when she heard her name being called. It was Letty.

Her aunt was walking with Miss Vikki and following three men. One of the men was Mr. Joe, and she didn't know the other man, but she stopped walking and forgot all about finding Midnight's kittens when she got close enough to see the man in the middle. He was walking like his foot was hurt, and his head was down, so she couldn't really see his face.

Suddenly the man raised his head, and when his eyes met hers Maya wanted to run away and hide somewhere safe, like Midnight's kittens.

"Maya!" Letty cried, when she spotted her niece standing near the door to the office.

"Christ!" Evan said angrily. "What's she doing here? Who the hell is supposed to be watching my daughter?"

Letty rushed toward Maya. She knelt down beside the little girl, trying to shield her from the sight of her father, bleeding and handcuffed.

Joe joined them a moment later.

"Ladybug," she said, her voice stern. "You're not supposed to be out here. You're supposed to be home with Isabelle."

"I saw Midnight. And I wanted to see where she hid the kittens." Maya peered around Letty's legs, watching as the ambulance attendants unfolded a wheeled gurney from the back of their vehicle.

Isabelle ran up to them, breathless. "Oh my God! Letty, I'm so sorry. I was looking at something on my Insta, and the next thing I knew, Maya was gone." She looked down at her charge. "Maya Papaya, you scared me!"

"It's okay," Letty said. "Please don't worry. She's fine."

"Sowwy, Isabelle," Maya said.

"What's going on out here?" Isabelle asked, pointing at the ambulance and the growing crowd of regulars who'd come out of their units to gawk.

"It's a very long story," Letty said. She reached down to pick up her niece. "Let's get you back to the apartment. I think you've had more than enough excitement for today."

"That's Daddy," Maya told Isabelle, pointing at Wingfield before hiding her head in Letty's shoulder. Evan Wingfield was sitting on the stretcher while the EMTs examined his foot. "Why is Daddy here?"

Letty looked at Joe for guidance, but he, too, was at a loss for words.

"He, uh, wanted to visit you, and bring you some new clothes," Letty began. "But I told him . . ."

Wingfield looked up just then, his eyes meeting Maya's. "Hey, baby," he called. "Daddy's here. I'll see you in a little bit, okay?"

"Nooo," Maya cried. She clamped her hands over her ears. "I don't want to go to Daddy's house. He's a bad daddy. He hurt my mommy."

Letty's scalp prickled.

"Do you want me to take her back to your place?" Isabelle offered.

"Wait." Joe leaned in, his voice calm. "Maya? Can you tell us how he hurt your mommy?"

"No!" Letty said, swinging Maya away from him. "Don't make her talk about it now."

"He pushed her down," Maya said matter-of-factly.

"That's enough!" Letty said.

But Maya kept on. "Daddy was yelling and saying bad words, and I was asleep, but then I heard Mommy crying, and I was going to give her a hug, like she hugs me when I'm sad."

"Let her talk, please, if she wants to," Joe said, his voice low. "This could be important. Please?"

"If she gets any more upset, we're stopping," Letty said, her eyes boring into his. "I mean it."

"Did you stay in your room that day, when you heard them fighting?" Joe asked.

"No?" Maya hesitated. "Mommy was crying and I was scared and I wanted some juice, but then Daddy was very, very mad. Mommy yelled at him to go away, and I wanted him to go away too, but then he yelled at her again, and he hitted her and she fell down. She had a boo-boo on her head."

Tears were flowing down Letty's face as she considered the unbearable act that the child had witnessed.

Joe's voice was gentle. "What happened next, ladybug?"

Maya ducked her chin. "I wetted my pants. I am a big girl and Daddy says big girls don't wet their pants, so I should be ashamed of myself."

"That's not true, Maya," Joe said. "Even big girls and boys have accidents sometimes," he reassured her.

"I wet my pants in PE the first day of junior high," Isabelle confided.

"And I had to take clean clothes to her at school," Joe said. "Hey, Maya? Did your daddy see you after he pushed your mommy?"

She shook her head. "No. I hid. I waited and waited a long time for Mommy to come and get me, because I was scared."

"Where did you hide?"

"Under the bed."

"Good girl," Joe said, patting her hand. "You're a very brave girl, Maya. Can you tell me what happened next?"

"It was a very long time," Maya said. "And then Letty got to my house."

"I'm glad Letty got there," Joe said.

"We took Mommy's car, because Letty said Mommy went to heaven," Maya said. "And now I live here, with Letty. And I swim in the pool and maybe soon I will get a kitten."

They heard the ambulance doors closing behind them, and Letty turned slightly to see that the EMTs had loaded Wingfield into the vehicle. Vikki Hill walked over. She pulled Joe aside.

"They'll patch him up in the ER, and unless there's an issue, he'll be transported to the jail."

"Maybe he and Rooney will have adjoining hospital beds," Joe said.

Vikki rolled her eyes. "Shit. That's not even funny. Garcia was going to meet them at the hospital. How about you call your partner Shauna, and tell her to make sure they don't let Wingfield anywhere near Rooney. By the way, he's already demanding to speak to a lawyer. Can you meet me at the jail after you get things settled down here?"

"Yeah." Joe nodded in Letty and Maya's direction. "Maya basically just told us she witnessed her mother's murder. Tanya and Wingfield were arguing, and she says she saw him push her down and she hit her head."

"For real? She's sure of what she saw?" the FBI agent asked. "Was Letty aware that Maya saw it go down?"

"No. Maya was awake and crying when Letty reached the scene, but I think she was hoping Maya didn't actually see her father kill her mother. As far as I know, this was the first time the kid has spoken about it."

Vikki pushed her sunglasses into her hair and kneaded her forehead. She watched as the ambulance pulled out of the motel parking lot, lights flashing but no siren. "What a cold-blooded piece of work that bastard is. He murders the kid's mother, hires us to kill the aunt, then shows up here with a pretty pink outfit to take her home to her new mama. He actually thinks putting Maya in a fancy preschool will solve all her problems."

Joe was only half listening. His eyes were following Letty as she and Isabelle walked over to the planter and parted the ferns to let Maya peek at Midnight and her kittens.

"What do you think will happen now? I mean, the only witness to Tanya's murder is her four-year-old kid. Will they let me and Letty testify about what she told us? Or would a judge put Maya on the witness stand?"

"I'm just a lowly Feeb agent, DeCurtis. Not a lawyer. Obviously, you and Letty will have to make some kind of sworn statement about what Maya told you."

Vikki sighed heavily. "But in the meantime, I've gotta go file a report because I shot a suspect who was getting ready to off an octogenarian. Christ, I hate paperwork."

56

AFTER ISABELLE WHISKED MAYA AWAY for a much-needed afternoon nap, the Murmuring Surf regulars lingered in the parking lot even after the ambulance had departed—a rapt audience for Oscar Jensen's first-person account of his recent ordeal.

He tightened a faded green-and-yellow-striped beach towel around his waist. "That guy was going to kill me." He pointed to the scarlet stain on his crepey skin. "He had his arm around my neck and like to choked me to death."

The crowd of women murmured their concern.

"And then Vikki—hey, it turns out she's an honest-to-God FBI agent! Then, she hauls off and shoots him right in the foot. Didn't even bat an eyelash. Pow! Just like on TV."

Oscar looked over at Letty, who was mindlessly picking up the bloodied bandages, gauze pads, and other detritus left behind by the EMTs.

"Hey Letty, Letty," he called. "That guy? I heard him say he's Maya's father. Is that right? How come he showed up here at the Surf? Was he trying to kidnap the kid?"

"Oscar!" Ava yelled, coming to Letty's rescue. "That's enough! Why don't you go back to your room now? Put some ointment on your neck and a sock in your mouth."

But Oscar was not easily discouraged.

"Man, what a weekend! First, I catch that prowler snooping around out here, then this morning, that Rooney guy tries to snatch Maya. . . ."

Ava threw a protective arm around Letty's shoulder. "Come on over to my place now, hon. You look like you could use some peace and quiet."

"And coffee?

"Definitely coffee."

She'd just settled in at the table in Ava's apartment when the downstairs door opened and a male voice bellowed up from below.

"Ava? Ava, are you here?"

Her hostess didn't turn a hair. "No," she hollered. "I'm not here. I'm off the clock. Come back tomorrow when the office is open."

But the intruder was not to be deterred. They heard footsteps on the stairs.

Merwin Maples walked into the kitchen, out of breath from the climb and brandishing a battered aluminum walker.

"Now Ava," he started. "This is an emergency. You see this walker? You see the legs? They're all banged up. This thing is ruined."

Ava poured coffee into a mug and handed it to Letty, then poured one for herself.

"What do you want from me, Merwin?"

"I think you need to buy Trudi a new walker, of course."

Ava laughed. "Me? How is this my fault? Your wife is the one who turned her walker into a weapon."

"But you're the one who rented to that lowlife Rooney in the first place. And you're the one who took up with Chuck, who invited that lowlife to move in here. I remember, I told Trudi, there's something fishy with that character and his so-called wife. What was her name again?"

Letty spoke up. "Her name was Tanya, and she was my sister."

"Oh. Well, uh, sorry to speak ill of the dead and all, but that doesn't change anything," he continued. "They were a gang of thieves."

"And Tanya also happened to be Maya's mother, in case you're interested," Ava said pointedly.

"Okay, but about the walker? These things cost money."

"I'll pay for the walker," Letty said. "Trudi probably saved Maya's life with it. Just buy a new one and save me the receipt, please. I'll reimburse you."

"Happy?" Ava said. She gestured to the door. "I'll let you show yourself out."

After they had the kitchen to themselves again, she went to a cupboard and brought out a tin of shortbread cookies. She lifted the lid, helped herself to a cookie, and offered one to Letty.

Letty dipped a cookie into the milky coffee and nibbled, remembering that she'd had no breakfast, or lunch.

"I'm sorry, Ava."

"For what? Merwin? You don't owe that old fool nothing."

"No. For . . ." Letty made an all-encompassing gesture with her arms. "All of it. If it weren't for Tanya, and me, by extension, none of this craziness would have unfolded right here on your doorstep. You did me a favor and took us in when I had no place else to go. You gave me a job and treated Maya and me like family. I want you to know that I'll understand if you want me to leave now."

"Leave? Why would I want that? You've been a godsend. Helped me out in the office. Got me thinking of ways to spruce up this old place, taught me how to use that damned new reservation software. You've made yourself pretty damn indispensable, Miss Letty Carnahan."

"I doubt that," Letty said.

"No, it's true," Ava insisted. "I'll admit, I've been in a rut these past few years. Hadn't had the energy or the gumption to give the motel the attention it needed."

"No . . ."

"Yes," Ava said. "Just between the two of us, I've started thinking maybe the time has come to sell the place."

Letty raised a surprised eyebrow.

"I get offers all the time. People dropping notes in the mail slot, sending me emails, or just knocking on the office door. It's developers who want to knock the place down and build another big resort hotel, or some of these damn hipster types who want to make it into one of those pricey boutique hotels."

Even though they were alone, Ava lowered her voice. "It's crazy the money these people are offering."

"It makes good business sense," Letty said. "You've got about three hundred feet of unobstructed Gulf-front property here. But would you really consider selling the Murmuring Surf after all these years?"

"Well . . ." Ava's voice trailed off. "The trouble is, I really love this old dump. I love all the families who started coming here when their kids were young, and now those kids are bringing their kids. They send me Christmas cards and birth and wedding announcements. And of course, our snowbirds, the regulars who've been wintering here for decades, they're like family. I hate to think about how they'd feel if I were to sell the Murmuring Surf. Where would they go? We're sort of the last of a dying breed here. And you know, every year or so, I'll get a call from someone's kids back home, telling me their nana or granddad has passed away, and they won't be joining us this winter. Or worse, we'll have one of our guests pass away while they're down here."

"That's happened?" Letty asked, horrified. "People have died, right here in the motel?"

Ava gave her hand a reassuring pat. "Maybe half a dozen times over the years. That's why I always ask our older guests for a phone number for their next of kin, up home. Just in case."

"It's none of my business," Letty said, "but if you still love running the Surf, why should you sell out?"

"I just think it's selfish on my part," Ava said with a shrug. "I'm sort of sitting on a gold mine here. If I were to sell, Joe could start up a business of his own if he wanted to, and Isabelle, she wouldn't have to worry about paying for college, or anything else for that matter."

"And what about you?" Letty asked.

"I guess I'd do whatever people do at my age. Retire. Take up crossword puzzles or knitting. Maybe travel."

Letty laughed. "I don't see you as a knitter or a puzzler."

"True. But this is Isabelle's last year at home. She'll head off to college in August. I haven't let myself think about what happens after that."

Letty nodded in sympathy. "That's exactly how I've felt, ever since the day I found Tanya—back in New York. I've been living day to day, not daring to think about what happens beyond tomorrow, terrified that Evan, or the police, would try to take Maya away from me. That was Tanya's biggest fear, you know."

"You're not much like your sister, are you?" Ava asked. "I mean, personality-wise."

"Tanya was like my mom. Beautiful, impulsive, a free spirit. I'm probably more like my grandmother, who helped raise us. We were pretty much on our own by the time we were Isabelle's age. I've always just been boring and dependable."

"Nothing boring about being dependable," Ava insisted. "I don't like to hear you run yourself down like that, Letty. You are every bit as beautiful as your sister was, but in a different way. You're sort of a wise old soul, aren't you?"

"That's what my grandmother used to tell me," Letty admitted. "I think me moving to New York to try and become an actress was just a way of trying to rebel against what everybody expected of me."

"Nothing wrong with spreading your wings and following a dream, especially when you're young," Ava pointed out. "I wish I'd done that, instead of getting married when I was just a kid."

"I'm not so young anymore," Letty reminded her. "I'm thirty-three. I don't have a college degree, or a career, or a home. What I do have is a four-year-old child depending on me to make better choices than her mother did."

"You will," Ava said, patting Letty's arm. "What's going to happen with Maya now?"

"As it turns out, Tanya had a will. And she named me as Maya's guardian."

"A will? And she wasn't but, what did you say? Thirty-two?"

"It was very unlike Tanya," Letty agreed. "She'd gone through a lot, but I think for the first time in her life, she was thinking about someone besides herself. I'm not saying she was a model citizen. I mean, she was a willing participant in Declan Rooney's scheme, and then she let Evan think he was Maya's father, but that was her idea of self-preservation."

Ava scowled. "God knows that rascal Rooney wasn't father material."

"And neither, as it turns out, is Evan Wingfield. I'm not naïve enough to believe that him being arrested today is the end of this story. He'll fight tooth and nail to get what he wants."

"Even from a prison cell? Even after he finds out he isn't Maya's biological father?"

"It was never really about Maya. This is about money. He's probably got a lawyer arranging bail right this minute."

"Would a judge really award custody of a child to a murderer?" Ava asked.

Letty drained her mug and stood up. "I guess we'll find out soon enough."

57

MAYA CURLED UP ON THE bed beside her with Ellie tucked in the crook of her arm. When her breaths became even and slower, Letty smoothed the child's curls, kissed her forehead, and eased away.

She fixed a cup of tea and took it and her phone out to the patio. It was midafternoon, sunny, and the breeze wafted through a strand of sea oats on the nearest dune. She scrolled through the call log on her phone until she found the number she wanted, praying the woman on the other end would pick up.

"Hello? This is Samiya. Who's this?"

"Sammi? It's Letty Carnahan, Tanya's sister."

"Oh, Letty!" the lawyer exclaimed. "I've been so worried. Are you and Maya all right? I've wanted to call, but didn't want to cause complications. . . ."

"We're fine. Now. I think I should catch you up with what's going on."

Letty gave Sammi a brief recap of the past week's events, ending with the most recent development. "Evan Wingfield was arrested down here this afternoon."

"Down here?" Sammi said.

"Right. I forgot you don't know where we went after Tanya was killed. We've been living in a little motel in Treasure Island, Florida."

"Treasure Island? You mean, like the Robert Louis Stevenson story?"

"Not quite," Letty said with a laugh. "It's a beach town near

St. Petersburg. There's a long story about how and why we ended up at the Murmuring Surf, but it was actually all Tanya's doing."

"The Murmuring Surf? It sounds charming."

Letty sat up and looked around. The tiny patio garden was alive with blooming jasmine and hibiscus and the herbs and flowers Harry Bronson had nurtured. She could see the pale turquoise waters of the Gulf of Mexico from here, and hear the rustle of palm fronds against her window.

"Actually, I guess it is pretty charming," Letty said. "The thing is, now that I know Evan is no longer a danger to Maya, I guess I need to figure out what happens next. For both of us."

"Yes," Sammi said. "Well, there's a lot for us to talk about, especially concerning Maya's future. As we expected, Mr. Wingfield filed notice that he intends to challenge your sister's will, and your guardianship. One quick question: has he been charged in connection with your sister's death?"

"Not yet," Letty said. She took a sip of tea. "But I think that will happen. Maya told us this morning that she actually saw Evan kill Tanya."

"Oh my. That poor child," Sammi said. "Will the police believe her?"

"I hope so," Letty said. "But it's the word of a four-year-old against an adult, who has every resource in the world to keep lying about his innocence."

"Well . . . you actually have resources too, you know," Sammi pointed out. "Now that you're no longer in hiding, I'm going to file an emergency petition with the court to release funds from Tanya's estate to help pay your legal fees and living expenses."

"You can do that?"

"Of course. As I mentioned the last time we talked, there's also a substantial life insurance policy. Maya is the primary beneficiary, and you are secondary. I was waiting to hear from you before I filed a claim, but if you agree, I'll file that claim immediately. In the meantime, as Maya's guardian, it's your responsibility to provide for her health and well-being. All reasonable expenditures on her behalf will be approved by the estate's executor and can be paid out of Tanya's estate."

"I forgot to ask. Who is the executor?"

"Do you know Tanya's friend Demetria?"

"The nutritionist?"

"Yes. She's a lovely woman. We've been in touch. She was devastated about the loss of your sister. I hope you don't mind, but I did tell her that I'd been in contact with you, and that although I didn't know your whereabouts, I felt that Maya was safe with you."

"I appreciate that." Letty stood up and walked inside to check on her niece, who was still asleep.

"Do you have Demetria's contact information?" Sammi asked. "I'll call her as soon as we hang up, and then I'll forward her information to you."

"Okay." A tiny green lizard was poised on the edge of the garden gate, its tail flicking backward and forward.

"I know it's a lot for you to process," Sammi said. "And I'll try not to overwhelm you with all the details. But do you have any idea when you'll be returning to the city?"

"To New York?" The question took Letty by surprise.

"Yes. We'll need to decide what to do with Tanya's town house. After the police finished collecting, um, evidence, I took it upon myself to have it cleaned. I hope you don't mind, but I thought, when you do return, it would be too upsetting for you to see things as they were."

Unbidden, Letty's mind returned to the foyer of the town house, to Tanya, lying on the cold marble floor as a pool of deep red blood seeped from her head, and to Maya, standing at the top of the second-floor staircase, wailing for her mother.

She shook her head to dislodge the brutal image.

"Doesn't Evan get to decide what to do with the town house? I mean, it belonged to him."

"Actually, the town house was one of the properties he conveyed to Tanya as part of his tax dodge," Sammi said. "I thought I'd explained that."

"Maybe you did. As you said, it's a lot to process."

"You don't have to decide right away," Sammi said. "But it would be good if we could begin the process of settling the estate."

"You're right, of course," Letty said, her voice trailing off. "And actually, now that Evan is locked up, I don't suppose there's anything keeping me down here in Florida. Maya turns five this fall, and I need to start thinking about kindergarten for her."

"I can recommend the school my son attends," Sammi volunteered.

"You've got kids?" Letty didn't know why she was surprised.

"Yes. Noah is six. His father and I divorced right before I got sober. Or rather, I got sober because I got divorced. At any rate, it's a small school, the teachers are very loving, and the curriculum is progressive, but not what Tanya would call 'too woo-woo.'"

"That sounds exactly like something my sister would say," Letty said, chuckling.

"Letty?" Maya called from the other room, her voice groggy.

"Oops. I'd better go, Sammi. Maya just woke up from her nap. I'll be in touch soon. Okay? And thanks again. For everything you did. For Tanya. And for me."

58

〜〜〜〜〜〜〜〜〜

I T WAS LATE AFTERNOON BY the time they reached the hospital.

They found Shauna Arthur sitting outside a cubicle in the recovery room, leafing through a magazine. "Hey," she said, greeting them. "Your boy's awake."

Vikki and Joe peered through the glass window into Declan Rooney's room. The head of the bed was raised, and Rooney's head lolled back against a pillow.

The patient's head was swathed in bandages, and his jaw had a gruesome-looking metal appliance affixed to it. One eye was blackened, the other was only visible through a tiny slit cut in a thick gauze pad. "Looks like he got run over by a train," Vikki said cheerfully.

"Or sideswiped by a walker," Joe agreed. He turned to his partner. "Thanks again, Shauna. We'll take it from here."

Rooney's head moved slightly, and when they opened the door his groan was audible through the layers of bandages.

"Hey, Rooney," Joe said. He held out a box of chocolate-covered caramels he'd picked up in the hospital gift shop. "Brought you a little get-well present."

The patient's lips moved and his response was vehement. "Fuck you."

"Oh good," Vikki said, pulling up a vinyl-covered chair and seating herself. "He's conscious and talking." She opened the box of candy and popped one into her mouth. "Since he won't be able to chew for a while, I'm sure he won't mind sharing."

Joe set the caramels on the nightstand, and then he took his phone from his pocket, swiped it over to record, and set it beside the candy. "Since you're awake, we thought you might like to answer some questions."

Rooney turned his head to face a wall with a bland framed pastel print of flowers in a pink vase. "Go away."

"Now, don't be like that," Joe said. "You know, if you cooperate, I can talk to the district attorney about maybe getting your sentence reduced. You're facing kidnapping and assault charges here, as well as breaking and entering, and theft by taking. Not to mention possession of a firearm by a convicted felon. And then there are the old fraud charges dating back to five years ago."

Vikki leaned closer to the bed. "Joe! Don't forget that little incident down in Immokalee."

DeCurtis smacked his forehead. "Oh yeah. I should catch you up on that. The cops down there found a body way out in the swamp. Somebody shot a guy and then set the car on fire. The corpse was in pretty bad shape by the time they found it, but fortunately they were able to lift your late buddy Chuck's fingerprint and identify him that way."

Rooney's shoulders lifted in a barely perceptible shrug. "Too bad."

"Yeah, it was too bad," Joe said. "He'd only been out of prison, what? A day or so?"

"Don't know," Rooney said. It sounded like he had a mouth full of marbles.

"We think you do know," Vikki said. "After Joe mentioned that you and Chuck liked to gamble at Indian casinos, the sheriff down there told us there happens to be a Seminole casino right there in Immokalee. They checked the casino's security cameras, and sure enough, they've got you and Chuck, on camera, at adjoining slot machines."

"You know what else?" Joe asked. "They've even got security cameras out in the parking lot there. Because sometimes, unsavory criminals like you take advantage of gamblers who've been playing poker and slots and drinking cheap booze for hours and hours. Anyway, it's a good thing, because the cameras show you getting into a vehicle and driving away with Chuck. And that's the last time anyone saw the poor dumb bastard."

Vikki crossed her legs and looked around the hospital room. "You know I think the jails and hospitals down here in Florida are probably way nicer than the ones in New York City, don't you? I've heard some bad stuff happens at Rikers Island."

"Probably so," Joe said. "Although I myself hate New York like the plague."

"New York?" Rooney shook his head slightly, looking confused.

"Yeah. That's where your girlfriend Tanya was living with her little girl, Maya. The same little girl you tried to snatch this morning," Joe said. "And don't try to tell us you haven't been to New York, or that you haven't seen Tanya, because we have video of that, too."

"No way," Rooney said. His words seemed to run together. "Neverbeenthere."

"Way," Vikki assured him. "In case you've forgotten, I'll jog your memory. This was back in late February. You visited Tanya in her town house. She seemed pretty surprised to see you, but you told her you'd tracked her down through her agent. Any of this ringing a bell with you?"

Rooney was silent.

"I'll bet it was a shock, seeing her after what, five years?" Joe said. "But the biggest shock must have been seeing that little girl, Maya. I'm guessing you didn't even know Tanya was knocked up when you and Chuck left her behind at the motel. Right? What happened? Did she call you that night and tell you we were arresting her and looking for you two?"

Rooney reached out his hand, groping for the foam cup of water sitting on the nightstand. Vikki handed him the cup. "I love these bendy straws they give you in the hospital, don't you, Rooney? I hope they give you a nice supply of them when they transfer you over to the jail."

"Did the doctors tell you how long your jaw will be wired up like that, Rooney?" Joe asked. "I bet it's gonna hurt like hell, riding in the back seat of a squad car all the way to New York. Those cruisers aren't exactly built for a smooth ride."

"I didn't do anything in New York," Rooney said, suddenly animated. "I went to see Tanya, that's all. You can ask the kid. I didn't kill Tanya."

"Okay," Vikki said. "Let's change the subject for a minute. Why'd you kidnap Maya? A guy like you doesn't seem like daddy material to me."

"I'm tired." Rooney closed his eyes, but Vikki snapped her fingers under his nose.

"You can sleep when you're dead, Rooney. Tell us why you took Maya."

His eyelids fluttered open. "After I saw Tanya, I was still in New York. I had . . . business. I saw in the paper that Tanya was dead. And that guy, Wingfield, was offering a reward for the kid's return. Ten thousand dollars. I thought maybe I could help."

"In other words, you wanted to cash in. So you tried to call Wingfield? We saw his number in your phone," Vikki said.

"I left a message, but he never called back. I was kinda between business opportunities, which was why I hunted up Tanya. But she swore she didn't know where the merch was. Anyway, I came back down here to look for it."

"You mean, you came *up* here to look for your loot. After Immokalee, where you killed Chuck. Did you get him to tell you where he hid the stuff? Is that why you broke into my room?" Vikki asked.

Rooney, feigning exhaustion, closed his eyes again. "My head hurts. You people need to go."

"Let's talk for a little while longer," Joe said. "Why grab Maya?"

"Mistake," Rooney murmured. "I saw her, looking for that cat, and I remembered the reward, and Wingfield. I still had his number in my phone. I figured I'd do a good deed. Reunite the kid with her father."

"You thought you'd snatch the kid and hold her for ransom. You knew Wingfield wasn't Maya's father. Tanya as much as told you so, although you had to have realized it the first time you set eyes on her," Vikki said.

Rooney snapped back to attention. "That kid could be anybody's. Tanya? She was always working an angle. She found a rich guy and told him he was the baby daddy. That's on her, not me."

"Get real," Joe guffawed. "Any idiot can tell that kid has your exact same eyes. She's yours, all right. So, did you get Chuck to tell you where he hid all your loot before you killed him?"

"I need you people to go away," Rooney said. "I think I got a concussion. I need some pain meds."

"Later," Vikki said. "Tell us what Chuck told you about the loot from your gold-and-silver-buying scam."

Rooney looked offended. "Hey, man! We bought that stuff fair and square. All those people? They came to us. We didn't have to twist anybody's arm."

"If everything was on the up-and-up, why'd you run?" Joe asked. "Why leave Tanya behind, holding the bag?"

Rooney probed his jaw with his hand. "Jesus. It's like they wired my face together with coat hangers. I'm probably gonna be scarred for life now."

"Don't try and change the subject," Joe said. "You ripped off those old people. You bought a thirty-thousand-dollar antique watch from Trudi Maples for three thousand dollars and told her that's all the gold was worth, but you damn sure knew its true value. You, Chuck, and Tanya operated your con for a good two weeks before we shut you down. We searched your room, after we arrested Tanya, but came up with nothing. Which was why the DA eventually let her walk. You and your pal Chuck were in the wind, but the loot—you didn't have the loot. Right?"

There was an extended quiet in the room. Vikki helped herself to another caramel and chewed loudly. "Damn, these are good. You might as well tell us the truth, Rooney. You're looking at a long stretch of prison time. Help us out, fill in the details, and Joe here will try to help you out. Maybe he can even talk the cops in New York into believing you didn't kill your baby mama."

"I never touched Tanya," Rooney repeated. "And you can't prove I did."

"Tell us what happened. Five years ago, after we arrested Tanya," Joe repeated.

"That crazy old bastard Chuck! We never should've hooked up with him. That was all Tanya. I think she had, like, daddy issues. We were doing good with the gold and silver thing. Making some solid buys. I wanted to move on to the next town. You know, before things got complicated here in Treasure Island. Tanya, she wanted to stay."

"You were already thinking of dumping her, right?" Vikki asked.

"It crossed my mind," he admitted. "I don't know why I always manage to get mixed up with chicks who are batshit crazy. That night, me and Chuck wanted to go to the dog track. Tanya was being a whiny pain in the ass, so we left her at the motel. I won a couple quinellas and a perfecta. A real winning streak. But Tanya kept calling and texting, so I just turned my phone off. Who needs that shit when you're winning? Am I right?"

Vikki rolled her eyes. "Totally."

"Chuck said he knew some girls who worked at a strip club over near MacDill. That's the air force base. He wanted to have some drinks and get laid, and I thought, okay, whatever. But that's when I turned my phone on and saw the text from Tanya. So we headed back over to the beach, to check things out. But the motel parking lot was crawling with cops. I said we should stop, but Chuck insisted we should go on back to Tampa."

"As if," Vikki said. "I'm sure you were super worried about Tanya."

"I knew Tanya could handle things."

"But the loot was back at the Surf, right?" Joe put in.

"The plan was we'd go back over there to the motel after things quieted down, and we'd get the stuff and blow town."

"But even the best-laid plans, right?" Vikki said.

"Huh? Anyway, we went back over to the club, and Chuck got shitfaced, and when he got like that, he turned mean. Like, crazy mean. We were on the way out of the club with the girls, and the bouncer said something to Chuck, and the next thing I know, that crazy bastard pulled a knife on the bouncer. The dude was half his age and twice his size! Then the cops came and things were getting real. I managed to slip away in the confusion."

"Lucky you," Joe said. "So, Tanya's in jail in St. Pete, Chuck's in jail in Tampa, and you're footloose and fancy-free. But you still don't know where the loot was hidden. Am I right?"

Rooney rubbed his jaw again. "I don't have to talk to you people. I'm in pain here." He reached for a cord tethered to the side of his bed and made a show of pushing the call button. In another minute, the door opened and a nurse popped his head in.

"Everything okay in here?"

"No," Rooney said. "Isn't it time for my pain meds yet?"

The nurse looked at the chart clipped to the wall near the door. "Not quite yet."

"How about something for my anxiety?" Rooney whined. "I feel like my blood pressure's about to shoot through the roof here."

"I'll talk to the doctor when he makes rounds," the nurse said.

"Never mind," Vikki Hill said. "We're leaving now." She stood up and helped herself to another piece of candy. "But we'll be back."

59

~~~~~~~~~~~~~~~~

FBI AGENT ALEX GARCIA WAS leaning against the wall outside a curtained-off alcove in the emergency room. He was still wearing the aviator sunglasses, but the loud plaid shorts had been replaced by staid khaki pants and a navy polo shirt.

"Joe, meet Agent Garcia," Vikki Hill said.

"Good job out there today," Garcia said, shaking Joe's outstretched hand. He nodded at Vikki and jerked his thumb in the direction of the alcove. "He's all yours. I'm gonna take off now."

Evan Wingfield was handcuffed to a gurney in a curtained-off alcove in the emergency room. His left foot was heavily wrapped and bandaged and his eyes were closed.

"Looks like he's asleep." Joe leaned over the bed, and with his thumb, opened the suspect's eye.

"Wake up, asshole," he said loudly.

Wingfield turned his head slightly. "Enjoy the joke while you can. I'm suing both of you for wrongful arrest and assault. And that's just for starters."

"Boo-hoo," Joe said.

"Maybe you'll become a jailhouse lawyer while you're locked up in prison for the rest of your life," Vikki mused. "I mean, from what I hear, you only get paid for billable hours in packs of cigarettes and commissary Hot Pockets, but it's probably a rewarding way to fill all those empty hours."

"Yeah. Sadly, I think his days as a dance instructor are probably over," Joe added.

Wingfield sighed heavily. "You're wasting your time here. I'm not talking to you."

Vikki nudged Joe. "Waste of time? When is it a waste of time to see a murdering piece of shit chained to a hospital bed?"

"With a bullet hole in his foot," Joe agreed. "It's a beautiful thing. Day. Made."

"Anyway, since we were in the neighborhood, we just stopped by to fill you in on the news," Vikki said. "I just got off a call with Cheryl Shapiro. She's the assistant US attorney in New York who's been heading up the investigation into your illegal Airbnb enterprise. Did I mention you've been the subject of a nearly-two-years-long grand jury investigation?"

Wingfield shrugged. "Fishing expedition. My real estate investments are entirely legal."

Vikki wagged her finger in his face. "You've turned whole apartment and co-op buildings into illegal hotels, which is illegal in itself. And then, to keep the city from shutting you down, you bribed corrupt city council members and two city housing inspectors to look the other way. I'm sure you must remember my quote 'predecessor'? Not the brightest light on the Christmas tree, that one. Or the most discreet. Bought himself a BMW convertible with the cash you slipped him at that diner you love so much. And yeah, we've got that on video. Along with all the meetings that you and I conducted there."

Evan Wingfield stared at her, but said nothing.

"It's called racketeering, slick, and you can look forward to being prosecuted under the RICO Act."

"He might not know what 'RICO' stands for," Joe reminded her.

"Oh yeah. It's the Racketeer Influenced and Corrupt Organizations Act," Agent Hill said.

"Anywho, according to Ms. Shapiro, those indictments are scheduled to be unsealed next week. In addition to the original charges, by the way, you'll be charged with solicitation for murder, in connection with trying to hire a hit man to kill Letty Carnahan."

"Dog and pony show," Wingfield said.

Joe glanced at Vikki Hill. "Did you deliberately save the best for last? I've been waiting for you to tell him about the murder charge."

The FBI agent's tone changed in an instant.

"Earlier today, when she spotted you limping off the beach, Maya was really, really upset."

"You put her there to see that on purpose," Evan said angrily. "What kid wouldn't be upset at seeing their father wounded? That was damned cruel. You had no right to expose Maya to that kind of trauma."

"Actually, that *was* an accident. Maya wandered away from her babysitter because she was looking for some kittens on the property," Joe said.

He flexed and unflexed his fingers. "Did you hear what she said when she saw you? 'No Daddy'? Maya was terrified because she knows what you are. A murderer. She saw you kill her mother. Yeah. She saw the whole thing. She told us how you showed up at Tanya's house. She woke up when she heard the two of you fighting downstairs."

Wingfield's eyes flickered for just a moment with a hint of emotion. "Never happened."

"You thought Maya was with Letty for their usual Sunday-morning playdate, right?" Joe asked. "But Tanya put her off, because Maya hadn't slept well. Nightmares. Your four-year-old was already having nightmares over your custody battle," he said. "Tanya texted Letty that you were coming over that morning, because you'd agreed to let her move to LA and take Maya with her."

"Tanya was delusional. I never told her that," Wingfield said.

"Delusional or not, she agreed to see you, alone, at home. Without her lawyer present. According to Letty, her sister was afraid of you. She wouldn't have let you in the door otherwise."

"Letty Carnahan is still bitter that I dropped her for her sister. She hated me, poisoned Tanya against me. She killed her sister and abducted my daughter. And probably, now, she's poisoned my own kid against me."

"No," Vikki said, poking Wingfield's chest. "*You* poisoned Maya against you. She heard you verbally abuse her mother on many occasions. And then, that Sunday, she heard the two of you yelling downstairs. She came out into the hallway just in time to see you hit Tanya and knock her to the floor, killing her. And then she went and hid under her bed, because she was afraid you would come after her."

"I never raised a hand to my daughter," Wingfield said. "I love Maya. I would never."

"She told Letty and me that she hid under the bed and didn't come out until Letty arrived and found Tanya's body," Joe said. "Seeing you—today? That was the first time Maya told Letty what happened that day. You must have triggered something powerful in that poor little kid."

Wingfield's face paled. "Maya has a vivid imagination. None of that happened. I never abused or hit her mother. She's four. Kids make up stuff like that."

"Yeah," Vikki Hill said, nodding thoughtfully. "We might have believed that. Except that we've seen video that proves otherwise."

"You're nuts," Wingfield said. "What video?"

"Tanya was no dumb bimbo, despite what you think," the FBI agent said. "You know that stuffed elephant your daughter carries with her everywhere?"

"Ellie. So what?"

"So Tanya hid a teeny-tiny little nanny cam in that elephant. So she could spy on you when you had custody of Maya."

Wingfield pressed his lips together and stared at the ceiling.

"We watched a video clip of you and Tanya fighting in her car on a day she was dropping Maya off at your place for visitation," Vikki said. "There's lots of that stuff, over hours and hours of video. Maya was crying because she didn't want to get out of Tanya's car. She was so upset she wet her pants. Sound familiar?"

"On advice of my attorney, I'm not speaking to you," Wingfield said.

"Here's *my* advice," Vikki said. "Rest up now, because as soon as the hospital releases you, you're headed to jail, where it's almost never quiet. But you shouldn't get too comfortable there, because you'll be headed back to New York just as soon as the homicide charges and extradition papers are filed."

"He's a lucky guy, facing murder charges there instead of down here," Joe said, addressing the FBI agent. "Being as Florida is a death penalty state and all."

They walked out to the parking lot together, pausing beside De-Curtis's pickup truck. "Are you headed back to the motel?" Joe asked. Vikki pushed a strand of dark hair behind her ear. "No. I gotta drive back over to Tampa. The SAC is coming into the office, and Garcia and I are gonna brief him before we get started writing reports. Then I've gotta get on another call with Cheryl Shapiro. I think they're setting up a press conference for midweek to announce the grand jury indictments."

"Busy day," Joe said. He pulled out his phone and looked at the call log. "My chief wants to be briefed on what all went down out at the beach this afternoon. Apparently, 'concerned citizens' have been calling in to report a police shooting. And I need to get back to that sheriff down in Immokalee and let him know we've got Rooney in custody."

"I'll see you around then," Vikki said. She turned to go, but changed her mind. "One thing. Back there, in the ER? I kept waiting for you to break the news to Wingfield that he isn't really Maya's father. But you didn't."

"It's not my story to tell," Joe said. "I'm gonna let you feds make that call. Or Letty."

Vikki Hill studied his face. "You feel sorry for him, don't you? Even after everything you know about what a cold, murdering piece of shit he is, you feel sorry for Evan Wingfield, because he's eventually going to find out that Maya isn't his."

"Me?" He unlocked the truck, opened the door, and climbed behind the wheel. "Nah."

She watched him drive away. "Sure you do," she said, under her breath.

60

~~~~~~~~~~~~~~~

J OE TEXTED HER AS HE was leaving the pizza place.

Dinner?

He waited a few minutes, tempted by the smell of hot yeasty crust, tomato sauce, and garlic. Instead of opening the box, he drove over to the Murmuring Surf and parked in the lot.

It was after nine, but he could see lights shining from inside her unit.

His phone finally pinged.

Can't. Maya's asleep.

Perfect. Be there in five. Bringing wine.

They ate the pizza on paper plates on the patio and Letty poured the red wine into juice glasses. She left the sliding glass door open in case Maya called out for her.

By unspoken mutual agreement neither of them discussed the day's earlier events.

Letty refilled her wineglass and sipped appreciatively. She plucked a blossom from the vine covering the patio fence and inhaled the scent. "You know, I'm gonna miss this place."

Joe reached for her hand. "Then why leave? Wingfield's headed back to New York as soon as the extradition papers come through. Rooney's locked up. You're safe now. Maya's happy. You've got a job. My mom loves you. Everybody here loves you."

She raised one eyebrow. "Everybody?"

"Well, maybe not Merwin. He hates everyone."

Joe tugged at her hand and patted his lap. "C'mere."

Letty put her glass of wine on the table and obliged, curling up on his lap, wrapping her arms around his neck, and resting her head on his chest.

"See?" He kissed the top of her head. "It's nice here. You should stay."

She yawned. "Could get awkward when you have to go to work."

"I don't mean right here, exactly. I get why you don't want to raise a kid in a motel room. But you could live with me . . ."

"Joe . . ."

"Just let me finish, please. I've been thinking about this a lot. My place is no palace, okay? I'm a single guy. But it's got two bedrooms and two baths. Maya could have her own bedroom. Okay, so the second bathroom is only a sink and a toilet, but I've been thinking I could put a shower in there, so she'd have her own bathroom. I know how to do plumbing. I had to learn it all, growing up here. I can do plumbing, electrical, tile, you name it. We could even add a second story if you want. The kitchen at my place sucks, I admit. But we could fix it up. You can design it, and I'll do whatever you want in there. New counters, floors, appliances."

"Joe," she tried again, but his enthusiasm was unstoppable.

"The best thing about my place is where it's at. I've got a fenced yard. There's a big old oak tree out there—at least I think it's an oak. I'm not so good on garden stuff. We could put a swing set under there for Maya, in the shade. And maybe a playhouse. She likes pillow forts, I bet I could build her a playhouse. And we'd get a dog. I always wanted one, but never felt good about having one before, because I'm at work all day, but with you and Maya there, we could get a dog. Hell, if she insists, she can even keep one of Midnight's kittens too. And did I mention it's waterfront? Just a canal, but it's deep water and I've got a dock with davits where I keep the boat. We'd go for boat rides. Dolphin-watching. Remember, we talked about that? And I'd teach Maya how to fish. And water-ski, when she's older . . ."

Letty touched her fingers to his lips.

"That is the loveliest offer anyone has ever made me. Truly. But Joe, we can't stay."

"Why not?"

Letty slid off his lap and stood looking out at the sky. "I talked to Tanya's lawyer today. I've got to go back to New York. There's so much stuff to settle with her estate. The most important thing is, we've got to get a judge to name me as Maya's legal guardian."

"But Wingfield isn't even her biological father," Joe protested. "He's going to prison, and if I have anything to do with it, he'll spend the rest of his life there. And besides, your sister left a will naming you as Maya's guardian. What is there to fight?"

"Tanya represented to Evan that he was Maya's father. His name is on her birth certificate. So right now, as far as the law is concerned, he is, in fact, her father. I'll probably have to get a DNA test to eliminate Evan as Maya's father."

"How long can all that take?"

"I don't know. Sammi says there'll be hearings, so I'll have to be there for that. And a judge may want to interview me, and Maya."

"Sammi?"

"Tanya's lawyer. She's the one who drew up the will for Tanya. And of course, Tanya didn't bother to tell Sammi that Evan wasn't Maya's biological father."

"Fine. So you guys live here, but you fly back up there for the legal stuff."

"It doesn't work like that," she said. "I can't keep ping-ponging Maya from place to place. She'll start kindergarten in the fall. I told you before, I need some stability in our lives. Especially now that we know she actually saw Evan kill her mom. I need to find her a good child therapist."

"We've got kindergartens right here in Treasure Island," Joe said. "And therapists. Letty, do you really want to raise Maya in a place like New York? C'mon? Where would you live? You told me before your old apartment was the size of the efficiency. Can you honestly tell me you want to go back to that?"

"I'll have to find a new place," she said.

"And what'll you do about a job? How are you gonna afford living in New York with a kid?"

A breeze had kicked up, and she suddenly felt chilly. Maybe it was the thought of spending another winter in the city. Of bundling Maya into a snowsuit, mittens, socks, and boots. Or maybe it was just the wind blowing off the Gulf. She had to keep reminding herself that it was technically still winter, even in Florida, in late March, when the nighttime temperatures dropped into the low sixties.

Letty crossed her arms and rubbed them to keep them warm.

"Tanya had a pretty big life insurance policy," she said slowly. "Of course, Maya is the primary beneficiary, but I'm the secondary. Sammi says the money will go into a trust to provide for Maya, but it'll be more than enough to provide for her housing and education and welfare. She says it'll also be enough to hire lawyers to make sure Evan never gets near Maya again."

"What about us?" The question hung there in the jasmine-scented air.

Letty wouldn't allow herself to go to him. If she did that, he'd pull her into his lap again, draw her into his plans for their future. She wasn't sure she was strong enough to resist the temptation.

"I don't know. I can't think about us right now. I want to, Joe. I want to want all the things you're offering. But the timing is all wrong."

She couldn't see his face in the dim light, but from the tone of his voice, which dripped icicles, Letty knew he was hurt.

"So that's it? You're leaving? How soon?"

"I've already told your mom about my plans."

"You told her, but not me?"

"Earlier today, while you and Vikki were at the hospital. I felt like I owed her. Fortunately, I don't have that much stuff here to pack up. I'll find an apartment for Maya and me, someplace that's month-to-month, no lease, so I don't have to make a long-term commitment."

"Yeah, wouldn't want to make a commitment now, would you?"

His words sliced right through to the bone, but she wouldn't let on to him that she was hurt.

Joe stood up abruptly. "I'd better go. I'm meeting with the district attorney in the morning, and we've got a conference call with that sheriff down in Immokalee, and there's a shit ton of paperwork to do."

Letty pressed her lips together to keep from begging him to stay. Instead, she gathered up the pizza box and the glasses and followed him inside. He picked up his keys and opened the apartment door to leave.

Vikki Hill stood there, her hand raised to knock. Her hair was mussed and her gym shorts and T-shirt looked like they'd been rescued from the dirty-clothes hamper. "You gotta come see this," she announced.

They followed her over to the efficiency. She unlocked the door, and pointed inside, where glittering heaps of gold and silver jewelry, sterling candlesticks and candy dishes and flatware, and gold and silver coins were scattered across the unmade bed and the floor, like a modern-day pirate's treasure chest had been dumped in the middle of a run-down motel room. Necklaces and watches dripped from the nightstand, where a nearly empty tequila bottle stood beside a pair of juice glasses.

"What the hell?" Joe asked incredulously.

"This is what Rooney was looking for when he broke in here," Vikki said. She held out her wrist, around which was draped a heavy gold men's wristwatch. "Is this the watch you said one of your regulars sold him?"

Joe slid it off her wrist and examined it. "It's a Rolex Daytona, kinda like the one Paul Newman owned, and it's monogrammed. Gotta be Trudi Maples's watch. How did you even find this stuff?"

With her index finger, Vikki pointed upward, at the ugly water-stained dropped acoustic-tile ceiling. One of the square tiles was missing, exposing part of the aluminum framework, and shards of it were scattered among the pieces of jewelry on the bed.

"It's the damnedest thing," Vikki said. "I was in bed reading and out of the corner of my eye, I looked up at the ceiling, and I noticed one of those square things up there was sort of bulging. I was afraid maybe there was a leak in the roof and the whole thing might cave in on me. I stood on the bed and tried to move the tile, but I couldn't reach it, so I went outside to look for a pole or something. I found one of those shuffleboard stick things, poked around, and dislodged the tile. When I did, all this stuff just rained down on me."

Joe was kneeling on the floor, examining the treasure. He stood up and held out an iPhone. "Did this fall out of the ceiling?" He tapped the phone's screen. "It's locked."

Vikki reached for the phone. There was a short knock on the door, and then it opened. "Hey Vikk, I think I left . . ." Alex Garcia, the FBI agent from Tampa, stopped short when he saw the other occupants in the room. His face reddened. "Well . . . shit."

Joe DeCurtis struggled to keep a poker face. He held out the phone. "Is this is what you're looking for?"

Garcia shoved the phone in the pocket of his jeans. "This is awkward as hell, so I am going to back out of here now, and we are all going to act like this never happened. Agreed?"

"Absolutely," Joe said affably. "See you around."

Garcia nodded at Vikki and left.

Joe waited until the threesome was alone again. "Not that it's any of my business, but that cockamamie story of yours was never going to work anyway." He pointed at the bottle of tequila, and the used glasses. With his toe, he nudged a torn foil condom wrapper that had been tossed on the floor beside the bed. "You forget I'm a trained law enforcement officer."

"You're a horse's ass is what you are," Vikki said. "Okay, it doesn't matter who else was here at the time, or how it happened. I noticed the ceiling tile looked weird. We, I mean, I found the shuffleboard stick, poked it around, and all that jewelry and stuff fell out."

Letty was peering up at the ceiling. "You know, when I was cleaning this place out so that Maya and I could move in, along with all the old television sets and mattresses and crap, I found an aluminum ladder. I didn't question it much at the time, but it makes sense now."

The door opened again and Garcia strode over to the nightstand, picked up a pair of Oakley aviators, nodded to the others, and started to leave. He paused at the door. "See you around."

Vikki Hill waited until she heard his footsteps echoing in the breezeway outside. "Not one word from either of you," she warned.

"*Chuck* was staying here, in the efficiency, after Mom kicked him out of her place," Joe said. "I'm guessing he hid the stuff in the ceiling, where he figured his 'partners' Tanya and Rooney would never find it, because he was probably planning on ripping them off."

"But he didn't get the chance," Vikki told Letty. "Joe and the other authorities raided the place while the boys were over in Tampa drinking and gambling and whoring around. Tanya texted Rooney to warn him that the cops were here. Being the selfless, noble thieves they were, they left her holding the bag—although not the loot. Rooney told us today that he and Chuck planned to come back here the next night, after the heat was off, to retrieve the goods. But instead, Chuck got busted and hauled off to jail. And Rooney had no idea where Chuck hid the stuff."

Letty picked up a delicate gold necklace with a dangling gold scallop-shell pendant. A large diamond was mounted in the center of the seashell. "All this stuff was up in the ceiling, this whole time." She leaned over and picked up a yellowing pillowcase. "Looks like this was what he kept it in."

Joe took out his phone and began photographing the evidence, but stopped after he'd clicked off a few frames. He pointed to a lacy black bra draped over a blade of the ceiling fan. "Uh, Vikk, you might want to remove that before I continue inventory of the crime scene."

The FBI agent calmly hopped onto the bed and removed the incriminating evidence.

"This could take all night," he finally concluded. "Let's just put everything in the pillowcase. I think I've still got a partial list in my files at the office of all the stuff we knew was sold to Rooney. But I'm telling you right now, this is a lot of merchandise. A lot more than they probably bought during the two weeks they were here."

"Rooney said they'd been operating in other parts of the state before they wound up here," Vikki agreed. "I bet there's easily a couple hundred thousand dollars' worth of jewelry here. Maybe more."

"It must have been driving Rooney crazy for the past five years," Joe said. "He knew it was here somewhere, but Chuck was in prison. That's why he tracked Tanya down in New York. And when she denied knowing where the stash was hidden, he went looking for Chuck."

"You can check the Florida Department of Corrections database online, which is probably what Rooney did," Joe said. "He saw Chuck was due to be released from prison, maybe even contacted him and offered to help him get set up again once he was out. We'll never get the truth out of Rooney, but the DOC will have a record of who visited Chuck, and who sent him mail."

"Poor dumb Chuck," Vikki said. "Talk about a fatal error in judgment."

Letty took a last look around the efficiency and shuddered. "It creeps me out, knowing all that jewelry and stuff was right here, right over the bed Maya and I were sleeping in. Which reminds me, I need to get back to her."

Joe went back to loading the goods into the pillowcase. "See ya," he said, not bothering to look up from his task.

61

~~~~~~~~~~~~~~~~~

ISABELLE SAT CROSS-LEGGED ON THE bed, watching as Letty folded the last items of clothing into her rolling suitcase. "That's it?" she asked, looking around the motel unit for other pieces of luggage.

"Yes," Letty said, zipping up the bag. "I was in pretty much of a panic when I left New York to come down here. I just threw some stuff in a bag and started to drive."

"I can't even believe everything that's happened since then," Isabelle said, picking up Maya's shopworn stuffed elephant. "It's all like something out of a movie."

"Not one I want to relive anytime soon," Letty said. She sat down on the bed beside the teenager. "Maya and I are really gonna miss you, Isabelle."

"I still think Mom's being totally unreasonable, not letting me go to New York with you guys," Isabelle said, pouting. "We've only got like a month of school left, and all my class stuff is just bullshit anyway. I could totally do, like, remote learning, and help you out with Maya."

"Sorry, I've gotta stick with Ava on this one," Letty said. "It's your senior year. You've still got prom and all the graduation stuff. You don't want to miss any of that. New York will still be there this summer. And if you still want to come, you know we'd love to have you visit."

"I guess we know who won't be visiting," the teenager quipped.

Letty sighed and went into the bathroom, pretending to check for anything left behind.

"He still hasn't called, has he?" Isabelle asked.

"No. Not since I told him when we'd be leaving."

"He's my brother, and I love him, but he's such a dumbass butt-head," Isabelle said. "I don't get why he's acting like this. If he loves you, and we both know he does, he should understand why you've got to go back to New York."

"It's more complicated than that," Letty said. She opened the closet and closed it, then went out to the patio for one final look at the beach. She found a thumbnail-size scallop shell that Maya had left there to dry, brushed off the sand, and tucked it in her pocket. A remembrance.

"Guess we'd better get moving if we're going to make our flight on time," Letty said, picking up her purse and her cell phone. "I know it's early, but sometimes traffic gets stopped on the bridge over to Tampa." She glanced at the phone screen for the tenth time in an hour, wondering if Joe would call, or text.

She hadn't seen him in two days, since she and Maya sat down in a conference room at the police station with Vikki Hill, so Maya could give a formal, videotaped statement about what she'd witnessed the afternoon of Tanya's murder. Joe had been in the room, of course, and though he'd been warm and solicitous with Maya, he'd been aloof, almost ignoring Letty's presence during the process, allowing Vikki to conduct most of the interview.

Isabelle glanced down at her own phone. "Hey. Mom just texted to say she and Maya had to go over to the rec hall. I think there's something going on with the air-conditioning thermostat." She reached for Letty's suitcase. "I'll just stick this in the car and meet you over there."

The motel was surprisingly quiet for a Friday morning. It was the first week of April. Several of the snowbirds had already departed to head back north, and the Murmuring Surf's reservation system was filling up with bookings for young families who'd be checking in for spring break and early summer stays.

Only 10:00 A.M., and it was already hot and humid. The morning weather report predicted the day's high would be eighty-two. She checked the forecast for New York City—rainy and low sixties. Letty wiped a bead of perspiration from her neck.

Zoey had volunteered to pick them up at JFK. She hoped her friend would bring along a rain jacket from the stash of Letty's belongings she'd been storing all this time.

Clothes were on the list of things Letty had been mentally scribbling all week. Maya had outgrown most of her old clothes that Letty had brought to Florida. She'd need real shoes—no more dollar-store flip-flops or cheap sneakers. And socks. Letty had been studying apartment listings and had narrowed her search down to two viable options in the East Village, both within walking distance of the kindergarten Sammi had recommended.

She pulled the rec room door open.

"Surprise!"

The room was filled with colorful balloons and streamers. All the remaining regulars stood in a circle around a table topped with a cut-glass bowl of red Hawaiian Punch and a chocolate-frosted sheet cake with pink and purple lettering that said GOODBYE LETTY & MAYA.

Letty felt her eyes fill with tears. Maya darted into the middle of the crowd. She was dressed in a fluffy blue satin and tulle ankle-length princess dress, her curls topped with a rhinestone-studded crown.

"Letty, Letty," she cried, spinning around in a circle and fluffing the multiple layers of tulle skirts. "Miss Ruth and Miss Billie made me a present because I am going away on an airplane. Look! I'm Elsa."

Letty was speechless.

"Billie designed it and sewed it herself," Ruth Feldman said proudly. "I found the crown at a costume store and bedazzled it."

"She insisted on putting it on right away," Billie said. "I hope you don't mind."

"It's fantastic," Letty said. "Billie, Ruth, what a wonderful gift. We can't thank you enough."

"Hey, let's give Letty our present now too," Oscar Jensen said loudly.

"Let's cut the cake and have punch first," Merwin said. "I'm taking Trudi to get fitted for her new walker in half an hour." He tapped Letty's arm. "And don't worry. I'm not gonna ask you to pay for it."

"Only because I read him the riot act," Trudi said, leaning heavily on the back of a folding chair.

Ava DeCurtis emerged from the rec room kitchen with a stack of paper plates and cups. "Okay, come on everybody. We'll present Letty with your gift, and then cut the cake and let her get on her way to the airport."

Isabelle brought out a large flat package wrapped in silver paper with a silver bow. "This is for you and Maya, Letty. Everybody here chipped in. Even some of the regulars who already went home."

"We all want you to have something so you don't forget about us. And the Murmuring Surf," Oscar said.

"Let me open!" Maya clamored, already tearing at the paper and letting it drop to the floor.

It was a large, period framed photograph with delicate pastel tinting. Letty recognized the building, and the retro neon sign at once. "Oh my gosh!" she exclaimed.

"That's one of the original postcards of the Murmuring Surf, from way back in 1937," Ava said proudly. "The old owners left 'em behind when we bought the place. I found a couple of 'em you missed when you were cleaning out the storeroom. I had one enlarged, and a lady I know hand-colored it. I hope you like it."

Letty clutched the frame to her chest. "I love it. It's the most thoughtful gift I've ever been given."

"Look on the back," Trudi urged.

Letty turned the frame around. Instead of a cardboard backing, the reverse of the postcard was also framed in glass. Her name, and Maya's, were written in the address side of the postcard. And on the opposite side, someone, probably Ava, she guessed, had written a greeting in bold black pen. WEATHER IS BEAUTIFUL. WISH YOU WERE HERE.

It had been signed by Ava, Isabelle, and Joe DeCurtis, plus all of the motel regulars.

"I don't know what to say," Letty whispered, choking up with emotion. "You people—every single one of you—have become so dear to me and Maya. We showed up here out of nowhere and you took us in and accepted us. . . ."

"Eventually," Ava put in, to good-natured laughter from the gathering.

"You saved our lives," Letty said. "Literally. I don't know what would have happened to us if it hadn't been for Ava and all of you here. After I lost my sister Tanya, I started telling people that Maya's the only family I have now, but that's not really true. All of you are like family to me. And we will never forget you. Or the Murmuring Surf."

"We don't intend to let you," Ava said loudly. "Go on, Oscar. Cut the damn cake and serve up that punch before we all get to crying and carrying on."

The regulars closed in on the cake and punch, and Ava slowly maneuvered Letty and Maya out the door and into the parking lot.

"Ava," Letty started.

"Never mind that." The older woman hugged her. "I already know what you're going to say, so save us both the heartache. You know you're like a daughter to me, right?"

Letty nodded.

Ava released her and pushed her in the direction of the white pickup truck idling in the loading zone. "Your ride's here," she whispered.

~~~~~~

62

J OE GOT OUT OF THE truck and opened the passenger-side door. He took the framed postcard from her and stowed it in an empty duffel bag on the floor of the front seat, then pushed the front seat forward and strapped Maya into her car seat.

"Mr. Joe, I got a new princess dress," Maya informed him, filling the awkward silence in the truck as they were crossing Tampa Bay on the Howard Frankland Bridge.

"It's the most beautiful princess dress I've ever seen and you are the prettiest princess I've ever seen," Joe told her. "I wish I had a crown like yours."

"Boys don't wear crowns," Maya informed him.

"What about the guy on the Burger King sign?" Joe shot back. "He gets to wear a crown."

"But he's a *real* king," Maya said. "Maybe you could be a pretend prince."

Letty smiled at the image of Joe DeCurtis in a crown. She glanced over at him. He kept his eyes straight ahead.

"I thought Isabelle was taking us to the airport," she said quietly.

"Didn't think you'd mind a last-minute substitute." He drummed his fingers restlessly on the steering wheel. "I've been kind of a dick to you, huh?"

"That's one way to put it."

"That's how my mother put it."

"She guilt-tripped you into showing up today, didn't she?"

"No! She, uh, cornered me as I was leaving work yesterday and, uh, enlightened me. It was my idea to show up today. I had to let Isabelle in on the plan."

"Okay. Do you mind if I ask what the plan is?"

He took a deep breath. "The thing is . . . I want you. I just want to be with you, whether that means we get married, or we don't, or whatever works for you. And Maya. And I get why you have to go back to New York. You can't just erase all the stuff that happened back there. I realize now that you've got to deal with it, and you can't pretend like none of it happened. I wish I could go with you and help you handle all this crap but . . . I know you don't need to be rescued."

She watched his face as he grappled with the right words, and noticed that they'd taken the exit ramp for the airport. Time was growing short.

"Maybe I'm the one who needed rescuing," Joe said. "I've been single for a long time, and I got so used to thinking about what *I* need and what *I* want, and I'm a cop, you know? I'm trained to help people and do good and stuff. And I'm not used to having people question my authority. Or my motives."

Letty nodded. "I get that. And for the record, I never questioned your motives." She turned around to check on her niece, who had fallen asleep in her car seat. "Unlike Maya, I think maybe you really are a real prince. Just not, you know, the kind who wears a crown."

He exhaled slowly. "So. We're good? You and me?"

"Yeah. We're good. And here's a question. Can you wait for me? I promise you, New York is not forever for us. Give me some time and some space, so I can figure out what's best for Maya and me and our future?"

"Am I included in that future?"

She scooted as far over in the seat as the seat belt would allow and kissed his cheek. "I don't think I could handle going back there if I didn't think you'll be waiting when I'm ready."

"I will be," Joe said. "Pick up the phone and call. Night or day. And I'll be there like a shot. Is that a deal?"

He slowed the truck as they approached the departures lane at the airport, waiting for a space at the curb. Letty began gathering her belongings, and as soon as he saw an opening, he eased over to the curb and flipped on his emergency blinkers.

Joe jumped out and pushed the seat forward as Maya blinked awake. He straightened her crown and lifted her out of the car seat, then reached in to retrieve their luggage. Letty took the two rolling suitcases, and he slipped the strap of the duffel bag over his shoulder, holding Maya in his arms.

He walked them as far as the airline's curbside baggage-check kiosk and waited while the clerk checked Letty's bags and issued their boarding passes.

A cop approached the truck on a Segway. Joe gave a sharp whistle, and the cop turned. "Gimme a minute, brother," he called. "I'm saying goodbye to my ladies."

He crushed Letty to his chest, with Maya sandwiched in between them. "I love you guys," he said. He kissed Letty, surprised by the tears rolling down her cheek. "You never answered me," he pointed out. "Do we have a deal? You'll call? And I'll show up?"

"Yeah," she said, laughing. "It's a deal. Goodbye, Joe. I'll call."

He kissed her again, his lips lingering on hers. "Hurry, okay?" he murmured. "Please?"

63

~~~~~~~~~~~~~~~

Five Months Later

"HAVE YOU SEEN THIS?"

The Manhattan assistant district attorney's name was Mallory Kennedy. She wore a chic cream-colored business suit, her hair in a short, natural cut. She unfolded that morning's *New York Post* on the tabletop.

MILLIONAIRE MURDERED HIS MISTRESS AFTER BABY MAMA DRAMA. A large color photo of Tanya and Evan, dressed to the nines for a charity fundraiser, accompanied the story.

"I've seen it," Letty said, quickly folding the tabloid and handing it back. She nodded toward Maya, who was busily applying stickers to a new workbook Ava had mailed. "It was plastered across the front of the newsstand across the street from our building. I was terrified she'd see it."

The diner's door opened and Vikki Hill walked in. She dropped into the red vinyl booth beside Maya. "Hiya, Maya Papaya!"

Letty stared. The FBI agent was hardly recognizable. Her hair was swept into a tight French knot, she wore makeup, black heels and a close-fitting navy pantsuit.

"You came!" Letty exclaimed.

"Miss Vikki!" Maya said, grinning. "Do you live here too, now?"

"For now," Vikki said, dropping a kiss on the child's head. "When did you get so big? What are you, eleven or twelve now?"

"I'm *five*!" Maya said proudly.

"Almost," Letty corrected. "It's next week, actually, but we've been celebrating her birthday for the past two weeks."

Letty touched the agent's hand. "I still can't believe you're here. And you're really going to go to court with us today?"

Vikki motioned to the waitress and held up her empty coffee mug. "Of course I came. I wouldn't miss seeing you-know-who get his comeuppance."

She looked over at Mallory Kennedy. "No nasty, last-minute surprises, right?"

"Not so far," the assistant district attorney said. "But I won't feel good about this sentencing until the judge signs off on everything."

The waitress brought the coffeepot and filled Vikki's mug, but Letty refused a refill. "I'm antsy enough. Any more caffeine and my head will explode."

Vikki sipped her brew. "I still can't believe you-know-who's lawyer insisted on making Maya testify in court about what she saw that day."

"It was horrifying," Mallory said. "But as bad as it was for her, I think hearing her tell it, in person, had much more impact than a video would have. You should have seen the look on the jury members' faces," she told Vikki. "The foreman, this sweet, grandfatherly-looking guy, looked like he wanted to personally string up you-know-who."

A second waitress bustled up to the table. Her left arm was covered in tattoos, and her short, vividly dyed red bangs made her resemble a pixie.

"Zoey!" Maya clamored, standing up in the booth.

"Sorry I'm a little late," the waitress said. "Art was under the impression I wanted to work a second shift today and I had to straighten him out." She untied her apron and stuffed it in her tote bag. "All ready to go, Princess Maya?"

"Yay!" the child said. She looked over at the FBI agent. "Would you like to go to the movies with us, Miss Vikki?"

"Maybe another time," Vikki Hill said.

"Thanks again, Zoey," Letty said. "I'll call you when I'm done."

"No hurry," the waitress said. "I think we'll go get our toenails painted after the movie."

The three women watched as Maya, dressed in her sparkling blue princess dress, walked out of the Lazy Daizy, hand in hand with Zoey, before they got back to the business at hand.

"Wingfield's lawyer saw the jury foreman's face too, which is why he went to my boss during the recess and asked for a plea deal," Mallory Kennedy said.

"Manslaughter, as opposed to first-degree murder," she added. "I told Letty it was up to her, but I did recommend we make the deal, just to get it over with."

Letty shredded a damp paper napkin in her lap. "I just had one condition. Evan has to admit that he killed Tanya. He has to sign a paper, or stand up in court and say it, or whatever, but I want him to say the words."

"And he will," Mallory promised. "His lawyer understands that anything else is a deal-breaker."

Vikki nodded. "Up to twenty-five years in prison, right? How old is Wingfield now?"

"He's forty," Letty said. "My nightmare is that he could get out much sooner, though."

"Not happening," Vikki said succinctly. "We just executed a search warrant for all of Wingfield's financial records. And it's a treasure trove. He's going down on the RICO prosecution. Bribery, conspiracy, bank fraud, tax evasion. And now that he's pleaded guilty to the manslaughter charge, that means it was a predicate act in furtherance of the racketeering stuff. My boss is a very, very happy lady. Wingfield is nailed, big-time. And in addition to the criminal and civil penalties, the government will seize his real estate holdings."

"What about prison time?" Letty asked.

"Well, the RICO prosecution could take another year or so," the agent admitted. "But he can get up to life imprisonment, on top of the state charges. He'll be an old, old man by the time he sees daylight again."

"We'd better get moving if we're going to get over to the court-house in midmorning traffic," Mallory said. She dropped some bills on the table and the three women went out into the glaring September sunlight.

The courtroom was a study in seasonal neutrals. The presiding judge sat on the bench in her somber black robe. Mallory wore creamy linen, and her counterpart, Evan Wingfield's lawyer, was dressed in a conservative charcoal pin striped suit.

But it was Evan himself who commanded Letty's attention. He was dressed in an orange prison jumpsuit and black rubber shower shoes. As he entered the courtroom, Letty took malicious satis-faction, noticing the halting gait that she felt sure was a result of Vikki Hill's bullet. His hair was cut close to the scalp, and he looked stooped and gaunt. Without Evan's favored trappings of wealth— the designer jeans, tailor-made dress shirts, and expensive Belgian loafers—he was a surprisingly ordinary-looking man, like an un-named extra in a made-for-television movie.

Letty wiped her perspiring palms on her skirt. It was one of the few remaining items of clothing Tanya had gifted her over the years; a blue-and-white Indian block-print cotton skirt whose hem brushed her ankles. She wore it with a gauzy low-necked white peasant blouse and navy espadrilles, and a necklace of blue and green plastic pop beads fashioned for her by Maya.

The court clerk was reading a document now, and the judge was speaking, but his words seemed to be swallowed whole in the high-ceilinged courtroom. Mallory stood and she shot Letty a reassuring nod. She read her statement in her high, clear voice. Letty heard the words, but her ears buzzed with a sort of electric energy.

Then it was Vikki Hill's turn. She was crisp and devastatingly professional, but Letty wasn't really paying attention to the gist of her statement.

Finally, the judge gestured at Evan. He directed him to stand, facing the spectator benches. Letty's eyes bored into him, but Evan's return gaze was blank, seemingly focused on a wall-mounted clock on the far wall.

Good, Letty thought. She hoped Evan Wingfield would watch clocks for the rest of his life. Let him mark all the seconds and minutes and hours as they ticked off in endless drudgery. She decided she didn't need to hear him speak after all, so she stood up, turned her back on him, and walked briskly out of the courtroom.

The heat and sunshine on the sidewalk outside were a relief after the arctic chill of the courthouse. Letty walked a few blocks, then hailed a cab. She called Zoey and told her about her plan for the afternoon. Then she called Sammi, who agreed to meet her at Tanya's town house.

"You sure you want to do this today?" Sammi asked, as she punched the security code into the new lockbox the real estate agent had recently installed.

"Yes," Letty said.

Her heart was thumping wildly as she stepped into the dimly lit foyer. Sammi flipped a switch and the immense crystal chandelier blinked on, its prisms catching the afternoon light.

The black-and-white-checkerboard marble floor was waxed to a high gleam. Letty let out the breath she'd been holding. There were no ghosts here. Only the faint scent of lemon polish.

"The real estate agent thinks it will show better furnished, if that's all right with you," Sammi said. "And of course, if you like, you can just sell it furnished and not have to bother with all this stuff."

"Let's sell it furnished," Letty said. Tanya had loved the opulence of her home, had reveled in how far she'd come since that long-ago double-wide in West Virginia, but none of the gilt-edged furnishings held any sentiment or attraction for Letty.

She and the lawyer walked from room to room, snapping on the lights, looking around, and then moving on.

They climbed the stairs and went into Maya's bedroom. The fairy-tale furnishings that Tanya had obsessed over seemed garish and overdone now. "You don't think Maya wants any of these toys or books?" Sammi asked, gesturing at the shelves overloaded with picture books and playthings. She pointed at the large walk-in closet. "What about all those beautiful clothes?"

"She's got Ellie, the only toy she really cares about," Letty said. "And she's outgrown all her clothes. Let's donate it all to a children's charity."

Sammi hesitated in the hallway outside Tanya's bedroom. "Do you want to go in there?" She gestured at the closed door. "I know this must be hard for you."

Letty's hand grasped the crystal doorknob. "I need to make sure there's nothing of Tanya's that she'd want Maya to have. Let's just rip off the Band-Aid, shall we?"

Inside the bedroom, she trailed her fingers over the mirrored dressing table arrayed with Tanya's cut-glass bottles of perfume and the row of sterling-mounted brushes and combs neatly arranged on the tabletop. Letty opened a deep drawer and stared down at all the bottles of foundation, the eye shadow palettes and eyeliner pencils and tubes of mascara. She closed the drawer and opened another, finding the small silver-mounted baby brush Tanya had used to brush Maya's curls before bed every night. She put the brush in her purse and closed the drawer.

Sammi stood near the enormous walk-in closet, gazing in. "It's like being back in Bergdorf Goodman's," she whispered, as though she were in a church instead of a dead woman's bedroom.

Letty smiled. "I'm not going to keep any of these things, but if there's anything you'd like, Sammi, please, help yourself. That's what Tanya would want."

"She was always so generous," Sammi said, stepping into the closet. "So spontaneous. If I commented on a pair of earrings she was wearing, or a pair of yoga pants, the next thing I knew, she'd insist on giving them to me."

"That was Tanya," Letty agreed. She went over to the freestanding jewelry cabinet in the middle of the closet and rifled through the velvet-lined drawers. She didn't know or care which pieces were costume or which were the real thing.

In the middle drawer of the case she spied a brooch she recognized, probably the cheapest piece in the jewelry box: a circlet of fake pearls. The faux-gold mounting was greenish with age. The brooch had been a Christmas gift to Mimi from their bopbop, and she'd worn it on Sundays, pinned to the collar of her church dress. Letty hadn't seen it in decades, and she'd certainly never seen Tanya wear it.

She fastened the pin to her blouse and turned to the racks of clothes and shoes.

Sammi was holding a pair of wickedly sexy sling-back black pumps with red soles. "These look like your size," she said. "And they're Louboutins!"

"Take them if you want them," Letty said. "I couldn't walk a step in those things."

"Really?" Sammi squealed. "They don't look like they've ever been worn. We could take all these designer shoes to a consignment shop. And the handbags too. Gucci, Prada, Chanel. They're worth a lot of money, Letty."

"You keep those and whatever ones you like," Letty said firmly. "I've been thinking. Since you know more about this stuff than me, take all the designer stuff, the jewelry, clothes, shoes, whatever to a consignment place. You keep part of the money, because you did the work, and all the rest of the money, and whatever is left of the clothes, I want to donate to charity."

Sammi nodded. "That's a great idea. I bet Tanya would like that."

"See if you can find a battered women's shelter, okay?" Letty asked. "Tanya would absolutely hate that anybody thought of her as battered. Or a victim. But that doesn't change the fact that she was."

She turned to the racks of handbags. There were dozens of them, lined up on shelves that reached nearly to the ceiling of the closet, many in soft flannel bags with the designer's name stitched or stenciled on the outside. She squatted down on the floor, reading the labels, shunting the bags aside, then stood and repeated the process, shelf by shelf.

Finally, she fetched a velvet upholstered bench from beneath the closet window, stood on it, and searched the top shelf. When her hand closed on the worn, pebbly surface of a particular handbag, she knew she'd found what she was looking for.

Letty set the pocketbook on the top of the jewelry cabinet.

"Louis Vuitton," Sammi said. She ran an appraising finger across the frayed stitching of the shoulder strap and peeked inside the bag. "And it's the real thing. See? Here's the date code. There's a huge secondary market for these bags. It's too bad about the condition, though. There are stains in the canvas lining."

"This one's not for sale," Letty said firmly. "She was so damned proud of this silly purse. She bought it with the money she earned from her first television commercial. At the time, she didn't have enough money in the bank to buy a full tank of gas. But she had to have a Louis Vuitton bag. She took it to all her auditions and casting calls. She said it was better than a good headshot. It meant she was a success."

Letty reached inside the bag and was surprised to see that it wasn't empty. She emptied the contents onto the top of the cabinet. A half-empty tube of Tanya's favorite Chanel lipstick, crumpled tissues, a plastic TicTac box, some faded Duane Reade receipts, and a prescription pill bottle tumbled onto the surface, along with a pale lavender sealed envelope.

The typed pill bottle label was for Tanya Carnahan, the drug's name was one Letty didn't recognize, and a single tablet rattled around inside. She handed it to Sammi. "It's an antianxiety med," Sammi said. "Looks like some doctor prescribed it not long after Maya was born."

Letty looked at the envelope, which was somewhat smudged and crumpled on the edges, but blank.

She slit the flap with her thumbnail and extracted a greeting card featuring a whimsical Victorian drawing of two little girls.

HAPPY BIRTHDAY!
I SMILE BECAUSE YOU'RE MY BIG SISTER
I LAUGH BECAUSE THERE'S NOTHING
YOU CAN DO ABOUT IT.

Letty recognized the handwriting inside.

Happy birthday, Letty Spaghetti—
xoxo Tanya Lasagna

"Oh wow," Sammi said, reading over Letty's shoulder. "How sad. I guess she just didn't get around to sending you this card. I wonder if she bought it right before . . . you know."

"No," Letty said firmly. "Tanya hadn't carried this bag in ages. The pill bottle, and the Duane Reade receipts, they're all from before and right after the time she had Maya." She turned to the lawyer. "Did Tanya ever tell you that we were estranged back then? We had a fight. Over Evan. After she told me she was moving in with him and she was pregnant with Maya. I was so furious. I didn't speak to her for more than three years—until I finally caved in and went to Maya's third-birthday party."

"I knew there'd been some kind of rift," Sammi admitted. "But I didn't press her for details." She tapped the card. "Look, there's writing on the back."

Letty turned the card over. Tanya's writing on the back was unlike the big, looped writing inside the card. This message was in tiny, cramped cursive.

Sissy—I'm so sorry for everything I did. Please don't be mad at me anymore. You and my baby are the only good things in my life. I miss you, Letty Spaghetti.

Letty tucked the card back into the envelope. A single tear spattered on the lavender paper. She put it inside the Louis Vuitton tote and brushed away another tear.

"All right," she said, her voice shaky with emotion. "Let's get out of here."

Sammi gave her a sympathetic hug. "Want to go get a drink? I know I could use one."

"You go," Letty said, slinging the Louis Vuitton tote over her shoulder. "Order a cosmo and drink it in Tanya's honor, will you? That's what she used to order when she first moved up here, you know. She never missed a rerun of *Sex and the City*. She thought drinking a cosmopolitan actually made her as sexy and sophisticated as Carrie and Samantha and Charlotte."

"What about you?" Sammi asked, as they locked up the town house. "What are your plans?"

They were standing on the brownstone stoop, looking down East Sixty-Third Street.

Letty pulled her phone from the pocket of her skirt. "I need to call a guy."

Sammi gave her a knowing smile. "I see. Keep in touch, okay? We'll need to finalize some paperwork, but that can easily be done online." She leaned over and pecked Letty's cheek. "I still miss her, you know? But seeing you helps. You're much more like her than you know. And that's a compliment."

"Thank you, Sammi."

Letty sat on the top stoop of the brownstone. The marble step felt cool beneath the fabric of her skirt. She scrolled through the contacts on her phone until she found the one she wanted.

The icon was a photo she'd snapped of Joe at sunset, standing knee-deep in the surf, silhouetted against the glowing orange sky with his fishing rod cocked, mid-cast, over his bare shoulder.

She hadn't talked to Joe since the night she'd arrived back in New York—just a brief call to tell him that she and Maya were okay. She'd sent a few emails and a couple of texts, but had been steely in her resolve not to call him.

Letty's finger hovered over the tiny icon on the phone screen. Maybe he wouldn't answer. She realized, with a start, that it was the

Friday of Labor Day weekend. Maybe he was working. Or out on the boat. Maybe he'd ignore her call.

Enough uncertainty, she decided. Enough hesitation, enough maybes. Nothing in life was promised to us, Mimi had always preached. She tapped the icon and held her breath.

Epilogue

THE FIRST PINK STREAKS OF daylight were visible in the eastern sky as the truck bumped over the crushed-oyster-shell pavement.

She found comfort in the sight of the blinking neon MURMURING SURF sign. She turned in her seat to check on Maya. The child was sleeping, her head tilted to one side of her car seat, Ellie clutched in her hand.

Letty rolled her window down and inhaled the scent of salt air.

When Joe switched off the ignition, she heard the distant whoosh of waves lapping at the shore. "We're home," he announced.

"Yeah," Letty said, smiling. "Home."

"You're sure this is what you want?" he asked, for what seemed like the tenth time since they'd left New York.

"I've had six months to think about it," she said. "And yes, this is what I want, for Maya, and for you and me."

"You're full of surprises, you know that?" he said.

"But not secrets," she replied. "No more of that." She ran her fingertips across the strap of Tanya's Louis Vuitton purse.

Somewhere south of the Chesapeake Bay Bridge, she'd summoned the courage to tell Joe about the remaining contents of her sister's go-bag.

"How much money did you say was in there?"

"There was about nineteen thousand," Letty admitted. "But I had to spend some of it—on the Kia, and living expenses."

"How much is left?"

"About eleven thousand, after I sold the Kia. But ever since Sammi told me about Tanya's will, I've been sort of sprinkling the money around."

Joe chuckled. "Sprinkling?"

"I'm calling it Tanya grants. I gave the girls at the Lazy Daizy, the diner where I used to work, two thousand dollars to split five ways. And I gave the doorman at our apartment in the Village a thousand."

"That's some sweet tips."

"I gave Zoey three thousand. I don't know what I would have done without her. And I've set some aside, as a gift to Isabelle. And the rest for your mom, for a vacation."

He looked at her in amazement. "I don't think she's ever taken a vacation. At least, not since she's been running the Surf, she hasn't."

Letty chewed her bottom lip. "You think I should have turned the money in to the cops in New York, don't you?"

"Not necessarily. You didn't know where the money came from. Tanya told you it was hers, and she specifically told you to take it if something happened to her, so you could take care of Maya. Which is what you did."

"I sold the push ring, by the way. Even after I paid the estate taxes, I made close to a hundred and fifty thousand dollars."

Joe let out a long low whistle. "Good for you."

"I've got an idea I want to run past you. But you have to promise you'll tell me your honest opinion, okay?"

"Okay."

Letty laid out the plan for him as the truck sped south. She'd discussed it with Sammi, who'd discussed it with Demetria, the executor of Tanya's estate, and with a real estate attorney Sammi had brought in for a consultation.

Joe hadn't bought into the idea immediately. But shortly after they'd crossed the Florida state line, a slow grin spread across his face. Letty closed her eyes and dozed off, dreaming of palm trees and jasmine blossoms, white sand and turquoise waves.

She awoke as they were crossing the bridge over Tampa Bay. He'd rolled the window down, and the sound of traffic startled her.

"Sorry," Joe said. "I was getting kind of drowsy and needed some fresh air."

"It's okay. We're almost there, right?"

"Another twenty minutes. I've been thinking about your idea."

"And?"

He nodded his head. "I like it. Okay, I love it. But only if it's what you really want."

"It is."

Joe reached over, took her hand, and kissed the back of it.

Lights clicked on in the Murmuring Surf office and the front door opened.

"Looks like the welcoming committee knows we're here," Joe said.

Ava looked down at the file folder Letty had presented to her. "I'm speechless. Are you seriously saying you want to buy the Murmuring Surf? And keep on running it?"

"No," Letty said firmly. "I want to help *you* run it. Unless and until you decide you want to retire. Or take up knitting or crosswords or whatever it is people do when they don't have to work anymore."

"Did you know about this?" she asked her son, who had been uncharacteristically quiet throughout Letty's presentation.

"Not until today. Or was that last night? It was definitely after we crossed that long damn bridge in Maryland. And I swear, it was all Letty's idea."

"And you're on board? I thought you hated living in a motel."

"I was a kid, what did I know? Anyway, the idea is, we wouldn't live here. You would, until you don't want to, that is. But you still haven't told us what you think."

"Be honest," Letty urged. She glanced over at Joe. "We'll understand if you don't want to sell. And there won't be any hard feelings, I swear."

Joe grinned. "I made her promise to marry me, no matter what your answer is."

Ava's eyes widened and she jumped to her feet. "Really? You're getting married?"

"Yeah," Joe said. He held out his left hand and wiggled his ring finger, which sported a band of silver foil from braided chewing gum wrappers. "How do you like my engagement ring?"

Ava blinked back tears, then swept Joe and Letty into a group hug. "I can't believe it. When? Where? Oh my God, I can't believe you're finally getting married."

"Me neither," Joe said, wriggling out of her embrace. "We'll get to the wedding details in a minute. But in the meantime, you still haven't answered the question. Do you want to sell the Murmuring Surf to Letty?"

"Actually, she'd be selling it to Maya," Letty said. "It'll be held in trust for her until she's twenty-one. I've run the numbers and it seems like buying the Surf would be a sound investment for her future. But only if the deal seems fair to you, Ava."

"And you wouldn't tear it down? And build condos or a hotel?" Ava asked, looking from Letty to Joe.

"No. That's not my intention at all. I have been thinking of ways we could improve and expand the property, like putting a second story on both the north and south wings," Letty said. "But that's for the long-range."

Ava ran her fingers down the column of numbers Letty and her lawyer had presented.

"This is even more money than those developers have been offering me," she said, looking up. "Letty, are you sure y'all can afford to do this?"

"Positive," Letty said, nodding. "We've already liquidated most of the real estate Tanya owned in New York. That and the money from her life insurance have been invested very conservatively on Maya's behalf. And the real estate broker texted me last night that we have a solid, all-cash offer for Tanya's town house."

"Then, yes," Ava said, nodding vigorously. "I'll sell. This is the best possible outcome, and one I never dreamed would happen. When do you want to do it?" She picked up a pen and hovered it over the contract. "Now?"

"We can go ahead and sign the papers now," Letty said, laughing. "But I thought you might want to hold off on the closing until after the wedding."

"When will that be?" Ava asked.

"As soon as possible. Before she has time to change her mind," Joe said.

"I was thinking, since this is what you call our slow, shoulder season, we should do it soon," Letty said. "How's next week?"

"That soon?" Joe looked taken aback.

"Are you getting cold feet?" Letty countered.

"Never." His kiss proved his point. "Where shall we do it?"

"On the beach," Letty said, pointing out the window of Ava's apartment. The sky was a brilliant blue. It was, she thought, the perfect omen.

"Anything you say," he agreed.

The bridal party emerged from the motel just at sunrise, and walked quietly through the early-morning darkness toward an arch at the water's edge that was wound with ivy and twinkling white fairy lights.

The groom stood, waiting, under the arch, dressed in a white linen shirt and navy blue board shorts and a lei of white orchids.

A ukulele player recruited for the event took a deep breath, and began strumming "Hawaiian Wedding Song."

The ring bearer and flower girl, Maya, led off the procession wearing her favorite blue tulle princess dress, now altered to fit, a rhinestone tiara, and an irrepressible smile that revealed two missing top teeth as she marched slowly toward her new, adoptive father.

Following close behind was Isabelle DeCurtis, in a blue silk sarong in the same shade as Maya's dress, with a white orchid tucked behind one ear.

Finally, Ava DeCurtis and the bride stepped onto the sand, with Letty's hand tucked into Ava's arm. Ava wore her flowered Aloha Bingo muumuu and a lei of orchids.

"Ready?" Ava whispered.

Letty nodded. "More than you'll ever know."

"Hey, Papa Joe." Maya called out the new name she'd picked out for him as she approached the arch, her arms opened wide. "We're getting married!"

"We sure are," he agreed, bending down to pick her up. Isabelle stepped to her brother's right, before kissing his cheek, and then the three waited while Ava and Letty approached.

Joe's smile broadened and his breath caught at the sight of his bride, walking toward him just as the sun peeked through the cloud cover. He thought of that first dawn, when he'd discovered Letty sleeping in her Kia in the Murmuring Surf parking lot. As exhausted and terrified as she'd looked, he'd seen something in that girl— *something pure* was the closest he could come to describing it to himself.

He could hardly believe the same woman was standing right in front of him, dressed in a slender bias-cut white silk dress that brushed her ankles. She wore a woven crown of white jasmine and tiny white orchids, and a circlet of imitation white pearls was pinned to the narrow spaghetti strap of her gown. He held out his hands.

Letty handed her bouquet of white orchids to Isabelle and took Joe's hands in hers. His were strong and warm, the thumbs and palms callused, and they dwarfed hers, making her feel safe. He was still wearing the "engagement ring" she'd woven after a convenience-store stop in Virginia a week earlier.

Her own engagement ring was a simple white-gold band with a modest solitaire-cut diamond that had been Joe's grandmother's.

"I love you," he mouthed.

"I love you too," she whispered.

"I love you three," Maya said, loud enough for the officiant and the rest of the family to hear it and chuckle.

The rest of the beach was deserted. All of the Murmuring Surf snowbirds had flown back north in the spring. The sole witness to the ceremony was a lone elderly female birdwatcher, who stood along the shoreline nearby, hands reverently folded over her binoculars as she watched the morning's event unfold with deepening curiosity.

Letty looked around at the small circle surrounding her as dawn broke. She'd felt lonely and isolated for so very, very long, but now, that was in the past. Joe's family, as the cheerful officiant they'd recruited from a nearby church reminded her, was her family now. And hers—meaning Maya—was his. And that was enough. In fact, it was more than enough.

"I do," she said, when the officiant nodded at her cue.

"I do," Joe said quickly.

"I do too," Maya added, just before Joe handed her off to Ava's waiting arms.

She was already in his arms before the pastor gave his blessing, already wrapped tightly in his embrace by the time he intoned "You may kiss the bride."

When she raised her head, she heard applause, and whistling. She looked over. The birdwatcher was beaming, stomping her sandal-clad feet on the hard-packed sand, and whistling. "Well done!" the stranger called in a high, quavery voice. "Well done!"

Acknowledgments

D EAR READERS: 2021 IS AN anniversary for me—
marking three decades of writing fiction. Many thanks to all of you
for buying and reading my books over all these years, and for
allowing me to do this work I love. Please know how much I missed
meeting my fans in 2020 when my book tour for *Hello, Summer* was
canceled. I fervently hope this virus will soon be wiped out, and I'll
be back on the road, hugging your necks and signing your books in
person. I was particularly grateful this year for all the booksellers
and librarians, who, when the world shut down last March because
of COVID-19, somehow still managed to put books into the hands of
readers. You guys are rock stars! I also have a heart full of love for
all those readers who joined our amazing Friends & Fiction community in 2020—both on our Facebook page, our Wednesday night
Facebook live webcasts, and our *Friends & Fiction* podcast. Please
stick around, all of you, because I have lots more stories to tell!

The best part of writing a book set in a vintage Florida motel is
doing the research—especially when it's gray and chilly in Atlanta.
I went knocking on doors one sunny February day on Anna Maria
Island and met Ken Gerry, the longtime co-owner of the White Sands
Beach Resort, who was incredibly helpful telling me about his
years growing up at a mom-and-pop motel. Huge thanks also to
Laurie Davidson of the Sunset Inn and Cottages in beautiful Sunset
Beach, and to Janet and Arthur Czyszcon, owners of the Page Terrace
Beachfront Hotel in Treasure Island, Florida.

Mary Balent Long, Esq., of Abrams, Davis, Mason, and Long

was once again invaluable when it came to research on the legalities of tax and estate planning. My dear friend and neighbor (and retired assistant US attorney) Sharon Douglas Stokes helped with research on federal racketeering charges, and retired FBI agents Wayne and Sharon Johnson of Atlanta were kind enough to tell me about their days with the agency—and advise on firearms.

I cast a net into the virtual waters of the internet and was fortunate enough to find Megan Wolleston who helped with research on the technical aspects of hidden video cameras.

As always, I am totally indebted to my publishing team. My editor, Jen Enderlin, and agent, Stuart Krichevsky, of the Stuart Krichevsky Literary Agency (and his crackerjack staff), my dear friend and marketing maven Meg Walker of Tandem Literary, and publicist Kathleen Carter of Kathleen Carter Communications.

In a year when the pandemic shook the foundations of our world, and their New York offices shut down, the team at St. Martin's Press: Sally Richardson, Lisa Senz, Dori Weintraub, Tracey Guest, Jessica Zimmerman, Brant Janeway, Erica Martirano, Anne Marie Tallberg, Jeff Dodes, Tom Thompson, Michael Storrings, and of course, their fearless leader, Jennifer Enderlin, were able to seamlessly shift to virtual offices. I am more grateful than words can convey for their dedication and enthusiasm through these troubling times.

When it came down to the hard stuff—the actual writing of this book, my 7 a.m. writing sprints with my author pals from Friends & Fiction—Kristin Harmel, Kristy Woodson Harvey, Patti Callahan Henry, and Mary Alice Monroe, saved the day.

On the home front, if you have to be on lockdown for months on end, I can think of no other human beings I'd rather be with than my family—Katie and Mark, Griffin and Molly, Andy and Meg, and of course, the captain of our ship of fools, my husband and love, Tom Trocheck.